"This page-turner is tightly written with a moody sense of place in the small coastal community, but it is the numerous twists that will keep readers thoroughly absorbed. A satisfyingly creepy psychological thriller."

—*Kirkus Reviews*

PRAISE FOR *IN THE DARK*

"White (*The Dark Bones*) employs kaleidoscopic perspectives in this tense modern adaptation of Agatha Christie's *And Then There Were None*. White's structural sleight of hand as she shifts between narrators and timelines keeps the suspense high . . . Christie fans will find this taut, clever thriller to be a worthy homage to the original."

—*Publishers Weekly*

"White excels at the chilling romantic thriller."

—The Amazon Book Review

"*In the Dark* is a brilliantly constructed Swiss watch of a thriller, containing both a chilling locked-room mystery reminiscent of Agatha Christie and *The Girl with the Dragon Tattoo* and a detective story that would make Harry Bosch proud. Do yourself a favor and find some uninterrupted reading time, because you won't want to put this book down."

—Jason Pinter, bestselling author of the Henry Parker series

PRAISE FOR LORETH ANNE WHITE

"A masterfully written, gritty, suspenseful thriller with a tough, resourceful protagonist that hooked me and kept me guessing until the very end. Think C. J. Box and Craig Johnson. Loreth Anne White's *The Dark Bones* is that good."

—Robert Dugoni, *New York Times* bestselling author of *The Eighth Sister*

"Secrets, lies, and betrayal converge in this heart-pounding thriller that features a love story as fascinating as the mystery itself."

—Iris Johansen, *New York Times* bestselling author of *Smokescreen*

"A riveting, atmospheric suspense novel about the cost of betrayal and the power of redemption, *The Dark Bones* grips the reader from the first page to the pulse-pounding conclusion."

—Kylie Brant, Amazon Charts bestselling author of *Pretty Girls Dancing*

"Loreth Anne White has set the gold standard for the genre."

—Debra Webb, *USA Today* bestselling author

"Loreth Anne White has a talent for setting and mood. *The Dark Bones* hooked me from the start. A chilling and emotional read."

—T. R. Ragan, author of *Her Last Day*

"A must-read, *A Dark Lure* is gritty, dark romantic suspense at its best. A damaged yet resilient heroine, a deeply conflicted cop, and a truly terrifying villain collide in a stunning conclusion that will leave you breathless."

—Melinda Leigh, *Wall Street Journal* and Amazon Charts bestselling author

THE
SWIMMER

THE
SWIMMER

A NOVEL

LORETH ANNE
WHITE

Text copyright © 2024 by Cheakamus House Publishing
All rights reserved.

Published by Montlake, Seattle

www.apub.com

Amazon, the Amazon logo, and Montlake are trademarks of Amazon.com, Inc., or its affiliates.

ISBN-13: 9781662525544 (hardcover)
ISBN-13: 9781662518911 (paperback)
ISBN-13: 9781662518904 (digital)

Cover design by Caroline Teagle Johnson
Cover image: © Jonathan Knowles, © Peter Finch / Getty

Printed in the United States of America

First Edition

For Melanie and Jay. Thank you for making such a welcoming office space available to me in your Australian home.

THE SWIMMER

September 27, 2019

A steady rain beats down on Chloe Cooper's bare head. She doesn't care that hair plasters her cheeks and cold water dribbles in through the gap between her raincoat and neck. She sort of wants it. The cold. The wetness. To be cleansed. For the water to wash away the darkness inside and to make her feel better. Or just *feel*.

Chloe hasn't been feeling things properly for weeks now. Yesterday in particular did not go well.

It's why she's here, at Jerrin Beach at 7:00 a.m., in a gloomy, dark dawn of rain and thick fog, standing on a patch of muddied grass beside the paved pathway that curves along a beach of gray sand.

She walked to the beach with Brodie on his leash from her apartment three blocks away, above the Persian supermarket. Brodie—barely a foot high and shivering wet in his little yellow rain jacket—circles around and around at Chloe's feet in his hunt for a suitable spot to relieve himself. She doesn't rush him. Brodie is fourteen years old, and even walking the three short blocks from home is probably too much for his little bandy legs. Once he's done, she'll carry him back.

He's getting uglier by the day, Chloe thinks as she watches him. He has bug eyes, a rather awkward overbite, rotting teeth, peculiar bald areas on his skin, and he stinks. Chloe cherishes him anyway. He's her mom's dog, and her mom is unable to walk the little critter any longer.

She's pretty sure no one else other than she and her mom could truly love Brodie. Which is why Chloe identifies with the dog. A bit anyway. She's not old and hopefully doesn't stink, but besides her mother, there probably isn't anyone in this world who would love and care for her, either.

Since her mom got really sick, Chloe developed a new routine—she's all about routines. They make sense to her. She departs the apartment at precisely 6:30 a.m.—rain or shine—while her mother is still asleep. It means her mom is alone for a short while, but Brodie needs his morning bathroom toddle. Chloe has always liked coming down to the beach to watch the moods of the sea, but two weeks ago she developed a new beach fetish. The swimmer.

Like Chloe, the swimmer adheres to a strict routine. At 6:50 a.m. she parks her small yellow car in the beach lot, then walks onto the sand. She heads for the rocky promontory that juts into the inlet, sets her towel on a rock, pulls on a neon-pink bathing cap, and tucks her long red-gold hair under it. The swimmer then slips out of her parka, exposing her wet suit underneath. She secures her swim buoy—a shocking lime color—to her waist with a line. She then fixes her goggles into place, fiddles with her watch, and wades into the salty water carrying the buoy at her side. By 7:00 a.m. she's swimming smoothly across Jerrin Bay—her pink cap moving like a beach ball across the swells as she is followed by the bigger lime-green balloon of her buddy buoy.

Her strokes are rhythmic, hypnotic. Strong. The swimmer seems so alone out in the sea, away from the shore, yet so at peace. So bold! So brave! For a short while each morning, Chloe imagines that one day she might be so bold, so free, as to traverse the moving, heaving, shifting watery landscape where anything could be lurking beneath. Killer whales, for example.

The swimmer's name is Jemma.

In the last two weeks Chloe has learned a *lot* about Jemma and her surgeon husband. They're her neighbors, and Chloe is a consummate watcher of people. Especially neighbors.

Brodie inches forward. His circling endeavor resumes. A baleful foghorn sounds. Chloe checks her watch: 7:11 a.m. and still no sign of Jemma. Perhaps she won't show today. Visibility is, after all, almost zero, and the clouds are so low it's impossible to tell where they end and the ocean begins. Plus, the monsoon rain is merciless, icy, and the tide is unusually far out. Dawn is also arriving later each day at this time of year.

That's the thing about the Pacific Northwest, Chloe. Even in midsummer the inclement weather can make days as dark as evening. Mist and gloom make it hard to see properly. People scurry with heads down, look inward. They nip into doorways, hide behind umbrellas and hats and under hoods. One can be invisible here. If one remains vigilant.

Her inner voices never shut up. Incessantly chattering, chiding, goading, tempting, manufacturing extravagant narratives about everything and everyone she sees around her. Including her neighbors. The voices rudely interrupt her at work with bright thought bubbles. They're an open background channel while she reads or watches TV. So annoying.

Perhaps the internal voices are just trying to make up for Chloe's external reserve. A counterbalance to her aloneness. Sometimes they utter snatches of phrases that make no sense to her but appear to be bits of memory she simply cannot place. Sometimes they talk in first person. *I should get more exercise.* Or in second. *You shouldn't do that, Chloe.* Occasionally they speak in a lofty omniscient. Or conflate with her mother's English-accented admonishments. *Be careful, Chloe. Don't share too much about yourself, even with people you think are safe. Cross the street if you see someone who makes you feel uncomfortable. Never draw attention to yourself. Don't wear bright colors. Don't trust people. People are never who they appear—there is Evil out there that wants to do us harm.* The voices always refer to Evil with a capital *E*.

The only things that quiet the interminable chatter are her weekend vodka and the odd sleeping pill. It's gotten worse since she turned forty just eleven days ago. Another foghorn moans. Rain pummels down harder. She shivers.

"Come on, Brodie," she whispers. "Hurry up and do your business. There's warm coffee at home. And treaties." Her mom will be waking soon and needing pain meds.

Brodie finally hunches his back, squats slightly, and strains.

Then she hears it.

The distinct *splish-splosh* sound of the swimmer's arms moving behind the curtains of mist. Anticipation ripples through Chloe. She squints into the downpour, scans the water, watching, waiting for her to appear.

Suddenly she spies the bright-pink ball of bathing cap being followed by the bigger luminous buoy. Lone spots of color against a canvas of battleship gray. The sight fills Chloe with a secret, vicarious thrill. The swimmer is only a few minutes behind perfect clockwork, alone in the salty swells of the inlet. How reliable. How consistent.

She moves slowly, steadily across the bay, shifting in and out of fog. A man on the beach throws a stick for his goldendoodle. He appears oblivious to the swimmer out there. Farther along the beach a couple walks with their hooded heads bent into the rain. Talking. Involved in each other's spheres. They don't seem to notice the swimmer, either.

Jemma enters the middle of the bay. She's quite far from shore due to the low tide. Brodie jerks against his leash. Chloe glances down. He's done his business. She reaches into her pocket for a poop bag and crouches to pick up his offering.

As she does, she hears an engine out on the water. Chloe's gaze shoots up. A Jet Ski emerges from the mist—blue and white with an orange streak down the side. The engine grows louder as it barrels at high speed toward the swimmer. Chloe tenses. *Jemma is directly in its path.* The driver hasn't seen her. She lurches up and steps toward the beach, shooting her hand into the air to yell for it to stop. Before she can get a word out of her mouth, she hears a dull *thuck* as the Jet Ski hits Jemma. Chloe freezes. Her knees go weak.

The sound of the engine shifts. The Jet Ski slows, circles back. The driver is going to help her. He's in all black. A wet suit. Black hood. Gloves. Goggles. The Jet Ski nears Jemma, slows further, then suddenly picks up speed again and heads away from her. It does a sharp U-turn, then guns back toward the swimmer, accelerating. It hits her harder the second time, a terrible dull thud. The Jet Ski lurches sideways from the impact. The driver corrects, then steers straight out into the fog. The Jet Ski disappears. The sound of the engine fades.

The swimmer's body lolls like limp seaweed on the swells. Her lime buoy is gone. Chloe can't see her pink cap. The fog thickens. A foghorn moans, and the rain redoubles its force, pattering loudly on the wet sand.

Chloe covers her mouth with her hand. She can't process what just happened. Can't move. She doesn't know what to do. Her gaze shoots to the man on the beach. He has a cell phone in his hand and is looking out to sea. He appears to be calling for help. The couple have also stopped and are staring out into the inlet.

Thank God. She can leave without making a scene.

"Brodie," she whispers, scooping him up quickly. "We've got to go."

She hurries away from the beach, disappearing into the mist between the houses. Behind her she leaves Brodie's twisted little poop.

IT'S CRIMINAL: The Chloe Cooper Story

THE VANCOUVER MORNING SHOW WITH AMY TEY

AMY TEY: We have some thrilling news on the entertainment front this morning. It's Criminal: The TV Show, produced by the talented Trinity Scott and Gio Rossi duo, will soon be coming to a streaming service near you with a brand-new season called She's Been Watching You: The Chloe Cooper Story, a true-crime retelling of a bizarre series of local events six years ago that ended in three shockingly brutal murders and a province-wide "manhunt" that brought its own stunning revelations. We're privileged to have Trinity Scott in the studio with us today. Welcome, Trinity.

TRINITY: Good morning, Amy. Thank you for having me.

AMY: You and Gio first made headlines with the blockbuster success of your series premiere, Beneath Devil's Bridge, which grew out of your true-crime podcast and told the tragic story of the murder of teenager Leena Rai. Then came your series on the Abbigail Chester killing. Now we have a chilling story about a married "it" couple, deeply in love by all appearances—the kind of relationship people write songs and stories about—who moved from Toronto to an exclusive Vancouver neighborhood to start a new phase in their lives after a tragedy. However, fate intervened when they crossed paths with a forty-year-old loner—Chloe Cooper—who became fixated on her new neighbors. The result was explosive. Toxic. Murderous.

TRINITY: Call it fate, if you will. But things might have turned out very differently had Jemma Spengler and her renowned oncological surgeon husband, Dr. Adam Spengler, never encountered Chloe.

AMY: You mean no killings?

TRINITY: Viewers will need to be the judge of that.

AMY: I've had a sneak peek at the trailer, and it looks to me as though this season of It's Criminal will hit all the notes. We have an "outsider," a "loner," who has trouble navigating social currents; a wealthy, "perfect" couple who are not quite what they seem; a parasitic fixation; stalking; spying; class differences; heinous secrets. And it all homes in on something strange and unsavory about being a woman fighting inevitable aging in society today. A true-crime "cul-de-sac" thriller, if you will. What am I missing here, Trinity?

TRINITY: At heart The Chloe Cooper Story is a tale of loneliness. Of longing. Of being invisible even in the middle of a city, or within a marriage. Of trauma and a desperate need to fit in. And the universal ache to be loved. All of which ends in violent murder. And more.

AMY: I understand this production is personal for you?

TRINITY: It is. Deeply. For reasons that will become clear.

AMY: Tease! Thank you for coming in, Trinity.

Amy Tey faces the camera.

AMY: Talking of teasers, viewers can catch a sneak peek of the new Scott-Rossi true-crime series by going to the It's Criminal: The TV Show website and clicking the preview link to The Chloe Cooper Story.

AFTER THE HIT-AND-RUN

September 27, 2019

Chloe has the television set in her tiny, rent-controlled apartment on the third floor tuned to the local news channel. She listens for something, *anything*, on the swimmer accident at Jerrin while she tries to follow her routine: feeding Brodie and cooking oatmeal for her mother, who is mercifully still asleep in the adjustable "hospital" bed in the living room.

Chloe takes the porridge off the heat, turns off the plate. Flashbacks from the hit-and-run pound through her brain as she struggles to pour a mug of tea. She adds a teaspoon of honey, and the spoon clatters to the counter. Emotion suddenly tightens her throat. She hesitates, then quickly opens the freezer, takes out a bottle of vodka, and pours herself two shots. She downs them quickly, pours two more, drinks those, too. She breathes in deeply, hands braced on the counter, waiting for the alcohol to ease her body and mind while she listens to the TV against the noisy hiss and hum of her mom's oxygen compressor.

Technically it's still your weekend, Chloe. Restaurant staff work odd hours, different to office workers. It's just a little early in the day, and that's okay—you need the "medication" to calm you down so you can think straight.

She mentally regroups, sets everything on a tray along with some fruit, a spoon, and a linen napkin. She carries the tray through to the living room and quietly sets it down next to her mom's bed. Her mother doesn't make a sound. A bolt of fear slams Chloe.

No. No, not yet. Can't let her go yet. Got to keep her living, because what will I do all alone?

Brodie finishes his bowl of soft food, wobbles on bowed legs into the living room, and stands at her socked feet. His bug eyes fix on Chloe.

"It's okay, boy," she whispers as she bends down to pet him. "It's all going to be okay. I promise."

She goes to the large living room window, folds her arms tightly across her chest, and stares through the rain squiggles on the pane at the angular concrete monstrosity that dominates the corner lot across the back alley. Jemma and Dr. Adam Spengler's house.

There are no lights on this morning. The garage doors are open. Both cars gone. Adam, a surgeon, often leaves for the hospital at incredibly early hours of the morning. Jemma departs for her routine swim a little later. Even though the Spenglers' house is only three blocks from the beach, Jemma drives her small yellow sports car to the Jerrin Beach lot.

She's usually back home and in her studio by now.

But today the studio is dark, empty, waiting for its owner, who routinely sits at her big white desk in front of her ring light, monitors, cameras, and microphones, creating Instagram content telling other women how to live their best lives, how age is just a number.

Chloe imagines Jemma's two little cavapoos—Boo and Sweetie—lying on the floor, facing the back door, eager for their favorite human to return. But she never will. Tears pool in her eyes. She swipes them away, trying to hold it all in.

The news anchor's voice cuts into her thoughts, and Chloe jumps.

"In terribly tragic news, we have just learned that a female swimmer was fatally injured in a Jet Ski hit-and-run off Jerrin Beach near Crow's Point shortly after seven a.m. this morning. Police are not saying whether they know the identity of the woman, who was crossing Jerrin

Bay in dense fog about fifty meters from the shoreline when—according to a witness—she was struck by a Jet Ski at high speed. Our crime reporter Kathleen Fairlie is on scene."

Chloe's pulse flutters as the footage cuts to a pretty brunette in a raincoat on the beach. She holds a mike. With her is a man in his sixties. He wears a blue jacket and cap and holds a very wet-looking goldendoodle on a leash.

"Mike Richards was on the beach when he heard—then saw—the Jet Ski. Can you tell us what you witnessed, Mike?" asks the reporter.

Mike points into the gray gloom. "She was hit when she was about midbay over there."

"You saw it happen?"

"I missed seeing the actual impact. I was throwing a stick for my dog when I heard the engine, then a kind of thudding sound. I looked out into the Burrard, but it took me a moment to realize what I was seeing." Mike struggles to control a hitch in his voice. "I—I saw the back of the Jet Ski as it roared off into the mist."

"It did not remain at the scene?"

"No. It fled off at super-high speed."

"Can you describe the watercraft or anything about the operator?"

"Like I said, I just saw the back end before the Jet Ski was swallowed by fog. It was very dark with the low clouds, too. I think the Jet Ski was white. There was a couple farther along the beach who also spoke to the police, but they didn't actually see the accident occur, either. There was one other person—a woman higher up by the paved beach path. She had a small dog. She might have seen more, but she vanished almost immediately."

Chloe presses her hand over her mouth.

The reporter faces the camera. "The Greater Vancouver Police Department is calling for this woman, or any other witnesses, to please come into the station, or to phone the number at the bottom of the screen. They say no detail is too small."

Chloe fixates on the number that appears on the screen. How long will it be before someone in this small neighborhood realizes it was she and Brodie out there? She was hoping the man or the couple would tell the police exactly what the Jet Ski looked like—blue and white with the dark-orange band down the side. And how the driver clearly hit the swimmer on purpose. Twice. Pressure mounts in her chest. A discordant noise begins to grow in her skull. Louder, louder. She needs more vodka.

"What's that about a swimmer, Chloe?" Her mother's voice slices into her thoughts. Chloe swallows and forces herself to compose her features before facing her mom. Her mother doesn't like surprises. Or change. Or strangers. Or visitors. She abhors anything that involves police. Her paranoia has only worsened as she's gotten sicker. The palliative nurse's words echo in Chloe's head.

Paranoia can be a natural part of the death process, Chloe. As in pregnancy and birth, there are clearly identifiable stages in dying. It helps if you as a caregiver can identify them.

"It's nothing, Mom. Just watching this ridiculous rain outside."

"Your voice sounds funny."

"It's all fine. I'll get your pain meds."

"I don't need meds. What was that on the news about a swimmer being struck and killed? Were *you* near the beach when that happened, Chloe?"

"Mom. I—"

"Good. Because the last thing we need is any involvement with cops. You *know* that."

"I—I saw it, Mom." Her voice cracks. A sob escapes her. "I *saw* it happen. They're calling for witnesses. They *will* find out I was there. I need to tell them what I saw, what I know about Jemma. And *him*. They need to know Dr. Spengler killed his wife."

"Are you completely *mad*, child? Are you also going to inform the police that you've been stalking the Spenglers? That you spy on them from this room with birding glasses, that you have a door code to get inside their house? That you've been in there, touched their things, put items in pockets just to mess with their minds, taken photos of the inside of their house? Do you understand what the detectives will do, Chloe? They'll start questioning *you*. And you know where that will lead. You *know*. The world doesn't trust people like you."

Chloe suddenly sees movement out the window. Dr. Adam Spengler's car is entering the far end of the laneway that runs perpendicular to the alley behind her apartment complex. A bright-blue Tesla. *Saving the environment one car at a time. Stupid.* The Tesla slowly approaches the Spengler house, windscreen wipers arcing against the downpour.

Chloe grabs her mother's birding binoculars from the side of the bed. She goes up to the window, adjusts the focus, and zeroes in on the car. Surprise ripples through her—Adam's Tesla bears a different registration plate today. A seasoned watcher like her notices details like this. This plate is a completely different color. Red, white, and blue. It's definitely not the vanity one he arrived with from Ontario, which was plain blue and white. She tries to zoom in closer. She can read the front plate's alphanumeric sequence: 2T C5662. On top, against a red background, it says: SCENIC IDAHO. At the bottom it reads: FAMOUS POTATOES. She frowns. *How strange is this?*

The Tesla turns into the driveway and enters the garage.

From this window Chloe has a partial view right into the Spenglers' garage, and she sees the driver's door swing open. Adam exits his car. He wears a dark hoodie and a cap. The hood is pulled over his cap, and the fabric hides the sides of his face. His cargo pants are olive green, baggy. It's most unlike the surgeon's usual attire, which is always streamlined and sophisticated, even when he's wearing his triathlon gear. He opens the rear door and extracts a large duffel bag. The zipper hangs open, and Chloe spies something black and bulky inside. *A wet suit?* She's certain it's a wet suit. She grows even more convinced it was him on that Jet Ski. Adam Spengler has just murdered his wife, and Chloe witnessed the whole thing.

She snatches up her mobile and hurriedly punches in the number from the television screen. A woman answers almost instantly. Chloe panics. Internal noise crackles through her head, and she can't properly process what the woman is saying on the other end of the line. She should hang up. Instead, she blurts out, "The husband did it. Dr. Adam Spengler killed Jemma Spengler with a Jet Ski that was blue and white with an orange stripe down the side. I saw the whole thing. He wore a black wet suit with a hood. Gloves. Goggles. He hit her twice—went back to make sure she was dead. Then he headed straight out into the Burrard. Into the fog. At high speed, heading toward the North Shore. They live at 1117 Crow's Road, off Main."

Sweating, she kills the call before the woman can ask for additional details, like her name. She's shaking so hard she can barely stand. She retches and clutches her stomach.

"You shouldn't have done that, Chloe," her mother warns. "My God, you will live to regret it. Mark my words."

"What's done is done," Chloe mutters as she hurries to the freezer to get more vodka, desperate to settle her nerves so she can think. She returns to the window with her glass full to the brim. She sees Adam inside his house now, putting on lights, moving around his expansive living area, the two little dogs following him. He goes to his liquor cabinet. Through her scopes she watches him pour a brandy. So early. Like herself. Totally unusual for him. He throws the brandy back, pours another. Chloe knows it's brandy from being inside their house. She even has photos of the Spenglers' booze cabinet in her phone. She's a bartender—it interests her what other people drink. And Adam usually drinks whiskey, not brandy. Her mind slides back to the day she first saw Adam and Jemma's moving truck arrive.

That was the day everything started to go wrong.

BEFORE THE HIT-AND-RUN

September 12, 2019

It's a sunshiny autumn morning filled with the hues of turning leaves, a sea breeze, and the scent of freshly baked bread wafting in through the open window from the artisan bakery on the corner of Main. It's the kind of day that fills people with an unarticulated sense of brightness and expectation. But Chloe feels bleak.

Her mom's health took a sharp downhill turn during another long, wakeful night, and she fears the end is nearing. Her mom's legs are frightfully swollen. The skin is red and stretched so taut it seems they can't possibly swell further without her flesh splitting open. Like a roasting suckling pig turning slowly over a firepit. This edema that has arrived with the end stages of cancer is really quite alarming. Her mom's abdomen appears even more distended today—larger than a woman about to give birth. The palliative physician told Chloe it's called ascites when fluid collects in spaces within the abdomen. Common in ovarian cancer. It's causing her mom pain, nausea, and vomiting, and affecting her kidneys and lungs. Above the sound of the oxygen compressor, Chloe also hears a new rattle in her mom's chest.

She paces up and down in front of the living room window, checking her watch, agitated for the home care palliative nurse to arrive with solutions, but the woman is not due for another hour.

"For heaven's sake, stop moving up and down, Chloe," her mother mutters. "You're giving me motion sickness."

"Can I get you anything?" She tries to fluff her mother's pillows and adjust the back of the hospital bed so her mom can see out the living room window better. Brodie stirs in the pile of blankets at the foot of the bed.

"Some lotion for my legs would be nice. They're really itchy today."

Chloe hurries to fetch a tube of calming cream, but stills at the sound of a loud beeping coming in through the open window. She looks out to see a monstrous truck backing slowly into the laneway across from her apartment. She pauses and watches. The truck has a moving company logo on the side. It stops in front of the driveway of the newly constructed house on the corner.

"It looks like the new owners are moving into Gloom House," she says. It's the name Chloe and her mom have given to the architectural monstrosity of concrete and glass that replaced Mr. Higgins's demolished little yellow cottage built in the thirties. Chloe wishes Mr. Higgins could have floated his house away on a raft of balloons like in the movie *Up*. Up and away to fulfill his dreams of adventure instead of going into a tiny, sterile room at the seniors' home near the highway. She felt so rotten about it she did a painting of Mr. Higgins's house floating up above the neighborhood, buoyed by a rainbow of giant balloons. She took it to him in the home, but by the time she arrived, they told her Mr. Higgins had gone and died. That's why she wants to keep her mom home for as long as possible. Institutions kill people. One way or the other.

"Can you see the van?" she asks when her mother doesn't respond.

"I can see, Chloe. I might be dying, but I'm not blind."

Chloe picks up her mom's scopes and zooms in on the van. "It has Ontario plates," she says. "That's a long drive across the country."

Her mother closes her eyes and says nothing.

Chloe sets the scopes down and seats herself near the end of the bed. She squeezes lotion into her hands and begins rubbing the cream gently into her mom's swollen, dry shins and cracked heels. Even her toes are fat, like little pork sausages. Her mother, who was so skinny all her life. This is a stealth illness. Women don't see it coming until it's far too late, and Chloe had no idea it would look like this, the battle with cancer. Obituaries always say that someone fought the illness bravely and lost, but she's pretty certain now you don't "fight" this. Not this particular kind her mom has. You just wait as it makes you incredibly uncomfortable, then consumes you wholly as it squeezes the life out of you.

She keeps an eye on the truck in the street below while she makes circular, stroking movements to encourage lymph flow, as the physiotherapist showed her.

"Thanks, Chloe, love," her mom whispers with her eyes closed. "Don't know what I would do without you."

She just nods because the lump in her throat makes it impossible to speak. She doesn't know how she'll survive without her mom. She tried. Sort of. A few years back she mustered the courage to escape the rural area of the interior where her mom raised her as a single parent after bringing her over from England as a toddler. When Chloe arrived in the big city, she got a job as a cashier at the Persian supermarket downstairs, even though she's not Persian and can't speak Farsi. But the owner was desperate for additional staff. He also happens to own the apartments above the row of commercial units downstairs. He allowed Chloe to rent this unit. After the supermarket job ended, she worked as a barista at a coffee shop down the road and became very, very good at learning the customers' needs and knowing exactly what they liked, and when. While there she began to teach herself mixology via YouTube videos. A person can learn just about anything from the internet, and Chloe is a proud autodidact. It's basically how she did her schooling.

Bill Zeigler, who owns the Beach House Restaurant and Bar, took a big chance on Chloe when she answered an ad for a bartender, and she's worked her damnedest to ensure he'll never regret it. She also started walking dogs part-time. Both jobs allow Chloe to move almost invisibly among people, and to be in places where she can observe them, study them, photograph them, paint images inspired by them, and conjure wildly self-entertaining narratives about them. All while never actually having to function as one of them. But her experiment at solo living was not long lived. Her mom was not quite done with her.

The diagnosis came fourteen months ago, and Chloe couldn't *not* bring her mother to live in her tiny apartment—or "flat," as her mom refers to it in her British accent. The "flat" is close to the cancer agency attached to the big Vancouver hospital.

Apart from those few brave solo months, it's always just been the two of them against the world for as long as Chloe can remember. A Big Bad World full of people and Evil always out to get them, or trick them, or seduce them. At least, this has always been her mother's view. But so firmly has Chloe's mind been imprinted with these notions that she can't seem to shake the sense that there really is a subversive, unnamed, amorphous threat out there, continuously hunting for the two of them.

Chloe replaces the cap on the lotion. Her mom appears to have fallen asleep. She covers her legs gently with a sheet, then goes to the window to watch the moving show at Gloom House.

Men in red overalls have rolled up the truck's rear door, and the inside is crammed to the ceiling with boxes. So. Many. Boxes. A thrill quivers through her. New neighbors. With brand-new belongings. So much to discover. A promise of distraction—something right outside her windows to occupy her sleep-deprived days and nights. What's inside those boxes? Who is moving in? What will she discover about them?

It's truly amazing just how much you can learn about people by watching—*really* watching. Like a mind hunter who profiles serial killers.

A bright-blue Tesla suddenly turns into the laneway. Chloe's pulse quickens. She grabs the binoculars and watches it park behind the moving truck.

It has Ontario plates, like the truck. But vanity ones. Blue letters against a white background spell DR SPENGR.

Chloe tenses with anticipation as the driver's door swings open and a tall, athletic man with gleaming black hair and dark sunglasses steps out. He stretches his arms and arches his spine as though he's been driving many miles. Placing his hands on narrow hips, he turns and studies the house. His feet are planted in a splayed, confident stance. His shoulders are squared. Chloe trains the scopes on his face. His wide mouth curves into a slight smile that screams *satisfaction*. There's a definite proprietary air in his posture. Clearly the Master of Gloom House has arrived. Brand new to the Crow's Point neighborhood and there he stands as though he already owns the street and all in it. The autumn sea breeze ruffles his hair, and something niggles through her body—a feeling of discomfit and darkness, and she can't quite pinpoint or catch on to it before it slithers back down into her subconscious. But the sensation leaves her unsettled about the man.

Trust your instincts, Chloe. Cross the street if your gut tells you that you are unsafe, Chloe.

The boxes are gradually unpacked throughout the day. The palliative nurse comes and goes with no real solutions. Various other cars and vans arrive at the house across the alley. One of them has an interior designer's logo on the sides. The other is the cable guy's. Another is an electrician's vehicle, and then comes a painting crew and a furniture store truck.

◆ ◆ ◆

September 14, 2019

Two days later, *she* arrives.

Chloe is carefully wrapping one of her art pieces for Bill, her boss—it's his birthday, and it's all she can think to give him—a painting of the outside of the Beach House as she observed it one icy winter's night, when she hears the cheeky toot of a car horn.

She glances out the window. A slender woman with massive sunglasses sits behind the wheel of a butter-yellow convertible. On the seat behind her are two little doggy crates. One pink. One blue. The car top is down, and the woman's hair is a wild windblown mass of red-gold spirals beneath a scarf with polka dots. Her skin is incredibly pale. As she exits the car, Chloe can see she is very tall, very thin, and oh so unbelievably elegant and stylish. She's the image of a timeless Hollywood movie star.

Chloe stares, open-mouthed, immobilized by the glamour that has arrived in the laneway. The black-haired man comes hurrying out of the house. The Hollywood goddess steps toward the man, opening her arms as though to hug him, but he stops her by placing a hand firmly on her slender shoulder.

The woman looks surprised. He leans forward, whispers something in her ear, then whips out a piece of white cloth. The woman appears to protest, but the man quickly ties the cloth over her eyes.

A blindfold!

He then takes the woman by the hand and leads her toward the ugly house.

And Chloe is utterly, wholly, completely hooked.

IT'S CRIMINAL: The Chloe Cooper Story

The screen shows a dimly lit room with a chair in the center. The chair is bathed in a golden glow from a lamp on the table beside it. A woman enters. She goes to the chair, sits. The lighting comes up. She angles her face toward the camera, and her bluntly cut black hair shimmers like a waterfall against her shoulders. Text at the bottom of the screen reads:

SAKURA OBA, CHLOE COOPER'S COWORKER FROM THE BEACH HOUSE RESTAURANT AND BAR.

SAKURA: I don't think any of us knew what to make of Chloe. She was . . . different. I mean, she was fantastic at her job. Very organized behind her bar. Military-precision stuff, and God help anyone who put things in the wrong place. The Beach House patrons loved her because she always knew exactly what they drank, and how they liked tiny individualistic tweaks to cocktail recipes. It made them feel seen, taken care of. That's basically what people want, isn't it? To feel as though they belong somewhere, special, cared for? She loved animals and was well known as a dog walker in Crow's Point. Just about anyone in the neighborhood would have seen her at one time or another, walking dogs. She was a fixture that blended into the background with her lack-luster brown hair, ordinary brown eyes. She was average build. Average height. Nothing especially noteworthy about her facial features. And I say this not to be mean, but to underscore how she was sort of . . . invisible. She spoke with a slight accent that was neither Canadian nor British. There, but not. And her phrases were occasionally odd, or overly formal, or even archaic at times. And while people maybe didn't notice Chloe, she always noticed them. In incredible detail. Watching. All the time. Absorbing. I—none of us would have expected what happened.

TRINITY OFF CAMERA: Did she have friends among her coworkers?

SAKURA: No. Like I said, she was just there. Part of the decor. No one paid her special attention or invited her to social functions, probably because she was so awkward outside of work. Once you took Chloe out of her bar domain . . . she just didn't know how to read social cues in the way most people do. She'd say weird things. Sometimes she seemed totally clueless; other times she came up with detailed knowledge about really obscure subjects. At times she acted judgy. Patronizing. As though she was superior and in possession of knowledge that us mere mortals were incapable of comprehending. She called herself an autodidact.

Sakura laughs.

SAKURA: I had to go look that up.

TRINITY OFF CAMERA: What about Stavros Vasilou, one of the other bartenders at the time? Did you not consider him a friend of Chloe's?

SAKURA: Oh, Stavros always made time for Chloe. He was kind—he made time for everyone. I did wonder at the time if Chloe misinterpreted his general empathy as something more.

A long pause. A change of facial expression and tone.

SAKURA: You know, I don't think Stavros could ever have imagined how crossing paths with Chloe would impact his life. Everyone was terribly shocked when he went missing like that. Just vanished.

Another long pause.

SAKURA: Those murders. They were so brutal. So bloody. Who'd have thought?

BEFORE THE HIT-AND-RUN

September 14, 2019

Blindfolded, Jemma stumbles behind Adam as he leads her up a small step and in through the house doorway. She senses a coldness and change in atmosphere as she enters.

She pulls back. "What about Boo and Sweetie? They've been in the car for hours. They need a bathroom break."

"Later. Come see first." Adam tugs her hand. "I want to show you how I furnished the place for you."

Jemma resists and whips off the blindfold. "Adam," she says firmly. "I'm *not* leaving them out there in the open car."

"The neighborhood is great. It's safe—"

"I'm getting them." She turns and exits the house. As Jemma makes her way back to her car, her heart pounds. She feels shockingly, disproportionately angry with her husband, and she knows it's partly because she's tired after the long drive.

"Christ, Jem," he calls after her. "I had it all planned."

She ignores him and reaches into the back of her car. She lifts Boo's crate out, then grabs the handle for Sweetie's. She holds the two crates by their handles at her sides and inhales deeply, tempering her emotions. Then, slowly, she turns and faces the house.

It's a modern and angular thing with big bare windows, and it squats over the small lot like a huge hostile alien that has consumed the entire corner parcel of land, along with whatever previous house and garden must have existed here. Some of the walls have been armored with trendy corrugated metal siding, as though girded for some kind of postapocalyptic onslaught. The garage doors consist of opaque window squares framed by heavy metal. The whole affair exudes an industrial aura. Any garden that once grew here—and she can see from the other older homes in the area what might have existed on this corner—has been replaced by pebbled beds and a spattering of enduring spiky plants that require limited human love and attention. Her gaze shifts down the laneway.

Some of the older neighborhood houses are still here—pretty rose and vegetable gardens out front, flowers and leafy trees—but everything is packed so tightly together. Claustrophobic. And part of their new view from this rear laneway is the back end of a row of commercial properties topped by apartments, complete with commercial vehicles parked among dumpsters. It's everything that their old estate, with its New England–style home on the shores of Lake Ontario outside of Toronto, was not. Emotion threatens to overwhelm Jemma. She's tired, she *knows* this. The drive has been interminably long.

But why did Adam not describe this to her better? Why did she allow him to keep this such a total surprise? Deep down Jemma knows why. She wanted to appease him for continuing with couples counseling. She's trying to be the good wife, the woman who makes compromises. That's why. And she regrets it. Profoundly. She would *never* have bought this place if she'd seen it for sale.

How is it possible that these homes backing onto this lane and bordering a commercial alley can cost in the millions of dollars? Is it *this* expensive to live in this city? Have they made a mistake? It's not like she and Adam don't have money. They could surely have afforded something more gracious-looking.

Her anger blooms. She tries to push it down.

It doesn't have to be permanent. Things can always change. Think of what your counselor said. Be positive. Try not to always default to negative. Be the woman you tell your Instagram followers to be. Walk the walk.

But Jemma knows her social media shtick is a con.

She starts to make her way back to where Adam stands waiting, but as she does, Jemma is hit with a sense of being watched. She stills, glances up. There's a woman in the window of one of the top-floor units across the alley. Sun glints off something she holds to her face. Binoculars?

No, surely not. I'm imagining things.

"Well, that was dramatic," she says as she brushes past Adam and sets the crates on the floor in the concrete entryway. She crouches down and opens the doors. "We're here, guys. Come out, babies. We—"

"What do you mean *dramatic*?" Adam sounds hurt, like a little boy who totally doesn't get it. Her husband might be a renowned surgeon with something of a god complex, but he's also a petulant boy perpetually seeking adoration from her, and from his daddy and mommy. Sometimes Adam reminds Jemma of a floppy-haired, guileless Hugh Grant character crossed with a James Bond persona. A brilliant, endearing, fit, good-looking, and talented sixty-two-year-old man-child.

"The blindfold was a bit much." She comes upright as Boo and Sweetie scamper into the open-plan living area downstairs and begin sniffing everything. "It's not like you hid anything from me from the car to the entrance hall."

He gets that look on his face. "Aw, Jem, you were supposed to leave it on. We need some levity in our lives. This is why we're making the change, right? Starting this new phase of our lives. Developing new habits, new patterning."

Her gaze goes to the giant mirror in the entranceway. She sees herself. Windblown. Downturned mouth framed by marionette lines. Furrowed brow. She instantly corrects this by tensing her features into a pouty half smile. She's shocked these days when she catches an unexpected reflection of herself. She's turning into her mother. This sours her mood further. Holding her face taut, she walks slowly into the expansive living area. The furniture is leather and pale Nordic wood, streamlined and sparse. Two large framed photos hanging on the dark-gray wall instantly snare her attention. Hailey and Jackson.

For a moment the image of their children in this new place undoes Jemma. Tears blur her vision, and she suddenly feels so incredibly exhausted. Not only has the trip been long, but the whole ordeal of the past years has been beyond punishing. She feels Adam's arm curl around her waist. He draws her into his body. Solid. Comforting. She leans into him, inhales his familiar scent, lets him wrap and enfold her into his being. He kisses her hair at her neck. His breath is warm, and she feels the beat of his heart against her torso. He's so alive. Strong. Vital.

"It'll take time, Jem," he whispers gently. "Grief is never linear. We knew it wouldn't be easy. But our moving west—this fresh start—is part of working through the losses, right? Baby steps."

She nods. But tears overflow and slide down her cheeks.

"Hey." He cups her face between his beautiful surgeon's hands and wipes away her tears with his thumbs. "It's going to be okay."

"I just don't know what the *purpose* of me is now, Adam."

"We're entering a new cycle in our lives, Jem. Metamorphosis takes time. And patience. We need to trust the process and just keep showing up day by day. You and I—we're discovering who we want to be as we grow older, wiser. Stronger." He hesitates. "Till death do us part."

She feels an odd niggle at her husband's use of those last five words. Facing age—especially as a woman in a culture where beauty is defined as youth—is one thing. But it's a little early to think about dying.

"It's easier for you, Adam. You still have your work," she says. "You have your new full-time position at the cancer agency. Saving people. Families hanging on to your every word. Respect. Worth. Value."

"You have your work, too, Jem. And value. You just need to focus on developing fresh content to go with the move. West Coast style." He grins. Hopeful. Expectant. "A new narrative for the new you."

She steps out of his reach, swipes away what's left of her tears, and gives a soft snort. "Instagram influencer? It's smoke and mirrors. It's as long as I can fake it, because honestly, who am I to tell other women how to accept their age, how to dress, eat, exercise, relax, vacation, be sexy? How to still 'have it all' and be their best fucking selves when it's a fucking crock of shit. Sixty is the new forty, my ass. It's still all about how to look *younger* longer. I've become part of the problem, perpetuating the narrative."

"You're just tired, Jem. And you're not sixty yet."

"Yeah, for another month."

"Tomorrow is a new day. After a good sleep, it'll all look different. I promise. It's just perspective. And you still have some old friends in the area, right? Like Sophia from your dance school days. And the new ones you've met online and at conferences. You should organize a dinner or something, invite them over. Come." He takes her hand and curls his fingers through hers. "Let's start the tour."

As Jemma is about to say the dogs still need to go outside first, Boo lifts his leg and aims a yellow stream of urine at the base of a designer leather sofa.

"Oh fuck!" Adam rushes forward. He scoops up the dog. "Damn you, Boo." He yanks open the glass slider and drops the dog out onto the deck.

"I *told* you they needed to pee, Adam."

"Then why didn't you let them outside at once? Look what he's done now." He gestures to the sofa. "Do you know how difficult it was to get that piece in that exact shade of leather?"

BEFORE THE HIT-AND-RUN

Adam immediately regrets his outburst. He *needs* Jemma to be happy here. He concentrates on controlling his breathing while Boo and Sweetie relieve themselves on the tiny triangle of lawn beyond the concrete patio. He lets them back in, closes the glass slider behind them.

"I'm sorry," he says to Jemma. "I just wanted it to be perfect. And to surprise you."

"It's okay. Why don't you show me around?" She tries to smile.

"Want to start up or down?"

"Up."

He leads her upstairs with Boo and Sweetie skittering behind them. "Main bedroom," Adam announces with a grand sweep of his arm. "Floor-to-ceiling windows everywhere in the house."

Jemma scans the room. Her features remain neutral. Adam feels a little dip in his heart. He clears his throat. "Walk-in closet. And the bathroom has a steam room and a small sauna."

Jemma enters the bathroom, turns in a slow circle, taking in the myriad of mirrors. "Very nice," she says. But her eyes don't seem to reflect her words.

Adam shows her the other upstairs bedrooms, then takes her back down through the kitchen and along a passage toward a guest bathroom and two more bedrooms. On the passage wall he's had the designer hang framed photos from happier moments in their lives. The kids at milestone stages. Birthdays. Family vacations. Him Jet Skiing with Jemma straddled behind him in a bikini, her arms wrapped tightly around his bronzed torso, a plume of Caribbean seawater arcing behind them. Huge smiles and laughter on their faces. A white-table dinner event on the lawns of their estate in Ontario. A skiing trip in the Italian Alps. Jemma in her race suit coming out of the water at an open-water endurance swimming event in Norway.

She pauses and regards the images. He waits for her reaction. She glances at him, and he sees emotion swimming in her eyes.

"They make you happy-sad?"

"Just sad. I—it's a narrative that isn't really true, is it, Adam?"

"What do you mean?"

She waves her hand at the images. "Those are the rare good moments we had with the kids. It doesn't tell the truth. It doesn't honor the pain and illness both our children went through for most of their lives."

"Jem, it's *supposed* to be about remembering the good moments."

"But is it? In doing this, are we actually trying to erase their struggles in a way?"

He bites down a spurt of frustration. This is exactly what their therapist has been counseling against—Jemma always zeroing in on the negatives, holding on to past pain, as though it might keep the kids' memories alive. He has been so patient. He's tried so hard. But it's been wearing on him. He's desperate now to help her find a new way forward, because if she can't, he won't be able to follow his own dreams without guilt. He chooses not to engage in this discussion now. It's best not to confront Jemma when she's tired.

"Come," he says gently. "Let me show you the home gym in the basement."

She follows him into a stunningly finished basement area walled with mirrors and furnished with top-of-the-line gym equipment, including free weights, stationary bikes, rowing machine, treadmill,

TRX, foam rollers, bands, balance balls, and a state-of-the-art sound system.

"Our road bikes are in the garage," he explains. "You can get a personal trainer in if you like. There's also an open-water swimming group that meets weekly in summer for social swims at Kits Beach. Plus, there's the Kits outdoor pool, and tennis courts."

"Looks amazing," she says quietly.

"Right?" Adam grins even as his uneasiness mounts. His desire to please her is kicking into overcompensating drive. "I saved the best for last."

"What's the best?"

He forces a bigger grin and tries to convey a sparkle in his eyes. "Well, you'll have to come see."

He takes her back to the main level and leads her toward a door off the kitchen. As she follows him, she says, "These windows really are huge—like half the house is windows. How do the blinds work?"

He reaches for the door handle. "That's the one little hitch. There was a screwup at the factory with the sizing and fabric, so the order is being redone. It'll all be in place within a few weeks." He opens the door.

But she comes to a stop. "A few *weeks*?"

"Won't be long."

"It's like being in a fishbowl, Adam. People outside will see everything happening inside, especially at night. I mean, look, even now, those apartments across the alley—anyone in those units can see right inside."

"Well, we can get some temporary screens that can be moved around. I'll order some tomorrow."

She regards him. Adam reads disappointment, irritation in her eyes. His neck muscles tighten. But he soldiers on. "Ta-da," he says with a flourish and an exaggerated sweep of his arm as he guides her into the next room. "Your home office, or studio. Or lady cave."

Jemma studies the white furnishings, the huge, gleaming white desk. The giant, framed poster advertising a North American podcast award ceremony in Vegas last year, where Jemma got an honorable mention for being part of an episode that won top honors in its category. Two matching dog beds have been positioned next to a cream leather swivel chair behind her desk. The ring light and microphone and giant curved monitors are all gleaming and new. In the corner is a gas fireplace. The floor-to-ceiling windows open onto a tiny personal patio, where the wide slats of an artsy industrial-looking metal fence provide some privacy from the alley.

She moves over to the bookshelves and touches framed photos of their children and images of dogs who have blessed their home over the years. Her hand goes to a new 360-degree PawGuardian cam that dispenses treats and shares pet photos directly to Instagram. Adam detects a small smile curving Jemma's lips. His chest feels instantly lighter.

"I put another pet cam in the living area," he offers. "And one in our bedroom upstairs." He knows how she likes to keep an eye on Boo and Sweetie whenever she's away from home.

Jemma goes to the windows and stares out. He sees her gaze going up to the apartment units across the alley.

"When the shrubs grow a bit, it'll feel more secluded. And when the blinds arrive, of course."

She smiles, leans up, and gives him a kiss on the cheek. "Thank you," she whispers against his ear. "It's perfect."

Her soft words, her pleasure, her warm breath against his ear send goose bumps over his skin, and Adam feels arousal in his groin. He cups her face and kisses her mouth. When she responds, surprise, then heat, spears through his belly, and he deepens his kiss, backing her toward a reading chair near the fireplace.

She resists, but only slightly, as Adam slides his hand beneath her blouse and unclasps her front-closing bra. When his fingers meet her nipple, he finds it hard, and he can't stop himself. He slides his tongue into her mouth and lowers her toward the chair. Jemma gives a small moan as she sinks into the cushions, opening her legs for him. He murmurs against her mouth, "We need to christen the place."

Jemma responds by reaching for his belt buckle and unzipping his jeans. He hurriedly sheds the rest of his clothes, and she does the same. Adam's mind narrows to only this moment, to the pure sensation of sweet physical pleasure as Jemma opens her thighs wide and draws him down and into her. It's been months, years even, since she's responded to him in this way. It excites him to a fever pitch, and he thrusts up inside her, moving harder, harder, faster, his breaths turning ragged as he forces her pale thighs open wider with his knees.

She suddenly freezes under him. "Adam!" she whispers urgently.

"What—what is it?"

"Over there, across the alley. Top floor. There's a woman in the window. She's watching us."

Frustration burns through him. He looks over his shoulder. Across the alley a drape moves slightly in the breeze at an open window on the third floor.

"I can't see anyone."

Jemma wriggles out from under him and grasps for her clothing on the carpet. She starts pulling it all back on.

His dick stands out, hard. He's frustrated. "Are you sure, Jem? I—"

"Of course I'm sure," she snaps. "She had binoculars."

"Come on, Jemma, *binoculars*?"

"Oh no—no you don't." She points her finger at him. "Don't you dare go there."

"Go where, for Pete's sake?"

"Go looking at me like that, like it's happening again, like I'm getting paranoid."

"Jemma, please—"

She storms out of her studio. Her little dogs scamper after her.

"Jesus," Adam whispers to himself as he flops naked into her white leather chair and just sits there for a while, looking out the bare windows at the unit upstairs across the alley. The drape billows again as a small wind gusts. But he honest to God can't see anyone standing there. Especially not a woman with binoculars.

BEFORE THE HIT-AND-RUN

Chloe quickly steps back behind the drapes. Her heart hammers—she's exhilarated by what she just witnessed through her mom's birding glasses. The new neighbors are exhibitionists with a high sex drive and no blinds, and suddenly the promise of days, weeks, months of entertainment spools like gossamer threads of happiness in front of her. She'll have something compelling to observe while sitting with her mother, or painting at her tiny desk in front of her bedroom window. A welcome distraction from the unbearable stress of waiting for her mom to die while desperately willing her not to.

That movie-star woman with the red-gold ringlets—*naked*—looked directly into her scopes, into her eyes. And Chloe looked back. They made contact. She vibrates with electrical energy and . . . guilt. Maybe a touch of shame.

She swallows, glances at her mother. Her eyes are closed. The oxygen compressor hums and whirs, mechanically feeding air into the nasal cannula. Her rosary is threaded through her fingers, as though her mom feels that if she slips away in slumber, at least Mother Mary and a means of penance for her sins will be with her.

A knock sounds on the door. Chloe jumps, and her gaze shoots to the door. The doorknob rattles. Chloe freezes. Her pulse races. She hears a key being inserted into the lock. She quickly checks her watch.

Bettina. Relief floods through her. She lost track of time and day. It's just the home carer arriving for her shift and using the key from the lockbox that George Vasilou—the Greek barber who lives one floor down—helped affix to the hallway wall so that if Chloe happened to be out, the shift workers could let themselves in without needing her mother to get out of bed.

"Oh!" Bettina says with surprise as she opens the door. "You're still here. No one answered, so—"

"I—I was just running late." Chloe starts making an overt fuss of gathering up her coat and hunting for her phone. "I couldn't find my cell. I was distracted. Sorry."

Bettina breezes into the flat, and in her wake flows the scent of freshly baked bread. Chloe feels blessed to have carers like Bettina on this difficult journey. Bettina is her mom's favorite. Kind and generous, gregarious.

"Hello, Raven," Bettina says as Chloe's mom's eyes flutter open. Her mom smiles weakly.

Bettina says, "I baked bannock and brought you some, like I told you I would when I was here last. You remember?"

Bettina is from the Squamish First Nation. She's reconnecting with her heritage and sharing it with her patients, and Chloe kind of really likes that. She wishes she knew exactly what her own heritage was, and where in the UK she actually comes from. Her mother never talks about it. She says it's a period *she* needs to forget. Well, Chloe has opposing needs. She needs to know how she fits into the world. But no amount of cajoling and whining and pleading over the years has ever wheedled a thing out of her mom. Chloe still has no idea who her dad is. Or was. She's come to the conclusion her mother might not even recall who fathered her offspring. Perhaps it happened on some drunken night. Perhaps he was—or is—a married man. Someone who might have given Raven Cooper and her infant daughter enough money to get on a plane to Canada and out of his and his family's hair. Chloe doesn't even know if Cooper is her mother's maiden name or a married one.

Maybe her father really is still out there. Maybe Chloe will find him and surprise him one day.

Hi. I'm your daughter. My name is Chloe Cooper, and I'm not creepy at all.

She suddenly remembers the empty vodka bottle and hurries into the kitchen to bag it and take it to the garbage. She doesn't want Bettina to see it.

"And you, Chloe, how are you holding up?" Bettina glances at her.

Chloe freezes—caught red-handed trying to sneak the empty vodka bottle into a garbage bag. Guilt flushes into her face. It shouldn't. She's an adult. She drinks only on her weekends. She forces herself to maintain a steady, nonchalant expression. "I'm doing okay." But as she says it, her voice catches despite her fiercest efforts.

"You sure? Do you need to talk to someone? There are support groups for family caregivers, you know?"

Bettina must smell the old vodka fumes coming off her. Shame rises hot in her chest. Immediately followed by self-loathing, self-disgust.

This is why you need routines, Chloe. Routines foster self-discipline. Without discipline you slide into dark and disorienting places. One day you will completely lose connection with reality.

"I—I know. Thanks. I'm heading off to walk the Mastertons' dogs down the road, then I'll be back to change and off to work this evening when your replacement comes."

"It's okay to ask for help, Chloe," Bettina says softly. "It does not denote weakness. On the contrary, it shows real courage. Strength."

Her mother's British voice snakes into her head.

Tell people too much and they use your vulnerability as a weapon against you, Chloe. Even if people seem kind, putting your innermost information into their hands can lead to it falling into the hands of Evil.

She nods and hurries out the door before she does something embarrassing, like cry.

As she goes down the stairs, she decides she'll walk the Mastertons' German shepherds slowly past Gloom House, where she might be afforded a good close-up of the activities inside. Then tonight, after work, when it's dark and the neighborhood windows morph into individual theater stages of yellow light through which occupants swim to and fro while attending to their private lives—when Chloe can see them but they can't see her—that's when she'll take Brodie out to pee again.

If the new neighbors are still awake, she will stand outside Gloom House in the dark for a while and watch them. With all that big glass, she's certain to learn quite a lot.

IT'S CRIMINAL: The Chloe Cooper Story

Drone footage shows an aerial view of Crow's Point. From the air the neighborhood is shaped like a triangle whose point juts into the Burrard Inlet. Jerrin Bay carves into the left side of the triangle, and Betty's Cove curves along the right-hand side. The Beach House Restaurant and Bar *sits near the rocky point and overlooks Jerrin Beach.*

The drone footage zooms down over the Spenglers' concrete home. It hunkers on a corner lot bordered by a laneway, the alley, and Crow's Road. The Spenglers' main entrance is on Crow's Road. Their garage and back entrance are accessed by the lane.

The drone moves and hovers over the roof of Chloe Cooper's apartment unit, then continues over the row apartments to show a view of Main Street on the other side. The drone zooms down in front of the commercial units to show a large and swarthy man who stands with feet planted wide and arms folded across a barrel chest. He's beside a red-and-white barber pole outside his barbershop. The man looks up at the drone camera as it approaches him. He sports an impressive handlebar mustache dramatically curled at the ends. His brows are heavy. He wears jeans, a white T-shirt, and as the drone camera comes even closer, viewers can see the gold-and-blue evil eye pendant hanging on a strip of leather around his neck.

Text at the bottom of the screen reads:

GEORGE VASILOU. BARBER. CHLOE COOPER'S NEIGHBOR.

The screen image fades to the interior of a traditional barbershop with a black-and-white-tiled floor, chrome features, red decor accents. George Vasilou sits in one of the barber chairs, dwarfing it. In his meaty hands he holds a tiny white espresso cup and saucer. He takes a sip of his espresso. In the mirror behind him, the reflection of a painting hanging on the opposite wall is visible. The painting is dark and somewhat abstract. It shows a woman with her feet trapped in rocks at the edge of a wild and stormy ocean. The woman's hair and dress blow and billow in a fierce wind. Also trapped inside the rocks are streaks and pools of gold.

TRINITY OFF CAMERA: You knew Chloe?

GEORGE: Probably better than most people in our neighborhood. She lived upstairs. I looked after that little dog, Brodie, when her mother went into medical distress and Chloe needed to get into the ambulance with her mom to go to the hospital. My nephew was friendly with her at the time.

TRINITY OFF CAMERA: Stavros Vasilou?

GEORGE: Yes. Stavros also worked as a bartender at the Beach House. That's where he met her.

TRINITY OFF CAMERA: What can you tell us about Chloe?

GEORGE: People said she was weird. A little creepy, or even crazy. But Stavros told me she was excellent at her job. Very precise. Ordered. She liked everything in certain places. When something was moved out of the right place, she'd get angry and scold her coworkers. And she knew all the patrons. She—it was like she made a study of them. Kept mental files on everyone. Sort of like an espionage agent.

TRINITY OFF CAMERA: So she liked to spy on people?

GEORGE: Focused observation. That's what she told Stavros it was. Sort of like detectives who know how to read little tells. They see signs and patterns others miss because they're not watching in the same focused way.

TRINITY OFF CAMERA: And she did this with the Spenglers?

GEORGE: She became fixated with Jemma Spengler. Their lives might have turned out very differently had they not moved in across the alley from Chloe.

TRINITY OFF CAMERA: Chloe gave you that painting on the wall?

GEORGE: As a thank-you for looking after Brodie. I—I think in retrospect, or I'm pretty sure, really, that it was done as a self-portrait, even if she didn't realize it at the time. I think Chloe felt trapped, like that woman in the painting. A woman who perhaps wanted to leave the rocks that trapped her feet and go into the sea. And all the veins and reservoirs of gold—they're the precious, enviable, valued, beautiful things in life— but they, too, are trapped inside those sharp, black rocks with her feet.

TRINITY OFF CAMERA: It's a sad painting then? Yet you keep it in your shop?

George is pensive for a while.

GEORGE: It's also quite beautiful. And a reminder. Part of a story.

TRINITY OFF CAMERA: A story that entwined your nephew.

George's dark eyes turn to look directly at the camera. He is silent. A determination tightens his features. He covers his evil eye pendant with a large hand.

GEORGE: If Stavros had never crossed paths with Chloe Cooper, he'd probably be here now, still. Coming to see me in my shop every Sunday. Same routine.

Emotion glints in his eyes.

GEORGE: But I believe our boy is in a good place now.

Another long pause. And then a smile.

GEORGE: I know in my heart he's in a good place. I—we all—also now know why Chloe Cooper had such an immediate and visceral hate for Dr. Adam Spengler. They were fated to clash.

BEFORE THE HIT-AND-RUN

September 15, 2019

The night is moonless, and it's near midnight when Chloe exits her building with Brodie tucked under her arm. She shuts the door quietly behind her and looks across at Gloom House.

Last night was a bust. By the time she returned from work, the new occupants were asleep, all the lights out. But early this morning, when she walked Brodie along the beach, she was delighted to see her new neighbor's bright-yellow sports car entering the Jerrin Beach parking lot.

From a distance Chloe watched the Hollywood goddess leave her car and go down to the rocks, where she shed her parka like a selkie skin. Mesmerized, Chloe watched her tuck her hair under a pink cap, pull on her goggles, then wade into the surging gray ocean in her wet suit. She swam all the way across the bay, then back, dragging her buoy behind her.

Chloe was transfixed. She can't swim, but in her dreams she can. It's as though she once knew how. But while her muscles seem to have some memory of it, her waking mind does not. Perhaps her dreamtime swimming comes from listening so often as a child to the audio version of a tale about a selkie. When Chloe was little, she actually believed she might be a selkie whose skin had been stolen—or hidden—leaving her unable to return to the ocean, or even remember her earlier form, and she was thereafter bound to remain on land, never quite knowing how to belong in the human world while she had this deep and inexplicably nostalgic yearning for the sea.

Watching her neighbor slide through the water with the ease of a seal spoke to something buried deep inside Chloe's core. Perhaps she and the Mistress of Gloom House are a mysterious kind of kin.

"Let's do this, Brodie," she whispers. She sets him down on the cracked paving and leads him slowly across the alley. Inside the Gloom House living room, she sees the flickering blue light of a television set—her neighbors are definitely still awake. She walks around to the front of the house on Crow's Road. It's the main entrance but there's only street parking out front. Chloe stops on the grassy verge and stands beneath a cherry tree. Brodie circles at the base of the tree, searching for a perfect pee spot while Chloe studies the entrance.

An outdoor light illuminates the front stairs and a tiny porch, and a milky glow shines through a rectangle of opaque glass that runs down the side of the wooden door. The architecture is quite hideous, in her opinion. Unwelcoming. Hostile, even. In the near future all the new houses of this design are going to look particularly dated to this period, and they will appear decidedly old fashioned.

Humans can be such peculiar herd animals.

With her phone, Chloe snaps a photo of the housefront. The flash blasts into the night. She freezes. Her pulse races. She didn't realize the flash was on. She stands motionless under the cherry tree, waiting to see if anyone noticed her. A cat emerges from under a car parked along the street. It stares at Chloe and Brodie, then slinks across the road and disappears under a parked van. A dog barks in the distance. No human appears.

Chloe leaves Crow's Road and rounds the corner into the alley. She glances up at her own apartment window. She sees the faint glow coming from her mother's night-light. It looks comforting. Safe.

Slowly Chloe walks Brodie along the thin strip of verge that runs beside the metal slats of the house's fence. He sniffs pee mail in the grass while she peers carefully through the fence gaps. Her heart beats a little faster. She can see her neighbors on a sofa, their bodies sunken deep into the cushions. Their feet are up on an ottoman. He has his arm around her, and she rests her head in the crook of his neck. Her long hair falls over the back of the couch. A little dog lies in her lap; the other is curled at her hip. They seem to be watching a movie.

Chloe shifts to her left and peeps in through another gap. There's a wineglass at the woman's side. The man cups a whiskey tumbler loosely in his hand. Classic choices—wine for the lady, Scotch for the man. Not terribly adventurous or risqué for exhibitionists who made love on a chair in front of a street-level window with no blinds.

The woman reaches for her glass and finishes her wine. Chloe wonders if they will visit the Beach House Restaurant and Bar. Surely it's only a matter of time before one—or both—steps into her domain? She shoots a few more photos through the gaps in the fence, secure in the knowledge she's deactivated her flash. The images will be grainy, but she might use them to sketch or paint a few pieces. As fascinated as she is with the selkie swimmer, the woman's partner gives Chloe a deeply uncomfortable feeling. It's like she knows him from somewhere before. The negativity she feels toward him makes her additionally curious about who these people are.

Curiosity killed the cat, Chloe. Your instincts are telling you this black-haired man means something Dangerous to you. You don't want to be a dead cat, do you?

She tugs Brodie's leash, leading him gently around the corner into the laneway. Almost instantly a vehicle rounds the corner at the far end of the lane, and headlights swing toward her. She gasps and jerks back into the shadows of a large bush, dragging Brodie with her. In her haste she knocks over a trash can, and the lid clatters like a cymbal onto the paving. As the sound echoes through the night, she quickly bends down, scoops Brodie up into her arms, and steps right back into the protective foliage of the leafy bush growing alongside the Gloom House driveway.

She remains motionless as the car crawls slowly down the lane toward her hideaway. Blood thuds in her ears. The driver appears to be searching for an address. As the vehicle nears, Chloe recognizes it as one of those sporty, newer Porsche models. Pearlescent white in color.

It stops in front of the Gloom House driveway. The headlights go off.

The driver's-side door opens, and the interior light illuminates a woman with a mane of shiny brown hair. Chloe's first observation is: *Beautiful woman.* She turns her head, and Chloe sees wide-set eyes. An aquiline nose, full mouth. The woman steps out of her car onto stiletto heels. She wears a fur coat.

Too warm for this weather. Crazy.

Chloe holds stock-still with Brodie in her arms as the woman swings her door shut. It makes a dull thud. In her hand is a bottle capped with foil and wire. Her coat falls open, and a thrill spears through Chloe— *She's wearing nothing underneath!*

Chloe can barely contain her excitement as the woman starts toward the rear-entrance door of Gloom House. At the same time an exterior light flares on and the front door opens. It's the man. He sees the woman. His jaw drops in shock, and his hand shoots toward her in a halting motion. The woman stops, as though confused. The man calls loudly back into the house, "I think it was just raccoons knocking over the garbage, hon! Going to take a look and clear it up. Don't pause the show for me—I've seen it before." He shuts the door carefully behind him and hurries up to the woman.

"What the hell?" he whispers as he reaches her.

Her smile fades. "Who were you calling out to?"

"Jesus, Gloria," he says softly as he draws the ends of her coat closed. "What the fuck are you doing?"

"I thought I'd surprise you at your new house with a special welcome, Adam." She holds up the champagne for him to see. "But it seems you already have company—who's inside?"

"Just—just come over here, away from the light." He grabs her hand, but she resists.

"Why?"

"I'll explain," he whispers. "Just—Gloria, come."

The two of them move closer to Chloe and Brodie's bush. Tension quivers through Chloe's body so intensely she fears the leaves around her will start rustling. At least Brodie is silent. He's basically deaf, and content to snooze in her arms. What will she do if they notice her? She can't very well step out of the bush suddenly and say: *Oh, hi, good evening, nice night for walking the dog. He's old. His bladder is not what it used to be.* That moment has long passed. She's fully committed now.

The woman—Gloria—glances toward Gloom House. "Who's inside, Adam?"

"It—Jemma's here."

"*What?*"

"Listen, I can explain—"

"Go on then. Explain to me why she's here. In *your* new house. You told me it was over with her. You promised. You—Christ, I don't believe this. You said you were moving out West, the new job, everything, because it was going to be just us. You. Me. Oliver. It was going to be our little family."

"Gloria, hear me out. Please. Jemma is vulnerable right now. I—I had to—"

"Had to what? Bring her out so she could live with you in your new house?"

He reaches for her arm, but she steps away, distancing herself from him. She stares at Gloom House, as if trying to process things. Then she spins back to face him. Chloe sees tears glistening on her cheeks.

"Two years," she whispers. "*Two years* we've been planning this. You told me two years ago she was vulnerable, that you were transitioning her slowly to the idea, and that you were both finally ready now."

He makes a lowering motion with his hand, indicating she should speak more quietly.

"Oh, you want me to keep it down? Hide in the shadows like some mistress?" She gives a harsh little laugh. "Right. Because clearly that's what I still am." She shakes her head. "God, I don't know why I trusted you so implicitly. Men. Fuck men. Fuck 'em all to hell!" She starts toward her Porsche on her impossibly high stilettos.

"Please, Gloria, I—"

She spins back to face him. "Exactly when *were* you going to tell me you brought your *wife* out?"

Chloe's phone vibrates in her pocket. Her breath catches in her throat. It vibrates again. She forces herself to hold still. At least it's on silent. But tension winds tighter. Who could be calling her at this hour? Her gaze shoots toward her window across the alley. The little glow inside is still warm. It all looks safe.

"I was planning to come to see you at the gallery tomorrow," he says. "I was going to tell you then."

Chloe's phone buzzes again. Perspiration prickles over her lip.

"Tell me what, exactly? That you've chickened out of a divorce?"

"Listen, she's been through a lot. We *both* have. She's still grieving. It just takes longer for some people, and it's not linear. I need to ease her into this, into being a single woman at this juncture of her life when she feels vulnerable for many reasons."

"Christ, you sound like your fucking therapist." She takes another step toward her Porsche, then pivots back again. "Does Jemma even know about us? About *me*?"

"I—ah—not yet."

"You said you'd told her."

Adam says nothing. A breeze blows, and the leaves around Chloe rustle. Her phone starts to vibrate again. Anxiety coils low in the pit of her stomach. She glances up through the leaves at her apartment window again. Surely her mother can't have woken yet? Not so soon after taking her heavy opioid meds?

"You *promised*, Adam. That you'd be present for Oliver, that you'd show up for him in the way you claimed your father never did for you. That's what this whole move was supposed to be about."

"I'm here, aren't I?" He holds his hands out at his sides. "The pieces are slotting into place, just a tiny bit slower."

She heaves out a breath of frustration. "So what's your plan now that she's here? Keep shuttling between two homes, but without the six-hour flight in between? You just wanted to make the deception a little easier on yourself? You want to be the renowned, virile surgeon who has, like, two wives? Perhaps there are more of us? Are there more, Adam?"

"Don't be ridiculous. You need to understand Jemma gave up her career, her entire life, for our kids, for my work. And she's still suffering from our recent loss. What sort of a man would I be to cut her deeper at a time like this? You surely should respect that in me, Gloria?"

"Oh, rich."

The buzzing in Chloe's pocket recommences. She has to get out of this bush, see who's calling.

He steps toward the woman, lowers his voice to a seductive croon. "Listen, I love you, Gloria. I love you and Oliver so much. More than anything. I just have a terrible fear that when Jemma learns I have another child, it literally might kill her. I don't want to be responsible for killing my wife. Come here." He tries to hug her.

She steps back and brandishes the champagne bottle at him. "I will not be *that* woman, Adam. Tell Jemma about me, finish it with her, or I'll walk away—I'll take Oliver. You'll never see him again. Make your choice."

She gets back into her car, slams the door shut. The engine growls to life, and the Porsche pulls away. Tires squeak as it rounds the corner into the alley. Brake lights flare in the night. And she's gone.

Wind gusts. Leaves rustle.

Adam stares after her. He drags both hands over his hair and mutters a curse. The door to Gloom House suddenly opens, and he spins round.

"Adam? What's going on? Is everything okay?"

"I—ah—all good, Jem. No worries." He starts back toward his house. "I was just sorting out the garbage can when a car stopped in the lane and some people asked for directions, and—" His voice cuts off as the door shuts behind him and Gloom House swallows the couple.

Chloe steps out of the branches and scurries across the alley with Brodie. She enters her building. As the door swings shut behind her, she checks her cell to see who called.

There's a new voicemail.

She hits the voicemail icon, presses *1* for the new message.

"Chloe," comes a husky, cracked whisper. "Help, Chloe . . . I . . . help. Need . . . can't . . . breathe."

Her mom! Panic strikes.

She pinions Brodie to her body and clatters up the stairs, stumbling, righting herself. She dashes down the hallway to her door, fumbles with a shaking hand to get the key into the lock, drops it. *Oh my God oh my God.* She scoops up the key, tries again. She flings open the door.

Chloe stills as she struggles to process the scene in front of her. Her mother is on the floor. Her limbs at odd angles. The nasal cannula has come out. Broken glass and spilled liquid surround her. Pills are scattered across the floor. Her mother is motionless. *Dead?*

"Mom!" She drops Brodie, rushes to her mother's side, falls to her knees. "Oh my God, Mom, what happened?" She feels for a pulse. Her mother is still alive, but barely. Her breaths come and go with a slow, wet wheeze. Her face is white as a ghost. She has an ugly gash on her head, and it's bleeding onto the floor.

"Mom! Can you hear me?" She pats her cheeks lightly. "Mom? Please, please, talk to me."

"C-Chloe?" her mother whispers, eyes fluttering open. "Is—is that you? Where . . . where were you, Chloe?"

"It's going to be fine, Mom. Hold on, just hold on. I'm getting help." She gropes in her pocket for her phone to dial 911. Her hands shake so hard she misses the *1*. She tries again, hears it ring. Tears wash down her face. "I need an ambulance! Hurry!"

BEFORE THE HIT-AND-RUN

September 16, 2019

The dispatcher takes Chloe's address, tells her to remain on the line, and informs her help is on the way. She asks Chloe to keep talking, to describe what's happening with her mother.

"She's got cancer. End—end stages, and she's fallen out of bed and cut her head, and she's ha-having trouble breathing. I—" Emotion overwhelms her, chokes her voice. *Focus. Focus. Do it for Mom.*

"She might have overdosed on medication as well. Hydromorphone." She sees more than one kind of pill on the floor. "She might have taken lorazepam, too. I—I don't know how much." Tears start coming. She should have been here. Her mother must have been in horrible pain. Chloe should have been giving her mother the correct meds; instead, she was in some stupid bush spying on the tawdry new neighbors—that *horrible* man and his mistress. She tries to insert the nasal cannula tube back under her mom's nose as she speaks, but can't because her hand shakes so badly.

The dispatcher asks if her mother is losing blood and says to apply pressure on the head wound. She asks if the apartment door is unlocked, and whether Chloe can find a safe moment to unlock it so the EMTs can get in. What about downstairs? Where is the most convenient entrance?

Chloe reaches up to pull a pillow off the bed. She tries to slide it under her mother's head as she tells the woman the ambulance will need to come around to the back alley. There is a building entrance there, where cars are parked. She says they can't access the building's front entrance on Main during nonbusiness hours.

She hears sirens. So many sirens. Coming closer, closer, louder. She begins to sob. She hears the sirens right outside now. The room begins to pulse with red light. The lights are probably probing into the big bare windows of Gloom House, throbbing right into the eyes of that ghastly man and his poor beautiful Hollywood goddess wife, who's being usurped by a nubile wench in a fur coat with a gallery and a little boy named Oliver, fathered by that man who makes Chloe feel so weird.

She pushes up from the floor and peers out the window. Firefighters in black uniforms are exiting a fire truck. *Why isn't there an ambulance?* Anxiety strangles her breathing.

"They're here, Mom," she whispers as she crouches back down beside her mother. "Help has come. Hold on."

This never would have happened if Chloe hadn't been out stalking. "I—I'm so, so sorry, Mom."

I can never rely on you, Chloe. Always doing stupid, creepy things. Look what you've done now.

Her mother's lids flutter closed. Her breathing slows to a strangled, high-pitched whistle.

The sound of heavy boots thunders up the narrow wooden staircase. Chloe hears the footfalls nearing her door. It swings open. Several big men in large, industrial boots with steel toes enter her tiny home. Fit, strong bodies. One has a big medical kit. Another carries oxygen.

It's a blur, all the questions about her mother: How long has she been like this? What medication has she taken? Is this sound in her chest new? They take her mother's vitals and ask Chloe to move the dog away, please, and to get farther back, out of their way, so they can work.

Two paramedics arrive. A dark-skinned man and a young white woman with a jaunty blonde ponytail who barely looks out of school. How can she possibly be old enough to save Chloe's mother? Chloe feels helpless as she clutches Brodie to her tummy and presses herself back against the bookshelf in the corner of her tiny apartment. Inside her head she hears her mother's strident British admonishments grow louder. Her voice seems to come from some far-off place and time when Chloe was tiny.

You can only blame yourself, Chloe. Sometimes you have to just accept it's your fault, that these are the consequences of your actions. This is what happens when you try to live vicariously through other people's more exciting lives.

Chloe thinks she hears a rooster crowing. She suddenly smells pig manure. In her mind the stink grows stronger. As though she's on a farm with livestock. Very deep inside her head she hears a terrible sound of a woman screaming. She squeezes her eyes tightly shut.

Is it a memory? It can't be real.

The woman's screaming grows muffled. As though Chloe has padded headphones over her ears. And she hears the beginnings of a familiar tale coming through the headphones. About a selkie. And calm slowly seeps back into her body. She begins to breathe. She's able to fully focus on what's happening.

The paramedics have gotten her mom onto some kind of stretcher so they can carry her down the stairs, because there is no elevator. They maneuver her out the door. Chloe grabs a bag with her mother's things and follows them down the stairs with Brodie clutched tightly in her arms. Outside, when she tries to climb into the ambulance with Brodie, they say she can't bring a dog. Chloe begins to cry.

That's when George, the Greek barber, appears at the ambulance doors. She realizes there are quite a few neighbors gathered outside in dressing gowns, watching the events.

"It's okay, Chloe," George says. "You go be with your mother." He holds out his hands. "Let me look after Brodie for you. Stavros will help.

He can tell your work what's going on. Call us when you can, to let us know how it's going."

She's immobilized with indecision, with fear. Someone from outside cannot be let into their bubble. How can she trust Stavros's uncle, the big, gruff, dark, hairy barber who tries to run the world from his shop on Main, with its classic red-and-white barber pole and gleaming chairs and checkered floor and chrome-rimmed mirrors and reviews that lure Gen Z trendsetters in search of a heritage experience?

He doesn't have a wife, Chloe. That's another reason not to trust him. And he's a foreigner. Her mother's voice inside her head turns self-righteous. *He cooks with too much garlic—you can smell it through the whole building. And he has that nasty Garfield of a cat that spends time in the shop with the clients.*

But Chloe does know Stavros. He's a fellow bartender at the Beach House. Stavros is awkward and rather ungainly and not terribly attractive. But he's kind and gentle. He's met Brodie. Brodie likes him.

Still, she's reluctant to let little old Brodie go. The paramedic says they need to leave, now.

She allows George to pry Brodie from her arms.

"His food is in the apartment," she says as she climbs into the vehicle. "And his bed, and leash—there's a lockbox. The code is—"

"It's okay, Chloe," George says in his growly Greek accent. "The dog boutique down the road will set us up. Brodie can spend time in the store."

"The cat?"

The doors start to close.

"The cat will be fine," George calls out. "Cat likes dogs."

The doors are latched shut. One paramedic is in the driver's seat. The other is in the back. He shows Chloe where to sit, indicates she should buckle up. She holds her mother's hand as they begin to drive, lights flashing and reflecting in store windows, the sirens wailing as they make the journey fast through the emptyish nighttime city streets to Vancouver General Hospital, which is affixed to the cancer center she has come to know so well.

53

BEFORE THE HIT-AND-RUN

September 16, 2019

Chloe sits in a beige hospital chair in the postsurgery waiting area. The room is clinical. Bland. Lit with fluorescent lights that belie the time of day or night. She feels numb, dissociated from reality. She could have been here hours or days—it all feels the same. Through the thick hospital windows, she sees a pale strip of lavender and yellow beginning to expand across the horizon. Dawn is coming, stirring the city awake. A heart of orange appears at the center of the yellow. The sun is peeping over the curve of the world. It's really quite beautiful, she thinks. Especially the lavender color and the way the yellow fades to peach. She should paint that one day—the earth revolving slowly into the pastels of a new day. Her mind returns to her plight.

She's terrified her mom won't come out of this huge gray hospital high-rise this time, that her chemistry can no longer be tinkered with, no longer adjusted with saline drips and medicines, setting her back into equilibrium like last time.

No, Chloe. Stop it. They took her into surgery. Surely they must believe there's something to be saved? Or why would they be operating?

She doesn't know why.

Maybe they told her and she's misplaced the information, or blocked it because she refuses to hear it. Everything that's transpired since she discovered her mom on the floor seems a bit of a jagged blur, to be honest.

What if her mom doesn't come out of this institution?

She'll be alone in the world.

Just Chloe.

Crazy Chloe Cooper, thirty-nine years old, with no one else in the universe. It strikes her suddenly that today is the day. Her birthday. That big portentous milestone day has dawned.

Today she turns forty.

She is now forty-year-old "creepy," "crazy" spinster Chloe Cooper—yes, she hears what people say about her. Even her mother calls her bad things. She's forty years old, and she always thought that when she reached this day, she'd surely have figured out how she fits into the world, or would understand why she's always felt "wrong."

She sees a surgeon in scrubs coming toward her. Scrubs cannot be a good thing. Surely if the operation had gone well he'd be in civilian clothes now? Changed and showered and ready to talk about future treatment? He comes closer. The corridor begins to narrow and elongate into an elastic tunnel, and the surgeon grows smaller and smaller, farther and farther back in the tunnel as her mind screams to make the tunnel even longer, thinner, so that it squeezes the surgeon out of her life, so he can never reach her sitting in the beige chair.

But the surgeon arrives at Chloe's feet. She tries to stand, but the surgeon makes a motion for her to stay sitting, and he takes the seat beside her.

BEFORE THE HIT-AND-RUN

As Chloe waits for an elevator, she studies the life-size photo images on the bank of elevator doors. One shows a senior man with dull skin, white hair, and a big smile. Another is a Black baby with outreached chubby arms. A different set of doors displays a pale-skinned child with a scarf over her hairless head. There's an East Indian woman in a sari. Another shows a teenage male of Asian heritage in hip-hop clothing. The messaging is clear: anyone in this world can get cancer. And if they're in this city, there's every chance they will end up right here. The cancer center, these wards.

The elevator bell pings, and a set of doors opens. She steps in. It's not a wide car, but it's deep to accommodate hospital beds. The doors slide closed.

Chloe begins the descent of the medical tower, trying to focus on nothing in particular.

The car stops two floors down. The doors slide open. A woman in scrubs wheels in a trolley of medical paraphernalia and a blood pressure monitor. She presses the button for the lower floor. The car stops again. The woman wheels out her trolley, leaving a waft of alcoholic-smelling sanitizer scent in her wake. The doors close, and the elevator hums slowly downward. Chloe imagines all the little microcosms of drama playing out right now, on each of these floors that she's sliding past, and beyond the hospital in houses and bedrooms, on the streets, in forests and on mountains all around the city, the nation, the entire globe, and it's so overwhelming she feels a carapace of protective walls creeping up around her.

You can't cry, Chloe. It's totally going to be fine. She's coming home, and that's the best one can hope for, right? Just a little more time in this life together, even if it's only a few days, or weeks.

Chloe grasps on to this idea like a lifeline, because the prospect of a completely solitary existence is simply unfathomable right now. The hollowness. She can't accept it. Not yet. She *will* continue the fight to keep her mom alive every step of the way. Maybe when the end finally does arrive, Raven Cooper's obituary will mention that it was her daughter who fought the battle with this disease. Bravely and fiercely, and she refused to give up. Her daughter kept Raven alive as long as she possibly could, giving her bonus days on this strange planet.

The elevator stops again, and the doors slide open. A tall man stands outside with his back turned to Chloe. He slaps his hand on the inside of one of the doors to hold the car open as he continues a loud conversation with someone unseen down the hallway. He's talking about golf. How very rude.

Instinctively Chloe shifts farther to the left side of the car before the man enters, because something about him spreads fine threads of disquiet through her.

When you get into a lift, Chloe, stand beside the control panel. If someone enters who makes you feel uncomfortable, if your spider senses alert you, you need to press every single button on that panel so the doors will open on every floor and give you more chance of escape.

"Okay," the man calls out. "See you at the club!"

He turns and steps into the elevator car. He's very tall, and Chloe automatically lowers her gaze. At her eye level she notices a doctor's ID card clipped to his breast pocket. Instead of stepping to the right-hand side of the car, allowing a decent bubble of space between Chloe and himself, he steps dead center, forcing her to squish even farther up against the side. Irritated, she glances up into his face.

He smiles.

Shock explodes through her body. *It's him.* A discordant noise starts in her head. It grows louder, louder, and Chloe feels a silent scream rising into her throat as she's seized by an overwhelming urge to hit all the buttons. She grits her jaw, fists her hands to control herself.

She's certain it's him.

The horrible man with the blue Tesla and mistress who lives across the road. Cautiously her gaze returns to the ID card. It reads DR. ADAM SPENGLER. He's the adulterer with a son named Oliver. The man who's going to dump that beautiful, willowy, pale-skinned goddess of a woman who is grieving, and it will kill her. He said so himself.

She returns her gaze to his face.

His eyes meet hers. They are the strangest, eeriest, palest blue, fringed by dense, pitch-black lashes that match his black hair. His teeth are unnaturally white, the canines pointy and a fair bit longer than his incisors, which gives them a slightly fang-like appearance.

Her brain spirals, and the edges of her vision grow ragged as an inexplicable fear serpentines up through her belly and snakes fire into her veins. She begins to shake. Her visceral reaction to this man terrifies her, because she doesn't understand it. She just knows on some molecular level that he's not nice. He's very bad and dangerous. She's encountered him before—she must have, but she can't recall how. *Was he one of the doctors who saw her mom?*

His smile deepens. "Morning."

All she can muster is a quick, tight nod.

He checks his phone, and they go down together in silence, all the way to the ground floor.

When the elevator stops and the doors part, Chloe bursts out and rushes into the hospital lobby. She makes directly for the revolving glass doors, panic nipping her heels.

Run, Chloe! Run! Run for your life!

As she shoots out of the revolving doors, she turns to see if he's followed her. But there is just a sea of people and staff flowing to and fro.

Of course he didn't follow you, stupid Chloe. Why would he? He's a doctor, for heaven's sake. Sure he is, Chloe, but he's also your cheating neighbor, and I told you to trust your gut.

She stands blinking into the rising sunlight for a few moments, then decides she'll walk home. It's far. It will take much longer. But she needs fresh air. It will help her decompress and clear her mind; plus, she cannot abide getting into a bus packed tightly with humanity right now. Besides, maybe if she lingers and draws out the walk and gets something to eat along the way, by the time she arrives home and picks up Brodie, her phone will ring to inform her that her mom is ready for release. She will then Uber back to the hospital to collect her mother. And it will be just the same as before.

As she crosses the street, she wonders whether she should stop and buy a gift for George as a thanks for watching Brodie. She has no idea what a Greek barber would like. Maybe she'll give him one of her paintings. Perhaps the one with the girl on the rocks by the sea.

IT'S CRIMINAL: The Chloe Cooper Story

The screen shows the interior of a dance studio with pale wood floors, mirrors as walls. Ballet barres are attached to the mirrors. Sunlight streams in through the windows. The space is empty until the studio door opens and a dark-haired woman walks in. She's in her late fifties or early sixties and moves like a lifelong dancer. Lean, lithe, ruler-straight spine.

She takes a seat on a stool. Lights dim while a spot shines only on her. Hers is not a classically beautiful face, but a striking one. Wide mouth, roman nose, dark brows, flashing black eyes. Her hair is swept loosely up onto the top of her head. The style underscores her defined jawline and prominent clavicles. A small gold chain with a pendant shimmers in the hollow of her throat.

Text at the bottom of the screen reads:

DANCE TEACHER SOPHIA MANCINI. OLD FRIEND OF JEMMA SPENGLER.

TRINITY OFF CAMERA: You've been Jemma Spengler's friend since her early Vancouver Dance Institute days? When she was Jemma Jayne Jarvis?

SOPHIA: We might have masqueraded as friends, but I can't say Jemma ever really had true friends. People said her husband had an inflated sense of grandiosity, a surgeon's god complex, but I believe Jemma was the real narcissist in that relationship. I met her when she was eighteen. She was beautiful, charming, a strategic thinker and uniquely talented dancer. But she was also cunning, manipulative, controlling, incriminating of others, and she was very adept at posing herself as a victim if things went wrong. She—Jem—was a challenging person. I used to put this down to her upbringing. Jem basically clawed herself out of the low-income trailer park she grew up in, and completely disowned her junkie mother and her past.

TRINITY OFF CAMERA: What about her father?

SOPHIA: She never really spoke about him. He died in a fire when she was around thirteen.

TRINITY OFF CAMERA: A lot of tragedy in her life.

SOPHIA: There was. People say it's why she was so driven to transcend it all. To succeed in spite of her past. But I think people should perhaps reframe that and ask why tragedy followed Jemma.

TRINITY OFF CAMERA: You both competed for one of the few coveted places at Toronto Dance Institute?

SOPHIA: She won it that year. Beating me and hundreds of other hopefuls from across the country.

TRINITY OFF CAMERA: And it was in Toronto that Jemma Jayne Jarvis first encountered Adam Spengler?

SOPHIA: Chicago, actually. Where Jem was performing. Adam was invited to the opening night by some medical benefactor—a connection to his wealthy parents. He met Jem in person at the party afterward. He was totally smitten from the moment he first saw her onstage. And she was utterly resplendent that night. The performance was televised, recorded—people can still see it.

> *The scene fades to an archived clip of a televised performance. A cone of spotlight falls on a dancer in white, alone on an otherwise dark stage. Her skin is alabaster, and her red-gold hair hangs in ringlets down her back. She's long and impossibly thin, and moves with the grace and power of a gazelle. Her white costume shimmers with silver threads as she leaps and spins and weaves and fills the audience with awe and emotion.*

> *The music crescendos, and drums begin to beat as three male dancers enter the scene. The final act is sensual, erotic, powerful. It depicts copulation, then death, as the dancer collapses and sinks to the floor like a puddle of melting ice. The lighting changes, and for a second all music stops. The audience appears electrified by the silence. One imagines being able to hear a pin drop in the auditorium that night. The image fades away, and the screen segues back to the studio interior.*

> *Sophia sits in silence a moment. She clears her throat.*

SOPHIA: She was mesmerizing that night. I think every man with red blood wanted to take Jemma Jarvis home after that show. No one did. She was wholly focused on her career, her passion, her dream to win a place with the Paris Institute. Bigger. Better. But Adam caught her eye at the party afterward. He asked her out. She declined. However, he was not a man who took no for an answer. Her rebuff just steeled his determination. He became laser focused on "owning" Jemma, this beautiful, ethereal creature that so many men lusted after. He flew to her performances around the States, and the world, when he could. He just kept showing up, and asking her to dinner, until she finally agreed.

Sophia pauses for a while.

SOPHIA: I think that's what won her over in the end—her need to be wholly desired, adored, and needed so desperately that the devotion became almost blindly obsessive.

TRINITY OFF CAMERA: And then came the day she was finally invited to study further, and perform, with the Marie Lacotte Institut de Ballet et de Danse Contemporaine in Paris.

SOPHIA: When she turned twenty-five, yes. Adam was three years older, and his medical career was also on the cusp—taking off. Plus, he'd just proposed. Jemma was caught between a career with endless possibilities of global fame and a marriage to a rising-star surgeon whose father was a well-known and respected federal judge and whose mother was a glittering Toronto socialite. The Spengler family had all the money she'd ever need. Adam's kind were everything Jemma's family was not, everything she aspired to. And as her decision loomed, Jemma discovered she and Adam were pregnant.

TRINITY OFF CAMERA: What happened?

SOPHIA: She made an extreme sacrifice. She gave up her dancing dream—her aspirations to global fame—for Adam and their baby. She ended up staying home to care for the child, thus freeing him to fully pursue his own career. Jemma told me at the time—we remained in contact via phone calls—that she refused to be like her own mother and her father, who basically rejected her. She was committed to embracing her child. They had a beautiful baby girl, Hailey. But Hailey was diagnosed with cystic fibrosis, which made life even more challenging for Jemma and Adam. Jemma devoted her entire life—her being—to caring for Hailey. With advances in medical care, the average age of death for cystic fibrosis patients has been steadily increasing. Patients can live well into adulthood now—some even into their thirties or forties—but Hailey developed an acute lung infection when she was seventeen. She was hospitalized and died of respiratory complications. Jemma and Adam were devastated. Jemma totally lost all sense of purpose. She confided to me that she felt she had nothing left—no child, no career, no sense of self. She became inconsolable.

TRINITY OFF CAMERA: But they had another baby? Even though Jemma was forty-three, she gave birth to Jackson?

SOPHIA: She was desperate to become a mother again, to fill that maw Hailey left in her existence. She and Adam consulted countless health-care providers and decided to opt for fertility treatments and try again, despite the warnings of complications with pregnancy at an older age. The resulting pregnancy was difficult because of age-related issues, but Jemma absorbed—even relished—the fuss and the imposed bed rest and devoted attention from Adam and his family and friends. When Jackson was born, he was underweight and sickly. He never really thrived. One illness after another. Jemma took to her role again of caring for an unwell child. Jackson eventually developed an acute and mysterious blood infection when he was fourteen. He died in 2017, two years before Jemma and Adam moved west to "start over."

Sophia is quiet for a long while. Her features turn pensive. She faces the camera directly.

SOPHIA: It was supposed to be a new phase in their lives—that move out West. They were trying to leave the tragedies of their past behind, to look forward, and do more things together. Or at least that's what Jemma seemed to think.

Sophia wavers, then takes a deep breath.

SOPHIA: But you've got to ask yourself what really happened to those kids.

TRINITY OFF CAMERA: What do you mean?

SOPHIA: It's almost like Jemma needed the drama. The attention that came with it all. And if Jemma didn't get what she wanted—if she didn't get the attention, the devotion—she turned vindictive. I mean . . . there's still an open question about what really happened to her old boyfriend who dumped her back in her Vancouver days. People can't just "leave" Jemma. Not without consequence. And she'd use others to get the thing she wanted.

Another long pause.

SOPHIA: Chloe Cooper really didn't stand a chance.

BEFORE THE HIT-AND-RUN

September 24, 2019

A fierce north wind pummels the shore, and the Burrard is awash with whitecaps as Chloe walks to the Beach House Restaurant and Bar for her shift. She took the past week off work after the 911 episode with her mom. Mornings were pretty routine during that period: walking Brodie to the beach, watching her neighbor swim, returning home to feed Brodie, cooking her mom's oatmeal, counting out her pills. The afternoons and evenings were where things got fuzzy. Chloe started drinking after lunch each day, while watching her neighbors' house and painting at her little desk, listening for her mom to call for help. By late afternoons Chloe was blissfully, numbly drunk. She must have functioned okay, because she got everything done, but in truth she really doesn't have a memory of what actually transpired during the times from midafternoon until she woke the following morning with a groggy head. She's glad to be returning to work now. She really does need the structure back in her life.

She pulls open the big restaurant door and is greeted by an immediate aura of warmth. The sight of the gas fireplace flickering in the corner next to her bar fills her with comfort. But as she steps into the entrance area, she notices something on the wall that stalls her dead in her tracks.

Bill has gone and hung her gift of the Beach House painting slap bang in the center of the wall above the hostess's stand. It's the first thing a customer will see when they walk in and pause at the sign that says PLEASE WAIT TO BE SEATED. Chloe's work—right in their faces, with all the time in the world to ogle it while they await a table.

She feels naked. Ripped wide open. Exposed. This image that came from deep inside her heart—this thing she painted privately at home—is now displayed for the entire neighborhood to see. An irrational and fierce anger begins a slow burn in her chest.

She glances around, trying to settle herself, trying to tell herself it's fine. It's really, really, ultimately going to be fine. Everything is perfectly normally completely okay. But all she hears is her mother's rebukes inside her head.

Christ, Chloe, you *gave it to him for a birthday present. What did you* think *he was going to do with it? Honestly, just when I believe you might finally have gotten it into your thick, dull skull to not draw attention to yourself, look what you've done. Your private feelings and emotions translated into glossy paint for all to gawp at? What'll it be next? More of your paintings hung around town? You* will *regret this, mark my words. The more of your vulnerabilities you put out there, the more opportunity you give enemies to weaponize them against you. You have got to stay in your lane, Chloe. It's the only way to be safe out there.*

"It's stunning, Chloe." A male voice butts into her mother's tirade. Chloe starts and spins round.

It's Stavros. George the barber's nephew. Too skinny. Too tall. Face too elongated. Glasses frames overly dramatically black and heavy. Ridiculously long sideburns and an unfortunate little soul patch below his bottom lip, as though he's channeling some jazz musician from the forties or fifties. A young and white Dizzy Gillespie, maybe. And his acne-scarred skin appears oily when he's working hard behind the bar. Stavros's breath always smells of those little aniseed mints he's perpetually sucking. Chloe prefers to *not* smell people's breath. Ever. Or to feel the warmth of it anywhere near her face. Unhygienic. Invasive.

"Why did Bill do that?" Chloe demands.

"Do what?"

"Hang it up there." She points. "Where everyone can see it?"

"Well, he *wants* everyone to see it. That's the—ah—idea."

"There's no reason to mount it right above the hostess's head."

Stavros angles his own head and gives Chloe a hint of a smile, which draws her attention to that provocative sprout of hair beneath his lower lip.

"Do you find this amusing, Stavros?"

"Bill loves the painting, Chloe. That's why he hung it there. He actually canvassed some of the staff, asking us where we thought it would look good. We all reckoned this was the best spot." He tilts his chin toward her rendition of the Beach House at night, windows aglow with yellow, people sitting at tables inside.

"By committee?" Chloe is horrified.

"Honestly, Chloe, it's brilliant. One of the customers who came in yesterday said it reminded him of a famous painting by Edward Hopper called *Nighthawks*."

She stares at him. She doesn't know about Edward Hopper, and she's not about to admit it. She'll google Hopper later.

"Seriously, where did you think Bill would hang it when you gave it to him?" Stavros asks.

"I don't know. At home, maybe. Or throw it away. I had to give him *something* for his birthday." Chloe likes Bill. She's indebted to him for giving her a start in the bar business. But before Stavros can answer, she makes a beeline for the bar, where she knows she will be safe behind the counter. In her domain. Her castle. With her arsenal of bottles and mixers and herbs and spices at her fingertips. Ingredients with which she can produce any variation of elixirs and potions to appease her patrons.

I know what you all like. I know exactly how much each of you drinks. All of you who live in this elitist little neighborhood enclave. I know your weaknesses. I see your lies. You're not as special as you all think you are.

Stavros, annoyingly, follows her. She keeps her face averted as she tucks her purse under the counter, shrugs out of her puffy jacket, and takes her black apron with its name tag off a hook. She loops the apron over her head and secures the ties behind her back.

"You should be proud of your work, Chlo. You have talent. Everyone says so."

"Don't call me Chlo, Stavros. My proper name is Chloe. And I don't see why people should talk about me behind my back. I know they do, but—" A weird emotion attacks out of nowhere, and her voice cracks. Tears threaten to come to her eyes. She doesn't know why she's suddenly reacting this way. It's as though seeing her painting up there has ripped away the protective veil of numbness she's been hiding under this past week, since the hospital episode.

You attracted attention. I told you—you would live to rue the day.

"Why are you so scared of the truth?" Stavros asks. "You're talented, Chloe. The photos of some of your other pieces that you showed me are stunning. And that painting you gave my uncle—"

"I am not scared, Stavros. What makes you think I'm scared? And for heaven's sake, just—just leave it alone, okay?" She turns her back on him and starts polishing glasses.

"Say, talking of birthday gifts, isn't yours coming up soon, too?"

"No."

"I'm sure you mentioned the other day that—"

"I didn't. You're wrong." She refuses to face him. She starts checking her inventory. No way on earth is she telling him she already turned forty in a beige hospital chair.

He's silent for a while. She wishes he would leave.

"Is it your mom, Chlo? Is she doing okay? How is she?"

"She's perfectly fine. Same as usual. The care worker will call if there's another emergency at home."

"And Brodie?"

"Brodie's fine."

"Okay, well, cool." He removes his own black apron. "Your shift. Bar's all yours."

He heads toward the kitchen with his peculiar bouncing lope, balling his apron up in his overly large hands as he goes. Her gaze follows him for a moment. Part of her wants to reach out, pull him back, say sorry, tell him she doesn't know what's overcome her.

Another part is relieved he's gone.

The whole thing is unnerving. Better to focus on getting her domain shipshape and regaining control. She checks her reflection in the mirror behind the bottles and smooths her brown hair. It's parted in a straight line down the middle and secured neatly in a little bun at the nape of her neck. No makeup. Clean face. Ready to blend into the bar background and simply serve. And observe.

About a half hour later, Chloe has hit her stride, and she's carefully pouring a third round of craft brew on tap for two men in their early thirties who sit at one end of her bar. They're talking about the physical attributes of their recent dates, and how everyone they know meets their partners online these days, instead of in places like this. As Chloe sets the full glasses in front of them, a kerfuffle of noise erupts at the restaurant entrance.

The men stop talking and turn to look as a woman's strident voice rises and carries into the establishment.

"Your website says you're dog friendly," the gray-haired woman says loudly. "So does your IG account. You even have posts with dogs in them. So why can't we bring these two in?"

Chloe edges along the bar to a vantage point where she can better see what's happening. Five women ranging in age from perhaps their late fifties to late sixties are arguing animatedly—and possibly drunkenly—with the host, who politely listens with his clipboard in hand. Chloe's heart almost stops.

One of them is her neighbor. The swimmer.

Her red-gold hair is piled elegantly on top of her head, and in her arms are her two little cavapoos.

"It's expressly why we came here," says the woman with the booming voice. She's stocky and tanned and strong-looking. She wears athletic gear, and her gray hair is cropped short and spiky. She turns to Chloe's neighbor. "I'm so sorry, Jemma."

"We *are* dog friendly, ma'am." The host has to raise his own voice to make himself heard over their fussing. "But only on the patios. You'd have to sit outside. We do have outdoor heaters if—"

"This is ridiculous!" exclaims the loud woman. "Have you *seen* how windy it is today? I specifically booked that window table at that far end over there." She points into the restaurant.

"We were not informed you were bringing dogs, ma'am. We do have an outside table that's screened from the sea wind."

The loud woman turns to the swimming goddess with the offending dogs. "Do we want to sit outside? What do you think, Jemma? Or shall we find somewhere else? We could always go back to your place and order in."

Panic swamps Chloe. *No. No!*

She can't let them leave. Not now!

This is a *sign*. The golden goddess—Jemma—has come to *her*. Into Chloe's own domain! A captive environment where she can learn all about her, especially within the context of a group of boisterous and tipsy friends. This—*this*—is her opportunity, and she simply cannot allow it to slip from her grasp. Not at this juncture of her life. Besides, she surely must find a way to tell Jemma about her husband and that woman, Gloria. Chloe quickly exits the area behind the bar and hurries to the group at the front.

"Wait!" she says in a polite but determinedly authoritative voice.

All turn, stare. The group falls silent. And waits.

Heat rises into her cheeks. *Keep a bland face, Chloe. You have an important goal. You must get them to stay.*

"If you all would like to sit at the long table by the bar." She points. "Over there by the fireplace. I know it's near the television, and it can be a little noisier, but it's right by the glass doors onto the patio. I can leave the door open a little while you sit inside—the dogs can be outside, almost right by you," she says directly to Jemma. *My God, she's even more alluring up close.* Her eyes are an impossible amber flecked with gold—a lioness's eyes—and her skin is translucent alabaster with a smattering of ever-so-fine freckles. Chloe's heart beats faster.

"It's basically like having them right at your feet," she says. "You can reach out the gap to pet them. I've had several customers do that. We even have clean and warm dog beds." She smiles her biggest smile. "We *are* actually dog friendly, you see. Well, as best as we can be with the current government health regulations for British Columbian eating establishments, which are really quite ridiculous, in my opinion."

No one says a thing. They're absorbing Chloe. Deciding whether she's weird, or overbearing, or too eager, or . . . something. The host is also regarding her oddly, because she really is acting out of character on this first day back at work after the hospital incident.

"Jem?" asks the loud woman. "What do you think?"

Jem *for short. How charming, how winsome.*

Chloe inches closer to the two cavapoos in *Jem's* arms. "Aren't you cute," she says to them, but she's careful not to stick her hand into their faces and pet them or anything. She *always* waits for a dog to invite touch. It's a sign of respect. Chloe cautiously glances from the dogs up into the face of their human. She really is tall, quite perfect. The kind of woman Chloe could never ever in her wildest dreams be anything like. She guesses Jemma must be in her late fifties, but she's very well maintained, with an obvious focus on self-care, so who knows. But one thing Chloe does know is that this woman needs to be saved from that beast of a man before he does something that kills her, like she overheard him saying. It suddenly becomes her new and sole task in life.

"What are their names?" she asks Jemma.

"This is Boo, and this is my Sweetie."

"Hello, cuties. Can I give them a treat? I have a jar of doggy biscuits on the bar. All-natural ingredients. Organic."

"Dog treats in the bar?" Jemma asks.

Chloe smiles. She has impressed the Goddess. "I love dogs—all animals, really. I'm a dog walker in this neighborhood when I'm not being a bartender. Shall I show you to the table?"

Jemma glances at her friends. "What do you think, guys?"

"It's really about you and the dogs, Jem. If you're good, we're good, right, guys?" The loud woman turns to the others. They nod and murmur agreement.

"Sure, why not," Jemma says.

And the "girls" follow Chloe into her domain.

Where she is in control.

BEFORE THE HIT-AND-RUN

Jemma settles her babies in the cozy beds right outside the glass sliding door, and once cocktails and prosecco have been delivered, and food orders have been placed, Jemma goes to the head of the table.

"Okay, you guys, everyone gather up this end." She makes a come-together motion with her arms. "I want a group shot of us for Instagram."

With her at the restaurant tonight—at Adam's suggestion—is Sophia Mancini from the Vancouver dance school Jemma attended in her late teens. Also here are three newer friends whom Jemma met at a social media influencer event in Vegas. One is Dot, a loud and occasionally foulmouthed seventy-year-old who was once a hard-living, heavy-drinking, very overweight chef before she underwent a mental and physical "transformation" with Natalie, her body-sculpting lifestyle coach. Natalie is also here—a world bikini-bodybuilding champ and viral sensation with clients around the globe, many of them inspired by Dot's metamorphosis at age seventy.

If Dot can do it, you can do it is Natalie's current shtick.

Dot's physical evolution was captured on film by Annique, a professional photographer who specializes in shooting women who have undergone Natalie's transformation program. Annique has also joined the party tonight.

At Jemma's summons the group of women quickly swallow fortifying gulps of their alcoholic libations, push back their chairs, and jostle and chatter and laugh hysterically as they attempt a group selfie. The pre-drinks and edibles consumed at Jemma's house before heading to the restaurant have rendered them loose-limbed and boisterous. Jemma holds her phone out as far as she can and snaps a photo. She examines the result and chortles.

"Oh God, I've cut half your heads off."

"Ask the bartender to take it," says Natalie.

Jemma goes to the bar. The mousy employee comes over to her. Jemma quickly takes in her appearance—brown hair, matching dun-brown eyes, dull skin, average height, neither slender nor overweight—and wonders whether she'd recognize this nondescript woman if she ever saw her again in the street. She's perfect for serving staff, the kind that blends nicely into the background and surfaces instinctively only when you need a refill, or something else.

Jemma's gaze dips to the name tag on the woman's apron. *Chloe.*

"Would you mind, Chloe?" She holds out her phone. "Taking a photo of our group?"

The bartender eagerly obliges. She takes several shots, various angles.

Dot says, "Everyone chant the slogan for Jemma's IG!"

In unison they call out, "Sixty is the new forty! Age is just a mindset!"

The bartender shoots one more with a wide angle, and Jemma suddenly becomes aware that other diners in the restaurant are overtly watching their noisy performance, then turning their heads to quietly discuss the women, heads bent low over their tables. Two men in their thirties at the far end of the bar ogle them, too. But not in a nice way. Their expressions are borderline hostile, as though a group of older women having an inebriated gathering in their presence both intrigues and disgusts them.

The bartender hands back her camera.

"Thank you, Chloe," Jemma says.

"Yes!" The group chimes in, raising glasses. "Thanks, Chloe!" They laugh loudly.

"No worries," Chloe says. But she lingers a moment, and Jemma wonders if she wants a tip. "Are Boo and Sweetie doing okay?" the woman asks.

"Oh, yes." Jemma smiles. "They'll survive. They have warm enough coats."

"Let me know if you need anything."

The food arrives, then more food. Drinks are poured and repoured and swallowed, and chatter grows louder as arms move and laughter flows and the women sink deeper into their own delicious, drunken bubble while the rest of the establishment blurs to oblivion around them.

Except for Jemma.

She feels off. Her mind strays to Adam. More and more she senses something is amiss about their move west. When she broached him about her discomfort, he said it's her state of mind. And, well, of course it is—she believes this big change might be a mistake.

She also has an uneasy sense he lied to her about the raccoons and the voices outside the other night. She's pretty sure she heard him talking urgently with a woman.

"So how was the wedding shoot?" Dot asks Annique. Jemma yanks her focus back into the circle of conversation.

"Interrrresting." Annique laughs and takes a swig of her prosecco. "That's my charitable description. The groom was older. He—"

"*Old* is relative," Dot interjects forcefully. Since her transformation Dot has been on a crusade, powering through and bulldozing down any vague hint of ageism or misogyny related to it.

"Older by how much, exactly?" Jemma asks, reaching for her wine.

"By thirty-nine years," says Annique. "He's sixty-five to the bride's twenty-three."

Jemma gives a harsh laugh. "Christ, he's almost my husband's age. And that bride is almost a decade younger than my own daughter would be if she were still alive."

Silence ripples over the party. The mood shifts.

"I'm just saying"—Jemma sips her wine—"it must be hard to swallow for the ex-wife."

"No kidding," Annique says. "Especially since the groom and ex-wife's daughters were part of Dad's new wedding entourage—all three older than his bride. The daughters also wanted to include their mother in the party—didn't want old Mom sitting home alone and brooding while they were whooping it up at Dad's nuptials."

"What do you mean by including Mom in the wedding party?" Natalie asks.

Annique says, "Well, they didn't want to seat Mom with strangers at some distant table, so she ended up at the main table, where she promptly got inebriated. You can imagine where it went from there, right? A scene from a bad comedy, with the ex proposing toasts to boob jobs, dermal fillers, Cialis, and Botox."

Dot slaps the table with her hand and throws her head back in a guffaw. Raucous laughter erupts from the rest of the group.

The guys at the end of the bar glance their way again. So do the other patrons. The looks on their faces seem to say: *Old crones. Harridans getting wasted. How pathetic.*

Or is this just Jemma's state of mind? Is she projecting her own feelings into everything?

The guys at the end of the bar suddenly swing their attention to the restaurant entrance. Their postures change—spines stiffen, shoulders square. Jemma's gaze follows theirs. She sees what's ensnared them. A young woman with long, lustrous, mahogany hair that cascades in waves over her shoulders has just stepped into the entrance area and is waiting to be seated. She wears tight, ripped jeans, trendy platform sneakers, big gold hoop earrings, and a cream sweater that skims the curves of her generous breasts and slender waist.

As the host leads her to a table, all eyes in the restaurant follow her. She's a siren of youth and sexual promise, pulling the attention of every red-blooded male in her wake, drawing envy from other females. That woman is everything Jemma is not. Not anymore.

As the siren reaches her table and the host pulls out a chair, she glances toward Jemma's party. She says something to the host, appearing to indicate she'd prefer to sit at the bar. The host brings her toward the bar. Her gaze catches Jemma's as she nears. The woman doesn't look away immediately. Rather, she brazenly holds Jemma's gaze, and Jemma feels an odd sense of connection, something very direct and personal. Almost confrontational. She swallows and watches as the woman sets her purse on the counter and seats herself on a barstool not far from the two men.

"That poor mother," Sophia is saying.

"How did the old dude and young bride meet?" asks Natalie.

"Tinder," says Annique. "I reckon ninety percent of my wedding clients meet via dating apps. Especially couples in the thirties range. And then there are the older or midlife-crisis men looking for a second time around—marrying very young brides who are often from immigrant families, or are looking to settle in a new country that has better opportunities than they left at home. To my mind, many of these young women are after financial security, and they offer their youth as a trade-off." She swigs back the rest of her prosecco and reaches for the bottle in the cooler. She pours herself another glass.

Natalie says, "So they're prepared to settle for Creepy Old Pedo, just so they can afford the lifestyle they want?"

"I tell you, not all the old guys are creepy," counters Annique. "Some are accomplished, wealthy, fit, good-looking athletic types, pumping it up at the gym and desperate to cling to some idea of youth after a midlife crisis of some sort."

"And they trade in the old wife because she's used up," Sophia says bitterly. "She's gone and given the best of herself to supporting his career while her own took a second place because she's the one raising his kids, being a good mother, trying to keep a beautiful home, trying to eat well, and to exercise, and to look her goddamn best for him, and finally time just robs her of everything."

Another mood-altering silence falls over the group. Attention turns to Sophia, whose eyes suddenly glitter with tears.

"This is so fucking clichéd," snaps Jemma. "I hope all those ex-wives take the fucking exes to the cleaners."

"I'm sure as hell taking mine to the cleaners." Sophia swigs back her cocktail and defiantly shoots up her hand, signaling to the bartender for another. "And, yeah, we fall in love, we marry, we start little families with our hearts full of dreams. Then the going gets tougher as the kids grow. But you keep soldiering on through various challenges, thinking it's all still perfectly fine, considering. You're driving the kids to soccer, still going on family holidays, everything seems *normal*, and suddenly you discover he's been having an affair behind your back for three fucking years. But I can tell you one thing." Sophia points her glass at the other women. "When it comes down to it, you need to treat divorce as a pure business transaction. You get the best lawyer you can. You fight to win the house. You win control of who sees the kids and when, and you take more than half his fortune and secure alimony for the rest of his life. But despite it all, ex-wives never *really* win, do they? He moves on, starts a new family, has new babies, but you can't—not in that way. So you obsess. You scroll through the new couple's social media accounts like you have an addiction. You park outside their house at night and watch through the windows. You follow him, or her, to the store, to the new kids' elementary school. You're the one left all alone. You no longer attract the male gaze. Not in that way."

Gently Dot says, "It's not always like that, Sophia."

She snorts. "Isn't it, though? Who in the hell wants to date a woman who has to ask her doc for 'old lady vag cream' to lubricate her vagina when it's drying up, and who just doesn't have the mojo at the end of a long day because the hormones are gone. I swear to you, it's nothing like the movies. It's nothing like the messaging social media accounts bombard you with."

Tears escape her eyes and her nose turns red. "Don't try to tell me that every senior couple is happily humping away at home. Sure, senior guy is swallowing his Viagra or Cialis, but he's not getting it off with Grandma. He's humping his twenty-year-old Tinder date at a hotel downtown."

Silence, awkward, presses heavily over the table. The music, the television, the other restaurant noises suddenly become noticeable, louder.

"Wow." Annique claps slowly. "You go, girl."

"In my opinion there are two kinds of husbands," Natalie declares in her smoky voice. "Those who you *know* are having an affair, and those cunning enough to keep their affair secret and get away with it." She raises her glass to make a point. "Dangle a fresh bit of tail in front of a man, and mark my words, midlife dude is not turning away." She throws back the rest of her drink. "Males are not biologically wired that way. Humans are programmed to propagate the species. When females can't do that any longer, the guys move on to someone who can. We might *think* we have free will. But the laugh is on us." She raises her empty glass. "Cheers. Oh, hey, bartender!" she calls out to Chloe. "Can you organize another round here?"

Sophia abruptly pushes her chair back and weaves hurriedly toward the washroom, bumping a barstool as she goes.

Jemma says, "S'cuse me a sec. I just want to check Sophia is doing okay. Can you guys keep an eye on Boo and Sweetie?" She reaches for her purse hanging on the back of the chair and tries to walk in a smooth and elegant line past the beautiful brunette on a barstool. As Jemma passes, she stumbles a little drunkenly on her heels, and she hears the young men whispering something derogatory behind her back as she passes.

BEFORE THE HIT-AND-RUN

Chloe notices Jemma push back her chair and hurry after her friend to the bathroom. She stares after her, wondering what happened. The voluptuous brunette sitting at Chloe's bar also turns to watch Jemma, then quickly asks for her bill, sets down her credit card, and tells Chloe she needs to freshen up. She gets off her stool and follows Jemma to the bathroom. Chloe's pulse quickens.

She glances at Jemma's table. The remaining women seem oblivious to the world around them and are now ordering desserts. A desire to protect Jemma surges with ferocity into Chloe's chest.

What should she do?

Like everyone else in the restaurant, Chloe immediately noticed the sexy brunette when she entered the establishment. The woman draws the male gaze in the way a corpse draws blowflies. At first Chloe wasn't 100 percent certain it was *her*.

But she is now—Gloria in all her glorious glory—Dr. Adam Spengler's other "wife." Or mistress. The mother of "Oliver."

It's also clear to Chloe that Gloria wanted to sit at the bar so she could closely observe Jemma.

Somehow Gloria must have known Jemma would be at the Beach House—possibly from her Instagram account—and Gloria had come to see, and be seen. Silent battle lines were forming, perhaps in preparation for some kind of love-triangle showdown.

When Gloria seated herself on a stool at her bar, Chloe set a bowl of mixed nuts, a napkin, and a coaster in front of her, and asked what she wanted to drink.

Gloria ordered a champagne cocktail and declined the food menu. It was clear she—like Jemma's group—had imbibed something alcoholic before arriving at the restaurant. As Chloe prepared Gloria's cocktail, she wondered where Dr. Adam Spengler was, and whether he knew what was going down at the Beach House tonight.

Gloria flicked her hair, keenly aware of the two men at the bar. She offered them a smile. It irked Chloe. This woman had already seduced Jemma's husband, and now she was flirting with more men? Hatred for the slut began to seep like cold ink into her veins.

The two guys—now bleary eyed and rosy faced—waved Chloe over. They ordered a second champagne cocktail to be delivered to Gloria.

The adulteress accepted with a nod and another smile. Gloria sank even lower in Chloe's regard. Women like her never paid for a thing. Those guys were assholes for even beginning to think they'd get anything in return. As Chloe prepared the second cocktail, a mean streak slithered into her heart, and she added double the amount of alcohol.

She set the fortified glass in front of Gloria with a mechanical smile. Gloria nodded to the men again, raised her glass in thanks, and took a big sip, then another.

"Even better than the first," she told Chloe in a deep, smoky voice. "This is such a *quaint* neighborhood and restaurant. Have you worked here long?" It was said in a patronizing way. Who in the hell was *she* to look down on anyone?

"A couple of years." Chloe noted the diamond cluster on Gloria's ring finger, and the matching clusters of little diamonds in her ears.

Gloria drank more of her potent cocktail, picked at some nuts and crisps while watching Jemma's table, and dabbed her bloodred lips on the white napkin. "Do you happen to know who the artist is who did that painting out front?"

Chloe went still. "Why?"

She reached again for her glass and took a bigger sip. Her drink was almost empty now. "Because I don't recognize it as the work of any local artist, and I tend to be pretty good at that kind of thing. I wouldn't mind seeing what else they've produced."

"Why?" she asked again.

Gloria laughed. "It's my business—art." She smiled. "I'm a dealer and a gallery owner. I'll ask the host on the way out who—"

"I did it."

She stared. "Pardon?"

"I painted it."

"You?"

Chloe started making another drink for Gloria, this time tripling the alcohol content. She set it down on a fresh coaster. "From the boys."

Gloria glanced at them. Nodded. They beamed back.

"Are you serious? *You* painted it?" She took a sip of her new drink.

"I don't look like a painter?"

A laugh again. Chloe could see she was getting quite tipsy.

"No. Not that—it's—I'm just delighted to meet you"—she peered closely at Chloe's name tag for the first time—"Chloe. It's a stunning piece. It reminds me of Edward Hopper's work. One in particular called *Nighthawks*. I haven't seen anything capture loneliness—a sense of someone being on the outside, looking in—quite like he does. But this comes close."

"That's what someone else said. The Edward Hopper comparison."

"It really is haunting. Do you have more?"

"I have lots. I paint all the time."

"Do you have a website, a portfolio, or do you work with a gallery? Do you exhibit your work anywhere?"

"No. They're just at home."

Gloria hesitated, and a hungry gleam entered her eye. "Any chance I could see some more of your paintings?"

"Not really. My—ah, my mom is home and not well. So—excuse me." Chloe took another order from a server and set four drinks on a tray for her to pick up.

"Do you have photos of your work?" Gloria asked when she was done.

Chloe regarded her. *Don't be blinded and seduced by vanity, Chloe Cooper. This is not a nice woman. She is no friend of Jemma's.*

But against her better judgment and her mother's warning inside her head, she unlocked her phone and showed Gloria her album of some of her work.

Gloria scrolled, silent. Her face changed. She looked up.

"Chloe, you really do paint loneliness."

Chloe wasn't sure what to say to that, so she said nothing.

"I mean, these images, all of them have a sense of an outsider, observing from a distance or looking into something. Into public places, house windows, private lives. They're beautiful and so incredibly, hauntingly lonely."

Chloe swallowed.

"And these ones—of the woman with her feet trapped in rocks—it's like the woman knows there is gold, or treasure, locked in the rocks under her. That something more is possible. But she can't release herself or the gold from the prison of her circumstance."

Chloe grew increasingly tense, anxious. Thankfully she was distracted by another order. When she returned, Gloria said, "Listen, if you ever feel like bringing a portfolio of your work round to my gallery—" She fished clumsily, drunkenly in her purse, and a tube of lipstick and a small bottle of perfume fell out and clattered to the floor. Chloe saw the perfume slide under a table. Gloria muttered a curse and handed Chloe her card. "My name is Gloria."

I know.

"Gloria Bergson of Bergson Gallery on the North Shore. My address is on there." She tapped the card with a long, manicured nail. "I would love to chat more, and possibly talk about representation. If you are interested."

Chloe studied the card. Sophisticated design. Clean lettering. She turned it over. On the back was a website address with an Instagram icon.

She glanced up and met Gloria's eyes.

Now I have your name and address. I know how to find you. I know where to come and watch you. I know what you like.

The woman got off her stool and wobbled. She steadied herself with a hand on the counter, seemingly surprised by her level of tipsiness. She then crouched down and gathered up her tube of lipstick, but couldn't seem to locate her perfume.

"Don't know if I dropped anything else," she said, coming to her feet.

"I don't think so," Chloe said, conscious of exactly where the perfume lay on the floorboards. Then as Gloria climbed back onto her stool, Jemma rushed past after her friend. Gloria saw Jemma, tensed, then quickly asked for the bill. She placed her credit card on the counter and hurried after Jemma.

Chloe now stares after Gloria. *What on earth is going to happen in the bathroom?* She glances down at the credit card, then notices the crumpled white napkin with a big smudge of Gloria's bloodred lipstick next to the cocktail glass. She snatches the napkin up, quickly places it in a ziplock bag, checks to see if anyone is watching, then sneaks it into her purse below the bar counter.

Always be alert for opportunities, Chloe. Seize them when you can. You never know how or when you might need something.

She'll retrieve the perfume later, when the restaurant starts to empty.

BEFORE THE HIT-AND-RUN

Jemma splashes cold water on her face while she waits for Sophia to exit one of the bathroom stalls. Jemma's complexion is flushed—two hot spots blooming at her cheekbones. It's not an attractive look. This is what wine does to her. She leans closer to the mirror to better scrutinize herself. The bathroom lighting underscores fine wrinkles and imperfections in her skin. It exaggerates the extra folds beginning to appear at her neck. Jemma pulls at her "turkey skin" and a melancholy sense of defeat descends on her, especially after the dismal conversation at the table.

There are two kinds of husbands. Those who you know *are having an affair, and those cunning enough to keep their affair secret and get away with it.*

She turns off the tap and rips a sheet of paper towel out of the dispenser. "You okay in there, Sophia?" she calls out as she dabs her face dry.

"Yeah. Out in a bit." Sophia's voice is thick, as though she's been crying. Jemma wasn't keen on seeing Sophia again. She considers her an old acquaintance and competitor rather than a friend. Sophia, in Jemma's opinion, is a failure. A loser. She couldn't cut dancing at a world-class level, and look at her now—teaching schoolkids to plié and barre fitness classes for stay-at-home moms and retirees. Seeing Sophia again reminds Jemma of her own career failures—her dreams lost to years of child raising and illnesses while Adam's star rose in the medical world. Jemma has also never quite trusted Sophia. She's a gossip. She showed a mean streak of jealousy back in the day. And she stole one of Jemma's boyfriends. Things didn't turn out too well for him in the end. Another part of Jemma feels Sophia's pain at being so unceremoniously dumped by her husband of many years.

Dangle a fresh bit of tail in front of a man, and mark my words, midlife dude is not turning away.

Jemma starts to apply some fresh lipstick. As she does, the bathroom door swings open, and the brunette steps in, carrying off her ripped designer jeans in a way only certain women can.

She comes up to the basin right beside Jemma's, turns on the tap, and begins to wash her hands. A natural beauty. Skin tawny. Flashing dark eyes. Luxurious, shiny hair.

The woman's eyes meet Jemma's in the mirror. A frisson—a sixth sense that she's being targeted, followed—tingles up Jemma's spine. The woman's gaze remains locked on Jemma's as a small smile plays over her full, wide mouth.

"Do I know you?" Jemma asks.

"Goodness, I'm so sorry for staring." The woman yanks a sheet of paper towel out of the dispenser, dries her hands. "I wasn't sure it was you at first. When I walked into the restaurant, I *thought* I recognized you from Instagram. It is you, isn't it? You have that @HiddenJems account, right? The *sixty is the new forty* thing about leaning into aging as a woman, and having no regrets."

Surprise washes through Jemma. "I—God, yes. I'm sorry I thought—"

"That I was being a creep?" She laughs. Husky. Warm. "I'm one of your followers. I mean, I don't go on the app a ton, but when I do, I totally love your content. You offer women like me something to aspire to, you know, for when we finally get to your age. It gives one hope. And the photos—stunning. Are you visiting Vancouver? I mean—wow,

I apologize if I'm being forward or anything. Please stop me if I am. But I know from your content that you live in the Toronto area." She digs into her purse and opens her own tube of lipstick.

Jemma, tipsy, is disoriented by this woman. She watches the color go onto her full lips. A glossy and violent red. Deep down in Jemma's core, warning bells start to ring.

The woman presses her lips together to evenly distribute the color. She examines the result in the mirror by angling her head. Appearing satisfied—*Who wouldn't be with looks like hers?*—she faces Jemma squarely.

"It's always so fascinating to have the filters pulled back, don't you think? And to meet the raw reality behind some of those accounts. I mean—oh, God, that came out wrong. I'm so sorry."

"No worries," Jemma says crisply. She's about to call out and tell Sophia she'll wait outside, when the woman flicks back her hair, and Jemma is suddenly reminded of a long, dark, wavy hair she found on Adam's coat last year. Her unease deepens. It's irrational. She knows it. But even the scent of this woman's perfume is suddenly surfacing an odd feeling of familiarity. Jemma's gaze goes to the diamonds on the young woman's ring finger, then to the matching cluster of sparkling stones at her ears. Cold slinks down Jemma's spine. She has the exact same matching set.

It can't be. It's not possible. How can you even let your mind go there?

But what are the odds? This woman showing up in the Beach House, approaching her so directly in the bathroom, wearing this jewelry. Jemma tries to swallow, but her throat has gone tight. She's suddenly unable to move.

"I saw you have your two little cavapoos with you," the woman says. "They're so photogenic on your IG posts. It always helps to use pets on socials, doesn't it?" She laughs her smoky whiskey lounge laugh again. "I don't have pets, but my son would adore a dog. His dad has been hinting about getting him one. Would you recommend the breed?

Are they good with kids?" As she speaks, she opens her phone and brings up a photo. She shows it to Jemma.

"This is my boy, Oliver."

A primal shock punches Jemma in the gut. The toddler in the photo is her Jackson. When he was little. Except it's not. She can't think, can't process what she's seeing as the boy's pale-blue eyes, fringed with the darkest and thickest of long lashes, stare back at Jemma from the screen. There's even a slight slant to the child's smile. A smile she knows with every molecule of her being.

In her mind, her memory, she hears the words, *Mommy, are you there? I love you, Mom.*

Jemma is afraid to look away from the image and to meet the gaze of this hateful person messing with her soul. Her eyes begin to water. She tries again to swallow.

"Oliver is just over two years old." The image vanishes as the woman shuts off her phone with a click. She slides it back into her purse.

Jemma glances up.

"It really was lovely meeting you. Face-to-face." She turns and saunters provocatively toward the door.

Jemma finds her voice. "What did you say your name was?"

A glance over her shoulder. Another smile. "I didn't." The door swings slowly shut behind her.

Jemma stares after her. She realizes she's shaking.

BEFORE THE HIT-AND-RUN

Jemma's brain reels. She didn't post anywhere online that she was coming here today, did she? Adam continually cautions her about telegraphing her locations via Instagram, especially since her account started going viral. She's usually so careful. But can one ever be too careful on social media?

With trembling hands, Jemma reaches into her purse and opens her own phone. She goes to her Instagram account, clicks on the last image she posted: a photo of herself in new gym gear. It's part of a promotion she's running in conjunction with a fitness-apparel company gunning for the aging boomer pool of women trying to hold on to their bodies.

There's no location signaling in the posted image that she can discern.

She clicks on the comments. And there it is. A note from @ SophiaDancer.

> Can't wait for our meetup at @
> BeachHouseRestaurant Saturday night! #welcom-
> etothewestcoast #olddancebuddies #crowspoint-
> beachlife #girlsnightout

Jemma closes her eyes and presses her phone to her chest. In her mind she sees the toddler's pale eyes. Identical to Jackson's. To her husband's. Those lashes. That black hair. All the same.

It's not possible. It *can't* be. It *has* to be a coincidence. It's just her insecure subconscious telegraphing things, seeing issues where there are none.

But there have been other signs, haven't there? Signs Jemma shrugged off in the same way she's desperately trying to now. That long dark hair on Adam's coat. The scent of that perfume in his shirt. The phone messages at strange times of the night that he claimed were emergencies from the hospital. His extended trips to Vancouver, the increase in conferences.

His name is Oliver.

He's just over two years old.

My son would adore a dog.

His dad has been hinting about getting him one.

Her knees start to buckle, and she braces her hands on the bathroom counter, breathing hard.

Not possible, no, no, no. More than two years? Could Adam have been seeing someone during those final months of Jackson's suffering? Through his death? Their own son's funeral, the mourning? Was there a deeper, more sinister intent behind his cajoling her to move out here? Did a *fresh start* mean something totally different to Adam? Was there a nefarious reason he so desperately gunned for a position with the cancer center? But then why on earth would he have wanted her here with him? Nothing makes sense.

A toilet flushes and Sophia exits her stall, red eyed, a little puffy faced.

"What was all that about?" she asks as she goes to the basin and turns on the tap.

Jemma doesn't even know where to begin. She's too embarrassed, humiliated, fearful to even voice it in case she makes something real that's still simply a figment of her imagination. She clears her throat, wipes a hand over her mouth, straightens her shoulders. "Are you okay, Sophia? I—ah—the conversation about divorce . . ." Jemma's words fade. She has no energy, no brain cells left for anything other than the white-hot focal point of suspicion still searing into her mind.

"Yeah, I'm fine. Just had a moment." Sophia pumps soap and lathers her hands. "Who was that woman you were talking to?"

"The—she was the brunette from the bar."

Sophia stills, stares at Jemma. "You mean that bombshell?"

Of course Sophia noticed her, too. The whole restaurant did. Tears threaten Jemma. She clears her throat again and nods.

"What did she want?"

"Just—nothing. Small chat."

Sophia finishes washing her hands and reaches for a paper towel. "You seriously look like you've seen a ghost, Jem. What happened?"

She *did* see a ghost. Jackson's. Looking back at her from a strange woman's phone.

"She just freaked me out, to tell you the truth. She apparently recognized me from Instagram and was totally stalkery about it. I'm actually concerned she could become an issue."

"Did she give you her name?"

"No. I asked. But she just walked out."

"Maybe the bartender will know who she is. Her name would have been on a credit card or something. We could ask."

"Employees can't just give out customers' names."

"Come." Sophia hooks her arm through Jemma's. "Let's go ask. Nothing ventured, nothing gained. The bartender mentioned that she was a dog walker, and you told us back at your place that you were looking for one, right? You could come at her from that angle."

BEFORE THE HIT-AND-RUN

Relief washes through Chloe as she sees Jemma and her friend returning from the bathroom, but then she notices the way both women fix their gazes intently on her as they approach her bar. It startles her and makes her brace with anticipation.

As they near, Chloe searches their faces for a sign of what might have transpired in the bathroom. Gloria exited before them, and in a whirlwind of fragrance and hair she settled her account and hurriedly left the establishment. Jemma now appears flushed, almost feverish. The friend looks like she's been crying. The friend nudges Jemma forward slightly, and Jemma actually appears nervous, which further unsettles Chloe.

"What can I get you ladies?" she asks.

"Actually, I—ah—this is going to sound weird," says Jemma, "but I was wondering if you perhaps know the name of that woman—the brunette—who was sitting here at the bar earlier." She hesitates, opens her mouth again, as if to offer an excuse as to why she wants the woman's name, then appears to leave it there, to test Chloe's waters.

Chloe is unsure. A million confusing images and feelings and voices crash through her brain at once.

This is it. She has come to you! She needs you. You know what her husband is doing, and it's incumbent on you to help her now, to find a way to break it to her. But tread carefully, Chloe. You will lose your job if Bill learns you gave out customer information sourced from credit cards. But you didn't! You already knew on your own who Gloria was when she walked in. This is your neighbor asking about someone who was talking out in public in the alley. Plus, Gloria gave you her business card in a personal capacity.

Jemma appears to interpret Chloe's silence as reticence. "Look, I know it's a tall ask, but—"

"She left this behind." Chloe points to the business card still on the counter. "Maybe that'll help?"

Jemma snatches it up, reads it, then shows her friend. The two exchange a hot glance. The friend says softly, "Gloria."

Jemma says, "Bergson. Bergson Gallery. North Shore." She glances up and locks her gaze back on Chloe. "Thank you," she whispers. Her gaze lowers once more to Chloe's name tag. "I really appreciate it, Chloe."

The way she mouths Chloe's name sends a warm flush through her body. "No worries." She feigns nonchalance as she puts a dirty glass in a rack. "Her card was just sitting there. It's not like I gave you anything you couldn't pick up for yourself."

Jemma hesitates as an idea seems to strike her. She studies the business card again and says, "You mentioned you do dog sitting, and walking."

Chloe's heart kicks. "I do. For quite a lot of people in the neighborhood. I have tons of references. Anyone in Crow's Point will vouch for me—I'm well known around town."

"Would you—I mean, I might need to be busy for the next day or so. Could you possibly come around to my house tomorrow morning? I mean, if that's okay with you? To properly meet Boo and Sweetie on their home turf, and to talk about a potential arrangement to walk them in the future?"

Pace yourself. Take a breath. You don't want to appear too needy or scary desperate.

"Tomorrow? Um—yeah, I think I could manage that. What's the address?"

"It's 1117 Crow's Road. Off Main Street. Do you know where that is?"

"I do." She smiles. "What time?"

Jemma returns the smile. "Say around nine a.m.? I'll be back from my morning swim by then."

"Absolutely. Can't wait to meet the pooches in their home space. I'll be there."

"Thank you so much."

Chloe watches as Jemma returns to the table of women, who are now faded and droopy around the edges and ready to go home. They settle their account with their server and wobble to their feet. They gather up their sweaters and purses and coats and cavapoos, and weave out of the restaurant.

From the door, Jemma gives Chloe a wave goodbye.

Chloe smiles proudly as she waves back.

She couldn't have imagined the evening turning out more perfectly. She scored a personal invite, right into the heart of Gloom House and into the life of Jemma Spengler. Chloe already knows what she will do first thing, once she gets inside, as soon as an opportunity presents itself.

BEFORE THE HIT-AND-RUN

Adam is still not home from the hospital when Jemma returns with Boo and Sweetie, and the house feels bleak, cold. She walked back from the restaurant, hoping to clear her thinking, but suspicion, jealousy, anger, pain continue to cloud her mind.

She opens more wine, lets the dogs out, and tries to phone Adam. Her call goes directly to voicemail. She thinks of Gloria Bergson and her son, then digs out some old photo albums of her kids.

Jemma turns the lights down low so she feels less exposed with the no-blinds situation, and she seats herself on the sofa. She sips her wine as she pores over the images of her dear children. Both Hailey and Jackson had Adam's eyes—that haunting, ultra-pale blue, fringed with the same dense, dark lashes. She lifts her gaze and allows it to drift beyond her reflection in the window up to the row of apartment units across the alley.

Most of the units have drapes or blinds drawn, and warm light glows behind them. But the unit where she saw the weird woman watching with binoculars does not have drapes drawn. There is a light on inside, but it's very dim. Jemma wonders if the woman keeps her lights low so she can spy out into the night without being easily seen. She curls deeper into the sofa with her dogs and continues to turn the thick album pages, which display snapshots of her life. She finds the particular photo she was searching for.

Jackson on his second birthday.

In the image his little cherub cheeks puff out in what at the time was a hysterical attempt to blow out the two candles on his cake. The photo morphs into the image of the toddler smiling from Gloria's phone. Her mind collapses in on itself as a hot rage erupts in her tummy and burns up into her chest. Jemma grabs her purse, digs out her wallet, and finds Gloria Bergson's business card. On the back is Gloria's Instagram handle. Jemma opens the social media app, punches in @ GloriaBeArt, and there she is. In all her fucking voluptuous, youthful, smug, superior glory.

Jemma starts scrolling viciously through her posts, one after another, her blood pressure rising as she hunts for some online clue, anything that might confirm her worst fears. Mostly she's searching for—and also desperately hoping *not* to find—a glimpse of Adam in one of Gloria's posts.

All she sees is one image after another showing Gloria from advantageous and flattering angles. In a bikini. Full, rounded boobs. Skiing in skintight pants. Straddled seductively on a Jet Ski. On an Iceland pony. Dipping into steamy pools filled by hot springs. At gallery openings. Among art celebrities. Smiling with local media personalities. Attending an opera in a strapless emerald-green gown, looking like fucking European royalty. Hiking. A picnic on a blanket with watermelon slices and little Oliver. Before she can go deeper, Jemma hears the low rumble of the garage doors opening and the electric whine of Adam's car driving inside.

Quickly she turns off her phone and hurries upstairs with the dogs scampering in tow. She'll give them a bathroom break later—she can't let Adam see her like this. She's too drunk, too emotional. Her face is blotchy and red. She needs to be in control when she confronts him about this. She needs a strategy.

Hurriedly Jemma shucks off her clothes, drops them in a pile on the carpet beside her bed, and quickly scrambles under the covers. She clicks off her bedside lamp. She pretends she's asleep as she hears Adam come up the stairs.

He enters the room, stills in the doorway. "Jemma?" he whispers. "You still awake?"

She tenses but remains silent. The dogs jump off the bed to greet him. He crouches down to pet them, whispering soft endearments, then heads directly into the bathroom. Jemma hears the shower turn on.

She flops onto her back and stares up at the ceiling, heart thudding. A plan of action—born of desperation, of hurt, of fury—begins to crystallize in her mind.

BEFORE THE HIT-AND-RUN

September 25, 2019

It's a big day for Chloe—she woke with a real sense of purpose this morning—and as she nears Gloom House, she ponders whether she should approach from the front entrance on Crow's Road, or go around to the rear laneway entry next to the garage. She decides that someone who technically doesn't know Gloom House would naturally favor the front door, near where Brodie relieved himself under the cherry tree.

She climbs the stairs, rings the doorbell. The chime triggers intense canine activity on the other side—she sees dogs' bouncing shapes through the strip of opaque glass as they yip with excitement.

The door opens.

"Morning, Chloe, come on in." Jemma's hair is still slightly damp from her swim. She wears a burnt-orange sweater that makes her eyes appear even more gold. But she looks tired today. Very pale. Still beautiful, but in a wan and vulnerable way. This only endears her further to Chloe. Her selkie swimmer needs all possible care and protection, and Chloe intends to do exactly that with what she has in her pockets. An anticipatory thrill quivers through her as she steps inside the house for the first time and inhales the atmosphere.

The dogs skitter around her feet. She gets down to her knees to greet them at eye level, ruffling soft fur, velvet ears; drinking in the doggy scent of them; noting their collars, and the little name tags and charms on them. Chloe really loves dogs. Cavapoo designer editions are no exception.

"They are such friendly and exuberant pups," she says, glancing up at Jemma. The lady of Gloom House nods. She appears somewhat distracted and distant, yet an aura of urgency also crackles around her, as though she's in a rush to be somewhere other than with Chloe. Disappointment whispers into her. The moment of connection she felt across the bar counter last night is gone. She tells herself she just needs time to build a solid rapport.

Chloe comes to her feet, notices the rear entrance across the living room. Beside it is a door she imagines leads into the garage. Raincoats and a man's jacket hang on hooks near the door.

"They seem to like you," Jemma says, glancing at her watch. "Is there any chance you can stay for the day, or at least come and go, and walk them, or let them out every couple of hours?"

Surprise ripples through Chloe. "I thought you just wanted to meet and discuss references—a possible future schedule."

"That was my plan, and I feel very forward for asking, but I called around this morning, and everyone vouches for you as a great dog person, and trustworthy, and—I trust you, Chloe."

Pride, affection, blooms in Chloe's chest. Excitement mounts. This is even better than she dreamed. She might have full access to the inner sanctum of Gloom House—free run for the whole day starting *right now.*

"Or are you working at the Beach House today?"

"Oh, only quite a bit later. I'm free for most of the day."

"Thank you! Shall I show you through the house?" She checks her watch again. "Or—ah—maybe you can just take a look around yourself? I have some early appointments, and I really apologize for rushing through this—"

"Not at all! It's totally fine. I'm sure the dogs won't need much."

"They have beds in just about every room in the house. It's all still new to us, but I usually let them out the glass sliders onto the deck over there." She points. "They can access a patch of lawn from the deck. The yard is completely fenced in. Water bowls are everywhere. Treats are in that jar on the kitchen counter there." She gestures to the kitchen. "And if you ever need food for them, they eat a raw diet, and their containers are labeled in the fridge. They're pretty low maintenance. If you can manage it, they would love a walk around the block or down to the beach sometime around midday."

Chloe nods. Her gaze shifts to the art on the wall behind Jemma. The pieces have no sense of movement, no *feeling*, in her opinion. Dr. Adam Spengler and the interior designer must have selected those. Her attention moves to two large framed photos. One shows a teenage girl in a field of sunflowers. The other is of a boy barely into his teens. Both have Adam's eerie eyes. A chill slides down Chloe's spine as she's seized by a sentient sense of Evil with a capital *E*. Her mind whips back to her encounter with Dr. Spengler in the narrow confines of the hospital elevator, right after she spoke with the surgeon, and a ragged noise—like a discordant jazz instrument—scrapes through her skull. Her breathing quickens. The walls feel as though they're closing in.

"Are those your children?" she asks with a nod to the frames.

"Yes." Jemma hesitates, then says quickly, "We lost them both."

Chloe's mouth opens to form the word *How?* But she bites it back and scrambles for a more appropriate response. "I'm so sorry."

Jemma doesn't elaborate. She grabs her purse off the kitchen counter and scoops a rain jacket and cap off a chair. "Are you sure you'll be okay, Chloe?"

"Maybe you could give me your cell number in case I need to call you in an emergency?"

"Oh, God, sorry. Yes. I—I'm a bit distracted today." She scribbles her phone number onto a pad from the kitchen drawer, followed by another set of four numbers. She rips off the page, hands it to Chloe.

"My cell. Plus the door code for the back door over there." She points. "It leads to the laneway. The dogs' leashes are hanging by the door. Yellow is for Boo. Pink for Sweetie." She starts toward the door that leads into the garage. "I'm not sure what time I'll be home today. But just lock the door if I'm not back before you need to leave. And, of course, please feel free to come and go during the day if you need to—just as long as the dogs get their bathroom breaks." She opens the door to the garage. "I really am sorry to rush. I—I have a bit of an unexpected emergency."

Chloe is *dying* to ask if the "emergency" has anything to do with Gloria and what transpired in the washroom last night. She's desperate to learn whether the business card she handed over has been of any assistance. But she needs to play her cards carefully, and be subtle.

"Honestly, anything I can do to help."

"Thank you, Chloe."

And Jemma is gone.

Chloe hears the little yellow sports car reversing out of the garage, followed by the rumble of the automatic garage door closing.

The dogs stare up at her expectantly. Chloe is elated. A world of discovery awaits.

"It's okay, guys," she says with a smile. "I'm good company, honest. Just ask my little Brodie. He's at home with my mom right now, right across the street. So, now, first things first."

She heads directly to the man's jacket hanging on the coatrack. From her pocket she removes a ziplock bag. She opens it, extracts the napkin stained with Gloria Bergson's bloodred lipstick that she took from the bar. She slips it into Dr. Spengler's jacket pocket.

From her other pocket she removes Gloria's travel-size perfume container that rolled under the table. She opens the lapel of the jacket and spritzes a robust dose of fragrance along the inside. She carefully replaces the jacket lapel in the position she found it, and she's filled with an immediate sense of satisfaction. Then Chloe is struck by an even better idea.

Quickly she removes the lipsticked napkin from Dr. Spengler's jacket pocket and heads upstairs. The dogs follow, curious. In the big bathroom off the main bedroom she locates the laundry basket. Inside the basket are several of Adam Spengler's white button-down shirts. She rubs some of the red lipstick on the inside of one collar. If she's lucky, Jemma will do the laundry and discover the lipstick stains. For good measure Chloe also gives the shirt a healthy spritz of Gloria's fragrance. Next she finds a pair of Adam Spengler's dress pants in the basket. Into one of the pockets she inserts a folded note she took the liberty of writing herself this morning. It reads:

Thank you for the amazing night.

Love you lots.

Your "other wife," Gloria.

P.S. Oliver sends kisses.

XOXOXO

Chloe heads back downstairs and reinserts the lipstick-stained napkin into Adam's pocket.

She steps back, congratulating herself. She just has to find a way now to suggest to Jemma that a wife should always check her husband's pockets. Once Jemma learns about her husband's affair, she'll have an advantage over her traitorous spouse. She'll be in a position to get rid of him, on her terms.

Next Chloe gets out her phone. She begins to take photos, meticulously documenting the entire interior of Gloom House, including the inside of the garage, where she finds an intriguing and colorful collection of car license plates from around the world displayed on one wall. She clicks. And again. Capturing the plates in detail.

BEFORE THE HIT-AND-RUN

Jemma sits in a brown rental sedan parked across the street from the Bergson Gallery. Rain has started to spit, and low clouds tumble down the flanks of the North Shore Mountains. Her mood mirrors the grim weather, but she's also grateful because it provides more cover for her stakeout. Her own vehicle is so bright yellow and far too distinctive for her task, so after leaving the dog sitter, she headed straight to a rental place downtown and asked for something ordinary and basically invisible. Like Chloe Cooper—a dull color, nothing memorable about her appearance. Provides reliable service.

On the passenger seat beside Jemma is her camera with a telephoto lens. Her goal is to learn more about Gloria Bergson and find something she can potentially use as proof or leverage when she confronts Adam.

The gallery is situated in a quaint and artsy commercial area near the quay—buildings new but designed to look somewhat Victorian. The gallery storefront is white with big windows that display artwork. Outside are pots with plants. One block down lies an older residential neighborhood—gorgeous period homes with lush gardens out front, peekaboo views of the city across the water.

People come and go along the sidewalks, with umbrellas shielding them from rain. A few customers enter the gallery. Jemma believes she can see Gloria in a cream sweater moving about inside. Time ticks on interminably. Rain falls harder, and pedestrian traffic grows quiet. She wonders if she should go inside.

No. Gloria clearly knows who she is. What purpose would that serve other than to humiliate herself?

She waits another half hour. She'll need a bathroom break soon. This turns her thoughts to Boo and Sweetie. They'll be requiring breaks, too. She reaches for her phone, opens her PawGuardian app to check the remote cameras in her house.

As the live images come up on the screen, Jemma sees Chloe moving around in her bedroom. Jemma's pulse kicks. She frowns, leans closer. Chloe is going through Adam's jackets and shirts in the walk-in closet. She's taking photos in there. *What in the hell?*

Jemma quickly rewinds some of the saved footage from earlier in the morning. She hits PLAY. And there is the dog sitter ferreting through their laundry basket upstairs. She watches Chloe put something in Adam's pant pocket before replacing the pants in the basket. Chloe then leaves the bedroom. Jemma switches to the downstairs cam. Chloe enters the screen and goes to the coatrack near the rear entrance. She sticks something white in Adam's jacket pocket.

What on earth is she doing?

But before Jemma can watch more, in her peripheral vision she detects Gloria exiting the gallery doors. Jemma tenses. Her heart beats faster as she watches Gloria pop up her umbrella and begin to walk down the sidewalk on her high-heeled boots. The woman heads in the direction of the pretty residential area with its lush gardens.

What to do?

Any minute Gloria will disappear down the sidewalk, and Jemma will lose sight of her. But if she follows in her vehicle and Gloria turns into a side street or enters another store, Jemma might be stuck in the middle of traffic with no immediate parking available. She makes a snap decision. She pulls her cap down low over her brow, tucks her hair into her raincoat, grabs her camera, sticks it in a big shapeless leather bag, and quickly exits the car.

Jemma slings the bag across her shoulder and hurries after Gloria Bergson, staying on the opposite side of the street.

Gloria enters the residential area. She walks another half block, then turns down a narrow street lined with magnolia trees and eponymously named Magnolia Lane. She stops outside a quaint double-story house with dormer windows. It's painted a rich teal color with white trim. Rosebushes and clematis creepers hang over the fence, and a small maple in the tiny front yard is dressed for fall with brilliant red leaves. Gloria opens the garden gate, enters the yard. The gate swings shut behind her as she makes her way along a paved path and climbs the stairs to a front door topped with a panel of stained glass. She opens the door and disappears inside.

Jemma steps under a bus shelter on the opposite side of the street. Rain drips off the shelter roof. She raises her camera and zooms her big lens in on the little plaque affixed to the gate.

BERGSON. 2210 MAGNOLIA LANE

Jemma clicks, then slowly lowers her camera. She stares. The woman actually *lives* in one of these pretty old houses with climbing roses? It's the kind of house she wishes Adam had bought her, instead of that vacuous and angular monstrosity hulking on the corner lot in Crow's Point. This is also a much nicer neighborhood—at least in Jemma's view.

A hollowness builds in her chest as she struggles to keep her mind from second-guessing anything, because a part of her still dares hope there's a rational explanation for Gloria Bergson that has nothing to do with Jemma's husband. Rain comes down a little harder.

A bus pulls up. Hydraulics hiss as the vehicle comes to a stop and lowers slightly for people to get off. A senior man struggles out with his walker while other passengers' blank faces stare through the rain-streaked windows. It gives Jemma a sense of being on the outside, suddenly no longer fitting in. Being cast adrift. An aging, dried-up husk of a woman with no more value or purpose. No kids left and no possibility to ever have more. Never will there be a grandchild to hold. Emotion fills her eyes, and her arms begin to ache with a need to embrace her lost children.

Suddenly she sees a blue Tesla, and her heart jumps as she notices the Ontario vanity plates—DR SPENGR. *Adam.*

His car slows outside 2210 Magnolia Lane, turns into the tiny driveway. Jemma's heart starts to thud. She watches her husband exit from the driver's side.

Swallowing, Jemma raises her camera to her face, but she's trembling so hard she needs to sit on the shelter bench in order to hold it steady. She clicks. And clicks again as Adam takes the stairs to the front door two at a time. The door swings open, and Jemma's heart clean stops as a little boy with pale skin and a shock of shiny black hair appears in the doorway.

Jemma's husband bends down, opens his arms wide, and the child flings his little arms around Adam's neck. He swoops the boy off the ground and comes back up to full height while madly kissing the toddler's neck. The child erupts into a mass of squirming giggles in his arms. Behind them, Gloria appears. They look like the perfect little family, framed by a halo of yellow light that spills out from the house into the bleak, rainy day.

Jemma clicks as Gloria smiles and places a hand on Adam's arm. She leans up to kiss Jemma's husband, who said he would be in surgery at the hospital today.

Jemma feels she might die. Right here in this bus shelter. There can be no doubt now. No explanation other than Adam and this woman have been seeing each other long enough to have a two-year-old son named Oliver.

As she watches in stunned shock from her bench, through her lens, through the rain, Adam sets Oliver down. Gloria, smiling, says something. Adam responds. Gloria's smile fades. She gestures angrily as she speaks again. Adam makes a pleading motion with his hands. They're arguing. Adam actually appears to be begging. Her husband *never* begs.

Jemma's mouth turns bone dry as she rapidly clicks a series of images, capturing the altercation. Gloria starts to push Adam out the door. He resists, but she shuts the door in his face while little Oliver cries at her feet.

Jemma's husband stands staring at the door. He appears to curse, then bangs loudly on the door with the base of his fist. No answer comes. He bangs again. Still no response. Adam heads back down the stairs to his Tesla.

From the protection of the bus shelter across the street, hidden beneath her cap and coat, Jemma watches quietly as her husband sits in the driver's seat, unmoving as rain squiggles over the car windows.

Jemma glances down the street. She sees several vacant parking spaces nearby. She decides to hurry back and retrieve her rental. If she can return in time—if Adam's Tesla is still parked here—she can wait in one of those spaces. And when he leaves, she will follow him.

BEFORE THE HIT-AND-RUN

"Adam, come on in," Narek Tigran says as he swings the door to his waterfront mansion open wide. His Lamborghini is parked in the sweeping driveway, and Narek is alone at his Vancouver property. Adam's old friend from university days has asked him to keep an eye on his estate while he's in Zurich, Sydney, and Dubai for business over the next nine months. Narek is of Armenian cultural background and a highly sought-after international corporate defense lawyer. Self-made and worth billions. He has several luxury homes around the world—this is one of them.

"Just a basic eye on the place every now and then is what I'm after," he says as Adam enters the house. "Can I get you something to drink before I show you the nuts and bolts of the place?"

"Ah—" Adam checks his watch. It's past lunchtime. And after his row with Gloria he could do with some fortification. "Yeah, sure. Thanks."

He follows his friend to the bar. While Narek mixes classic martinis, Adam is distracted by a framed photo of Narek's young and incredibly beautiful wife—Sharie—a Parisian model he met in Dubai. Young enough to be Narek's daughter. Younger even than Narek's son. Possibly younger than Gloria, even. His last words with Gloria echo through his entire being.

"I was so happy to see you here, Adam. I thought it meant you'd made a decision. That you'd finally told her about us."

"I have made a decision, Gloria. It's just that the timing is still not quite right. Jemma is still vulnerable. I need you to understand that—"

"Bullshit. I refuse to be a kept mistress. I'm not falling for it anymore. You've been lying to me for—"

"I never lied."

"Yes, you did. You've been making hollow promises for two whole years. You could have spent those years with us. You could have been watching your son grow up. Seen his first steps, been there for his birthday parties, his first day at day care. I'm done. Get out. Go. I'm serious—don't set foot here again or even contact me unless she's out of your life. And if I haven't heard from you by Christmas, it's over for good."

"Gloria, please, I love you—"

"Yeah, and I love you, too. But not like this—not anymore. I refuse to be that *woman. A victim. An afterthought. Second best. I have pride, and I'm not going to waste my life and my youth on this."*

And the door shut in his face. Oliver howling.

Adam is gutted. Afraid he might actually lose her and his son.

The two men go out onto the massive, covered patio that looks over the Burrard Inlet. Narek turns on the gas table fire and the outdoor heaters. They sit and watch the rain over the water. On the other side of the inlet are Jerrin Bay and the Crow's Point house he bought primarily for Jemma. This, Adam realizes, is the narrowest part of the crossing—perhaps five to seven kilometers directly across to Jerrin Beach. He sips and wonders if he could swim it as part of his endurance training. He'd need a support craft—either a motorboat or Jet Ski. Mostly for protection from other vessels. The biggest worry for an open-water swimmer is being hit by watercraft. Swimmers are notoriously difficult to notice from boats. It's why triathletes like him use personal buoys. For visibility. His thoughts turn to Jemma on the other side of that water, and his mood worsens.

"What's troubling you, Adam?"

He snaps back to the present moment. "It's nothing."

Narek points his martini glass at Adam. "I know that look on your face."

Adam inhales deeply. He needs to act. He cannot, in his heart of hearts, lose Gloria and Oliver, and she's set an explosive clock ticking—time is running out.

"When you and Babette got divorced . . . how did you tell her? How did you broach the fact you wanted to leave?"

Narek narrows his eyes. "Have you met someone else?"

"It's not like that."

"Come on, Adam. You can square with me."

"Okay, there is someone. Has been for a while."

"What's 'a while' mean?"

"Over two years."

"And you love her—this woman?"

"Deeply. Wholly. We have a son, Narek."

He whistles softly, eyeing his buddy. "And Jemma doesn't know?"

Adam sucks in another huge breath of air. "No. I haven't told her. Although I get a sense she might be starting to suspect something." He rubs his brow hard. "It's been rough, you know? First losing Hailey like that. Then Jackson's protracted illness hit her hard, and she . . . we didn't have sex for ages. It was like her body was there, but she wasn't present. And I was struggling, too. Lonely." He sips, his eyes going distant as he stares out over the gray water in the direction of Crow's Point across the fjord. "I tried the couples counseling thing, but by the time we started therapy, I'd already met Gloria. At a hotel in San Diego. She was there visiting art galleries, and I was on a medical convention. And—" He heaves out a sigh. "The chemistry was instant. Electric." He meets Narek's gaze. "She made me feel fucking alive, Narek—I mean truly *alive*—for the first time in years. And young. I—I have so much life left to give, to live still, and with Jemma . . ." His voice fades.

Narek sips, pensive. "It was the same when I started seeing Sharie. As far as I know, Babette wasn't aware of our affair. I think it came as a huge shock. But one thing I've learned is—and I know it's a tough thing to say—but my advice for you is to tell Jemma. Straight up. The sooner the better. It's better for them—the women. They're better off in the long run ending things. Everyone is better off leaving a dead relationship."

"What's she doing now, Babette?"

"She went back to university, some continuing-education thing. She's got a part-time job. She volunteers for things—the food bank, reading to seniors at a long-term care facility. And she's joined a writers' group. She always wanted to write, so she's trying that."

"Is she happy?"

"What is happiness, my friend?"

He nods, contemplative. "I do love her, you know—Jemma. But, like, in a different way. We've traveled a long, rough road together. I guess I sort of love them both."

"No, you don't. You want to own them both. You're just reluctant to give up something you feel belongs to you."

"That's bullshit."

Narek laughs. "But true. You've always had a bit of a god complex, Adam. Wait—" He shoots his hand up in a halt position. "Before you bite my head off, what brilliant surgeon doesn't? You make life-and-death decisions. You save people. Patients worship you. You're entitled to some arrogance, in my book."

"You can't function in this job with too much empathy," Adam says defensively. "Compartmentalization, intellectualization—it helps protect the emotions, keeps you in the game for the long haul. Less chance of burnout." He takes a big sip. "And I don't want to hurt her."

"I get it. But you *are* going to hurt her by hanging on to something that saps the life and joy out of both of you. Stay in the marriage too long, it goes toxic. And no one wins. Yeah, it's a tough conversation, and the fallout is rough at first—really rough—but it gets better, easier. I promise." He smiles. "And, brother, that freedom when she finally lets you go—it's fucking worth it."

"Serious?"

"Totally serious. Way I see it, we humans are herd animals. A bull, my friend, needs many cows. The more young cows he can mate with, the more calves, the stronger and bigger the herd. And the bull can keep going with younger cows. Come." He gets to his feet. "Let me show you the place."

They walk from the home gym, with its wall-to-wall windows overlooking the water, to the wine cellar, to the great big media and entertainment room, and through the many bedrooms. Narek shoots Adam a wicked, conspiratorial grin. "Feel free to use the place, Adam, entertain. Bring her here if you want. Try the wine, the sauna, the hot tub, all the toys. The keys and the place are yours while I'm away. And let me show you the boathouse and watercraft."

They walk under a covered walkway through the garden toward the waterfront, which boasts a small and private pebbled beach.

"Garden service comes once a week, hot tub and pool maintenance and the housecleaning services have all been scheduled. Basically I just want people around the neighborhood to know someone has eyes on the place, and if there are problems, there's a list of maintenance personnel to call." He creaks open the boathouse doors.

Inside are two Jet Skis on hoists. One is black with white stripes down the sides. The other is blue and white with a bold orange stripe. "That one needs some servicing, I'm afraid." Narek points to the black-and-white craft. "Otherwise everything else is in working order. Gas containers there. And hanging up over there"—he points—"snorkeling and diving gear, the SUPs, wet suits. Everything you need." He grins. "Too bad we're heading into winter, eh? But it'll be good come spring."

Narek hands Adam a bunch of keys. "All labeled. You have access to everything, including the garage."

BEFORE THE HIT-AND-RUN

Jemma sits in her rental outside Narek's driveway, diagonally across the street in the shadows of a large cedar. The neighborhood is densely forested with tall conifers, lush shrubs, and it's full of crannies and nooks and—right now—rain, mist. She slinks down in the seat, her cap pulled low over her brow. But her hands grip the wheel even though she is stationary. Her mind reels as she continues both slotting pieces together and fighting the emerging picture. The depth, the scope of her husband's betrayal, is dizzying. She feels nauseated. Terrified. And enraged.

She tries to draw in a deep breath, then exhale slowly. As her swim coach taught her—*to relax the body. To focus. If you can't breathe fully, you can't win. You can't swim. You can't pace yourself and go the distance, the sheer lengths you need to.*

She knows Narek from meeting him through Adam in Toronto many moons ago. He's joined them for dinner on the odd occasion over the years with his wife, Babette. Jemma knows Narek has several estates around the world, and she long ago briefly visited this one with Adam when they came through Vancouver to depart on a cruise. Adam told Jemma a few days ago that Narek had asked him to keep an eye on the property while he went away on business. She also knows what Narek did to Babette—the same thing Steven did to Sophia. And Jemma recalls *clearly* how she felt at the time she learned that Narek had traded in his gentle, lovely wife—mother of their children—for that featherbrained model from Paris. At the time Jemma felt smug. She believed it could never happen to her. She believed her love and hold on Adam were solid. Unbreakable.

We fall in love, we marry, we start little families with our hearts full of dreams. Then the going gets tougher as the kids grow. But you keep soldiering on through various challenges, thinking it's all still perfectly fine, considering. You're driving the kids to soccer, still going on family holidays, everything seems normal, and suddenly you discover he's been having an affair behind your back for three fucking years.

Dangle a fresh bit of tail in front of a man, and mark my words, midlife dude is not turning away.

The echo from their conversation at the Beach House reverberates through her mind.

You need to treat divorce as a pure business transaction. You get the best lawyer you can . . . you take more than half his fortune . . . But despite it all, ex-wives never really *win, do they?*

Jemma's death grip on the wheel tightens as her jaw clenches.

She will *not* cry.

She will not shed one wretched tear. She *refuses* to be a victim—it's just not going to happen. Because Adam will *not* leave their marriage. She won't allow it. She has leverage, and she'll not flinch in using it. And if she can't keep him, neither will Gloria.

BEFORE THE HIT-AND-RUN

When Jemma returns home, the dog sitter is gone, and there's a note from her on the kitchen counter.

Hi Jemma!

I had to leave to get ready for work and walk my mom's dog. Boo and Sweetie were amazing. We got two walks in, and they've had treats, and I took them out for a bathroom break just before I left, so I imagine they will be fine until their dinnertime.

Happy to dog sit anytime!! Feel free to call.

Chloe

There's a phone number at the bottom of the page. Jemma glances at her babies snoozing in their beds. They seemed tuckered out, content. It's a relief because her mind is wholly consumed with thoughts of Adam and his mistress and their toddler son. The fact Adam has a little boy utterly guts Jemma to the core. She goes to the wine fridge, takes out a chilled pinot gris, uncorks it, and pours herself a fat glass. She takes a sip, and then something strikes her.

The PawGuardian footage.

What in the hell was that about?

She takes another swig of wine, finds her laptop, opens it on the coffee table, and rewatches the footage of Chloe Cooper rummaging through the laundry basket upstairs and putting things in Adam's pockets. Jemma frowns. She saves the footage and goes upstairs to the bathroom.

She scrabbles through the laundry until she finds Adam's dress pants and shirt. She pulls them out and stills at the sight of a red stain on the inside of his white collar. It looks like lipstick. She recalls Gloria in the washroom, painting her full lips in the mirror. A violent bloodred. Same color as this. Her heart beats faster. She sniffs the shirt. The smell of Gloria's perfume from the Beach House bathroom assails her senses. Her heart stumbles at the memory of their conversation and the shocking image of "Oliver" on that whore's phone.

She drops the shirt to the floor and rummages through the pockets of her husband's pants. Her fingers connect with a crumpled piece of paper. She slowly removes the paper, smooths it open, and reads the words.

Thank you for the amazing night.

Love you lots.

Your "other wife," Gloria.

PS: Oliver sends kisses.

XOXOXO

What on earth is that dog walker / bartender up to?

Pulse galloping, Jemma hurries back down the stairs and makes for the coatrack in the hallway. She feels in Adam's jacket pocket. Empty.

She tries the other. The movement of the jacket fabric releases a waft of the same fragrance. Jemma gags. And her fingers touch something. She takes out a used napkin. It has an embossed BEACH HOUSE logo in one corner and is stained with the same shade of bloodred lipstick.

Gloria used this to wipe her mouth?

Jemma stands there, thinking. The bartender gave her Gloria's card with the gallery address. Gloria sat awhile at Chloe's bar, drinking, picking at a bowl of snacks. She must have used this napkin and Chloe saved it? Does Chloe Cooper know that Gloria is Adam's mistress? How?

Jemma recalls how she came to invite Chloe Cooper into her house. Had Chloe somehow manipulated the invitation, insinuated herself into their house?

A chill crawls down Jemma's spine. What in the hell does that creepy plain Jane want?

Jemma glances at the napkin and note in her hand. Clearly Chloe Cooper wants Jemma to think the worst of Adam. The woman left these clues, presumably for Jemma to find. For some reason she's trying to communicate the news of Adam's affair to Jemma without coming straight out and saying it, and she's planting evidence that Jemma can use against her husband. How weird. How very intriguing. And then something strikes Jemma.

Maybe I could use you *in some way, Chloe Cooper. Maybe I should cultivate our relationship further, learn more about who and what you are, and what you might be capable of.*

BEFORE THE HIT-AND-RUN

Adam arrives home in the early evening. He told Jemma it was a workday, and after Narek's he took a long drive up the Sea to Sky Highway to think, followed by a brutal workout at the gym with his personal trainer. It was a good decision. He was able to physically thrash things out, and he's come to a decision. Narek is right. So was their marriage counselor: it's better in the long run for *all* parties if there is honesty, transparency. He needs to tell Jemma for her own sake. If he lingers in this dead-end relationship, all of them—he, Jemma, Gloria, and Oliver—will suffer. Oliver will bear the real brunt of it. He owes this to his little boy.

When he steps through the door, gym bag in hand, he hears soft jazz. It fills the home with an unexpected ambience. He smells something delicious cooking, with garlic. It instantly makes his mouth water. Adam realizes he's barely eaten all day. He shrugs out of his jacket, hangs it up, and cautiously enters the living area, gym bag still in hand.

The dogs skitter across the floor to greet him, but his focus is on Jemma. She's relaxing on the sofa with a glass of wine in front of her, dressed in a soft cashmere sweater of dove gray over black pants. Her hair is freshly washed and hangs loose and shiny around her shoulders. She appears . . . content. Adam stills. Even now she's very beautiful. But it's an abstract observation. It's not accompanied by instant arousal. It's familiar. Nothing compared to the physical excitement that seizes him when he lays eyes on Gloria. But he hasn't seen his wife relaxing like this in a long, long time.

"Hey, hon." He hears the lilt of a question in his tone.

She smiles, reaches for her wineglass, and regards him as she takes a slow sip.

A warning bell begins to clang in Adam's mind. Something's off. She's *too* relaxed. Or perhaps she's finally settling into the home a bit. Which would be a good thing. It'll be easier to leave her if she's in a healthy mental space.

"Smells great in here."

"Made your favorite. Beef Wellington," she says.

His gaze goes to the dining table. It's set for two. The good crockery. Linen napkins. Flowers. Candles flicker, and a bottle of red breathes alongside two wineglasses. His brain races. What has he forgotten? A special occasion? A birthday, some anniversary? He can't recall. Anxiety begins to build in him.

He forces a smile, then suddenly notices she's wearing the same diamond jewelry set he gave Gloria. A chill slinks through his belly. "Have I forgotten some occasion?"

She comes to her feet, gives him a kiss on the mouth. "Just thought we'd celebrate the true beginning of this next phase of our life together, now that we're a little more settled in the new place."

He swallows. She smells different. And it strikes him—she's wearing the same perfume that Gloria loves. His heart begins to beat faster. He's imagining things. And even so—it's not going to matter because he *has* to tell her. Tonight. Now. It can't go on any longer. Gloria has left a tiny window open for him, and if he doesn't act soon, he'll lose everything and be stuck in this cul-de-sac of a marriage.

"Right," he says, stepping away to place his gym bag at the base of the stairs.

"Can I pour you a drink?" she asks.

"Sure. I'll start with Scotch."

Jemma goes into the kitchen to fetch a glass. "So how was your day?"

"Oh, the usual." He thinks of his conversation with Narek as he takes a seat in the living room. She brings him his Scotch and picks up her own glass.

"Cheers. To us." She holds her glass out.

He meets her gaze, and his brain scrambles for the best choice of words as he raises his glass and chinks it against hers. He sips, then carefully sets his drink down. "Jem, we need to talk."

"This sounds ominous. What's wrong?"

"Take a seat, will you?"

Worry creases her features. Slowly she sits opposite him. She fixes him with her gaze.

He inhales deeply and leans forward, clasping his hands. Tension tightens his neck. His gut is a ball of acid. The last thing he wants to do is hurt her, but he has to make that first cut. Narek's words snake through his mind.

It's a tough conversation, and the fallout is rough at first—really rough—but it gets better, easier. I promise. And, brother, that freedom when she finally lets you go—it's fucking worth it.

"I—look, I know the timing of this is really awkward. With the move, and our plans, and coming on the back of all the counseling. But I did try, Jem. I really was *trying* to make it work, and—"

"What are you talking about?"

"I—I think you're still not happy. And neither am I, and we both know our marriage, I mean the intimacy, it hasn't been there for a long time. The spark. And . . ." Words defeat him. He drags his hands over his hair. "We've both had a lot on our plates for the last few years, and . . . I think I lost a sense of myself a bit. I need some time, you know, to think."

Jemma's jaw drops. Her eyes go wide. "To *think*?"

"Look, I *know* you've been frustrated, too, Jem. These past years have taken so much out of us—they've gutted us, and . . . I just need time to reset."

A look of shock, horror, seeps into her features. His anxiety triples. "Do you understand?"

She tries to find her voice. It comes out rough. "So this move out West, this new phase—"

"I was trying. Really trying. I—"

"Is there someone else, Adam?" Her words are suddenly crisp.

"It's not like that. I—"

"Just answer the fucking question."

He blinks. "Whether I've met someone else is not the point. It's more of—"

"Don't bullshit me." She surges to her feet. "Is. There. Someone. Else?"

"No, Jem. I—"

"Liar. I saw you today. With *her*. Gloria. And Oliver."

Blood heads south in his body. He feels dizzy as his mind folds in on itself.

"I know, Adam. About the diamonds." She wiggles her hand with the ring cluster at him. "What was it? A two-for-one special that Christmas? One jewelry set for the wife and one for your whore? Yes, I know about Oliver, and the gallery, and the little house on Magnolia Lane. Did you buy that for her? How long has it been going on? How many fucking months or years have you been screwing her—because it's more than two if you have a two-year-old son." Her voice cracks. Her eyes glitter with fierce emotion, and her cheeks flush. Anger rolls off her body in waves he can feel.

"Jemma, I—I'm sorry. The last thing I wanted to do was hurt you. I couldn't tell you while we were going through—"

"Through the pain and hellish nightmare of our son's fatal illness? Through his last days of struggling for his life on this earth? Through his funeral? You were sleeping with this woman, making a new baby, while we were burying our son, grieving for *our* son? While I was struggling to come to terms with the fact I could never try again—never have more children—never be able to fill that hole in my soul? That hollowness consumed my entire being, and you were busy making a fresh little backup family for yourself?"

"Jemma—"

Her hand shoots up. "Stop. Just stop. I need to know why you convinced me to move out here, why you made promises about a new phase, about doing things together. What was—" A cough-sob escapes her throat. She turns away from him, fighting to control her emotions, tension in her back.

She clears her throat and says quietly as she faces him again, "What was that about, Adam? How could you take me away from a home and environment that grounded me, and bring me out here—stick me in this ungodly, awful concrete house—while the whole time you intended to leave me?"

Adam quickly downs his drink in one gulp, desperate for false courage. *It gets better, easier. I promise.* "I didn't tell you because I *couldn't* hurt you, Jem. I thought you'd be ready before now, but you weren't. And—and I figured that if I set you up here—"

"That you could have both of us? As a chickenshit move because you were too much of a coward to tell me?"

"I figured I could transition you more slowly to the idea of my new relationship, while still keeping an eye on you, Jem. Helping you out when you needed. Being close by."

"Jesus." She curses bitterly, softly. "We had a pact. A marriage is a promise. A deal. A pledge. Until death do us part."

"I'm so sorry, Jem."

"I sacrificed *everything* for this marriage, Adam. For you, for the children. I gave up my career, my place at the Lacotte Institut in Paris so *we* could have Hailey. So we could marry. Do you know how many would have *killed* for an invite to a dance school like that? It was my last big shot at my dream of being on a world stage, but one of us

123

had to be home for Hailey after her diagnosis." She beats her fist on her chest. "Me. I could have *been* somebody, Adam. And you know it. I took the blow, so you could pursue this"—she waves her hand at the window—"this medical career that has now brought you here, to the cancer agency in Vancouver. Where you can be with *her*. That's what this whole big move-out-west thing is, isn't it? To be with Gloria Bergson and your new son. I got used up over the decades, spent on our family, only to be spat out and lose it all, for *this*?"

"That's not fair, Jemma. One of us needed to work. We needed the income. It was a team effort."

"Exactly. *A team*. And now that I'm all used up, and you still have your big-shot surgeon's career and viable sperm and your new child—how old is your slut, anyway? Early thirties? Same age as Hailey would be had she lived?"

Guilt washes up through Adam's chest. It twists with anxiety, conflict. He almost starts backing down in the face of her anger, but he remembers Narek's words—no one will be happy in a dead-end relationship. It'll turn toxic. He *will* lose his son and the woman he's come to love with all his heart. They'll *all* lose.

"Jemma, if you don't like it here, I'll help you move back to Ontario. I am so sorry. I—it was a mistake, this move out West, this house. I—"

"I can't believe that some part of your selfish, narcissistic brain allowed you to think it could actually just carry on with me here."

Adam's resolve hardens. He cannot back down now. He's come this far. He has to push through—the first cut will surely be the worst.

"We both know it hasn't been working for a long while. We tried. And now we both need to face the fact that it's over. It has been for a long time."

She stares at him as color drains from her face, leaving her sheet white. Her eyes seem to sink into dark hollows in her head. She begins to tremble. "Do you love her?" she asks very quietly.

"I do, Jem. Very much." He wavers. "I—I'll pack some things now. I'll move out tonight. I will—"

"No."

"What?"

"I said no. You're not leaving."

"What do you mean?"

"We have a pact. You made a promise. A vow. In sickness and in health. Until death do us part. I will not allow you to leave this relationship."

"Why would you even want to try to make me stay, Jemma, if you know my heart is with another woman, with my son? How will that make *you* happy?"

"I believe in honoring a vow, Adam. It's a matter of principle. And if you dare even attempt to leave this marriage, I will pick up the phone, and I will call the media, and the Ontario fraud unit, and the College of Physicians and Surgeons, and I will tell them what you did all those years ago."

Adam reels. He feels dizzy. "You wouldn't."

"Try me."

His mouth goes dry. "That was forever ago."

"Fraud is fraud. And even if there is some kind of statute of limitations on what you did, the college will ensure you lose your license to practice. The media will have a field day. You'll lose everything you worked for, Adam. Everything I helped you work for."

"You were in on it, too. You *knew* what I was doing. You'll also go down."

She barks a harsh laugh. "You know better than that. My *alleged* knowledge isn't going to make me an accessory. But you? You could be criminally charged in addition to being fined hundreds of thousands of dollars. No one looks lightly on a doctor—a beloved surgeon—defrauding a provincial health insurance plan. You took in well over two million dollars over a period of three years by false billing, overbilling, and charging for procedures and tests that were not necessary."

Horrified, Adam says, "You sound like you've rehearsed it all."

"I've had time to think about how to pitch it to a journalist, and the cops."

"For Pete's sake, Jemma, we needed that money. We—you and me—did it for Hailey. We *had* to. We couldn't afford things back then. The medical treatments in Switzerland would have completely bankrupted us."

"You could have asked your parents for help."

"You know I couldn't."

"Oh, right, you were too proud, too desperate to prove to Daddy and Mommy that we were not struggling financially. You thought your father would use it as another opportunity to degrade you and to drive home how you would never live up to your dead older brother. His favorite son."

Anger explodes in Adam. He lurches to his feet, points his finger at Jemma. "Stop. Stop it right there."

She falls silent, regards him. Waiting.

His heart thuds. His skin is hot. He's breathing hard. "You wouldn't do this, Jemma. You don't have proof. It's all in the past, and—"

"I do have proof. I kept copies of everything."

"What?"

She says nothing. Her eyes burn into his.

His jaw drops. "Why would you even do that?"

"In case of an occasion like this."

Adam glowers at her. His mind spins. It doesn't make sense. Why would she have felt she needed insurance, leverage against him? He'd been wholly committed to her and to Hailey—their little family—at the time. And all the while she'd been scheming and keeping open a back door in her mind? His world tilts. "You wouldn't do it," he says quietly.

"Try me," she says again. "Either you end it with her. Tomorrow. For good. Or I make those calls, Adam."

BEFORE THE HIT-AND-RUN

September 26, 2019

Adam's hands are tight on the wheel of his car, his shoulders tense. He has two more days off work—he's taking a three-day weekend—and when Jemma went for her morning swim, he left the house to drive to Langley, where Sophia's dance studio is located.

If Jemma does in fact have evidence of his past fraud—as she claims—and she takes it to the authorities, he *will* lose everything, including perhaps his freedom if he goes to prison. He could lose Gloria, too. If he loses Gloria, he loses Oliver.

He turns off the highway, enters a stream of traffic, slows and stops at a red light. How can he allow Oliver to learn his father is—was—a criminal? The child would never understand why Adam did what he did to help pay the crushing costs of experimental medical treatments in an effort to extend Hailey's life span with cystic fibrosis.

The light turns green. He depresses the accelerator and follows the GPS directions to Sophia's studio. It was to no avail anyway. Hailey caught a bad respiratory infection. Because of her comorbid issues, she was unable to fight it off. It stole her life. Too early, too young, and it broke both him and Jemma.

Emotion thickens his nasal passages, burns into his eyes. He turns down a side street and slows to a crawl as his navigation system informs him he is nearing his destination. Adam turns into a small parking lot and comes to a stop outside the Barre and Beyond Dance Studio. For a while he sits in his car, thinking.

He needs a way out of the marriage. He has every intention of making it work with Gloria—he's never felt clearer or more fierce about this goal than he does now. Perhaps Sophia, one of Jemma's oldest friends, who has gone through her own divorce, might be able to talk some sense into his wife, or at least help her see there can be light on the other side.

Adam exits his car and makes his way to the studio entrance. Through the windows he sees little girls in leotards and tights holding on to a barre and pointing toes in front of mirrors. He waits outside until the class is over. Sophia lets him in as the girls stream out, full of laughter and chatter.

"Thanks for seeing me," he says as Sophia pours him coffee in a small kitchenette off the studio.

"It's been a while."

"No kidding. When was it that we last saw you at our old place on the lake?"

"When I last visited my brother in Toronto." She hands him a steaming mug. "Your phone call this morning has me intrigued, Adam. What can I possibly do for you?" Sophia takes a seat at a small table and gestures for him to do the same.

He sits, sips his coffee, then decides to get straight to it. "It's Jemma. I—I told her yesterday I've been having an affair, and that I want out of the marriage." He explains the situation.

Sophia's face reveals no single emotion. Her gaze—dark, intense—remains steadfast and locked on his. He begins to feel uncomfortable and shifts in his chair.

"So, I—I was wondering if I could ask you about your divorce, because there are some similarities. And—"

"You mean because Steven was also having an affair? With a younger woman? Because they also now have a child?"

He moistens his lips, decides it's best to remain transparent if he wants honest answers in return.

"I mean, you *are* better off, happier now, right? Now that it's over?"

She shakes her head slowly, gets up, goes to the window. She stares out, her arms folded tightly across her chest. Her spine is ruler straight. Despite her age, Sophia still has a long dancer's neck, a physical grace.

She says, not looking at him, "What makes you think I'm happier?"

"Are you not?"

She faces him. "What do you really want from me, Adam?"

"Could you talk to her? Tell her it'll be okay? Ask her what the point of staying in a dead marriage is, especially with someone who loves another woman. How can that make her happy? It'll make life unbearable. For both of us. If you can just talk to her, explain to her there *is* life at the other end of divorce—like there is for you—maybe she'll . . . feel better."

"I don't understand why you brought Jemma to Vancouver, Adam. Why the new house? Why all the talk about a new phase in your lives and doing new things together if you knew you wanted to leave her?"

"I couldn't leave her behind in Ontario, all alone. I didn't want to hurt her."

She huffs. "So you uproot her, rip up her foundations, *then* hurt her?"

"I wanted to wait, Sophia. Honestly. But she found out somehow."

"Gloria—that's your mistress's name, right?"

Surprise washes through him. "How do you know?"

"Gloria showed up in the Beach House restaurant the other night. She sat at the bar and watched our table, then confronted Jemma directly in the bathroom."

Adam feels blood drain from his head.

"Your mistress must be getting weary of not being seen, Adam, of being kept in the shadows. Funny how people have a need to be seen, noticed, acknowledged. It makes them feel real. She apparently showed Jemma a photo of *her* little boy. Jemma says he looks exactly like Jackson. Let me guess—your mistress is putting on the screws? She wants to break your marriage since you can't do it yourself."

Adam blows out a chestful of air and rubs his face. He curses softly. "I wondered how Jemma found out about it. I had no idea Gloria did that."

Sophia pulls a wry mouth and reseats herself at the table. "Good luck with all of that." She reaches for her mug. "If I can tell you one thing about Jemma—people don't leave her. They don't abandon or dump her."

"What do you mean?"

Sophia takes a long, slow sip of her own coffee. Her gaze holds his over the rim of her mug.

An edginess—a whisper of foreboding—curls through Adam's stomach. He leans forward. "Sophia, what in the hell do you mean?"

She sits back. "Your wife is a narcissist—you know that, right? She has a pathological need for attention, adoration, exclusivity. She'll do just about *anything* to keep focus on herself. Have you ever wondered why Jemma and I never stayed close after she left Vancouver for the Toronto institute in her early twenties?"

"I'm listening."

"I had a suspicion she was responsible for the death of my new boyfriend at the time. He used to date Jemma, but dumped her for me. Somehow he still ended up going on a hike with her, along a cliff above a water-filled quarry near her old trailer park home." She pauses. Her gaze lasers into Adam's. "He slipped on loose rocks, fell, hit his head on the way down, and drowned. At least, that was her story. Autopsy revealed nothing suspicious. No one could prove otherwise."

"Christ, Sophia, you can't think she—"

"And what about her father? He abandoned Jemma and her mother. Next thing he dies in a fire that consumed his trailer? The door was locked."

"She told me about that. She said he was drunk. That the fire department believed it was a lit cigarette that fell onto a mattress."

"There was some question about whether the door had been locked from the outside."

"This is absurd."

"Yeah. Right. You think I'm just saying these things because I'm jealous of Jemma? Vindictive because she won that Toronto scholarship over me? Because that's *her* narrative." Sophia leans forward. "What about Jackson?"

"What about my son?"

"The rumors."

"For Pete's sake, Sophia, *what* rumors?"

"You do recall that my brother was a nurse at the hospital where Jackson was admitted and readmitted over the years?"

"Yes, I remember."

"Jackson was always brought in for some mysterious ailment or complication. Doctors were always stumped. Jemma—the devoted, long-suffering mother—always at her son's side. Making all the sacrifices, trying to do everything for her child. And your son was completely dependent on his loving, beleaguered mother. Jemma was the epicenter of Jackson's world, and of *your* attention."

"What rumors, Sophia?" Adam says quietly.

"You're a doctor. You know about Munchausen syndrome by proxy."

He comes to his feet. "This is ridiculous."

"Is it, though?"

"Your brother heard these rumors? At the hospital?"

"There was talk among the nurses. One of them brought the history of Jackson's many hospitalizations and strange sets of symptoms to the attention of a doctor, and raised their concerns. But there was no evidence, and who wants to accuse a grieving mother unnecessarily? It's risky territory. But it fits her psychological makeup, Adam, and I'm sure you can see it." She checks points off her fingers. "A caregiver who appears devoted, caring, extremely distraught over a child's illness.

Someone who might exaggerate symptoms in several ways—either by lying about them, altering or tampering with tests, or giving false urine or blood samples that are not the child's. Someone who might even suffocate, starve, or cause infection in a dependent through the use of toxic substances. The typical profile is someone who appears friendly and helpful with health-care providers. She'll bring the child into the hospital, and once admitted, the child's health starts to improve, but when he goes home, complications return." She pauses, watching him. "There is no cure for someone with Munchausen's, is there? Because before there can be treatment, there needs to be admission of a problem, and someone with the syndrome will continue to lie and deny there is—or was—an issue."

Adam feels as though he's going to throw up. "Are you accusing my wife of killing our son?"

She shrugs. "It was just rumors."

"And Hailey?"

"Maybe Jemma learned her behavior through her experience with Hailey, Adam. Maybe she was at such a loss after Hailey passed that she *needed* to relive it all." Sophia pauses. "Maybe that's why she was so desperate to try for another child. Having a sick child and being the center of need and attention was a way for your wife to keep going. It became a way for her to justify to herself the loss of her stellar career, the years she'd sacrificed for Hailey and your career."

Adam stares at Sophia. His pulse races. His skin prickles with perspiration. As much as his brain refuses to process these heinous accusations about his wife, another part of Adam's mind can see it. Because things start to make sense. Things he's avoided interrogating within himself.

He rubs his mouth hard.

"You see it now, don't you?"

"Why are you even still friendly with my wife?"

"I'm not really. To be honest, I think I actually disgust Jemma. To her I represent the personified image of a failure, at least in terms of being a dancer, and a woman who can't hold on to her husband."

"Yet you went to the dinner with her."

"I suppose I have my issues, too. I wanted to see what she looked like after this time, after the loss of both children. Perhaps I was hoping to discover she was doing terribly, looking old and washed up—as a way to make myself feel better about myself and my own choices. My own losses." She hesitates. "My own wasted youth." She leans forward again and lowers her voice.

"Be careful, Adam. Consider the ferocity of drive and ambition she mustered to pull herself out of that trailer park. She's not who people think she is. Not even you, her husband."

BEFORE THE HIT-AND-RUN

Adam lies in bed, listening to the wind mounting outside. The weather is turning foul, a bad front blowing in. The forecast warns of heavy rain and fog over the next three days. Despite this, Jemma told him before going to sleep she would still be going swimming in the morning.

She's soundly asleep beside him now, breathing the deep breaths of relaxed slumber. Hate festers to a pitch inside him. How can she act like nothing is wrong? As though he can just continue as before, because if he doesn't, she'll destroy him.

When did they cross the line, exactly, from passionate lovers into indifference, and now red-hot hate and ultimatums of destruction?

When he arrived home after visiting Sophia, Jemma asked if he'd been to tell Gloria it was over. He lied. He said yes. Jemma said, "Good." And she carried on making dinner, humming to music, sipping her wine, acting like yesterday never happened at all. As though Gloria and Oliver and his affair never existed. And now never would. How was it even possible that she could compartmentalize things like this?

His mind goes to Sophia's talk about Munchausen by proxy. He feels ill. Desperate. He tosses, turns, punches his pillow. Outside the wind grows stronger and begins to moan through the corners of their big gray concrete-and-glass house. It rustles through the trees, tearing dead leaves from their branches, hurling them into a tumbling clatter down the street. He imagines the sea heaving and tossing, as unrestful as he is. He hears rain begin to fall.

"Adam?" she whispers.

He startles, but says nothing.

"You awake?"

He holds his breath, hoping she'll go back to sleep. But he feels her hand, warm, slide onto his belly and down the front of his pajama shorts. She cups him between the legs, begins to move her hand back and forth. Adam scrunches his eyes shut tight, willing her to stop. She moves more rhythmically, harder. When she finds he isn't responding, she comes closer and throws one warm and naked leg over him. She whispers in his ear, "Adam, make love to me."

He feels nauseous. He clears his throat. "It—it's been a long day, Jemma. I'm tired."

She grinds her pelvis against his hip and pulls down his shorts. She straddles him and moves against his groin. His eyes burn. He's repulsed. He can't do this.

Jemma goes still. "You did tell her, didn't you, Adam? You told her never to see you again?"

"Yes."

"You *sure* you're not lying to me?"

Her question hangs in the darkness. A threat. A fucking sword of Damocles, under which he dare not move lest he cause the thread to break.

"I told you I did," he says finally as he tries to roll away from her, but she clamps her knees firmly on either side of his hips.

"Prove it to me, then. Prove it's all over with her." She moves rhythmically over him again. Tears of frustration prick into his eyes.

"Jem—" He tries to keep his voice soft, his tone modulated. "Please, I—just need some time."

"You didn't tell her."

"I promise, I did. It's all over. But she didn't take it well. And Oliver—it was a really rough day. I need to sleep. I—I'll be functional again tomorrow."

"We'll just cuddle then." She spoons her naked body around his and wraps her arm over his chest. Adam tries to swallow. He feels trapped, revolted by his wife's forceful attempts at intimacy. It's as though his entire world has ended. Thunder rumbles in the distance. Rain begins a steadier beat against their windows. His thoughts return to Sophia, and what she said. And the more he chews on the horror of her accusations, the more he believes Jemma might have poisoned—killed—their son. If not intentionally, then through her actions to keep him ill and in need of her. And then something went too far, or wrong. This might explain the depth and breadth of her unresolved grief over his early death. Because she perhaps *knows* she's guilty. At least on some level. And now she can never replace Jackson in the way she replaced Hailey. And the fact he now has a new child when she can't—it's making her dangerous.

Has he always been willfully blind to what she is? Because it feels as though Sophia today lifted the hood on his marriage and shined a light into the inner mechanics, and he can suddenly see what he perhaps always knew was there—the ugly, gritty, oily, dark underpinnings of the machine. And now that he's peered in, he can't unsee the grimy angles and rot, because so much of the past is suddenly making sense.

He doesn't dare confront her with this, either. A person with Munchausen by proxy is usually incapable of admitting, even to themselves, the truth. It could just make his wife even more volatile, more dangerous to him. To Gloria. And to Oliver. This last thought makes his heart race so fast he fears it'll burst out of his chest.

Could Jemma do something to hurt his son? Would she try in order to keep his attention limited to her? Would she hurt Gloria?

He can't have this. He cannot live like this. A prisoner to her threats. Adam no longer has any doubt in his mind. If Jemma sniffs out his lie—if she learns he has not dumped Gloria—she *will* turn him in for fraud. He's between a rock and a very hard place. A possible criminal conviction and loss of his profession—his calling—on one hand, or the loss of Gloria and Oliver and all his dreams for their future as a little family on the other.

Adam turns restlessly again in his bed and punches his pillow once more. The rain beats down even harder, wind lashing it in a stream against their massive windows with no blinds. As he lies there, watching the rain rivulets snaking down the panes as they catch refracted light from the streetlamp outside, he drifts into a place of lucid dreams—a space that hangs partway between wakefulness and sleep, where Jungian monsters creep out of the dungeon of the unconscious—and it's here a plot begins to take shape. At first Adam believes it's just a dream, that he's controlling it, directing it, but as he comes more awake again, he realizes it's the only answer. He needs to make it reality.

THE HIT-AND-RUN

September 27, 2019

Adam carries his gym bag into the garage. It's almost 5:00 a.m., pitch dark and pouring outside. He left a note on the kitchen counter, telling Jemma he has a very early emergency hospital call due to surgical complications—an infection has developed in the blood of one of his patients. He doesn't know when he will be back. In reality no one expects him at work since it's day three of his weekend.

Inside the garage, Adam carefully lifts a pair of vintage plates from his collection off their hooks on the wall. He crouches down in front of his car, unlocks his Tesla license plate mount, slides it forward. He unscrews the bolts securing his Ontario vanity plate to the mount, then replaces it with a red, white, and blue Idaho one. He chose the Idaho registration because he has a pair of plates, and because they're a more recent edition than the others, and less likely to draw unwarranted attention on the roads. It's not legal, of course. If he's pulled over in a routine stop and the plate is run, it will amount to a traffic violation. But Adam is more concerned about playing it safe and not having his Ontario vanity registration captured by any CCTV cameras on the Lions Gate Bridge over the Burrard, or anywhere else along his route along the North Shore. Blue Teslas are common in these parts, so that fact alone won't single him out as the driver should his car be snagged on camera.

He repeats the process at the rear of his car.

Adam places his Ontario plates on the floor behind his driver's seat. He pulls a black cap low over his brow, and he covers the cap with the voluminous fabric of his dark-gray hoodie.

As he pulls out of his garage, rain pummels his car, and his wipers come on. It's windy and dark out. Fog makes tunnels of his headlights and forms halos around the neighborhood streetlights. He can't see anyone in the laneway, and when he turns onto Main, he discovers the roads are almost deserted apart from a few buses and early commuters braving the darkness and stormy weather.

The bridge is fairly clear. He's over in minutes and soon driving along the North Shore highway. He takes the Eagle Cove exit and twists down into the curving, steep, forested roads toward Narek's estate on the water.

It's around 5:30 a.m. when he arrives, and he's grateful for his Tesla's quiet engine and the densely treed nature of the neighborhood. He parks in the circular driveway and sits in his car for a moment, rain thudding on his roof, windows misting. Anxiety snakes through him. He fears Jemma might end up *not* swimming in this weather. But he also knows his wife. Once she sets her mind to a routine—be it exercise, a diet, or another goal—she's frighteningly rigid about keeping her commitment to herself. It's Jemma's way of controlling her world, so Adam believes there remains a high probability she will actually swim.

Wind gusts suddenly, and the tall conifers on Narek's estate sway in the dark shadows around him, bombing his car with pine cones and bits of debris. He inhales deeply, checks the time. It's 5:37 a.m. His mind turns to Gloria, as it so often does in the morning, and he imagines her naked and warm and asleep in her bed, her dark hair splayed over her white pillows. He thinks of little Oliver with his cheeks pinked as he breathes the deep breaths of sleep, cuddled with his favorite stuffy basset hound. Oliver, who wants a real puppy. Adam promised his son that when he moved in, they would get a dog. He will not let him down.

He *has* to do this.

Especially with this foggy-weather window. It's now or never. Jemma has left him zero choice. He either ends up in a federal prison, or he stays in another kind of prison in his marriage with Jemma—the woman he has now come to believe killed their boy. Either way, he loses Gloria and his new son. But if he does this . . .

He swings open his car door and steps into the downpour. Water drips off the bill of his cap as he takes his bag off the back seat. Adam shuts the door and pats his pocket to ensure he has the keys that Narek gave him. Using his flashlight, he makes his way around the side of Narek's house. A shadow darts in front of him. Adam freezes. His heart thuds like a drum. He pans his light into the bushes. Two yellow-green eyes glow back at him. Relief is instant. It was just a cat. He listens carefully for what might have spooked the cat, but all he hears is rain, wind in the boughs, and the gentle hush and crush of rocks in the wavelets down on the beach.

He proceeds cautiously to the rear of Narek's mansion, then ducks under the covered walkway that leads down to the beach and the boathouse, his flashlight poking a beam of muted light into the mist.

Outside the boathouse door, Adam sets down his bag and holds the keys under the beam of his flashlight. He selects the one tagged for the boathouse. He unlocks the door, creaks it open, steps inside. Carefully he shuts the door behind him. Only once he's safely inside does he switch on the interior light. The boathouse springs to life.

The Jet Skis gleam in front of him, hanging in their cradles from cables and a hoist mounted on the boathouse ceiling. He recalls Narek pointing to the black craft.

That one needs some servicing, I'm afraid. Otherwise everything else is in working order. Gas containers there. And hanging up over there— snorkeling and diving gear, the SUPs, wet suits. Everything you need.

Come spring, when he's free, when some time has passed, he might visit the estate with Gloria and Oliver. They will swim and play with all the toys. A lightness of golden promises blooms in Adam's chest and firms his resolve. It's too bad that the black Jet Ski is not operational, because it would be a preferable option—less distinctive. But the other will have to do. Adam finds the controls for the winch system and begins to lower the blue-and-white craft with the orange stripe down to the rails on the ramp.

Once the craft is lowered, he checks the fuel. All good. Heart beating faster now, he removes his clothes, folds them, and leaves them on the boathouse bench. He pulls on his swimming wet suit, zips up the back. Next he dons his hood, booties, and the gloves he uses for very-cold-water triathlon training swims. He puts on his goggles. They'll help with the rain and wind, as well as obscure his features.

Adam opens the boathouse doors to the water and switches off the light. The craft itself is not equipped with lights, as per regulations, but the dawn has brightened enough to see, and he will use his flashlight for the crossing—because of the mist—until he reaches Jerrin Bay on the other side of the inlet.

He slides the craft down into the water, mounts it, starts the engine. It grumbles to life beneath him, water coursing through the impellers. These craft do not have external props like boats do, so any damage that needs to be done will have to come from blunt impact. Speed will compound the force.

Adam steers out into the small bay. Nerves spark through him. He fears the sound of the engine will attract attention. He peers at the densely forested shoreline. Most people are still asleep, and the noise of rain on their houses helps cover him. The properties abutting Narek's are all also over two acres apiece. And should anyone peer out their window, they will see thick mist.

He revs the engines and heads steadily and carefully into the fog. From his last visit to Narek's he knows the tankers that wait in the bay to enter the port usually lie farther to the east. Using the compass on his watch, he navigates a direct line toward Jerrin Bay.

Within minutes he begins to glimpse the mist-shrouded lights along the shores of Crow's Point. As he nears the bay, he cuts his flashlight and slows his engine. He moves into the shadowed lee of a rocky promontory that juts out behind the marina and the Boathouse Restaurant. He cuts his engines, checks his watch, and waits on the surging tide. As the seconds and minutes tick by, Adam grows more and more agitated. He begins to shiver from cold. Or perhaps it's jitters from fear, from second thoughts.

Dawn begins to seep more light into the gloom, turning the sea and fog into tones of gray upon gray. Tense, he waits. Rain doubles down, patterning the gunmetal water. A seal breaks the surface and peers at him. Adam jumps. His heart races faster. He begins to worry she won't actually come out. Perhaps it is too bleak, too cold for his wife. But then he hears what he's been waiting for.

The gentle and rhythmic *splish splosh splish* of a swimmer's arms moving into the bay.

THE HIT-AND-RUN

Jemma takes a fast sip from her coffee mug and sets it on the dresser. She opens yet another drawer and rummages through it, searching for her bathing cap. She can't find it anywhere. She checks her watch. She's starting to run a bit late now, and she's irked—she has a live Instagram interview booked for later this morning. She wants to be home in time to shower and dry her hair and prep properly before logging on. This is what happens when she drinks too much the night before and doesn't set her gear out before retiring to bed. She really is a creature of habit and routine, and when it's broken, it rattles her. She feels out of control. Jemma detests that feeling. This is why these past two years, and recent days, have messed so badly with her head.

She could always call her swim off, but she also needs it to clear her mind before her interview. She always feels amped and empowered after rigorous exercise, possibly because of her dancing background. Plus, Jemma wants to be able to say online—to the world—*Look at me—how good I look at my age. And how do I attain my physique, my glow? I swim. And this morning I did three kilometers in open water, wild swimming in the rain and the mist. I swim daily, early in the a.m. I'm all about showing up, building habits.* She will then launch into the importance of committing to—and achieving—small daily goals, each and every day, because consistency is the key to attaining a dream. Those who show up win.

Jemma strives to be an influencer who actually walks the walk before she talks and tells other women how to live. Which is another reason it's so critical for her to hold on to her marriage. She absolutely *refuses* to be the dumped, rejected, washed-up wife, a victim. But she holds the trump card now. Adam is at heart a self-centered man. He's all about survival. He will not choose criminal prosecution or being struck as a surgeon over being with his mistress when it cuts down to the wire.

She finally decides to grab a new cap. She swigs more coffee and shimmies into her bathing suit and then her wet suit. In warmer weather she dons her wet suit at the beach, but in this cold and rain, she's fine to drive with it under her Dryrobe. She grabs her towel, a woolly hat, a scarf, and the preprepared flask of extra-hot coffee. She adds swim booties for today. She might even wear neoprene gloves. Although on days like this the ocean can be warmer than the air, which is probably the case, given the fog. Jemma hurries down the stairs.

"Be back soon, guys," she says to Boo and Sweetie as she pulls open the door to the garage. She tosses her bag onto the passenger seat of her vehicle, climbs in, buckles herself into the driver's seat, and opens the garage door with the remote. Within minutes she reaches the Jerrin Beach parking lot. As she slows her car, Jemma notices the tide is very far out along the shallow flats, and visibility is very low. She makes another snap decision.

A few moments later, she's tucking her long hair into her bathing cap, securing her buoy to her waist, and wading out into the gray water. Sans gloves. Because the inlet is in fact warmer than the air. Jemma dips her hands into the seawater, acclimating to the temperature, then splashes water over her face before sinking in down to her neck. Water rapidly seeps into her wet suit, filling the spaces between the neoprene and her skin. She breathes calmly, then allows herself to float face down, arms out, suspended in time and water as her body adjusts to the change.

She begins to swim, one arm with bent elbow arcing over the surface as the other pulls firmly beneath. She moves smoothly through the gentle rise and fall of the swells, rain drumming down on her back as she breathes deeply, rhythmically. Endurance swimming is all about controlling breathing, staying calm. Tensing up uses too much energy. Gradually, steadily, she moves into the center of the bay, and a calm begins to fill her.

THE HIT-AND-RUN

A lime-colored buoy emerges from the curtains of mist as the swimmer moves toward the center of the bay. She rises on a swell, and Adam is able to discern her pink-capped head. His mouth goes dry as he flexes his hands around the controls, waiting for her to move farther out and into the very center of the bay. His goggles begin to fog from the heat of his perspiration despite the cold. The rain drums down. Mist swirls and shifts like a sentient curtain around him as he floats up and down on the swells. The buoy is almost at the center. Adam's heart pounds. He waits one more second for her to reach the very middle of the bay, which is the farthest point from all shores and from safety and refuge. And as she does, he clenches his jaw, narrows his eyes, and guns the engine.

The Jet Ski shoots forward with a rooster spray of power. He focuses solely on her capped head gliding slowly forward. He doesn't think, can't, just grips the controls, aims, and rides at full speed.

The hull of his craft slams into her body, and the thud judders through Adam's bones, almost throwing him off as his Jet Ski bounces and veers sideways. Blood booms against his eardrums. Every molecule in his body vibrates with the explosive shock of the hit. He rights himself, decreases engine power, and slows. He doesn't want to, but he glances behind him. His throat clamps closed. Blood darkens the water, and her body is limp. But as he is about to turn away, she moves, lifts her head slightly, and raises her right hand from the water. A plea for help. Adam panics. He glances toward shore, but he's so hyperfocused he doesn't really register anything other than the fact she's still alive.

He gives the engine gas and moves away from her, circling out wide as he gathers momentum. He turns to face her again, gritting his teeth as he revs the engine to full speed. This time he's physically prepared for the explosive impact. This time he hits her square in the center of her skull. He rides over the back of her body and smashes through her buoy. Adam regains the equilibrium of his craft and aims for the open water and the North Shore. His pulse races so fast he fears he will die. He's dizzy. Within seconds he's enshrouded once more by mist, invisible from the shores of Crow's Point. He slows ever so slightly to check the compass bearing on his watch. Once he sees he's on a direct path across the narrowest neck of the Burrard, he knows his path should be clear of big ships. And there's very little likelihood of encountering any other small pleasure craft in this weather, at this time of the gloomy dawn.

As he nears the shores of Narek's estate, Adam starts to shake. And sob. He cannot believe the horror of what he's just done. He loved her once. So much. They shared children. A full life.

Go. Go. Focus. Keep moving forward. Your only choice now is to follow through. If you lose courage, if you falter, it will all be over. Think of Gloria, of Oliver. Stay in control. Falter now and you will still lose them.

He nears the residential bay and slows to a putter as he navigates slowly into the small cove shadowed by tall conifers—pine, cedar, hemlock. Adam sees no movement along the private beach. The forest of vegetation is dense. A muffling buffer. And fog is still heavy in this corner. He believes he's safe.

He approaches the boathouse and enters. Adam dismounts and has trouble standing because he's shuddering so badly. After a few faltering attempts, he manages to secure the Jet Ski into the cradle, and he winches it up. He unrolls a hosepipe, turns on the tap, and thoroughly rinses the Jet Ski. Urgency crackles through him as time ticks. He needs to get back over the bridge and be home before authorities identify his wife.

Hurriedly Adam changes back into his clothes and bundles his wet gear into his duffel bag. Quickly he scans the interior of the boathouse to see that everything is back in place. He knows he'll be in deep shit if any CSI-type team gets in here. But his job is to ensure that never happens. He'll lie low for a while, and maybe he can return later, when things die down, in order to clean things up better. He clicks off the light, exits the boathouse, locks the door.

Adam heads back over the bridge. He's still shaking so forcibly he can barely drive. He's a fucking wreck of a mess. A couple of brandy shots at home will settle him. And he needs a shower. He needs to be ready for when the police finally identify the body, and come knocking at his door with the terrible news of his wife's tragic accident at sea.

IT'S CRIMINAL: The Chloe Cooper Story

*The screen fades to an interior with a leather chair posi-
tioned in a spot of light. A bulky woman in her late sixties
enters the room as the lighting brightens. She wears a
navy blazer over a white blouse and black pants. Her
dark-brown hair is streaked with silver and cut in a lob.
Her face is hard. Her jaw is firm, but her brown eyes are
liquid, warm, kind.*

Text at the bottom of the screen reads:

RETIRED DETECTIVE MAEVE HAVERS,
MAJOR CRIMES, GREATER VANCOUVER
POLICE DEPARTMENT.

MAEVE: The postmortem revealed cause of death to be exsanguina-
tion—massive blood loss caused by severe blunt-force trauma to the
head and torso. It was the second impact that killed her.

TRINITY OFF CAMERA: So she was still alive before the Jet Ski
circled back?

MAEVE: Her injuries were consistent with that scenario, so yes. A coordinated, interagency search for the Jet Ski was immediately initiated. It included the Canadian Coast Guard, the GVPD marine unit, plus other law enforcement agencies along the North Shore directly across the water from Jerrin Bay. A CH-149 Cormorant helicopter was also dispatched to conduct a search—it has more capabilities in inclement weather. But everything was hindered by heavy rain and dense fog. The shores along the Burrard Inlet—which is essentially a fjord—contain a myriad of bays, coves, smaller inlets, and marinas both public and private. The suspect could have gone a thousand different places. To the south the Burrard stretches toward False Creek, English Bay, past the Capilano River mouth, under the Lions Gate Bridge, widens into Vancouver Harbour—which contains Canada's largest port—and goes all the way to the Indian Arm and up to Port Moody. To the west it opens into the Georgia Strait, from where the Jet Ski could have headed to any number of small islands in the gulf.

TRINITY OFF CAMERA: So the Jet Ski essentially vanished that morning—a ghost into fog.

MAEVE: Correct. We put out additional calls for information and witnesses via news media and various social media accounts. We received hundreds of tips, but nothing actionable. Apart from one unusual call—an anonymous one—that came through to our line.

A graphic showing sound bars appears at the bottom of the screen as a recording of the call plays. A woman's voice, shaky, breathy, says:

"The husband did it. Dr. Adam Spengler killed Jemma Spengler with a Jet Ski that was blue and white with an orange stripe down the side. I saw the whole thing. He wore a black wet suit with a hood. Gloves. Goggles. He hit her twice—went back to make sure she was dead. Then he headed straight out into the Burrard. Into the fog. At high speed, heading toward the North Shore. They live at 1117 Crow's Road, off Main."

There is a moment of silence as the haunting echo of the words hangs in the space. The camera returns focus to Detective Maeve Havers.

MAEVE: The call came from a forty-year-old woman named Chloe Cooper, who lived across the alley from the Spenglers.

TRINITY OFF CAMERA: How did you identify and locate her?

MAEVE: We knew from a witness at the homicide scene that a woman with a small dog was on the beach walk at the time of the hit-and-run, but she left the scene in a hurry. A neighborhood canvass quickly revealed that Chloe Cooper—a local Crow's Point resident—routinely walked a small senior dog down to Jerrin Beach and along the paved walkway at around 7:00 a.m. each day. We visited her apartment, and on questioning she admitted to making the anonymous call. It emerged over the course of our investigation that Chloe Cooper had developed a parasitic fixation with Jemma Spengler, and she'd been at the beach every morning—including that fateful day—to watch her swim.

TRINITY OFF CAMERA: So Chloe was a person of interest?

MAEVE: She definitely became a very key person of interest after the other violent murders.

Detective Maeve Havers pauses.

MAEVE: A province-wide hunt for Cooper was initiated after she fled.

TRINITY OFF CAMERA: When you and your partner visited Chloe Cooper's apartment, did you meet her mother?

The detective's eyes narrow. She is silent for a moment.

MAEVE: Well, that's where things really got interesting. Cooper was not quite what met the eye.

AFTER THE HIT-AND-RUN

Adam turns into his driveway with his wipers arcing in vain to swipe away the deluge of rain. As he waits for the garage door to open, he hears sirens wailing toward the beach. Twitchy, he scans the lane to see if anyone is watching him. Shock slams into him. That woman is up there in the third-floor window, and this time he sees the glint of scopes in her hands. Jemma was right. Shit. Is she going to become a problem now?

Adam enters his garage, throat tight. He glances at the empty space left by Jemma's car, and the image of her crushed skull and bloodied body floats up into his mind. His stomach contracts as he imagines authorities finding her damaged body. He wonders how long it will take for them to identify her.

Jemma's buoy doubles as a dry bag. She usually tucks her car fob and phone inside the airtight compartment before inflating it fully to swim with. He knows he punctured the buoy, but it could still be attached to her body by the line, and there's a chance the keys and cell phone are still in there. Her phone is password protected, but her fob could lead cops pretty quickly to her parked car in the beach lot.

He wonders if the police will return her car directly to him, or whether crime scene techs might check it out first. But why would they? He can't see any reason for them to view her vehicle as a crime scene. He'll sell it. He's pretty sure Gloria will not want his dead wife's things. A wave of emotion suddenly slams Adam, and he drops his face into his hands and begins to sob. Big, snotted heaves shudder through his body. Christ. He must corral himself, get a grip on his emotions. The police could be here anytime now.

He gets out of his car, removes his bag. In his haste to leave Narek's boathouse, he hasn't zipped it up properly, and the wet suit gapes out. He remembers the woman in the window, glances out of the garage toward her window, and swears. From the angle of her vantage point, she has a partial view right into his garage. And she's still up there, scoping him out.

Who is she?

He steps back out of her line of sight, aims the remote, and the garage door trundles shut. As he enters the house, Boo and Sweetie scamper up to him and jump and yip for attention. Another punch of emotion slams his gut. He regards the dogs. They're going to take it hard. He'll need to rehome them. Perhaps he can find someone who will pamper them as much as Jemma did.

He drops his duffel by the door and heads straight for the booze cabinet. First step is to quell his nerves so he can act calm when the cops arrive. He pours a half glass of brandy and swallows it straight down. He coughs, and his eyes water as he pours another. He drinks this down, too. It burns like all hell, but already he can feel a warm sense of bonhomie branching through his chest and leaching into his veins. He pours one more for good measure.

As he raises the glass to his lips, he hears more sirens. Coming down Main. He hears them turning into Crow's Road. They wail down to the beach. A chopper begins to thud above the clouds. Tension twists through Adam. They're hunting for him. And for the Jet Ski—the murder weapon. He suddenly recalls the fraudulent plates on his Tesla.

He sets his glass down and rushes back into the garage. With fumbling fingers he removes the Idaho plates and replaces them with his regular Ontario vanity plates. He tucks the Idaho plates into the duffel bag with his wet suit. As he brings his bag inside, he hears more sirens. He stills to listen.

They wouldn't have identified the body yet. Would they? He doesn't really know how long it could take. He has got to stop shaking—be ready. He catches his reflection in the mirror and feels ill at what looks back at him. A sweaty, gray-complexioned murderer in his sixties who looks every bit his years and then some.

Get yourself together, man. When those cops knock, you need to present as the calm, cool, collected, worshipped, unsuspecting Dr. Adam Spengler. Every inch the renowned surgeon. Only after they break the news of your wife to you will you exhibit classic symptoms of shock, after which you will appear utterly devastated as you project a slow comprehension that your wife of thirty-four years is never coming home. That she is dead. Gone for good.

He's going to need another wretched shot of brandy. He sets his duffel down, retrieves his glass, and as he raises it to his mouth, he hears a vehicle enter the back lane outside. He tenses. Stills. Listens. The car comes to a stop outside their house. Adam is unable to move. The police? Already? He hasn't showered. He reeks of booze. He—he'll have to tell them he was on a bender last night. That he's hungover. That this in his glass is the hair of the dog.

A car door slams. He swallows and turns very slowly to face the back door. A dark shape moves outside the opaque window that runs down the side. He hears the pinging of the door code being punched in. His brain scrambles in confusion. *What the—*

The door handle turns. The door swings open.

Jemma steps inside. Wet hair, carrying her bag.

The whiskey glass slides from his fingers and explodes into crystal shards at his feet.

AFTER THE HIT-AND-RUN

Jemma stares at Adam. His face glistens with sweat. His jaw is slack, his eyes wide. He looks as though he's seen a ghost. She notices glass shattered on the floor around his feet and a reek of alcohol.

The dogs come up to her, but Boo and Sweetie appear muted, as though sensing something is wrong. Slowly, with one hand, she sets her bag of swimming gear down. In her other hand she clutches her swimming cap, which fell out of her bag when she removed it from the car. Adam's gaze is locked on the orange silicone cap in her hand. He reaches to brace himself on the counter.

"Adam? What is it—what's wrong? Did something happen at the hospital?" Outside more sirens rise and scream down Crow's Road toward the ocean. A helicopter thuds overhead in the mist somewhere. She was forced to drive home via a detour because the road to Jerrin Beach has been cordoned off by cops. She saw ambulances and fire trucks, too. Something massive is going down in that bay.

"Why are you drinking? What in the hell's going on?" She moves toward him, but he cringes away from her, as though terrified.

"Adam?"

He rushes to the bathroom. Jemma hears her husband throwing up. Confusion swirls through her mind. When they went to bed last night, everything seemed in her control. And this morning—his note on the counter—was nothing unusual. He often visits the hospital for rounds in the very early hours. Jemma follows him to the bathroom. The door is shut. She hears the toilet flush inside and the taps begin to run.

She knocks on the bathroom door. "Adam? Are you okay?"

"Fine," he calls out. "Give me a sec. Drank too much last night."

Jemma frowns. They'd enjoyed cocktails together, followed by two bottles of wine, and Adam had chased it all with a glass of cognac, presumably to shore up his regrets over dumping Gloria and her offspring. But his alcohol consumption should not have resulted in *this* kind of hangover, surely?

Jemma returns to the hallway to retrieve her swim gear. She needs to rinse out her wet suit. As she reaches for her bag, she notices Adam's duffel near the door. The zipper is open, and inside are two red, white, and blue car license plates on top of a wet suit. She furrows her brow, crouches down, and examines the plates. They're his Idaho ones. He got them to commemorate a whitewater rafting trip they took there. Jemma feels his wet suit. It's wet. She moves the wet suit aside and finds a neoprene hood, gloves, and booties, along with Adam's swimming goggles. All wet. Her pulse quickens. Nothing makes sense.

She enters the garage and sees a gap in his display of vintage plates. Presumably that's where the Idaho plates hung. Jemma turns to his Tesla. His Ontario vanity plates are still on the vehicle. She rubs her mouth, puzzling over these facts. She hears the helicopter above the house again. The thudding of the rotors vibrates through the building. It's a big one—like military big.

When Jemma reenters the living room, Adam is crouched down and cleaning up the broken glass and spilled booze. He doesn't look at her.

"Adam?"

His hands go still. He takes a slow breath, then comes to his feet and faces her.

"Sorry, Jem. I—it's been really rough on me. You know with breaking it off . . ." His voice cracks.

She just stares at him.

He clears his throat. "I couldn't sleep, so I got up and did some more drinking in the night."

"You went to see patients this morning while *drunk*?"

"No. God, no. I just needed to get out and get some air."

"Your car was gone when I left—does this mean you drove while impaired?"

"Jus—just a few blocks. And I felt pretty clear at the time. It's the shakes that hit me when I got home, so"—he shrugs—"hair of the dog and all that. I—I just didn't expect you to walk in and see me like that. Drinking in the morning. I got spooked."

She glances at his duffel bag again. "I always come home after my swim around this time."

"I—I'm just not thinking clearly." He goes into the kitchen, opens the door that contains the garbage bin, and tips the shattered crystal shards from the dustpan into the bin. He replaces the dustpan and brush in the cupboard under the sink. "I'm going to take a shower." He clears his throat; then, as if on second thought, he meets her gaze. "I'll be fine, Jem. I—ah—how was your swim?"

Irritation crackles through Jemma. "It's been tough for *you*? Think about how I've been feeling, Adam, since I learned the sheer depths of your betrayal. Swim was fine. I was running late because I couldn't find my lucky pink cap. I had to use another one. And the tide was so far out this morning that I decided to swim the smaller bay east of Crow's Point. It meant I wouldn't have to go so far out into the Burrard. I prefer to stay closer to the shoreline, especially in weather like this." She pauses. "Did you hear all those sirens? And that chopper? There's some massive police incident at Jerrin Bay. Probably lucky I chose another swim route."

He pales, and it appears as though he's going to throw up again. "Yeah. I wonder what's going on. Do you want to shower before me? I know you have that Instagram live thing in a few?"

"Yeah. Maybe you can use one of the other showers?"

"Sure." Adam immediately heads toward the passage.

"Adam?" she calls after him.

"What?"

"Did you swim this morning?"

Silence hangs for a moment. He doesn't turn to face her.

"Just went for a drive. Like I said."

"What's with the wet suit and car plates by the door?"

Another beat of silence.

"I forgot to rinse off my gear after my last open-water swim. Been sitting in my trunk. I went to get it, saw that two of the plates had fallen off the wall. Need to rehang them. Just picked them up on my way in."

A dark seed of unease unfurls low in her gut as she watches her husband disappear into the passage. A beep from her watch makes her jump, and she realizes her interview starts in twenty minutes.

AFTER THE HIT-AND-RUN

In the guest bedroom Adam closes the door and clicks on the TV. He finds the local news channel and keeps the sound low, relieved to hear the shower turning on in the bathroom upstairs.

He fixates on the screen as the image cuts from the anchor's desk in the studio to a brown-haired reporter standing in the rain at Jerrin Beach.

"Police have confirmed that a female swimmer was struck and killed in a Jet Ski hit-and-run in Jerrin Bay just after seven a.m. this morning. However, they are not at this point saying whether or not she has been identified. According to a witness she was wearing a pink bathing cap and swimming with a lime-green swim buoy."

Adam's vision blurs. He begins to shake again but forces himself to keep watching.

"According to the witness, the Jet Ski fled the scene and headed north into the fog." The reporter in the raincoat points to the misty ocean behind her. "Police are asking anyone with any information whatsoever—no detail will be considered too small—to please call the tip line at the bottom of the screen. Meanwhile, a massive search for—"

Adam clicks off the TV. He can smell the stink of his own sweat—an acrid odor that comes with fear. He sinks momentarily onto the edge of the guest bed and stares at the blank screen. In his mind he sees the orange swim cap clutched in Jemma's hand.

I couldn't find my lucky pink cap. I had to use another one. And the tide was so far out this morning that I decided to swim the smaller bay east of Crow's Point.

Adam drops his face into his hands. In his mind he sees the swimmer with a pink cap moving through the mist. The memory of hitting her reverberates through his bones. He sees her hand rise out of the water, calling for help. Tears fill his eyes.

He killed someone else. He—a surgeon, a saver of lives—has murdered the wrong woman, an innocent woman. In cold blood.

AFTER THE HIT-AND-RUN

Jemma has showered and blow-dried her hair, and is dressed in slim jeans topped with a soft lavender sweater. She is now positioned in front of her monitor with her ring light and microphone in her new studio, a mug of freshly brewed coffee and a notebook at her side. Her dogs are curled in their beds under her desk.

She hears the big chopper thudding in the clouds somewhere as she moves her mouse to click the link to her interview. Disquiet burrows deeper into her as her mind dips back to the misty, rainy scene she passed on her way home—cops setting up a barricade to Jerrin Beach and diverting traffic. Ambulances and fire trucks. She wonders what happened. As she waits for the link to load, her thoughts flick back to Adam. Seeing him drunk and shaky and sick early in the morning is not something she's witnessed before. But then he's never been forced to break up with a whore he professes to love.

Another thought hits Jemma. Did he sneak off to see Gloria this morning? Was he lying about his wet suit and those Idaho plates? How could *both* matching plates have just fallen off the wall?

"Hey, Jemma!"

She jumps as a cheery face with bright-red lipstick under a mop of blonde curls smiles from her monitor. Charlene. An Australian wellness guru and Instagram sensation out of Brisbane, who has a world-wide following, particularly of *women of a certain age* looking to *age gracefully and with acceptance and screw the patriarchal narrative around older women.*

"Charlene—"

"God, am I ever glad to see you in one piece. I was worried for a hot minute," she says in her Australian accent.

"What do you mean?"

"The news this morning—Jerrin Bay. The Jet Ski hit-and-run? I just spoke with a friend who lives in Vancouver, and she told me about it. For a godawful few moments I thought the swimmer killed was you—apparently she was swimming across Jerrin at the same time you told me you like to swim, and she was wearing a pink cap and swimming with a lime-green buoy. I mean, I know there are basically, like, three different colors of buddy buoys on the market, but I saw your recent posts of yourself in your wet suit, wearing a pink cap, and you have a lime buoy. So I sort of panicked for a second. Thank heavens you're okay."

Jemma stares at Charlene's red lips. The sound of the chopper drums into her brain. Rain drums on the patio outside. Blood drums in her ears. She tries to swallow, then clears her throat.

"How—what happened exactly?"

"You don't know about it?"

"No. I just got home from . . ." Her words die on her lips.

"Look at me here in Queensland telling *you* what happened in your own backyard across the world." She laughs, but her features turn serious as she reads something in Jemma's face. "Apparently some guy—the witnesses think it was a guy—in a wet suit and hood rode a Jet Ski full-on into the swimmer, then fled into fog."

In her mind Jemma sees Adam's wet suit and hood by the front door, the red, white, and blue license plates in his bag. His shocking appearance. The drinking, shaking. How he looked like he'd just seen a ghost.

"Ready to get started?" Charlene asks.

"I—ah—did they find the Jet Ski and driver?"

"Last I heard was the Coast Guard and marine units were still searching."

Her pulse starts to race.

No. Ridiculous. Not possible . . . is it?

She issued him an ultimatum. Threatened to disclose his past crimes, which would 100 percent cost him his medical license, if not his freedom. What if Adam had *not* broken up with Gloria?

No. No way in hell would he try to *kill* her in order to keep his mistress and his son. Would he? But Jemma was supposed to be swimming across Jerrin Bay. At that time. In a pink cap. She saw the way Adam fixated on the orange cap in her hand when she walked in the door.

"Who was she?" Jemma asks Charlene. "The swimmer who died?"

"I have no idea. That's why I was worried about *you*. Listen, we're running late—ready to jump in?"

Jemma swallows, nods. But her mind has burrowed into dark places, and that strange, unarticulated feeling in the pit of her stomach is growing. From her bare windows, through the rain, through the metal fence slats, she sees a nondescript brown sedan creeping slowly past their fence, as though searching for an address. Two occupants inside.

Charlene says cheerily in her Australian accent, "And today, for our listeners around the world—don't even *ask* about the time difference— we are privileged to have as our guest Jemma Jayne Spengler. Good to have you, Jemma. Welcome to *Be Your Best*."

Jemma straightens her spine, lifts her head, and elongates her neck to offer her best jaw angle and less of her aging throat. "It's a pleasure to be here, Charlene. Thank you for having me."

She hears the doorbell ring, followed by a loud banging. Her dogs begin to bark wildly as they charge to the door.

The doorbell chimes again. More banging sounds. Louder. Someone begins to yell.

AFTER THE HIT-AND-RUN

Adam stands in the shower and lathers and scrubs his skin red for the third time in a row, as though it might scrape away the sick, filthy, ugly, black evil that oozes from his pores like coal tar. As he rinses shampoo from his hair, suds pooling at his feet, he hears something—a banging? Downstairs? He stills, listens, hears it again. Quickly he turns off the water. He hears it more clearly—banging and the doorbell ringing. His heart kicks into his throat. Panic whips through his brain. There's no reason anyone should show up at *his* door in this kind of time frame. Is there?

He grabs a robe off the hook on the back of the bathroom door, punches his arms into the sleeves, and secures it around his waist as the banging continues, louder. He hears someone yell. He exits the bathroom, peers out the bedroom window into the lane. There's a brown sedan parked across his driveway. The banging sounds again.

As he hurries down the stairs, he hears a man call out, "Adam Spengler, this is the police. Can you open up, please?"

He freezes on the stairs. What should he do? Run out the other door? Even though every molecule of his body screams to do just that— flee—he also knows it would be stupid. He'd look guilty as hell. It would all be over.

"Adam Spengler? Can you open the door, please?"

He swallows, proceeds cautiously down the stairs, and pads on bare feet to the rear door. He opens it.

Two people stand outside. A tall, very skinny man with buzz-cut white-blond hair and a chunky woman in a blazer with silver-streaked brown hair. Adam is incapable of processing much more than this. He recognizes his symptoms—he's firmly in the grip of fight-or-flight mode, his amygdala battling to override logic. He grasps the door handle firmly, bracing himself.

"Adam Spengler?" the woman asks.

"Who wants to know?" He glances from her face up to the tall man's face. Their features are set in grim lines. Eyes serious.

The woman says, "I'm Detective Maeve Havers with the Greater Vancouver Police Department's Major Crimes Unit." She shows him her ID. "And this is my partner, Axel Pederson."

Sweat prickles across the top of his lip. He tries to swallow. "I'm Dr. Spengler. Yes. What can I do for you, Officers?"

"Can we come in?"

He holds tighter to the door, draws it in closer. "Can I ask why?"

"We're investigating an incident that occurred in Jerrin Bay this morning. We're canvassing everyone in the neighborhood, asking everyone a few questions."

"I haven't been anywhere near the bay this morning."

"Is your wife home, sir?" Detective Pederson asks.

There's no way they could know, surely? How would they have traced this back to me so soon? How do they know I even have a wife? How do they know my name? They can't be knocking on every door in Crow's Point, addressing every resident by name—can they?

"Sir?"

"I—ah, yeah, my wife is in her studio. Working."

"We'd like to speak with her, please," says Detective Havers.

"She's in the middle of a live social media interview."

"We can wait. Perhaps inside?" says Detective Pederson.

Panic strikes a hatchet into his chest. Adam quickly runs possible scenarios through his mind: What if they see something incriminating in plain sight inside his home? Before his shower he, while Jemma went into her studio, hung his wet suit, hood, and gloves in the garage to dry. He also removed his entire vintage license plate collection from the wall, boxed all the plates up, and secured the boxes in the back of his car to await a trip to the dump. He casts a quick, furtive glance over his shoulder.

Thankfully the door that leads into the garage is closed. Reluctantly he steps back and allows the major crimes detectives into his home. As they brush past him, he's sure they can smell the booze exuding from his pores despite his scrub in the shower.

The detectives stand in the middle of his open-plan living area, out of place in their bulky coats and heavy boots that have clearly been tromping all over the sand beach. The woman's gaze sweeps across the interior of his home, her eyes beady and dark and hungry, like those of a raptor seeking prey among the tiny details of his abode. The man, however, watches Adam.

Adam rubs his mouth. "I—I don't know how long she'll be. She could be a while."

"We've got time," says the man.

"You got me out of the shower. I was busy showering." Adam silently curses for repeating himself.

You're a fucking world-class oncological surgeon. You are respected, worshipped. These public servants should be looking up to you—act like yourself, man.

"Feel free to go and change," says the man. "We can wait here."

"I'd prefer to wait with you," he says.

"Mind if I use your bathroom?" asks the woman.

Adam's alarm bells start clanging. He knows the drill. He's seen enough cop shows on TV to understand that a cop asking to visit the bathroom is a way to snoop in someone's house without a warrant. But he also can't refuse. He would look as guilty as sin.

She regards his face, eyes unblinking, waiting for an answer.

"Sure," he says. "Down the hall." He jerks his chin in the direction of the passage.

"Mind if I take a seat?" asks Detective Pederson as his partner heads off to the bathroom.

"Are you going to ask for a full breakfast, too?" Adam quips.

"I wouldn't say no to a coffee."

Adam's blood pounds harder as anger crawls into his cocktail of fear, anxiety, guilt. But he bites back a retort. It will not serve him to provoke the people charged with power to put him away for life. Acting like a jerk might also arouse their suspicions. His thoughts turn to Jemma, and another kind of terror slams through him. She doesn't know about the swimmer hit-and-run yet. His mouth goes dry. If Jemma learns about the death from these cops, and begins to suspect him—

The door leading to her studio swings open, and Jemma enters. Her face is white. Adam tenses.

"Oh." Jemma stops dead in her tracks. Her gaze whips from Adam to Detective Pederson on the sofa, then to Detective Havers, who at that moment appears from the hallway that leads to the bathroom. Jemma frowns. "What's going on?"

"I'm Detective Maeve Havers," the woman says to Jemma.

"Detective Axel Pederson," says the skinny man on their sofa, still wearing his coat.

Jemma exchanges another glance with Adam. "Why are they here?"

"These officers are investigating a fatal incident that occurred at Jerrin Bay this morning."

Jemma's gaze shoots between the cops. "I just heard about it from my friend—a swimmer was struck by a Jet Ski that fled the scene. It's all over the news, apparently. I was swimming at another bay—Betty's Cove this morning, and on my way home I saw the road was cordoned off, but I had no idea at the time what happened."

Detective Havers says, "We're canvassing the neighborhood for witnesses, or any other information that might be helpful in both identifying the victim and locating the driver of the personal watercraft."

Jemma swallows. Her gaze finds Adam's. He suddenly can't breathe, and his heart thuds so hard against his ribs he fears he will pass out. He breaks Jemma's gaze and says to the cops, "So you're still searching for the Jet Ski driver? You don't know who the swimmer was?"

The cops remain silent. Observing them both.

"I can't believe it," Jemma whispers, taking a seat. "I have been swimming Jerrin Bay daily since we moved here. Today was the first time I swam somewhere else. It—it could have been me." She turns to Detective Havers. "And you don't know who it was—who was killed?"

"As I said, we're still working to identify the victim, Mrs. Spengler," says Detective Havers. "We were hoping you might help." She jerks her thumb back to the hallway. "I saw from the photos on your wall that you're an open-water swimmer. And since you mentioned you regularly swim across Jerrin Bay, do you have any idea who else might have been swimming across there this morning? Another swimming buddy, perhaps, or fellow enthusiast you might know?"

"No. I'm sorry. We're pretty new to the neighborhood. I did join the local open-water swimming association, but I have yet to attend any meetups. Have you tried contacting them?"

"Our colleagues are working all angles."

Pederson says, "Do you guys own a Jet Ski?"

"No," Jemma says.

The cops look at Adam.

He shakes his head.

"Do you know anyone with a personal watercraft?" Pederson says, taking a small notebook and pen from his pocket.

"Like my wife said, we're really new in town, so no." In Adam's mind he sees the interior of Narek's boathouse. He tells himself there is nothing that will lead the cops there as long as he is careful in what he says.

"When did you move into Crow's Point?" asks Havers.

Jemma says, "I arrived on the fourteenth. Adam was here two days before me. So it's only just over two weeks."

Pederson makes a note in his book. "And have you signed up for membership at any local marinas, or yacht clubs that moor or rent Jet Skis?"

"No," Adam says. "Why are you asking this?"

"But you do know how to operate a Jet Ski." Havers directs her statement at Adam.

"What makes you say that?"

She tilts her head toward the hallway. "Vacation photos on the wall."

Adam curses inwardly. He knew he should never have allowed her to use the bathroom.

"That was in the Caribbean," Jemma says quickly. "It was maybe four or five years ago." Jemma gets up and comes to Adam's side. She slips her hand into his and curls her fingers very tightly through his. "I'm really devastated by this news." She glances up at Adam. "I mean, that totally could have been me, with my pink cap. I have the same lime-green buoy as the dead swimmer, too. By the grace of God it was Adam who suggested I swim the smaller bay closer to the shoreline this morning." Adam tenses at his wife's startling lie in his defense. "He thought it would be safer in this foggy weather." Her grip on his hand tightens, as though in warning. "My husband stayed home to have coffee ready. We both had too much to drink last night—celebrating an anniversary of sorts. As you no doubt can tell, Adam chased the hair of the dog this morning."

Detective Havers nods slowly as she regards them.

Pederson says, "What was the anniversary?"

"Start of a fresh new phase in our lives. A renewed commitment to our marriage, right, love?" She looks up into Adam's eyes. Her grip on his hand is a vise.

He feels as though he's going to be sick. Because it's at this exact moment he realizes Jemma thinks he might have tried to kill her, and it's dawned on her that he killed an innocent woman instead.

There can be only one reason she's covering for him now, instead of fleeing from him in fear that he might attempt to take her life again. She believes she now has the ultimate weapon to control him. His guilt. For murder.

"Right, hon?" she prompts.

He manages a small grunt.

"Will there be anything else, Officers?" Jemma asks the cops.

"Not for now, thank you," Havers says. "Here's my card if you think of anything that might be of help." She holds it out to Jemma. She takes it. Pederson comes to his feet, and Adam shows them both out.

He stands in the doorway, watching them leave. But to his surprise, they don't get into their unmarked vehicle. They start walking across the alley to the building on the other side.

Detective Pederson glances back at him. Adam quickly, quietly, shuts the door. But he knows—he just knows—they're going up to the third floor of that building across the alley to speak to the woman in the window with the binoculars.

AFTER THE HIT-AND-RUN

Chloe is drunk.

She hit the vodka hard after making the anonymous call to the police, after witnessing Jemma's horrific death in the water. The selkie goddess is gone. At the hands of her Evil man. Chloe is overwhelmed by the ghastliness of the murder. It knifes into her soul, pierces the heart of her childhood security bubble, where the selkie fairy tale that always comforted her and made her safe in the face of unarticulated ugliness has been shattered in real life, in real time, as she watched with her own eyes.

She is on the floor with her back propped against the wall beneath the window, next to the oxygen compressor with its comforting hiss and rumble. Brodie has crawled into her lap. Chloe takes another sip of neat vodka and strokes his wiry pelt. At least she has Brodie, and booze, and she is beginning to feel blessedly numb. At last.

She squints up at one of the several paintings she did of a woman with her feet trapped in rocks by the sea. A cold ball of depression sinks low into her belly. That woman will forever be locked in rock, unable to enter the freedom of the surging sea, those veins of precious gold sealed in the granite at her feet forever unreachable—full of wealth and promises that will never be realized. Chloe is unsure why Jemma's death feels like the end of her world. One thing she does know for certain is that since she made the call to the police tip line, she's been unable to look out her window at Gloom House again. She cannot bear the thought of those poor little dogs trapped in that concrete monstrosity, alone with that awful man.

Her mother stirs in the bed above her. "Chloe? Where are you? I can't see you."

"Down here."

"Where? What happened? What's wrong?"

"I'm fine. Everything's fine. I—it's going to be okay. I promise." But she knows it's not. She can't go on like this. She swallows the last of the vodka in her glass, and her eyes burn as it sears down her throat. She coughs, and her stomach heaves as the alcohol hits, but she nevertheless reaches for the bottle and sloppily tips more into her glass, splashing some on her thigh.

As she lifts the glass to her lips, she hears a hard banging on her door. She jerks, then stills. Her gaze moves slowly, blearily to the door. She squints at it and angles her head. The banging sounds again. Confusion churns through Chloe's brain. Bettina? One of the other caregivers? Why don't they use the key from the lockbox?

What day is it?

She moves her unfocused gaze up to the hospital bed. Her mother hasn't stirred. She doesn't seem to hear the banging—gone back to sleep under the pile of bedding. Chloe shoves deaf Brodie off her lap and gets onto all fours. She tries to steady herself on hands and knees, tries to stop the room from spinning. She reaches for a chair. Holding it for balance, she pulls herself to her feet, wobbles.

"Chloe, someone's at the door," her mother mumbles.

"I—I got it, Mom." She fixes her gaze on the door and lurches toward it. She reaches the door, places her hand on the knob, pauses. God, she feels terrible. Was the swimmer's death all a dream? But even as she wishes it were a fiction, in her mind she sees it play out again. In a loop. Over and over. The Jet Ski making a U-turn, coming back, faster. She feels the thudding sound in her body. It happened. It's real.

The loud knocking sounds again. "Chloe Cooper? Are you home? Can you open up, please?"

Fear strikes. It's not one of the caregivers. She doesn't recognize the voice.

"Chloe Cooper? This is the police. Can you open up, please?"

Chloe panics, and she can't think what to do.

"Chloe Cooper? We'd like to talk to you about what you saw this morning. We think you can help us. Please open up."

Slowly, like syrup, her brain turns this over. Somehow they found her. They know she saw. Maybe she should let them in, tell them about Dr. Spengler so they can take him away and lock him up and throw away the key. She slides back the dead bolt, unlocks the door, opens it a crack. And blinks out.

"Chloe Cooper?" a woman in a blazer asks. A long skinny man stands at her side.

Chloe nods.

"I'm Detective Maeve Havers, and this is my partner, Axel Pederson. We're with the GVPD Major Crimes Unit. Can we come in, please?"

See, Chloe? What did I tell you? That you would rue the day you made that call. You stupid little runt, how could you believe you would stay anonymous? Honestly, what are you going to tell them now? That you're a stalker? A snoop? That you have access to their house? You photographed it in detail and you planted fake evidence in his pocket? Now look what happened. She's dead. Dead dead dead. This is your fault.

"My mother doesn't like visitors. She's . . . unwell. It—it's not good for her to get visitors." Brodie comes up to her feet, sensing her need for support. Chloe picks him up and stumbles sideways. She regains her balance by holding on to the door.

The woman cop glances at Brodie, and says, "People in the neighborhood have identified you, Ms. Cooper, as the dog walker and witness who left the scene at Jerrin Bay this morning. We believe it was you who placed an anonymous call to our tip line, and we really need to talk to you about what you witnessed. Could we come in?"

"I—I've done nothing wrong." Her voice shakes.

"We're not here for you, Ms. Cooper. We only need to know what you saw."

Indecision, conflict, torques through Chloe.

"If you can describe the Jet Ski to us, we will have a better chance of hunting down and catching that bad guy, and putting him away, Ms. Cooper. And I think you want that. I think that's why you made the call."

Chloe does want that. She nods and opens the door fully. The two large police officers enter her tiny apartment, and the place shrinks around them.

They look at her paintings on the walls. They take in the disarray of her apartment, the vodka bottle and half-empty glass on the floor next to the humming oxygen compressor. They turn their gazes to her mother in the hospital bed.

Chloe feels scared. She wants them to leave already, so she blurts out, "I know it was him. Dr. Adam Spengler. He's been having an affair with a woman called Gloria, and they have a little son, and he wanted to get rid of his wife to be with them, so he killed her. I saw his car returning this morning with fake Idaho plates. I saw the wet suit in his bag." She points shakily toward the window. "You can see their house out there, on the corner. You can see everything. I—I use my mother's birding glasses."

The woman cop regards Chloe. Silence fills her apartment, thick and heavy and vibrating.

"The thing is, Ms. Cooper," the cop says slowly, quietly, her eyes fixed on Chloe, "while we have not yet identified the swimmer who was fatally struck this morning, we do know it wasn't Jemma Spengler. Mrs. Spengler is very much alive."

Chloe's mouth falls open. She squints at the cops, trying to pull them into focus. "Are you sure? How can that be?"

"We responded directly to their residence after you placed the call and gave their address. Jemma Spengler is not dead. But we're interested in knowing why you thought she was."

AFTER THE HIT-AND-RUN

Chloe lurches to the window and peers through the rain at the Spenglers' house. All the lights are on. She can see them. *Both* of them. In the middle of the living room, and they're arguing—waving hands at each other. She braces her fists on the windowsill as the blurry barrier between reality and fiction dissolves before her eyes.

Did she even see what she saw this morning?

Was it a different day that she walked down to the beach with Brodie? Did she drunkenly imagine it all? What day is it, anyway? Maybe she should be at work, or taking her mother to the hospital. Panic strangles her throat, and she begins to pant.

"Ms. Cooper?"

She spins around, mouth open. The detectives stare at her. She points toward Gloom House and struggles to form words. "J-Jemma was in—in the sea. I—I've been watching her swim every day. I saw . . . He hit her. Twice. On purpose." She realizes her voice has gone high, and her whole body shakes.

"Why don't we all sit down, Ms. Cooper," the woman cop says, "and let's take it slowly. One step at a time. Okay?"

Chloe considers this. She glances at her mom. That terrible sound begins again inside Chloe's brain because the detectives' gazes follow hers to the bed, and she suddenly sees what they must be seeing.

She wants to explain that the reason her mother is sleeping so soundly—and hasn't yet drunk her tea, or eaten the oatmeal congealing beside her bed, is because she had a rough night, but now that the meds have finally kicked in, she's out like a light. Because one compartment of Chloe's brain still refuses to believe a word of what the surgeon was trying to tell her on the morning of her birthday in the hospital. Another compartment in Chloe's brain—the part that gets louder and obnoxious when she's not drinking the vodka—knows exactly what the two police officers are seeing in the bed, in this apartment.

Very gently the lady cop says, "Please sit, Ms. Cooper. How about Detective Pederson waits outside while you and I chat? Would that be easier?"

Chloe nods.

The detectives exchange a glance. Her partner hesitates, seems to understand something, nods, leaves. The door closes softly behind him.

Chloe picks up Brodie and sits on a chair. She cuddles Brodie in her lap. Close. Tight. Stinky. Safe. She glances again at the hospital bed, *willing* her mother to appear among the heaped-up bedding to offer some instruction, guidance. Chloe has been hammered by her mom for her entire life with the idea that law enforcement means bad things. *Anyone* strange inside the house means bad things.

He will find us, Chloe. He will find you. *Because if you let people in, they will see how you live, and they will talk, and it will give Him clues— little Hansel and Gretel breadcrumbs that will guide the Monster to where you hide in the dark, dark forest.*

He? A Monster. Evil.

It's the first time her mother inside her head is being more specific about what is hunting them.

"Ms. Cooper? May I call you Chloe?" the officer is saying.

Chloe drags her mind back to the present. She nods.

"I see the hospital bed here, and the oxygen compressor going. You mentioned your mother not liking guests in the house?"

She nods again, strokes Brodie's wiry fur more forcibly.

"Can I ask where your mother is right now?"

The noises in Chloe's head crash with a terrible sound of cymbals and discord. She begins to sweat. Very carefully she says, "She's not here right now."

"Where might we find her?"

She breaks eye contact, looks down at Brodie. "In the hospital." She sucks in a deep breath, and with great effort, she says, "My mother died on my birthday."

A beat of silence.

"I'm so sorry, Chloe. When was your birthday?"

"Eleven days ago."

The detective nods slowly. Her eyes turn soft and kind. They remind her of Stavros's eyes.

"I really am sorry. It can be very hard to let go sometimes."

Chloe nods once more.

The cop leans forward, elbows on her knees. Her hands clasp together, and her eyes are direct and totally focused on Chloe, like she matters. "Were you at Jerrin Beach with your dog this morning?"

No point in lying now. Detective Havers already knows. "Yes."

"You made the anonymous phone call?"

She nods.

"Can you tell me what you were doing at the beach, and exactly what you witnessed this morning?"

She can hear the helicopter in the sky again. She thinks of Gloom House hulking across the alley with its big window eyes. Of Jemma alive. Arguing with that man. Her mind slides back eleven days, to her birthday, to the surgeon explaining how her mother had died in surgery. How they tried to save her. It was the day she encountered Dr. Adam Spengler in the elevator. The raw fear and anxiety that came with seeing him in the flesh—being confined in that car with him—instantly surge into Chloe's chest, followed by a deep sensation of Evil swirling like a cloak around her shoulders, and a sense she's encountered him before.

"Chloe?"

"I was walking Brodie. He's my mom's dog. We were there just after seven. I like to watch her swim."

"Jemma Spengler?"

Chloe moistens her lips. The taste of vodka in her mouth is terrible. She can smell it all over herself. "Yes. She swims every morning at seven. In a pink cap. With a lime-green flotation device."

"That's why you were convinced it was Jemma Spengler in the water this morning?"

"I guess so."

"Tell me what happened next."

"I watched her swim into the center of the bay, like she always does, and that's when the Jet Ski appeared out of the mist. It was blue and white with an orange stripe down the side. The driver wore all black. A hood, too. Gloves. I thought he hadn't seen her because he was going so fast in her direction. But after he hit her the first time, he slowed, and checked. She raised her arm toward him, as though to ask for help. But he circled away, then doubled back at full speed and hit her again. The thud was awful. I heard it from the beach. He took off into the fog."

"What direction?"

"Straight toward the other side of the Burrard."

"When you placed the call to our tip line, you said it was Dr. Adam Spengler who hit his wife. What makes you think it was him on the Jet Ski?"

"I didn't know it wasn't Jemma."

"But what made you think it was Jemma's husband on that Jet Ski?"

"He's having an affair with a woman named Gloria Bergson, and they have a son, and she runs Bergson Gallery in North Vancouver, and I overheard them arguing one night in the alley when I took Brodie out to pee. Gloria told him he had to finish it with Jemma, or he would never see her and his son again." Chloe draws in a huge, shaky breath as she struggles to get it all out in one go before she can't. "Gloria said he had to make a choice. And—and I know he's a bad man. He's Evil."

The cop's brow crooks up. "What makes you think Adam Spengler is an evil man?"

Heat rises in her face. She draws Brodie closer to her belly. She desperately needs another swig of vodka and can't wait for the cop to leave so she can completely numb everything. Chloe reckons if she just tells the detective everything as fast as she can, she'll be gone quicker.

"Chloe?" the cop prompts.

"Because I saw him returning home after the Jet Ski accident. He had different license plates on his Tesla. Red and blue ones from Idaho. I saw them with my mom's binoculars. And he wasn't wearing his usual kind of clothes. Had camouflage cargo pants and a hoodie on, and a cap. Dark colors. Like some gangster. The hood hid part of his face. And when he took his gym bag out of the back of his Tesla, I could see what looked like a wet suit inside. If you take a look out the window, you can see there is a partial view from here into his garage."

The cop takes a small notebook from her blazer pocket and makes a series of notes, then gets up and goes to the window.

"Go on," she says quietly while she looks out into the alley.

"He has a whole wall of registration plates hanging in his garage." She faces Chloe. "And how do you know this?"

Her stomach knots as her mother's voice rises in her head again.

Are you going to inform the cop that you've been stalking Jemma and Adam? That you spy on them, stalk them, stand outside in their bushes at night, that you have a door code to get inside their house? That you've been in there, touched their things, put things in pockets to mess with their minds, taken photos of the inside of their house? Do you know what the detectives will do, Chloe? They'll start questioning you. And you know where that will lead. You know. The world doesn't trust people like you.

Chloe's mouth flattens into a straight line to ensure no more stupid words come out.

The policewoman's gaze goes to one of the swimming paintings Chloe created of Jemma with her pink cap and lime buoy in the gray sea.

"Is that Jemma Spengler in the paintings?"

She nods.

"Does she always wear that pink cap and swim with the yellow buoy?"

"It's lime."

"But always those colors?"

"Yes."

Detective Havers says, "You have very keen interest in the Spenglers, Chloe."

"I—I just happen to notice a lot of things about people. And they have no blinds."

A knock sounds on Chloe's apartment door, and it opens. The male detective peers in and says, "Maeve, we have a tentative ID on the victim. Her husband called from Kelowna after seeing the news. Says his wife was in Vancouver, and she texted him early this morning to say she was going to do a training swim in Jerrin Bay." He looks pale. Features grim. "Her car has been located in the Jerrin Beach lot."

"Give us one sec," Detective Havers says to her partner. He holds her gaze for a moment, steps out, closes the door again.

Detective Havers says, "Chloe, I really am sorry for your loss." Her gaze flicks to the oxygen compressor humming at Chloe's side, feeding air into the nasal cannula that lies on the bed. "And I can see you're having real trouble accepting she's gone."

Chloe stares firmly at nothing in particular, clutching Brodie too tight. Tears slip down her face.

"Were you caring for her for a long time?"

She nods.

"Grief can be devastating. I know. I'm going to leave you a number for social services, Chloe. They have counselors who specialize in this sort of thing. Will you call them? Talk to them? Or would you prefer I took you someplace now?"

You've already told this cop too much. You should never believe the fake facades people put on. They can be so crafty. Just tell her what she needs to hear, then she'll go away.

"I'll call," Chloe says. There is definitely no way she will. Chloe knows she is having problems, but she's functional. If she is able to adhere to her routines, she can be *highly* functional. If she tells some mental health worker that she's struggling, they might take her away from her home, from Brodie, and lock her in an institution like the one Mr. Higgins went and died in when he had to leave his yellow house on the corner. No way is she going to allow that to happen.

Detective Havers scribbles something in her notepad, rips out the page, and hands it to Chloe. Her gaze locks on Chloe's. "Call the number. It will help." A pause. "And Chloe, we might need to speak to you again, okay?"

"Okay." *Now please go.*

"If you think of anything else, this is my card." She holds Chloe's gaze as she hands it to her. "Call me. Anytime. Okay?"

Chloe takes the card and nods.

AFTER THE HIT-AND-RUN

Jemma faces her husband of thirty-four years, and he glares back at her from the doorway. The tension, silence, inside the house is hot and thick.

"Where *were* you this morning, Adam?" she asks very quietly. "While I was swimming in another bay?"

"I told you, I just went for a drive." He makes an abrupt beeline for the booze trolley and pours himself a whiskey. He swallows it down.

Jemma's stomach tightens into a ball of acid. "I think you drove over the bridge, Adam. To the North Shore, from where the Jet Ski came. And that's why you needed those Idaho plates, isn't it? That's why your wet suit is wet."

"What the *fuck* are you insinuating?"

She struggles to control her voice, but it starts to tremble. "You tried to kill me."

"Jesus, Jemma. Are you mad? How could you even *think* that?" He takes a step toward her, but she rapidly steps back, raising both hands in front of her.

"Stay the hell away from me."

"Jemma—"

"My God, it's true. Isn't it? Where—where did you find a Jet Ski?" Even as she asks, the answer hits her like a load of bricks. Emotion floods into her eyes. "Narek," she whispers. "You went to Narek's estate this morning. He has Jet Skis in his boathouse. Right across the Burrard from Jerrin Bay."

"That is not true. I—"

"Prove it to me! Let's go into the garage, right now. Show me your car's navigation history."

He glowers at her, spins around, pours another drink, and downs it.

"Did you even break up with that whore?"

"Her name is Gloria," he snaps. "She has a name, Jemma."

"Well, *did* you?"

"Of course I did. I told you."

"I don't believe you. I think you tried—no, you *believed* you actually succeeded in killing me, getting rid of me. Your little problem. Your obstacle. Gone. When you came home, you thought you were free to carry on with that slut. *That's* why you were so shocked to see me arrive home, with an orange cap in my hand."

A mixture of rage and something akin to fear explodes across her husband's features, twisting his face into that of a monster she no longer recognizes. He swallows yet another drink, and Jemma warns herself to be careful. He's tried once to murder her. He actually went through with it. What's to stop him trying again? The fact that the cops are near, maybe? That they are actively searching for him, and might already suspect him for some reason? Otherwise, why *did* they come here asking all those questions about Jet Skis?

She needs to be careful. He's drinking too much, too fast. This man she thought she knew so deeply, so very well, Jemma no longer knows at all. She has no clue how far she can push him and still survive.

"You've lost it, Jemma, you know that?" He points his glass at her. "Your imagination has finally gone off the rails. I had *nothing* to do with that swimmer's death. But you—you're the one who's dangerous. I think you killed our son—you poisoned Jackson."

Her heart stops. Her jaw drops. Her brain spins. Jemma reaches for the back of a chair to steady herself. "*What* did you say?"

"I went to see Sophia. She told me what her brother and the other nurses at the Toronto hospital feared. They believed you were making Jackson sick. That you were altering tests, poisoning him. Did you miss the attention so much when Hailey died that you wanted another child so you could do a repeat? You are sick, Jemma. *Sick*."

"How *dare* you? It's lies. All lies and ridiculous rumors that were never proven and never will be, because they're not true."

He takes another step toward her.

"Get away from me. You tried to kill me once. What's to stop you trying again?"

"I would never, I—" Emotion swamps him. He sets his glass down and drops into a chair. He slumps over, buries his face in his hands, and rocks, moans. "I could never do that again. Never."

Jemma feels bile rush to her throat. Very quietly she whispers, "Again? So you really did do it. You tried to eliminate me but killed an innocent woman instead. You are a murderer, Adam, a cold-blooded killer, and if the cops find out, my God, you're going away for the rest of your miserable life. Never mind financial fraud, this will finish you. Completely."

He looks up. His face is bloated, blotchy, tearstained. "So why didn't you tell the detectives the truth, Jemma? Why did you lie for me and say I was home?"

"I—I was still processing. I . . ." Her voice catches. She blows out air. "I didn't want them to think that my renowned surgeon husband was out driving his Tesla while stinking drunk. I—I didn't want what I was beginning to fear to be true." As she talks, she moves to the coffee table, snatches up the TV remote, and clicks on the news channel.

They both stare in simmering silence as an image of a reporter on a fog-shrouded Jerrin Beach fills the screen.

"We've just got more breaking news coming in on the Jerrin Bay hit-and-run." The reporter holds her earpiece as though listening to someone in the studio, then glances up into the camera. "We have just this moment learned the identity of the person killed by a Jet Ski this morning. The victim's husband came forward when he heard on the news that a swimmer had been struck. Her name is Marianne Wade. She's a beloved and well-known Ironman triathlete, a swim coach, and a mother of four young children. She lived in Kelowna and was doing a last training swim this morning before she was due to fly out of YVR to Hawaii to participate in the Waikiki Wild Water Epic—an endurance swim of ten kilometers that she won last year."

Jemma goes stone cold. She turns to look at Adam.

He's motionless, staring at the TV.

AFTER THE HIT-AND-RUN

Adam comes out of the bathroom, where he rushed to throw up again. His limbs are weak. He wants to die in this instant. How can he possibly reconcile being a surgeon, a saver of lives, with also being a killer?

Her name is Marianne Wade . . . a swim coach, and a mother of four young children.

"Going for a walk," he yells to Jemma, who is still riveted to the television in the living room. He needs to escape her accusatory glare, and he's desperate to find a space where he can think clearly and process things.

She doesn't answer. His anxiety deepens, because now he fears she will use her knowledge to control him, and he'll definitely now lose Gloria and his son. He gets his rain jacket and exits through the rear door. He stands for a moment in the pouring rain and looks up at the window across the street.

Did that snoop up there tell the cops she saw something? His Idaho plates, perhaps? Even if Jemma does keep her mouth shut, that woman in the window could be a real problem for Adam. He needs to find out who she is.

He walks the three blocks to the beach. The mist has cleared a little, and the rain is softer, but the sky and sea remain bleak and heavily gray. The wet sand appears almost black, and helicopters still hover above the clouds in search of him.

He walks slowly with his hands in his pockets along the paved pathway to where a small crowd gathers with umbrellas near a large tree, coats flapping against the sea breeze. Adam sidles into the crowd. His pulse stutters when he realizes why these people are here. They're leaving gifts around an impromptu memorial that has been started at the base of the tree. Bunches of flowers, cards, stuffed animals, and other mementos have been placed around a framed photograph of a sunny-looking woman with tousled sandy-blonde hair and a huge, toothy smile. The frame has been slipped into a plastic sleeve to protect it from the rain. The sign alongside it reads:

WE LOVE YOU, MARIANNE.

SWIM WITH THE DOLPHINS IN THE SKY.

R.I.P.

Adam goes cold. He stares at the photo. The woman he murdered smiles back at him. She holds a race bike in front of her, and four young kids surround her. Her children. All towheaded. Tanned. Blue eyed. All so vitally alive. Their happiness snatched away. By him. Emotion surges into his chest, and deep inside his belly he begins to shake as tears blur his vision.

He's not a killer.

How could he have done this? Who has he become?

If he could turn back time, he would *never* dream of doing this again. He was blinded by passion, by rage. By Jemma's threats. By the raw fear of losing what he loves, his future. His child.

He acted to save himself from a life trapped with an aging wife who has turned bitter and jealous and who threatens his existence at every core level. A wife who might actually have killed their son. He got on that Jet Ski in a desperate bid to rid himself of the noose Jemma has become around his neck.

But he failed. And he destroyed other lives instead. And now his own life is unraveling anyway, in ways far worse than he could have imagined.

The sound of the chopper grows louder. He wonders if they're using some kind of infrared or digital technology to see through the low clouds over the water. He glances toward the beach. He sees uniformed GVPD officers and forensic techs in boiler suits, still on the rocks where they brought the woman's body out. While he watches them, the hair on the back of Adam's neck begins to prickle and stand up as he is filled with a sense of being watched.

Slowly he turns and scans the crowd. He notices a plain-looking woman in a khaki raincoat at the outskirts of the gathering. She holds a leash attached to an old-looking dog. She snares Adam's attention because she is staring straight back at him. Direct. Unabashed. She doesn't even attempt to glance away as their gazes meet. Adam swallows as he's seized by an uneasy sensation. He heard on the news there was an additional witness who left the scene—a woman with a senior dog.

Could she be the one? Another thought strikes him.

What if she's also the woman across the alley in the window—and that's why the detectives went up to visit her? What if she actually followed him down here to the impromptu memorial?

AFTER THE HIT-AND-RUN

Chloe stands at the fringe of a motley group clustered around a memorial to the woman she saw being killed on purpose this morning.

The woman's identity was only recently released, and already these people have brought photos and trinkets and little stuffed animals. Apparently Marianne Wade was well connected with Vancouver's open-water swimming and triathlon community. A beloved coach and competitor who volunteered for many charities.

What a waste, thinks Chloe. There are plenty of other people who should die first. She can personally think of several.

Dr. Adam Spengler, for one.

Her mind returns to the cops who came inquiring about what she witnessed. Chloe has been mulling it all over since the detectives left. Given that Marianne Wade was wearing a pink cap like Jemma usually does, and traversing the same route at the same time Jemma does, trailing a lime buoy, it *still* could have been Adam Spengler who made a terrible mistake by thinking Marianne was his wife. And what if he tries again? Jemma's life might *still* be in danger.

Surprisingly, dealing with the police didn't end in disaster or with Chloe being arrested, as her mother always claimed it would. Instead, Chloe was rather moved by the kindness Detective Havers showed her. Had her mother perhaps done something in her past that she was trying to hide from law enforcement? Could this explain her fear?

Chloe hasn't asked herself these questions before, but things are stirring deep inside a place that feels like memories, but also not. While there remains zero chance Chloe will seek the help of social services, she did finally unplug the compressor after the cops left. She did say out loud to Brodie that her mother was gone. And it made it all horribly, heavily real.

The apartment filled with a terrifying silence. A lonely silence. She tried to fill the void by opening the windows to air the place, and by hurriedly stripping down her mother's hospital bed. She stuffed the bed linens into the washing machine, and as it began to chug, she poured the rest of the vodka down the drain in the kitchen sink. It's a workday tomorrow anyway. She needs to clear her head. Maybe it's even a good thing Detective Havers came. At the least she stopped Chloe from sinking downward into a complete drunken—and possible deathly—spiral.

As the washing machine began the spin cycle, Chloe dared peer out the window at the Spenglers' house again. She saw Adam leaving on foot in his rain jacket. Brodie also needed to pee. So she grabbed her jacket, the dog, and his leash, and hurried in the direction she saw Adam going. She found him on Crow's Road, in the distance, making his way toward the beach. So she followed him.

As Brodie sniffs the wet grass at her feet, Chloe studies Dr. Spengler standing among the group.

He's like one of those serial killers on TV who revisits the scene of the crime. Or who attends the funerals or burials of their victims. As she stares at him, that inexplicable urge to flee rises once more in her veins. But this time the fear slams into another compulsion: a hot and fierce desire to do something—anything—to out him. Punish him. To save Jemma from him. Blood begins to thrum against her eardrums as she fixes her gaze on the man.

His hands dig deep into his pockets. His head is bent forward, and his shoulders slump as he regards the image of the dead mother and her children.

Suddenly, as though sensing the intensity of her gaze, he glances up and looks her way. Their eyes meet across the crowd. Shock ripples through Chloe. His face is flushed, puffy. And she realizes he's been crying—his cheeks are sheened with tears. Or is it the rain?

He holds her gaze. Chloe's body begins to hum. She's incapable of looking away, and the connection feels intimate, like a threat. Her body temperature rises.

"Chloe?"

She gasps and spins sideways. It's Stavros. In his nylon jacket from Walmart with his precious Seattle Mariners baseball cap on his long head.

"You shouldn't sneak up on people like that, Stavros," she snaps, heart hammering.

"Sorry, didn't mean to spook you." He shuffles from one big foot to the other, hands in his pockets as though he's cold. He really should wear a warmer jacket. If Chloe had spare money, she would buy him one, since he can't seem to be bothered to do so himself.

"Terrible, terrible thing." He jerks his chin toward the memorial. "About to start my shift at the Beach House in a few but thought I'd come down and pay my respects. Not sure how busy the bar is going to be with the beach road blocked off by the cops like that. Or maybe everyone will feel a need to drink by the warm fire inside, and look out over the bay. It's all over the news—got a TV crew in the restaurant right now." He hesitates. "Are you okay? You look like shit, Chloe."

Her mouth flattens. Emotion suddenly surges and threatens all her control. Everything that has happened since she witnessed the swimmer being hit pushes down on her shoulders with a phenomenal, unbearable weight. Chloe can't help the words that shoot out of her mouth.

"I—I saw it, Stavros. I witnessed it this morning. Saw it happen."

"Christ." His eyes narrow onto her. "Was it you, Chlo—the woman with the dog who disappeared from the scene?"

She nods as tears flood into her eyes.

"You speak to the cops?"

She nods again. Her tears spill onto her cheeks, and she turns away in shame, humiliation.

"Hey?" He touches her arm.

She jerks away.

"Chloe?"

She can't face him. He will see her tears. She begins to sob.

Stavros wraps his arm around her, drawing her closer. Chloe freezes, and her body stiffens like a board. Panic rises. She abhors people touching her. She's not accustomed to this. But he strokes her hair, and she can't help crying harder, leaning into him just a little. And the panic begins to slide away.

"It's okay, Chlo—let it out, just let it all out."

A strange warmth blossoms in her chest. It feels comfortable in his arms. In the way her small apartment feels comfortable. She doesn't pull away.

"I'm going to call Fatima," he says gently. "She can take my shift. We're going to go somewhere dry and have a coffee or a hot chocolate, okay?"

The prospect of a warm mug of something sweet in a nice dry place feels compelling. Her other option is to return to her deadly-silent apartment and the bare hospital bed, which she will need to have collected by the Red Cross that loaned it to them.

"Okay, Chloe?"

She wipes her nose and nods.

Stavros makes the call on his cell. It takes a mere minute or two.

"Sorted," he says.

A short while later they are seated on a covered patio nearby under some outdoor heaters. They're outside because she still has Brodie with her, although he's zipped up and warm inside her coat, his little heart beating against her tummy. Alive and comforting.

Stavros orders her a hot chocolate with cream on top and tiny marshmallows. He has a mocha, also with cream. He asks for a slice of seasonal apple pie to share.

"I think the occasion calls for something extra," he says as he sips and gets cream stuck in that stupid little hair thing under his lip.

Chloe wraps her hands around the big mug. It's warm, and it fills her core with a rare sensation of comfort and belonging.

She focuses on the creamy, chocolaty, sweet taste.

"How's your mother, Chloe? I should have asked."

Panic stabs her chest again. She meets his gaze as she tries to say something. Can't. She tries again. It comes out a strange animal noise.

A line furrows into his brow. "Is your mom okay?"

"She's dead."

A beat of silence. He blinks. Chloe can hear the rain on the awning, soft voices from people talking nearby in shocked tones about the swimmer. Wind gusts, and the patio awning flutters like beating wings.

"What?"

"She died."

"When?" he asks quietly.

"She—she never came out of the hospital, Stavros. She died in surgery that day." She bites her lip and carefully sets her mug down using both hands because she's started to tremble again, and she is loath to spill.

Another moment of silence passes as he processes this. The line in his brow furrows deeper—thank heavens he's removed that Mariners cap. His eyes change and go very soft and liquid. His lashes are long, she realizes, and quite thick.

"You mean, when you came into work after the 911 episode, and you said—" He lets it drop, gets to his feet, comes around to her side of the table, and sits on the bench beside her. He takes her hand. "I'm so, so sorry, Chloe."

She manages a nod.

He leans forward and wraps his long, wiry arms around her. And just holds. Although every instinct in Chloe screams to move away, she once more allows his touch. He smells of the mints he likes to suck, and something like cedar trees. Again, the tears come. And Chloe lets them. Never in her life has she been hugged and just held this way. And for the first time she feels just a little bit safe in the world.

AFTER THE HIT-AND-RUN

As soon as Adam leaves for a walk, Jemma clicks off the TV news and hurries into the garage.

She feels his wet suit draped over a hanger behind his Tesla. It's definitely damp—no doubt in her mind. The hood, too. She sniffs the suit. No sour smell. If the wet suit was in fact crumpled wet into his bag and left in the trunk for a while, as he alleged it was, surely it would have a lingering whiff of odor? She hesitates, then tests it with the tip of her tongue. Salty. The taste of the sea. Her pulse quickens.

She spins to face the wall with his display of vintage plates.

Shock crackles through her. The wall is empty. Every single plate is gone. Including the ones she saw in his bag from Idaho.

Jemma peers into the windows of his Tesla. On the rear seat are two big cardboard boxes. The car is locked. She goes back into the house to locate the Tesla key card. She yanks open the kitchen drawer where they keep spare keys and other odds and ends, and as she grasps the bifold wallet containing the key card, she remembers something—Adam coming home with a bunch of tagged keys after he'd visited Narek's place. She recalls him putting them into the drawer on his side of their bed.

Fearing Adam will return any moment, Jemma runs up the stairs with a sense of urgency. She finds the bunch of keys. Each is labeled. She fans through the labels: *Garage. Pool room. Storeroom. Wine cellar. Boathouse.* She pauses on the boathouse key. Her brain races. Although she's only ever visited Narek's North Shore estate once with Adam, she knows the billionaire owns personal watercraft.

She makes a snap decision, rushes downstairs, grabs her jacket and purse, and summons the dogs into the garage. Once the dogs have hopped into her car, she unlocks Adam's Tesla and opens the tops of the boxes in the back. He's boxed up his vintage plate collection. She finds the Idaho plates among them, removes them, closes the box tops, and places them in the trunk of her own car. She takes his wet suit off the hanger and gathers up his hood, booties, and gloves, too. She bags them in a black garbage bag and stashes the bag in the trunk along with the plates.

Jemma climbs into the driver's seat of her car, draws in a deep breath, opens the garage door, and exits into the lane.

Rain patters on her soft top, and the wipers arc across her windshield as she takes a route through the core of downtown Vancouver. She feeds with the traffic onto the bridge. As she drives, she listens to the radio for news on the swimmer murder and updates on the hunt for the Jet Ski driver. According to the news, the police have located the witness who left the scene. She's a local dog walker who saw the Jet Ski circling back and hitting the woman a second time, *as though to ensure she was dead.* Jemma clenches the wheel. Her neck is wire tight. Her eyes burn as she listens to the newscaster read out a description of the personal watercraft: white and blue with a dark-orange streak down the side.

Within forty-five minutes she's on the Upper Levels Highway and turning onto the off-ramp that leads down into Eagle Cove, where Narek's lush estate hugs the water.

She's looking for proof—both fearing she'll find it and also hoping she won't, because it still seems impossible that her surgeon husband of thirty-four years actually went through the actions of trying to kill her. Another part of her brain is churning over the possibility that he did, and what this might mean for her now, and for their marriage she was trying so desperately to save, to hold on to.

She parks in the sweeping bricked roundabout driveway and tells Boo and Sweetie they need to stay in the car. She steps out into the misty rain, so much softer now. Towering conifers drip all around her.

Jemma follows the flagstone- and moss-covered pathway around the side of the house, and ducks onto the covered walkway that leads down to the boathouse. In her fingers she tightly holds on to the key tagged *Boathouse*, ready to open that door.

When she reaches it, she slots in the key, turns it. The key moves smoothly in the lock. Jemma pulls open the big door.

She inhales as the salty, cool air of the wooden interior wafts over her. She hears the soft slap of water against the ramp. Anxiety winds through her as her eyes adjust to the dimness. As things begin to take shape, she discerns a light switch on the wall to her right. She clicks it on. The inside fills with brightness. And she sees them.

Two shining Jet Skis pulled up on hoists mounted to the roof.

One is black.

The other is *white and blue with a dark-orange streak down the side.*

Jemma's pulse begins to gallop. Her mouth turns dust dry. She stares at the craft with the streaks of dark orange—one on either side— and her mind returns to Adam's wet suit, and the Idaho plates now in the trunk of her car. And the description on the news.

And she knows. She just knows in the core of her bones. That's the murder weapon right there, hanging from the roof of Narek's boat-house, and she would bet her life that if she accessed Adam's Tesla's navigation history, she will find he drove over the bridge to the North Shore in the very early, dark hours of the stormy morning.

Staring at the blue-and-white Jet Ski, Jemma extracts her phone from her pocket. She shoots several images of the watercraft from different angles. Slowly she walks closer to it, and she reaches up to touch the bottom of the craft. She runs her fingertips along it and feels a dent, and then another, and some splintering of the hull. Bile rushes to her throat. She notices something else—a tiny scrap of pink silicone is trapped in the splintered part of one of the dents. Her body spasms at the thought of this thing slamming into the skull—the pink cap, the head—of a swimmer. Of Adam doubling back to crush her again. Deliberate. Calculated. Premeditated.

Jemma moves to the boathouse doors that open to the sea. She unlocks them and opens one side. She stares at the water, which stretches across to Crow's Point and Jerrin Bay. A chill trickles down her spine.

Dr. Adam Spengler, her husband, the renowned oncological surgeon, has in cold blood murdered an innocent mother of four young children—there is no longer a shred of doubt in Jemma's mind. He tried to eliminate her so he could be with Gloria. He killed someone else instead.

This is powerful leverage. But also dangerous knowledge for her to possess.

IT'S CRIMINAL: The Chloe Cooper Story

The screen shows a man in his late fifties. He wears a black coat and is seated at a table on a coffee shop patio. His features are not handsome but characteristic, erudite: gaunt cheeks under high cheekbones, a prominent nose, dark brows, intense brown eyes, a small goatee. A confident man with an aura of presence. The text at the bottom of the screen reads:

DR. NOAH GAUTIER. CRIMINAL PROFILER, OR "MIND HUNTER," RENOWNED FOR HIS SKILL IN DECODING THE MINDS OF SERIAL KILLERS AND CRIMINALS WITH DEVIANT BEHAVIORS.

NOAH: All three of them—Jemma and Adam Spengler, and Chloe Cooper—began to unravel in visceral but different ways from that moment. And it set them on a collision course with each other. A deadly one.

TRINITY OFF CAMERA: Can you speak more to what you mean by unraveling?

NOAH: It was that day that Chloe Cooper was forced to acknowledge out loud to a police officer, and to herself, that her mother, Raven Cooper, was really dead. Up until that point Chloe had been desperately trying to keep Raven alive in some way. It tipped her into uncharted psychological territory. Raven and Chloe exhibited complete codependent behaviors as a result of their pasts. Chloe didn't know a world where it wasn't just her and her mom. For the first time ever, she was alone. And in admitting her mother had passed, she was also allowing herself to become vulnerable. In that sense, the old Chloe was unraveling in order to permit a new Chloe to enter. It was frightening, and it felt dangerous to her. And possibly also exciting. All of this also cracked open a vault of buried memories and sensations she had no narrative for.

Adam Spengler, on the other hand, went—in the space of one morning—from lifesaving surgeon to cold-blooded killer. He was facing his abyss. His personal dark night of the soul. And he knew that everything he was trying to attain would be destroyed by the fact Jemma knew what he had done. He began to unravel.

Jemma Spengler was a deeply troubled woman with a pathological need to be wanted, revered, loved exclusively. When it dawned on her what her husband had done, she faced a choice—either fight tooth and nail to hold on to her husband and the security of her marriage, or face the fact her husband was deeply in love with another woman, that he wanted her dead, and that he was fully capable of killing her.

TRINITY OFF CAMERA: So this made Jemma dangerous to Adam?

NOAH: They all become dangerous. When humans are pushed into fight-or-flight survival mode, they become capable of diabolical things. The psychological triggers for each of them were all there. Each fed on the other, and it locked them onto a path to brutal murder.

BEFORE THE MURDERS

Jemma returns to her car parked in Narek's driveway and rummages in the back. She finds a small paper bag among the cloth grocery bags she keeps in her vehicle for shopping trips. Inside her purse, in her makeup bag, she locates a set of tweezers. She hurries back to the boathouse, careful not to slip on the wet moss. Once inside the boathouse, using her tweezers, she carefully extracts tiny pieces of pink bathing cap silicone from the splintered areas of the Jet Ski hull. She drops these into her paper bag. She also finds a blonde hair in the splintering. Carefully she pulls it loose with her tweezers, and places the hair in the bag with the silicone. She folds the top over. If police procedural shows on TV are correct, DNA is better preserved in a paper bag than a plastic one, and she's certain there will be some DNA on these bits of evidence, perhaps even microscopic amounts of Marianne Wade's brain. She shudders as she tucks the bag inside her jacket to protect it from the rain.

Leaving the boathouse as she found it, she relocks the door and takes the bag back to her car. Once inside her car with her dogs, Jemma phones Dot.

"I need a lawyer," she tells Dot. "You mentioned the other day you knew someone good."

She jots down the name and number Dot gives her.

"Everything okay, Jemma?" Dot asks.

Jemma hesitates. "Not really. But I'll catch you up later. There's something I have to deal with right away. And—Dot, thank you. I really appreciate it."

She kills the call and immediately punches in the number Dot gave her. She stresses to the receptionist the highly urgent nature of her business, and she manages to get an emergency appointment at the law firm Dot recommended.

Her next stop is a twenty-four-hour storage unit rental facility in North Vancouver's industrial area near the train tracks. She rents the smallest unit possible, and inside the unit she places the Idaho plates, the garbage bag containing Adam's wet suit, hood, gloves, and booties, and the paper bag of evidence she collected.

She drives home to find Adam still gone. Upstairs, from a small safe at the back of her closet, where she stashes her valuable jewelry, Jemma retrieves a thumb drive she brought from Ontario.

Jemma opens her laptop, inserts the thumb drive, and copies the photos she took of the boathouse onto the drive. She also prints out several of the images that show the Jet Ski, plus the interior of Narek's boathouse.

The day is turning toward evening when she drives into town to see the lawyer.

BEFORE THE MURDERS

When Jemma returns from the lawyer and enters the laneway behind their house, it's dark. As she is about to turn into her driveway, she sees a woman with a small senior dog crossing the alley at the far end, and moving toward the door of the building with the residential units upstairs. Something familiar about her body movements makes Jemma slow, then stop, her car.

The woman opens the building door, glances furtively down the alley, and Jemma catches sight of her profile under the outdoor light. Surprise ripples through her body. It's Chloe. The dog walker / bartender.

Jemma watches Chloe enter the building with her dog. The door closes behind her.

Her blood quickens. She's aware that the two detectives crossed the alley and went into that building after visiting their house. She glances up at the third-floor window. A light goes on. A form moves across the window. Same coat, same hair color as the woman who entered the building.

The spy in the window is Chloe.

She's been watching their house since the day they moved in, with binoculars, even. It was her who observed Jemma and Adam making love in her studio. How much has Chloe seen of their lives? Of their arguments, their meals, their television watching? Made all the more accessible to her because they still don't have goddamn blinds, thanks to Adam.

Jemma drives into her garage and sees Adam's Tesla is gone. She sits in her car as the garage door rumbles closed behind her vehicle. A chill sinks deeper into her veins as it dawns on her that not only has Chloe Cooper been spying on her and Adam's every movement, but the woman has even been *inside* their house. She took photos inside their home. She still has the key code to the back door. And Chloe is obviously aware Adam is having an affair with Gloria, who sat at her bar. Why else would she plant those things in Adam's pockets? Who did she anticipate would find them, if not Jemma? It was also Chloe who gave Jemma Gloria's business card with the gallery address.

Unease crawls over her skin as she recalls how insistent the bartender was that their group not leave the restaurant that night because of the dogs, and how eager she was to befriend Jemma, and how she offered Boo and Sweetie treats.

The woman is flat-out creepy. A stalker. A snoop. But is she dangerous?

Maybe not to Jemma, but perhaps to Adam—the cheating husband?

And why did Detective Havers and Pederson go into her building? To question her because she claimed to have witnessed something— Adam coming or going perhaps? Possibly with Idaho plates. And like a streak of lightning, it slams into Jemma—Chloe Cooper, a dog walker, must be the local Crow's Point dog walker mentioned on the news—the one who apparently walks her senior dog along the beach path every morning at around 7:00 a.m.

She is the one who witnessed Adam killing the swimmer? No wonder the detectives showed up at their house to question Adam.

Jemma exits the car with Boo and Sweetie. She lets them out into the yard and pours herself a glass of wine. She stands in the dark house, at the window, sipping her wine, watching the window across the street. An idea begins to take shape. But she needs to be certain—she needs to learn more about that woman in the window up there.

Jemma reaches for her phone. She texts Chloe.

Hi Chloe! Jemma Spengler here. Are you able to come around anytime soon to talk about a longer-term dog sitting arrangement?

Barely seconds pass. Jemma's phone pings.

I'd love to. Any time in particular?

Jemma glances up at the lit window across the alley.

What about now? My husband is out and I sure could do with a glass of wine after all the horrendous news today. Care to join me?

BEFORE THE MURDERS

Chloe trembles with anticipation as she rings the doorbell to Gloom House and hears the dogs bark inside. Pet sitting is one thing, but not in her wildest dreams could she have imagined being invited to drink *wine* with the selkie goddess. Things are changing for her. Even Stavros asked her on a "date" after their hot drinks on the patio. Perhaps life at forty really will be different, and she will finally figure out how she fits into the world.

Jemma swings the door open wide. "Chloe, hi. Come on in!"

She appears flushed, a little disheveled. Distraught, even. Most unlike a Hollywood goddess. Chloe steps in and the dogs jump up for attention. She crouches down to say hi to Boo and Sweetie while Jemma shuts the door.

"Sorry if I come across distracted," Jemma says as she smooths her hand over her long hair. "But I've had a day and a half. Which is also why I need wine and company. Come through to the kitchen."

Chloe removes her shoes and follows Jemma on socked feet. Two glasses already await on the granite counter, along with a half-drunk open bottle of Louis Latour Ardèche Viognier. As a bartender, Chloe knows her wines, and this is a fine choice, in her opinion. She wouldn't expect less from Jemma. Chloe doesn't customarily drink wine—vodka is more affordable and delivers maximum bang for the buck. But if she were flush like the Spenglers, she would most certainly drink exceptional imported wine.

"Take a seat." Jemma indicates the counter stools.

Chloe lifts herself up onto one and feels a burst of warm satisfaction as she gazes into the kitchen. Here she is, in the inner sanctum, primed for a cozy chat woman to woman with Jemma behind the counter, looking like a Nicole Kidman character with her fair skin, red-gold hair, and elegant limbs.

"Is white okay?" She holds up the Louis Latour. "Or something else—a red, a cocktail, perhaps?"

"Oh, the Viognier is lovely."

Jemma sloshes a large amount into the glasses, picks up her own, and raises it by the stem. "Cheers, Chloe."

"Cheers, Jemma." She smiles.

They sip. Outside the rain increases. Inside the gas fire flickers, and the dogs curl into their beds near the hearth. It's one of those cool fall days in a city where tomorrow could just as easily turn beautiful again. Or it could remain ugly for weeks.

"Thanks for watching the dogs for me. I was wondering if it's something you might be interested in doing on a regular basis," Jemma says.

Chloe takes a gulp of wine. "Of course! How often are you thinking?"

"Hmm, maybe three days a week. Just for the late mornings into the lunch hour. I'm going to be busy in my studio, and I'd love someone to take them for a walk, basically. Do you live close by, Chloe?"

She shifts on her stool. "Oh, pretty close."

Jemma regards her. Her eyes seem intense, as though she's hunting for something in Chloe's expression. It's the wine, thinks Chloe. It's the stress of the detectives being here. And Adam Spengler himself is undoubtedly a source of great stress. The urge rises afresh in Chloe to tell this woman about her unfaithful husband, to explain she believes he killed the swimmer and Jemma might still be in danger. Chloe wonders if Jemma found the clues, and how to broach this. She takes another big sip of wine—it's going down awfully well. She clears her throat. "Did you manage to find Gloria Bergson? After I gave you the business card?"

Jemma looks panicked for a brief instant, but almost as quickly her face slips back to something more neutral. She reaches for her glass, drinks deeply. "Actually, yes. I, ah—thank you for that."

Chloe waits, hoping Jemma will offer more.

She suddenly swigs back the rest of the wine and says, "Would you like a refill? I have a few more bottles of the Louis Latour."

"Sure, yes, please," Chloe says.

Jemma goes to the fridge, selects a chilled bottle, and opens it on the counter. She refills their glasses generously. "There's actually something I've been needing to get off my chest, Chloe. Can I trust you?"

"Of course."

She regards Chloe for a moment, as if deciding how much to say. "I—does Gloria Bergson come into your restaurant often? Is she a regular of yours?" Her hand shoots up in a halt sign before Chloe can answer. "I really don't want to press you to talk about customers, if it's a problem. I—I was just wondering how well you might know her."

Her heart quickens. Jemma must have found the clues. "Well," Chloe says carefully, "the first time I spoke with Gloria was that night you and your friends came in."

"So she hasn't been there before?"

"Not on my shift. But I—I have seen her around elsewhere."

"Where?" A sudden bite sharpens her voice.

Chloe hesitates and twirls the stem of her glass as she studies the shimmering gold in the wine. "I don't know how to say this, Jemma." She meets the selkie goddess's eyes. "But when I saw her elsewhere, she wasn't alone."

Sharp interest burns into Jemma's face. "Who was she with?"

"I—it doesn't feel right for me to say. But—"

"Adam? Did you see her with my husband?"

Chloe swallows. "I think I might have spoken out of turn."

Jemma seats herself on a stool, leans over the counter, and her gaze lasers into Chloe's. Her voice turns low, urgent, quiet. "I found some things in Adam's pockets, Chloe. I think—I'm pretty sure they're having an affair."

Delight ripples through Chloe. *Yes! It worked!*

"She's a horrible woman," Chloe says, "cheating with someone else's husband. I hate her, to be honest. I hate most cheats."

"So you do know that she's cheating with Adam?"

She nods.

"So you hate my husband, too?"

"I—I didn't mean to imply th—"

"It's okay. I feel that way about him myself at this point." She drags her hand over her hair, then curses softly—rather beautifully, actually. "I'm so sorry, Chloe. I didn't invite you over to off-load on you. It's just been consuming me. I'll shut up now."

"No, please don't. I—I mean, a cheating husband can be dangerous."

Jemma goes still. "What do you mean?"

"Just that one needs to be careful, you know? Like, what if he wants to get rid of a wife so he can be with a mistress and start a new family."

Energy, hot, fierce, crackles up around Jemma, and it fires into her eyes. "Do you *know* something? Did Gloria say anything? Did you overhear them discuss something bad?"

Chloe's brain tumbles over itself as tension bands across her chest. She doesn't want Jemma to know she's a stalker. She can't flat out say she believes it was Adam on that Jet Ski who killed a woman while trying to kill Jemma. Can she? Besides, how does she know for certain it was him? Apart from the fact she saw the photos on the passage wall the last time she was inside Gloom House—images of Adam driving a Jet Ski. And she saw him arrive home with fake plates and a wet suit in his bag, and a strange hoodie and cap over his head. Plus, she overheard Gloria noting that they have a child, and giving him the ultimatum. Which is motive, to her mind. And when you watch people—really observe them and make a study of them—you tend to see links between things that others don't.

Carefully, Chloe says, "I overheard her saying that Dr. Spengler—Adam—needed to make a choice, or she would leave him."

"Where? When?"

"Ah—in the parking lot near the restaurant when I was walking home," Chloe lies. She feels hot now. Uncomfortable. She's gone too far in her desire to bond with Jemma. She needs to change direction a little. "Actually, she's invited me to her studio."

"What?"

"She wants to see some of my art."

"Gloria does?"

Chloe nods.

"What do you mean, *art?*"

"My portfolio. She saw my painting hanging in the reception area at the Beach House, and she asked who painted it, because she really liked it. She then asked if I had more. She said I paint loneliness like Edward Hopper."

Jemma sits back slightly, wineglass in hand, appraising Chloe. "Wow. I know of that painting. It's famous."

Chloe beams, and her chest puffs with pride. "When Gloria was at the bar, I showed her some photos of my other work, and that's when she gave me her card. Implying that maybe I could have a show or something, or that she potentially wants to represent me."

Chloe can literally see heightened interest quickening through Jemma: Her carotid artery at her neck stands out a little, beats faster. Pinkness increases over her cheeks. Her pupils dilate, and there is tightening of her body posture. Chloe can also feel her altered energy. It crackles around them both, enveloping them, filling the room with a silent, hot intensity.

"Are you going to?"

"Going to what?"

"Take her your portfolio? Show her samples of your work?"

"No. I don't think so. I—"

"Why not?" Her gaze remains hot, persistent.

"I just paint for me. I don't think I want people to gawp at my work, you know? Have them sit there and read all sorts of things into it."

Jemma tops up the wine. And for a moment she seems to suddenly shut off, as though she's gone deeply internal, thinking. She flicks a glance at the door as though expecting her husband to return any moment. Chloe thinks of him crying at the memorial, and she wonders where he's gone now.

"I need to know more about this Gloria," Jemma says as she lifts her glass toward her lips, then stops midair. "I *need* to know just how serious this is, Chloe," she says quickly. "I wonder . . . is there any chance you could do me a huge favor? I mean, please feel free to say no, because it's a big ask . . . then again, maybe it's too big. No, it's—it's unreasonable."

"What is it?" Chloe asks, eager to please, thrilled to be asked anything at all.

Jemma inhales deeply, then blows out a momentous breath and sets down her wineglass. "What if you *did* take her your portfolio? And went to visit the gallery? And while there, you did some digging for me—just questions. About herself, where she lives. Her family, any children, her significant other, whether she owns the gallery—that kind of thing? Because if you got to know her a bit, you could perhaps tell me more? I mean, you could help me as well as get something out of it yourself, like a potential show, or gallery representation."

"I don't know, Jemma. I don't really want my art—"

"It would really help me, Chloe."

That band of tension torques tighter across Chloe's chest. This would be stepping *way* out of her comfort zone. But she's also desperate to please Jemma, and to be her friend. And to save her from Adam. Maybe she *should* do it. Maybe turning forty really is going to be a magical year of saying yes to things, and becoming someone new, with friends and a place in the world.

"I'd have to acquire a big enough portfolio case. And it would be tricky going via bus with a large portfolio in hand. I'd probably need to pay for an Uber, and—"

"Chloe! I'll drive you, of course I will. I'll drop you right outside the gallery. Well, not *exactly* outside the door, because I don't want her to see me, of course."

"Of course not."

"And I'll wait down the road for you while you go inside and check out the gallery and Gloria. Remember, you'll be interviewing her as much as she might be interviewing you for a business arrangement, if she likes your art."

"I—I don't know, Jemma."

She appraises Chloe. "Have you got photos of your paintings on your phone?"

"I do."

"Can you show me?"

Reluctantly Chloe opens her phone, locates the album of her work, and hands it to Jemma.

She scrolls through. Leans closer, moves fingers to make one bigger. Silence thickens around her. Chloe hears one of the dogs scratching its collar. Rain ticks against the window. Like a clock. *Tick tick tick.*

Jemma glances up sharply.

Chloe braces.

"God, Chloe, these are stunning. Is this—who is this swimmer with the pink cap in the bay? It looks like Jerrin Bay."

Shit. Heat fires into her face. She reaches for her phone, almost tugging it out of Jemma's hands.

Jemma waits, watching her face.

Chloe breaks the gaze, glances down at the counter. Her pulse races. "I—I walk my mom's dog along the beach every morning around seven, and there's always a swimmer there. I loved the sight of her moving across the bay. The—the freedom." Slowly she glances up, swallows. "I later recognized it was you."

Very quietly Jemma says, "Were you the witness of the hit-and-run, Chloe? The one the police were looking for?"

Emotion pricks into her eyes. She nods.

"Is this why you said my husband might be dangerous? You thought someone—he—was trying to hit *me* in my pink cap."

She nods again.

Jemma leans forward and takes Chloe's hands in hers. Her skin is soft and her bones are fine.

"I need your help, Chloe. Please. Can you help me?"

She nods.

"If you show that swimmer painting to Gloria, and she wants it for her gallery, you could tell her it's a painting of Jemma Spengler. You could inform her that Jemma was supposed to be in the bay with a pink cap, and someone else was killed instead, and you could watch to see how she reacts. It could lead to something. Some information. Would you do that for me?"

Some part of Chloe is incapable of resisting Jemma's magnetism and intensity now, even though the idea of taking her swimmer painting into Gloria's gallery utterly terrifies her.

Don't trust don't trust—

Shut up, Mom. Let me have a friend.

Stupid little bitch. She's using you.

But my art is good. I could make money. Gloria said so. This could be beneficial for me, too. You always tried to stop me from doing anything, becoming anything, because you were scared that I would leave you alone, right, Mom?

You're vulnerable, Chloe, now that I'm gone. You cannot be trusted to make big decisions by yourself.

But Jemma is vulnerable, too, Mom. She needs my help.

Rubbish. Look at what she's asking you. Is it making sense to you?

Shut up. GO AWAY! You're DEAD.

Silence.

Chloe nods again.

Jemma squeezes Chloe's hands. "Thank you. Thank you so much. You are a good friend. Why don't you call her now? Ask her for an appointment?"

Friend.

The word hangs.

Something unravels a little more in Chloe, and possibly it's the wine, too.

"Okay," she says hesitantly. "I'll call Gloria. If—"

The back door opens. The dogs jump from their beds and rush to it. Adam steps in.

Surprise whams through Chloe, and she lurches to her feet, knocking her counter stool over with a crash to the floor.

Jemma stiffens and her face changes completely. Tension mushrooms into Gloom House.

Adam steps forward. He looks awful.

"Where've you been?" Jemma asks.

"To off-load some things at the dump. And for a drive." But his gaze is not on Jemma. It's fixed solely on Chloe. "What is *she* doing here?"

"I should go," Chloe mutters as she hurriedly gathers up her jacket and scurries to the front door, where she came in, and where her shoes are.

"Adam, some respect, please. Chloe is my guest."

"Do you know who she is?" Adam points at her. "She's that woman from across the street. She's a goddamn sick Peeping Tom."

Jemma hurries over to Chloe. "I'm so sorry," she whispers as she opens the front door and bundles Chloe out. "Please, don't mind him. Just—" She holds Chloe's gaze and lowers her voice even more. "Just help me, okay? You can see I need help."

Chloe nods quickly as the door to Gloom House shuts in her face. Rage twists into her belly as she turns away from the house and descends the front stairs. She walks into the night, Adam's words beating like a drum through her brain.

She's a goddamn sick Peeping Tom. A goddamn sick Peeping Tom. Sick Tom. Sick. Sick.

IT'S CRIMINAL: The Chloe Cooper Story

The screen shows a bald and stocky man in his late fifties sitting at a restaurant table with a view over Jerrin Beach and the bay. His eyes are bright blue and filled with light. A Dionysian flush colors his cheeks. The text at the bottom of the screen reads:

BILL ZEIGLER, BEACH HOUSE RESTAURANT
AND BAR OWNER. CHLOE COOPER'S BOSS.

BILL: Chloe applied for a position when we were severely short-staffed, and she came with excellent references from her barista job. I'd frequented the coffee shop where she worked myself—she had an uncanny knack of recalling everyone by name and knowing exactly what they were going to order, sometimes even before they did. Or so she made it seem. She was awkward socially. And had no bartending experience. When she applied, she told me she was self-taught. I was skeptical—but desperate for staff—so I sat at the bar with a colleague, and we asked her to mix up an array of drinks. She had an encyclopedic knowledge of cocktail recipes and the histories of various drinks. I've never seen anything quite like it.

Bill Zeigler pauses. His gaze goes out the windows to the sea where the swimmer was killed.

BILL: You know, I come from a background where I had to build myself up from nothing. My parents were immigrants to this country with professional skills that didn't translate well to the local job market, so they settled for less and struggled to feed a family of three boys and a girl. Then we lost my mother when I was twelve, and . . . times were hard. Really rough. There were several occasions when the Zeigler kids had to visit the food bank or rely on school lunch programs. This is why food—feeding people—is important to me. As is giving those who are less privileged a chance at success. Chloe, I suspected at the time, came from a challenging background, and she didn't have a formal education. I hired her anyway, or perhaps because of it. She became one of my best employees. She never let me down. And then she gave me that painting of the Beach House for my birthday.

Emotion glints in his eyes.

BILL: Sometimes we think—or like to think—that we know or understand people, but can we ever truly know one's interior landscape? Can we ever comprehend all the drivers from a past life that have shaped someone? Not in my wildest dreams could I foresee those precursors that shaped themselves into Chloe Cooper. Or how the events of those September days in 2019 would trigger her.

BEFORE THE MURDERS

"What the fuck was *she* doing here?" Adam demands of his wife as she shuts the door on the woman from across the alley. Anger, anxiety, beats through his body with each thump of his heart.

"She's Chloe Cooper, the dog walker I hired. I was working out an arrangement."

"Do you realize who this 'Chloe' is?" He points out the window. "She's that busybody freak who's been spying on us with binoculars."

"Where were you, Adam?"

"She's dangerous, Jemma. She—"

"She what? Suspects what you did? Are you worried she'll tell the cops something you want to keep hidden? Like how you drove out of here with Idaho plates and a wet suit?"

"What are you talking about?"

"You know exactly what I'm talking about. Where've you been? You look like something the dogs dragged in."

"I went for a walk, like I told you. Down to the beach. When I came home, you weren't here, so I took the car and did a run to the garbage dump, then went for a drive."

"To the dump? To get rid of the Idaho plates, perchance?"

He stares at his wife, hatred consuming him. She glowers back. They're a Mr. and Mrs. Smith—two circling assassins wondering who will strike first against a ticking clock with a timer set by the detectives' visit.

"I saw that your entire vintage plates display is gone from the garage, Adam."

"I was tired of them. So I got rid of them." He shrugs out of his wet jacket and dumps it over the back of a chair.

"But you didn't dispose of the Idaho ones."

"What do you mean?"

"I have those, Adam."

"What?"

"Stored in a very safe place. I removed them from the box of plates in the back of your car. I also have your wet suit, hood, and the gloves that you wore this morning."

Blood drains south in his body. He feels lightheaded, dizzy, as though he's peered over the edge of a precipice into a black maw, and he's not going to be able to stop himself from being sucked down into it. He's not going to be able to hide what he did from his wife. She knows—somehow she knows exactly what he did to that swimmer.

He brushes past her to get a drink. As he reaches for a bottle of Scotch, she says behind him, "I want you to look at these."

He ignores her, pours a whiskey. Slugs it back. It burns into his chest as he pours another.

"Adam. Look."

He turns to face her, drink in hand. She has placed images—photos—on the counter. Printed on regular printer paper.

"What are those?"

"Come see."

He edges toward the counter. It takes him a nanosecond to register what they are. Photographs of the Jet Skis inside Narek's boathouse. His gaze flares to Jemma's as shock stalls his heart.

She points. "Blue and white with a streak of dark orange." She fixes him in her gaze. "That's what the choppers were searching for." A hint of a sadistic smile creeps crookedly over her mouth. "And I know where it is, Adam. We both know."

His breathing quickens. He wants to ask how, but *how* matters less than the fact that she knows.

"What are these images worth to you?" she asks.

He doesn't know what to say. Denial is useless.

"And do you know what else I have stored in the safe place?" she asks. "Tiny scraps of pink silicone from a swimmer's cap that were embedded into the dents and splinters on the hull of this Jet Ski." She taps the image of the blue-and-white craft with her nail. "I bet there's DNA—maybe even bits of Marianne Wade's brain—on that silicone. And I'd wager that some CCTV camera somewhere captured images of a bright-blue Tesla with Idaho plates traversing the Lions Gate Bridge very early in the morning before the swimmer was struck and killed. And then recrossing the bridge afterward."

Adam sinks onto a chair.

Jemma swears softly. "Christ, you really did do it. You formed a premeditated plan to kill me, and you acted on it. And here I am, still hoping you might offer me some explanation—*anything*—as to why this could not possibly be true." She pauses, regarding him steadily. "You never did break it off with Gloria Bergson, did you?"

"What do you want from me, Jemma?" His voice cracks. He's beyond exhausted, drained. Broken. Finished. The thudding sensation of hitting—killing—a woman, the image of her hand lifting in a plea for help, begins to pound on a loop through his body and brain.

He's doomed. Terrified of what comes next. And the only thing he craves is the gentle comfort of Gloria's arms around him, the feeling of his son's warm little body against his. But even they won't want to know him when this gets out. They will not come and see him in prison.

"I visited a lawyer today," she says quietly.

He just stares at her.

"I left in his care a sealed envelope that contains a key to the storage locker with your Idaho plates, the silicone cap traces, your wet suit, and copies of these photos." She points at the images with a long-nailed finger. "Plus Narek's address along with detailed instructions to deliver these items to Detective Havers in the event of my sudden death. Also inside the locker is a thumb drive with records of your past financial and medical fraud. If you even *think* of trying again to get rid of me, you will be done, Adam. So very done."

A flicker of hope licks through him. Because there's an unspoken corollary in her words, and she's dangling it like bait before him. She's saying she might keep it all secret, under lock and key, if he behaves. He might yet stand a chance of staying out of prison.

"I'll never try to hurt you again, Jemma," he says softly. "I don't know what got into me. I couldn't do anything like that again."

"Yes, you could."

"I wouldn't ev—"

"Get rid of her, Adam. For good. Do to her what you tried to do to me."

Adam searches his wife's face, her eyes. Very quietly, darkly, he says, "What do you mean, Jemma?"

"Kill her."

Blood drains from his face. *"What?"*

"Eliminate her."

"You cannot be serious."

She says nothing.

Adam's mind splinters into a million different directions. Sophia's words echo through his brain.

Your wife is a narcissist—you know that, right? She has a pathological need for attention . . . exclusivity. She'll do just about anything *to keep focus on herself . . . I had a suspicion she was responsible for the death of my new boyfriend at the time . . . He slipped on loose rocks, fell, hit his head on the way down, and drowned . . . And what about her father? He abandoned Jemma and her mother. Next thing he dies in a fire that consumed his trailer? The door was locked . . . There was some question about whether the door had been locked from the outside . . . You're a doctor. You know about Munchausen syndrome by proxy . . . There was talk among the nurses. One of them brought the history of Jackson's many hospitalizations and strange sets of symptoms to the attention of a doctor, and raised their concerns. But there was no evidence, and who wants to accuse a grieving mother . . . But it fits her psychological makeup, Adam, and I'm sure you can see it.*

Horror leaks ice into his veins. He begins to shiver with a cold sense of dread. Is *this* who he's been married to the whole time? Has she really killed before? Will Jemma actually try to force this ultimate ultimatum?

Not in his worst nightmares could Adam have foreseen *this* as the trade-off—the price—for staying out of prison: killing the woman he loves, the mother of his child.

He can't. He won't.

Not ever.

"Jemma, I—I'm not a killer."

"Oh, but you are, Adam. You've proved it. You killed Marianne Wade. Just do it again."

As he opens his mouth to answer, a loud rap sounds on the back door, followed by the doorbell chimes. The dogs begin to bark, and he hears a woman's voice yell, "Mr. and Mrs. Spengler! Detective Havers here. Can you open up, please?"

BEFORE THE MURDERS

"Go on. Open it, Adam," Jemma orders quietly.

Adam, still stunned, gets up, goes to the door, cracks it open. Detective Maeve Havers stands on his doorstep, illuminated by the outside light. Detective Axel Pederson is walking around the front of the garage, trying to peer in through the opaque windows set into the door.

Adam leans out to call to him. "What can we do for you, Officer Pederson?"

"We have a few more questions," says Detective Havers.

He turns to her. "Like what?"

"Do you mind if we come in?"

"Actually, we—ah, we're really busy." Jemma's calmly uttered, horrendous demand is snaking around and around in his brain, and he can't even begin to think straight.

Get rid of her, Adam. For good . . . Kill her.

Havers eyes him, weighing him. He feels stripped. Naked. As though the detective can see right into his crumpled, damaged, loathsome soul, the murdering doctor that he is. His hand tightens on the door.

"Do you drive a blue Tesla, Mr. Spengler?"

"It's *Dr.* Spengler," he says in a desperate bid to cling on to some semblance of normalcy, some shred of his identity, some tiny sense of control.

She waits. Her partner comes closer out of the gloom. Rain droplets shine on his black coat. The cops regard him, waiting for him to answer the question.

He clears his throat. "I do drive a Tesla. Blue," he says.

"Can we perhaps see it? Have a look inside your garage?"

"Why?"

"Traffic cam caught a blue Tesla going over the Lions Gate Bridge early this morning," says Pederson. "We have reason to believe this vehicle is of interest in our Jet Ski hit-and-run investigation."

Havers adds, watching him, "The Tesla had Idaho plates."

Adam's brain scrambles for why the police would have singled out that particular Tesla on the CCTV footage. And what would have made them link it so quickly to him? Then it strikes him, and it's so damn obvious. It's her—the woman in the window. Chloe Cooper. She noticed the different Idaho plates on his car when he returned, and she must have told the police. They must have then gone back to search for CCTV confirmation, and found it.

But why would the cops or Chloe Cooper think Idaho plates in themselves had anything to do with the hit-and-run?

Jemma comes up behind him. Adam feels trapped like a mouse, terrified his wife will divulge everything to the cops. He clears his throat again. "Well, it wasn't my Tesla on the cam, then. Because I have Ontario registration—a vanity plate."

Jemma says quietly near his shoulder. "We have yet to change over to BC plates."

"You wouldn't mind us taking a look in your garage, then?" Pederson asks.

An iron vise of tension clamps around his ribs. He can't breathe, and he hesitates. But he also knows refusing will make them even more suspicious of him.

"Fine, whatever. Let me get my jacket, and I'll let you in through the garage door." He's not inviting them inside, not this time. Not with Jemma's photos of Narek's Jet Skis on the kitchen counter.

He gears up, steps out into the rain, and opens the garage door. He enters, switches on the light. They step in behind him. Jemma follows like a loaded gun pointed at the back of his head, her trigger primed in case he slips.

Do to her what you tried to do to me. Eliminate her.

The two detectives walk slowly around his car. Check the plates. Peer in the windows. Taking their sweet time.

They turn to look at Jemma's car, and he begins to feel a slight easing of breath. But then Maeve Havers stops and faces the empty garage wall, where his registration plate collection once hung. She regards the wall in silence. Seconds tick by. Pederson, meanwhile, watches Adam. He tries not to swallow, or blink, or react in any way, but it makes his skin crawl, and his eyes start to water.

"What was on the wall here?" Detective Havers asks.

He fights an urge to glance at Jemma. Did *she* tell them about his display? Is Jemma messing with him? Double-crossing him? How else would they even know to look at his wall?

"Nothing. Why?" he asks.

The detective purses her lips, glances at Jemma. He tenses. But Jemma doesn't say a thing. Havers returns her attention to his Tesla. Adam fears she'll ask to see his navigation history. He will insist they need a warrant before they can do that. He's pretty damn sure that right now they have nothing to secure one.

But Havers just nods. "Thanks, Mr. Spengler."

Irritation spurts through him at her refusal to use his medical title. But he bites back the impulse to correct her. It does, however, remind him of how intensely his profession defines him, and how he cannot entertain losing it, because it's his identity.

The detectives exit into the soft rain and darkness. But as Adam is about to shut the garage door, Havers steps back into the light. "Are you guys members of any marinas on the North Shore?"

"You asked us that already," Jemma says.

"We asked about local marinas. Not North Shore ones."

"We aren't," Adam says.

"Any friends on the North Shore with personal watercraft?"

"No," Jemma says quickly. Then adds, "So you think the Jet Ski definitely came and went from the North Shore, then?"

"We're pursuing all angles. Thank you again for your time, Mr. and Mrs. Spengler."

As the detectives climb back into their unmarked brown car, Adam shuts the garage door, and he and Jemma return inside.

As soon as he is sure the detectives have gone, he spins to her. "Is this you—did you tell them something about the plates on the wall?"

"No."

"Then how would they know?"

Her gaze goes to the window. Adam follows it and sees a shape. Upstairs. Third floor.

"Well, Chloe was inside here, alone, looking after the dogs the other day," Jemma says. "She could have seen the plates on the wall, as well as on your car. And she is the one who witnessed the swimmer being hit, Adam. She told me. She said she thought I was the swimmer who was struck, because she sees me every day traversing that section with a pink cap." She pauses. "Adam?"

He glances at Jemma.

"Chloe believes you tried to kill me. She might have told the cops that."

"Christ," he whispers. "Why would she believe that?"

"It doesn't matter why. The fact is she does. She's crazy. She could have told them anything, and now the police have you in their sights."

"So what in the hell was she doing here, drinking wine with you?"

Jemma says quietly. "Come sit down. Have a drink. Calm down."

"*Calm down?* Are you out of your mind? Give me any ultimatum you fucking well like, Jemma, but it's not going to make one iota of difference, because it's not *you*, but *Chloe*, who's going to do us in."

She smiles.

"Why are you smiling?"

"Because you said *us*."

He stares. His chest is so tight with panic he's almost panting. His armpits are drenched. He can smell himself, sour with the stench of fear.

"It's going to be okay, Adam. I have a plan."

"What?"

"Please, sit first." She tops his glass up with whiskey and brings it to him. "Here, have a drink."

Adam hesitates. Part of him wants to flee. Another part is filled with mortal dread. Yet another piece of Adam's soul wants to hear what his wife has to say, because he can't believe she was actually serious in her demand that he kill Gloria. So he acquiesces and takes the glass from her. He sits and swigs down half the contents. She seats herself opposite him.

"I know how you can do this, Adam."

"Do what exactly?"

"Get rid of Gloria. Eliminate her for good."

A wave of nausea rises from his gut. "I told you, I can't. I won't. I'm not a killer."

"And I must remind you that you are. You need to do this, Adam, in order to buy my silence, to put me back into the center of your life. You must prove to me you're committed to 'us,' and the only way that can happen is to have her—Gloria—off the scene. Gone. Completely."

"I can't believe you mean this."

"I'm serious, Adam. Do it, or I'll tell Havers and Pederson you killed the swimmer."

"Christ." He drags a hand over his hair. "Do you realize that even if I did do this, I'm the first person the police would suspect, Jemma. It's always the boyfriend, or husband. It's not like I'd get away with anything. I'll still be convicted for murder. I might as well just confess to hitting the swimmer."

She leans forward. "I'll tell you how we'll do it *and* get away with it. We'll use her. Chloe. The crazy dog walker. I have an idea that'll make all our problems, including Chloe, go away." Jemma waves her hand

225

with a dismissive flick toward the building across the street, like she's discarding a speck of dirt.

He stares at his wife, still unable to process. She actually looks animated. A cold and terrible sense of doom seeps into Adam's veins. Jemma *is* serious.

Lethally serious.

BEFORE THE MURDERS

Jemma watches her husband closely, energy—adrenaline—mounting in her body.

"What do you mean, 'use Chloe'?" There's a slight quaver in his voice.

She leans forward in her chair, gaze locked on his. Quietly she says, "Adam, you can do this, and I will help you do it. If we stick together, we are unstoppable. We can survive anything, even the tightening noose of a homicide investigation. After all, couples who kill together stay together, right?"

Slack-jawed, he stares at her, almost blankly, like a boy who doesn't or can't seem to understand.

"But first you need to tell me some things."

"What things?"

"What are Gloria's gallery hours?"

At the mention of his lover's name, Adam is galvanized. He lurches to his feet and goes to the cabinet to refresh his drink. As he pours more whiskey, he says, "What do you mean by *making Chloe go away*, along with our problems?"

Jemma can see that he's trying to buy time, searching for a way to escape.

"Sit down, Adam."

He glowers at her, drink in hand.

"I mean it. I need you to sit and listen carefully, and for you to give me the information I require."

Very slowly, reluctantly, hesitantly, he reseats himself.

"Tell me what her gallery hours are."

"I don't know the gallery hours, Jemma."

"Of course you do."

"Look them up."

She regards him. Tension rises. "Do you want to stay out of prison, or would you like me to call Detective Havers?"

He moistens his lips, inhales deeply. "The doors open at eleven a.m. Monday through Sunday. Close at six p.m."

"Is she always there?"

"No. Why is this—"

"Answer me, Adam. You need to focus. This will help you focus."

"You're sick, you know that?"

She sits back in her chair, crosses her legs, and pins him with her gaze. Jemma keeps her arms relaxed on the armrest. Outwardly she projects composure, and she sees this scares him. Good. But inside her anger is deep and wild and desperate. Calmly she says, "I'm not the one who followed through on a plan to murder my spouse—and believed I'd succeeded. I'm not the one, Adam, who killed an innocent, beloved mother of four in cold blood by smashing in her skull."

He swallows and looks gray.

"What days is Gloria personally in the gallery, and when she is there, what other staff are also present?"

"She's there Wednesday through Sunday. She likes to work the weekend shifts because she sees a bigger volume of prospective buyers."

Her jaw tightens. She fights to temper herself. "Go on."

"She has two employees who stand in for her on her days off, one on Mondays—the other does Tuesdays. The remainder of the week, it's her and an admin assistant, who knocks off at five p.m."

"So she's alone in the gallery between five and six p.m. on those days?"

He sips his drink and regards her over the rim. She can almost hear the wheels of his brain turning, scheming, seeking ways to second-guess her.

"What if she wants to meet with artists?" Jemma asks. "And look at portfolios?"

"I don't know."

"Of course you know, Adam. You and Gloria have been intimate for more than two years. You share a child."

He breaks her gaze, stares into his drink.

"Adam?"

Slowly he glances up. "She prefers to meet with prospective clients at the end of the day, when the gallery is quiet. Around closing time—often right after. She'll lock the front of the gallery—the showroom—and invite them through to the back, where she has a framing studio, tables, a kitchenette, and an office. She likes to offer the artists wine, coffee, snacks, or whatever while she examines their artwork."

"What about security cameras?"

"Only in the front," he says quietly. "No cameras in the back."

"Outside?"

"Nothing outside, but the showroom CCTV cams have a view of the sidewalk through the front windows. The place is alarmed. She activates the alarm when she leaves."

"What is at the rear of the premises?"

He inhales shakily. "A parking bay and delivery entrance."

"Did you set her up in that business, Adam? Do you own part of it, or do you pay rent? How does it work?"

"How is this relevant?"

"What about her pretty little house on Magnolia Lane? Did you buy that for them, too?"

He looks shocked.

"I *need* to know, Adam. I need to hear it from you. *Your* admission, *your* words—the depths of your duality, your betrayal, while you brought me out here under false pretenses to park me in this godforsaken house. If we want to get past this and move forward as a team, tell me if you bought that house and business for her."

He nods slightly.

And Jemma is steeled. A ferocity of purpose coalesces around her heart. It sharpens her mind and courses a resilience through her blood. Her determination to follow this through is 100 percent solidified. "So the delivery entrance at the back is accessed by an alley?"

"Yeah. It runs behind the block of buildings that house the gallery."

"You have keys?"

He looks away. Nods.

"When you do use those keys, which door—"

"The back door, okay? Satisfied? I sneak in the fucking back way. For *you*. To hide it from you, so you wouldn't be humiliated, shamed. I was going to end it properly, tell you, Jemma."

"But you didn't, did you, Adam? For more than *two years*, you lied. And kept lying."

His chest heaves and falls. An ugly sheen has developed on his skin. She checks her watch calendar.

"We do it tomorrow."

"Do what, exactly?"

"What I said. You get rid of Gloria. Tomorrow. The sooner the better, because the cops are closing in and time is ticking down with every second we wait. If we do this, and we keep that Jet Ski and other evidence out of sight, they won't be able to prove your connection to the hit-and-run homicide. And remember, the burden of proof lies solely on them. Without it, they can't touch you. But I need to set up some things."

He blinks as though unable to comprehend.

She leans forward and grasps her phone off the coffee table. She places a call.

The phone on the other end rings three times before it connects. Jemma hears a tentative "Hello?"

"Chloe! It's me—Jemma. Have you done it yet? Have you made the appointment with Gloria?"

"I—no. Not yet. I—"

"You should do it right away. I know it's late, but even if you just text her, you can inform her that you'll be in the area with your portfolio on Sunday, the day after tomorrow. Ask her if you can stop by around six p.m. And I'm sure she'll want to see you, Chloe. Your work truly is spectacular. And she'll be at the gallery at that time."

"Sunday? I have work in the evening."

"Can you get someone to cover your shift? This is really important to me, Chloe. And I am available to pick you up at that time, and drive you over, drop you off. Like I said, I'll wait for you down the road, and then bring you back home."

Jemma hears the woman hesitate. But she's also seen the neediness in the dog walker's eyes, the pathetic way she fawns on Jemma. That strange woman will do this to buy a connection. Jemma is pretty certain of it after assessing her over drinks.

"Okay."

"Text me as soon as you have an appointment. And, Chloe, thank you. You're a good friend."

"Anything I can do to help, Jemma!"

She kills the call and sits back in her chair, phone in hand. Her lips curve into a smile.

"What have you just done?"

"If my plan works, that weird Chloe Cooper, that woman in the window, will be charged with stabbing Gloria Bergson to death. And you won't. Because you will set Chloe up to take the fall. And as far as your Jet Ski homicide goes—if you follow through with our plan, I promise to have your back all the way, Adam. Together—as a team, a couple—we'll ensure that no Idaho plates, or wet suit, or other evidence will ever be found. And when things calm down, we'll return to Narek's place and get rid of that Jet Ski before the detectives even get wind of the boathouse. Once it's over, it'll be just you and me. We'll be free to go back to our lives, and the way things were. Till death do us part." She smiles as warmly, encouragingly, as she can.

He clears his throat and scrubs his fingers through his hair. "I can't—I can't do anything to hurt Oliver. I can't take his mother from him. I just can't."

"You *can*, Adam. Plus, think about this—with Gloria gone, you still remain Oliver's father. That will never change. We can get custody, Adam. Oliver can come live with us. We'll have another child."

His mouth opens as horror fills his eyes.

BEFORE THE MURDERS

While Jemma gets ready for bed, Adam goes into the bathroom downstairs. Quietly he shuts and locks the door. He flushes the toilet and turns the taps on full so they make a noise, and he calls his lawyer's office in Ontario. It's ridiculously late back East now, and he's also beyond exhausted, but he needs to leave a voicemail while he can, while Jemma is out of earshot.

When the call connects and Adam hears the prompts, he leaves his detailed message. When he hangs up, his hands tremble. He splashes water on his face and stares at himself in the mirror.

He doesn't recognize the trapped and doomed specimen of a human who looks helplessly, hopelessly back at him.

But he's a survivor, he tells himself. It's time for triage. Number one—keep from being arrested, do not get charged, stay out of prison.

He will play along for now, placate his wife, buy time. Because he's certain to get a window of opportunity at some later point. And he'll take it.

But he also has to hedge bets.

Adam turns off the taps, dries his face, and heads up to bed.

BEFORE THE MURDERS

September 29, 2019

Chloe waits at the bus shelter on Main, clutching the handle of her awkwardly large portfolio case filled with her art. Jemma suggested the shelter pullout as the easiest place to pick her up, and Chloe is totally fine not to be collected outside her back door and have it underscored that she lives across the alley. Adam Spengler's words worm through her head.

Do you know who she is? She's that woman from across the street. She's a goddamn sick Peeping Tom.

Chloe inhales deeply and wonders if Jemma will broach this issue with her. It makes her nervous. Her mind goes back to the day Jemma arrived, and how she looked right into Chloe's binoculars when she was naked and making love with Adam in her studio. Perhaps it doesn't matter that much to Jemma—some people *like* being seen. Exhibitionist sorts. Or perhaps she's now so desperate for Chloe's help with Gloria that she's prepared to overlook this oddity.

You're wrong, Chloe. Listen to your gut, to the little whispers. Something is not right with those people in Gloom House. You might rue this day—

Enough! Let me be!

She shuts off her mother's voice and checks her watch. Jemma is late. Chloe needs to be at the Bergson Gallery right at 6:00 p.m. Gloria seemed thrilled to have Chloe come in with her work. But now the sun is lowering, and the autumn air is turning cold, and fallen leaves skitter with gusts of wind down the sidewalk. Anxiety twists through her chest.

A bus pulls in. The hydraulics hiss as the doors open. People get on and off. Stores across the street are closing. She glances at her watch again. Jemma is not coming. She's been stood up. Figures. Story of her life. This was a mistake anyway.

Chloe starts to walk home just as a white van with tinted windows pulls into the bus bay, and stops. The passenger window slides down.

"Chloe!"

She frowns and peers into the van to see Jemma at the wheel.

"So sorry I'm running late. Hop in."

Chloe hesitates. Her reptilian brain is hissing, balking. White vans are the choice of serial killers in all the cop shows and true-crime stories. White vans bring bad things. But smiling at the wheel is her selkie goddess, welcoming her inside.

"Where's your sports car?" Chloe asks.

"I had alternator trouble. It's at the shop, which is why I'm running a bit late. But we can still make it. Open the rear sliding door. You can put your portfolio in back, and hop on up in front."

Chloe slides open the van door. The inside smells newish, or freshly detailed. In the back is a big gym bag. Chloe notices some blue nitrile gloves poking out of the bag, along with some clothing.

Jemma sees her looking and says, "It's a rental that a cleaning company uses. They loaned it to me in a rush."

Chloe nods, shuts the side door, and climbs into the passenger seat, feeling uneasy. But there is soft music playing inside, and it's cozy and warm. Jemma waits for her to buckle up, then grins. "Ready?"

She nods.

Jemma puts the van in gear and pulls into the stream of traffic. They join the flow feeding into the city center.

Chloe notices Jemma is not wearing her usual style of clothes. She has loose-fit jeans on and a baggy gray sweatshirt. Her gorgeous mane of hair is very tightly plaited into a ropy braid that hangs down her back. No makeup.

"Is everything okay?" Chloe asks.

Jemma flashes her a look. "Yes. Apart from the damn alternator. Why?"

"Oh, no reason."

She laughs. "You mean my apparent lack of self-care? That's what happens when your car breaks down and you desperately need to find a garage and a rental in a rush, and your husband is no help because he's working at the hospital." Jemma heaves a breath out, as if finally unwinding now that they're on their way. "I just didn't have time to fix my face and change." She throws another sharp glance Chloe's way. "I so badly didn't want to let you down, Chloe."

"Where are Boo and Sweetie?"

"Home. I fed them early. They'll be fine until we return."

Chloe settles back into the passenger seat. Disappointed, and still a little thrown. She dreamed about driving over the bridge in the yellow sports car with Jemma and the two little designer cavapoos. She's never done anything as glamorous as that.

"I could have canceled with the gallery," she says, suddenly overwhelmed, and needing to back out.

"No. Not at all. I honor my commitments, especially with friends."

Friends.

That word again. A faint warmth thrums back into her body.

Chloe, you're not listening to the whispers. Cross the road if something makes you uneasy, move away. While you still can.

When has her scaredy interior voice actually saved her? When have the motherly warnings and admonishments done anything other than hold her back from participating in life? Maybe she really does need to interrogate her own intuition better, because she might have slid into an interior narrative that is not serving her. At all. Look what happened when she went against the grain and agreed to go with Stavros for hot chocolate, and allowed him to touch her. He asked her afterward whether she might want to go with him to a small jazz club in two weeks, to listen to a musician he likes. And then came the wine-evening invitation with Jemma, and a request for Chloe to be on her team to help dig up intel on Enemy Gloria.

It's all made Chloe feel as though she might finally belong some-where, or fit into some group. She might even get recognized as an "emerging artist."

Baby steps, Chloe. Just get through this meeting with Gloria. Help Jemma out. Assist her in getting rid of that awful husband. Then it will be just the selkie goddess across the alley, going swimming every morning, possibly drinking wine with Chloe on summer evenings with the dogs—including Brodie—on the grass.

They make surprisingly good time over the bridge onto the North Shore.

Jemma can't locate easy parking right near Bergson Gallery, so she drives a little farther and pulls into a loading bay with a sign that says No Stopping.

"Is this okay?" Jemma asks. "Not too far?"

"Oh, it's fine—the gallery is just a block or so down." Chloe is nervous again now.

She gets her portfolio out of the back, and Jemma says through the window, "There's an alley behind the gallery with loading bays. If you exit via the back of the building and turn left into the alley, and then walk to the end where it intersects with the street, I'll be waiting right there."

"Are you sure?"

"Of course! There will be plenty of empty bays at this time on a Sunday evening. Nice and quiet." A fast smile. "Please just get me some dirt on that woman."

Chloe walks the two blocks to Bergson Gallery. It's definitely quiet—most of the stores are already closed, and it's getting dark early as the days grow shorter. The area has an abandoned feeling right now, and rain begins to spit. But up ahead the gallery emanates a warm glow into the gathering gloom. And she is going to go in. She will do what she can to save Jemma from that hateful Adam Spengler.

She's a goddamn sick Peeping Tom.

Chloe's resolve firms at the reminder of his taunt. She pushes open the door and is greeted by a friendly tinkle of little bells.

THE MURDERS

Chloe steps into another world. The gallery interior is bright and airy and humidity controlled and filled with breathtaking art—the aura is both warm and incredibly classy. She stands in the entrance, clutching her portfolio case, suddenly overwhelmed.

Gloria pops out of the door at the back. "Chloe! Welcome. Thank you for coming."

Gloria appears to be alone in the gallery, and Chloe is instantly struck by how beautiful and stylish she appears—so different from her edgy sex-appeal shtick that she sauntered into the Beach House with. No doubt her goal that night was to goad her lover's wife, but clearly she sold herself short. Because in here she's the sophisticated, understated empress of her art emporium. She's dressed in cream cashmere that sets off her rich, dark hair, and she wears minimal makeup on her olive-tawny skin, which is smooth and unlined. She's definitely much younger than Jemma.

"I am so happy you reached out to me, Chloe. Please, come on in."

Chloe edges forward, and her gaze is drawn to the art on the walls. The work in here is exceptional. It sucks her in on every level, and for a moment Jemma's waiting in the van slides to the periphery of her mind. Chloe can't believe Gloria thinks her paintings could belong in a place like this. Is it actually possible? That her work might be displayed among these pieces? Has her world truly turned around at the magical milestone age of forty?

Gloria falls silent, allowing Chloe to absorb the artwork as she goes to the gallery door, locks it, and flips the OPEN sign over to CLOSED.

After a few moments she breaks into Chloe's awe. "I'd love to see what you brought in your portfolio. Why don't you come into the back, where we can lay your canvases out nicely on the tables? We also have some easels onto which we can prop some pieces to get a good look."

She follows on Gloria's heels into a brightly lit studio off the gallery showroom, where framing equipment hangs and tools line a shelf. There are several long tables, more framed art, excellent overhead lighting, an office area, and a kitchenette with a bar-height table and stools.

"Would you like coffee, tea, wine, something sparkling? I'm partial to prosecco myself—especially at the end of a week, and it's been a busy week."

"Sure, thank you. Prosecco would be lovely."

Chloe feels as though she's Alice who has slipped into Wonderland as Gloria swans over to the fridge and takes out a charcuterie-and-cheese board and a bottle of sparkling wine.

"Why don't you hang your coat up in the rear foyer—the hooks are near the back door—then you can spread out some of your pieces over there." She tilts her chin toward the tables as she pours two glasses of bubbles.

Chloe hangs her coat in a utility room off the studio, then returns to unzip her portfolio case. She begins to carefully lay her canvases out on the large workshop tables. She's included one of her swimmer paintings, two different aspects of the girl in the rock, and several studies of building exteriors at night that invite the viewer to look voyeuristically into lit windows with unsuspecting occupants inside. Night-stalker images. One shows the outside of a coffee shop with patrons at tables inside. The other is a hair salon with women in chairs as stylists chatter and work with their hair, and the third is the exterior of a neighborhood house similar to Mr. Higgins's place, which was demolished. Chloe feels these echo the mood and tone of the Beach House painting Gloria loved.

Gloria brings the two champagne glasses over, hands one to Chloe, and her attention turns to the canvases. She falls silent as she sips and scrutinizes the pieces one by one.

Chloe's heart hammers. She downs half her prosecco in search of liquid bravado, the bubbles filling her chest with an instant softness and her body with a sense of goodwill. The edges around her mind turn supple and relaxed.

Gloria lifts her gaze and penetrates Chloe's. Her eyes are alight with fire, and a hungry electricity rolls off her. She reminds Chloe of a predator who has suddenly spied prized prey, yet she's restraining herself so she doesn't spook it, preferring to move carefully as she closes in on the kill.

"Chloe," she says gently. "These are truly haunting." She touches the edge of the piece with the house. Inside a yellow square of window, an old man hunches at a table in front of a single plate of food and a cup. There is a cat on the floor beside him. The man looks across the table at an empty chair on the opposite side, as though he sees and yearns for someone who once sat there and kept him company, and is now gone.

"The emotion that comes through these—you really do capture aloneness, Chloe. A sense of longing, yearning. I think this is something everyone can identify with," Gloria says. "This is art each one of us can see something of ourselves in."

Chloe swallows another swig of prosecco. "I—I suppose I never thought about everyone being lonely. Just some people who live on the periphery of things, always looking in from the outside, into lives that appear warm and connected, as though something is wrong with them, and they don't fit into those lighted windows." Her skin goes hot. How did those words even come out of her mouth? She's ashamed. Embarrassed. Exposed. Somehow, being inside this gallery with this woman who loves her creations—it's made the place appear briefly safe enough for Chloe to speak honest thoughts.

"Do you know of the Portuguese word *saudade*?" Gloria asks.

Chloe shakes her head.

"It doesn't really have a direct translation in English," Gloria says, "but it refers to an emotional state of deep, nostalgic longing for something or someone that is absent, or far away. A bittersweet, melancholic, or poignant yearning for things gone." She moves to the painting of the girl looking out to the stormy sea. Alone. Stuck.

"There's also a word in German, *Sehnsucht*, used to describe an indefinable and intense yearning for a person, or place, or an experience, or state that is unattainable or beyond one's current reach. Like *saudade*, it's associated with nostalgia, melancholy, unfulfilled dreams—a concept much explored in German literature, philosophy, and psychology, and often considered a fundamental part of the human experience." Her gaze meets Chloe's again. "This loneliness resides deep inside every one of us, whether a person is in a relationship, a marriage, or a group, or a city—it's a shadowy part of who we are as humans. That's what I see in your work."

Heat increases in Chloe's cheeks as a paroxysm of joy flutters through her heart.

Gloria says, "Your work will resonate with anyone who has ever felt isolated in this world, or who feels that everyone except them has a secret formula for fitting in. I think—"

"I do have more," Chloe says quickly. "I mean, if you feel it's not enough. I have lots. I paint all the time. Some of my pieces are in a storage room in the basement of our building."

"Really?"

She nods. But before she can speak more, Chloe's phone pings in her pocket. She frowns. It pings again—the signal for texts.

"Go ahead, take it while I top our glasses up," Gloria says, reaching for Chloe's now-empty flute in her hand.

Chloe extracts her phone from her pocket, and her heart kicks when she sees the texts are from Jemma. She turns her back to Gloria and opens up the messages.

How are you doing? Everything okay?

NO RUSH! Just want to nip out for a coffee and was wondering
if I had time—if you are still going to be a while?

Chloe quickly texts back.

Plenty of time! I think she likes the work.

Then she recalls why she's really here—at Jemma's behest. Her pulse
quickens as discord twists through her head. She hesitates. Then types
again.

I will msg when we're wrapping up. Thank you.

Gloria comes toward Chloe with freshly filled glasses of bubbles.
She glances at Chloe's phone as she hands her a glass. "Everything okay?
You need to be somewhere?"

"No. It's fine. And—ah—and you?" She slides her cell back into
her pocket. "Are you sure you have time for me?" Her brain scrambles
for a way to raise questions about Gloria's son, her lover, her affair with
Jemma's husband. "I mean, maybe you have family waiting for dinner
or something. Do you have kids?"

Gloria's face lights up. "Oliver. My boy. He's two." She smiles with
obvious love. "He has a full-time nanny, though, and she feeds him
an early supper. We'll have mom-and-son time when I get home. And
bedtime stories."

"What kinds of stories does he like?" Chloe was going to ask
about Oliver's father, but the dissonant part of her brain is reluctant
to pop this delicate, beautiful bubble of a dream she is in with Gloria
right now.

"Oh, gosh, all stories—anything goes. We're reading some old folk-
lore, and he—"

"I used to love the folktales about selkies when I was a child. I think that's why I have this"—she grins as she tries the new word on for size—"*Sehnsucht* for the sea. I can't swim and I didn't grow up around the ocean, but I have this indefinable sort of longing to be in it and near it."

"You definitely captured that in this swimmer painting. I'd love to talk about a possible partnership, Chloe."

Jemma's words float up in her mind.

Show the swimmer painting to Gloria . . . tell her it's a painting of Jemma Spengler . . . inform her that Jemma was supposed to be in the bay with a pink cap, and someone else was killed instead, and you could watch to see how she reacts.

"That swimmer is actually a painting of—"

A noise sounds in the utility room, stopping her. Gloria's head turns. They both listen. It sounds like a key rattling in a lock. The back door opens and shuts in the utility room. "Gloria?" calls a male voice. "You here?"

Gloria's face changes. Chloe tenses.

A man steps from the rear room into the studio. "Ah, there you are."

Shock knifes clean through Chloe's core. She stares. Her heart gallops.

Dr. Adam Spengler.

He's even larger and more imbued with an aura of Evil in this gallery space than in the tight confines of the hospital elevator. Or inside Gloom House. And he's sucking out all the oxygen. She can't breathe. An overriding urge to flee fills her body. At the same instant she realizes he's dressed weirdly again—the same gear he wore when he returned with the Idaho plates on his car and the wet suit in his bag.

"Adam," Gloria says breathlessly, a smile broad on her beautiful face. "You—you're here. Does this mean you have good news?" She looks expectant, as though she's anticipating he will say something huge, something marvelous. Momentous. Life changing. It strikes Chloe then—Gloria Bergson thinks he's finally broken it off with Jemma.

Adam smiles and turns to Chloe. His extra-white smile morphs into a fixed grimace that bares his long eyeeteeth. "Well, this is a surprise. Hello, Chloe."

"You know each other?" Gloria asks.

He takes a step toward Chloe. Every fiber in her body snaps tight. Her gaze rockets to the door that leads to the utility room and the back exit.

"Chloe is Jemma's dog walker," he says patronizingly, taking another step toward her. Chloe sees his hand go to the side pocket of his cargo pants. His eyes are intent on her. He slides his hand into his pocket and grasps something. Every internal voice in her head screams: *Go. Flee! Run! Danger, Chloe! Run for your life and hide Zoe!*

Zoe?

She sparks into action and bolts for the door to the utility room and back exit.

But he steps into her path as his hand moves in front of him with something in it. She stills, panting. He's blocked her exit. In desperation, Chloe reaches and feels behind her for something to defend herself with. Her fingertips touch metal. Cold. Hard. A framing tool of some kind. She curls her fingers around the handle.

She hears Gloria's voice expressing alarm, but she can only see Adam Spengler's ice-blue eyes as they lock on hers. He lunges forward abruptly, raising his hand, and Chloe sees exactly what's in it. It's pointed at her—coming at her. She grips and swings the heavy tool from behind her back around and up in front of her body with a ferocity fired by a need to survive.

The tool connects with the side of Adam's face at the same time as he sinks a needle into her arm. The jolt of the impact with Adam's skull shudders through her bones. She drops the tool with a thud to the floor. He stalls, stares at her in shock. Blood starts to dribble down the side of his face. He staggers sideways, reaches for the wall. Gloria screams. Chloe takes the gap and darts for the door, but instead of surging forward, her legs begin to buckle like jelly under her, and she slumps to the floor. Panic sears through her stomach, but all she can do is lie helplessly on the floor, looking at the room sideways from the ground up. The room starts to spin and sway. She feels drunk, can't form thoughts. Everything has turned syrupy, thick, and moves in slow, sickening, waving motion.

Chloe tries to raise her hand but can't move it off the floor. She sees the dark shape of Adam Spengler getting onto his hands and knees, crawling, then pulling himself up into a standing position using the wall. He takes a carving knife out of his cargo pants pocket on the side. Gloria screams words. Chloe can't make sense of what she is screaming. With every ounce of her energy, Chloe tries to drag herself up off the floor. But she slumps back down.

IT'S CRIMINAL: The Chloe Cooper Story

The screen shows a brown-skinned, slight woman in her forties. Her dark hair is parted in the middle and shaped into a bun at the nape of her neck. She sits in a room with a view into a garden filled with flowers and a red-leafed tree.

The text at the bottom reads:

GABRIELA BAUTISTA, OLIVER BERGSON'S NANNY.

TRINITY OFF CAMERA: You worked for Gloria Bergson?

GABRIELA: I was Oliver's carer. I started when he was only three months old. He was like a son to me.

TRINITY OFF CAMERA: You were also the one who found the bodies—can you walk us through what happened that day, Gabriela? And please, take your time and stop if you need to.

Gabriela nods.

GABRIELA: Gloria told me she was going to be staying a little late at the gallery that Sunday, to see the work of a potential client. It was a common practice of hers. I gave Oliver his dinner, but by his bath and bedtime, his mother was still not home. This in itself was not terribly unusual. Sometimes her meetings turned into dinners out, or she entertained at her gallery, or went to shows, or stayed out some nights if her boyfriend—Oliver's father—was in town, that sort of thing. But she would usually phone to let me know. I tried to call her so she could say good night to Oliver, but I got voicemail. I thought maybe her cell battery had died or she was out of range or something, so I left a message and went to bed. When I got Oliver up in the morning, his mom was still not home.

Gabriela pauses.

GABRIELA: That's when I got worried. I phoned her again, and there was still no answer. So I fed Oliver his breakfast, dressed him—put on his puffy jacket and a knitted cap and scarf and gloves—it was a chilly Monday morning. And I got him into his stroller, and we walked down to the gallery. I . . .

Gabriela's voice fades. She inhales shakily.

TRINITY OFF CAMERA: Take your time, Gabriela. Start with what the neighborhood looked like that Monday morning as you and Oliver walked to the gallery.

GABRIELA: It was a clear sky. Wind blowing the clouds away. Very cold in the shadows of the buildings. Commuter traffic was starting to build. Some stores were opening. People hurrying to buses and down to the sea bus. Autumn leaves blowing off trees. Oliver—he was excited. He was reaching out his hands, saying, "Mommy, Mommy."

TRINITY OFF CAMERA: He knew you were going to his mom's gallery?

Gabriela nods.

GABRIELA: He loved to visit there—always got excited. He . . . when we reached the gallery, I saw the sign on the door said Closed. I felt very anxious at that point. I cupped my hand against the glass and peered inside. I couldn't see anything unusual. The back door of the showroom area that leads into the framing studio was still shut. She wasn't there. But . . . something felt wrong. I pushed Oliver around to the lane at the back, and when I reached the bay where the deliveries are made, I saw the rear door was slightly ajar. That made me frightened.

Gabriela hesitates.

GABRIELA: I sort of froze there in the alley with Oliver in his stroller, just staring at the door, not knowing what I should do. I glanced down the alley, looking for someone who could help me look inside, but there were no delivery guys—no one outside at that time yet. So I pushed Oliver up to the door, and left him parked there, outside, as I stepped up the stairs and pushed the door open wider. I couldn't see anything— it was dark. So I stepped inside and flicked on the light switch. The first thing I registered was a red handprint on the wall by the door and streaks of red on the floor. Like drag marks. It took my brain a few seconds to realize it might be blood. I—I . . . went from the utility room into the studio and clicked on the light in there, and . . .

Gabriela pales at the memory. She takes a few moments to regroup and compose herself.

GABRIELA: I'm sorry. I'm still triggered.

TRINITY OFF CAMERA: Are you okay to continue? To tell us what you saw?

Gabriela nods and inhales deeply.

GABRIELA: Blood. So much blood. Congealing. Streaks running down the back of the door that leads into the gallery showroom, streaming down from the handle, on the handle. And everything was in a mess. Like a hurricane had hit. Things all over the place—overturned stools, broken glass, a prosecco bottle lying on the floor, painted canvases on the floor and under the table, wet with blood and liquid. And—and there were two bodies. One lying in a pool of blood near the kitchen cabinets, and another—Gloria—in a crumpled heap at the bottom of the blood-streaked door. As though—as though she was trying to escape, but the door was locked.

IT'S CRIMINAL: The Chloe Cooper Story

CLIP FROM GLOBAL TV NEWS ARCHIVES DATED
MONDAY, SEPTEMBER 30, 2019

*A reporter in a mustard-colored wool coat stands at
the end of an urban block with a mike in her hand.
Behind her the road and sidewalks have been cordoned off with police tape that flaps in the breeze.*

REPORTER: We are near the Bergson Gallery in North Vancouver,
where the Lower Mainland's Integrated Homicide Unit—iHit—is
attending the scene of what a source close to the investigation says is
a violent double homicide that occurred sometime late on Sunday or
possibly during the early hours of this Monday morning.

> *The camera pans down the street. Marked police
> cars with flashing bar lights can be seen outside a
> building, along with a coroner's SUV and a white
> forensic identification unit van. The camera zeroes
> in on two detectives. One is an older woman in a*

black coat, who stands talking to a very tall man
with short white-blond hair.

REPORTER: No word yet on the identities of the victims, but the gallery is owned by Gloria Bergson, a local single mother of a two-year-old boy. It was the boy's nanny who made the gruesome discovery earlier this morning. An iHit spokesperson is expected to hold a news conference later today. Meanwhile, the source close to the investigation tells me two detectives from the Greater Vancouver Police Department—Detectives Maeve Havers and Axel Pederson— have joined the iHit team. Havers and Pederson, both with the GVPD's Major Crimes Unit, are also currently investigating the Jet Ski hit-and-run fatality that occurred on Jerrin Bay.

GLOBAL TV ANCHOR: Is there any indication that the gallery homicides and the Jerrin Bay death are linked?

REPORTER: Nothing at this point, but we will continue to bring our viewers breaking news as we receive more information throughout the day.

The screen fades to show Detective Maeve Havers
in a chair.

MAEVE: It wasn't our jurisdiction. North Vancouver is the RCMP's—or Royal Canadian Mounted Police's—responsibility. But when I heard the news and saw the location—Bergson Gallery—it struck a note. When we first visited Chloe Cooper's apartment, she told me that Dr. Adam Spengler was having an affair with a woman named Gloria Bergson who runs Bergson Gallery in North Vancouver, and she claimed at the time that Dr. Spengler planned to leave his wife for this woman. She said she believed it was Spengler on that Jet Ski, trying to kill his wife.

I immediately contacted the lead investigator in the gallery homicide case, informed him the owner of the gallery, Gloria Bergson, had come up in the course of our Jerrin Bay death investigation. When my partner and I arrived at the gallery, we learned there were two victims, both deceased. There was evidence of a violent altercation—stabbing and blunt-force trauma. A bloody carving knife was left at the scene, and there was no sign of forced entry. There was also clear evidence a third person was present at the time of the attack.

First impressions were that the assault and deaths occurred on Sunday evening or night, after the gallery closed for the day—the CLOSED sign on the door was turned to face the street. Identities of the two victims were not confirmed at that point, but it was assumed one of the slain bodies belonged to Gloria Bergson. There was ID found on the second body, and the lead investigator informed me they were in the process of trying to locate next of kin for a formal identification. It was at that point it became a joint investigation, and my partner—Axel Pederson—and I were tasked with the job of informing next of kin once located.

IT'S CRIMINAL: The Chloe Cooper Story

The screen shows a tall, well-built, dark-haired actor playing Dr. Adam Spengler. He wears camouflage cargo pants, a dark, baggy hoodie, and running shoes. A belt bag loops across his chest. He stands under a sign that says MAIN STREET. An Uber pulls up, and he climbs into the car. Text at the bottom of the screen says:

FICTIONALIZED REENACTMENT OF THE HOURS LEADING UP TO THE BRUTAL GALLERY DEATHS, SUNDAY, SEPTEMBER 29, 2019.

TRINITY SCOTT VOICE-OVER: From evidence obtained throughout the course of the double-homicide investigation and subsequent court testimony, we have been able to dial back in time to show a reenactment of Dr. Adam Spengler's movements prior to the event. From the iHit interview with Adam's Uber driver, we know Adam was picked up on Main, one block up from his house, early on the morning of the murders.

The screen fades to show the interior of an Uber vehicle. The actor playing Adam Spengler gives his destination as the cancer agency attached to Vancouver General Hospital.

DRIVER: You having a good day?

ADAM: Had better. Here, stop outside the center here. And can you wait? I'll be a few minutes.

DRIVER: It's your dollar, sir.

Adam glances down the street, checking to see whether anyone notices him. He then hurries into the building. Several minutes later he exits. The Uber driver notices his passenger's hand hovering nervously over his belt bag, as though there is something of high value in there—something acquired in the medical building. Adam climbs back into the Uber and quickly instructs the driver to deliver him to an address near Narek Tigran's estate in Eagle Cove.

DRIVER AS HE ENTERS EAGLE COVE: Fancy neighborhood. Never driven a client down this way.

ADAM: [Mumbles something unintelligible]

DRIVER: You live down here?

ADAM: No.

DRIVER: Work here?

ADAM: Yeah. Uh—maintenance.

DRIVER: Must be a good gig.

ADAM: Here, you can stop here.

The driver pulls over on the street lined with dense conifers. Adam pays in cash. He exits the Uber and waits for the car to leave and round the corner before he jogs a short distance to Narek's driveway. He stops and glances furtively down the street, as though checking to see if anyone has seen him. He then jogs down the long driveway to the four-vehicle garage. Breathing hard, he removes a set of keys from his pocket and unlocks and opens one of the garage doors.

Inside are a small red Corvette, a black Hummer that Narek has been meaning to off-load for years, a black Cadillac Escalade, and a white utility van used mostly by Narek's estate staff.

Adam drops to his haunches behind the van. He opens a small container he brought with him, and he greases up the plates so the alphanumeric sequence is obscured from CCTV cameras. He climbs into the van, finds the key fob in the glove compartment, and starts the vehicle. He checks the gas. The tank is full.

He reverses the van out, closes the garage door, and drives back across the bridge toward Crow's Point. He passes his house and begins searching for street parking close to the Jerrin Beach lot. He does

*not enter the beach parking lot itself by choice. He
locates a spot on the street and eases the van into it.*

*Adam climbs out, locks the van. For a moment
he stands in shadows as he scans the street for possible witnesses. When he's certain the coast is clear,
he crouches down and places the fob up inside the
rear wheel hub. Adam comes erect, checks the time.
He pulls his cap down low over his brow and walks
briskly home via a back route.*

TRINITY VOICE-OVER: In Adam's belt bag he carries a syringe and
several vials of Ketalar, or ketamine hydrochloride. He picked them up
at the cancer agency. It's a drug familiar to the surgeon. Later in the day
he will call another Uber and ask to be dropped off one block down
from the Bergson Gallery. He doesn't need a vehicle of his own, because
the plan is to return home with Jemma once it's all over.

AFTER THE MURDERS

Chloe tries to open her eyes, can't. She's floating, dizzy. Detached from her body. Dissociated from place or time. Has she been dreaming? She tries again. Her lids are thick and crusted, but she sees a slit of light. Bright. Hurts. She shuts her eyes again as she struggles to figure out whether it's day or night, and where she is. She's on her back—is she in her bed? She moves her left hand, feels the cold hardness of a bare floor beneath her.

Panic licks through her tummy.

She tries to move her right hand. Pain sears through her palm as something sticky slides out of her hand. It clatters along the floor. She tastes blood in her mouth. She explores her lips with the tip of her tongue—her bottom lip is swollen fat, slit open. Panic licks more fiercely. Her head thuds with pain in time with the beat of her heart as a wave of nausea washes up through her chest. She tries to lie absolutely dead still for a moment, fighting to not throw up, just listening. Feeling. She hears faraway sirens and an almost indiscernible soft hum from fluorescent lighting. Confusion tips her panic toward terror as she is seized with a sense that something very, very bad just happened.

Move, Chloe. Move. Urgent. Danger. Got to get to safety.

She lifts her throbbing right hand in front of her face and opens her eyes again to peer at it. Her palm is sliced open. Bleeding. She folds her hand into a ball. Pain mushrooms and rolls up her arm. Her upper arm, she realizes, is stiff—as though she's been punched there. Carefully

Chloe rolls onto her side and raises her head. The world sways, then comes into blurry focus. She's in a room. Lights on. She discerns a dark shape through the legs of a trestle table. Confusion spins her head again. She shuts her eyes once more, steadies her breathing, tries again.

This time she identifies the form. A man. Slumped on the floor against kitchen cabinets on the other end of the room. Limbs at odd angles. Blood pools under him. Black hair. Large man.

A bolt of memory strikes her.

Adam.

Shock slices across her throat. Her heart starts to race. She scrambles onto all fours, sliding in blood. Her own blood? Sticky. Gelatinous. Still vaguely warm.

Desperation, tears sear into her eyes.

On hands and knees she crawls closer to Adam. He's curled in a fetal position, as though clutching his belly. Another memory slashes through her. A weapon in his hand. Coming at her. The sound of screaming. Hers? Someone else's? In her mind she sees a blade. She recalls striking at someone.

She glances back to the area where she was lying. A knife rests in a puddle of blood. A big kitchen carving knife. Black hilt. That's what was in her hand?

A sob of desperation shudders through her body as she reaches up to grasp the edge of the tabletop. She struggles to pull herself into a standing position, but her feet slip in blood and some other liquid, and they slide out from under her. She crashes back down to the wet floor. She smells alcohol—sour wine—and the blood. Reminds her of the meaty smell of a butcher's shop her mom once took her into when she was little. Chloe realizes that she's lying among her own canvases—paintings of swimmers and houses. Saturated. Destroyed. Her own signature at the bottom right of her swimmer canvas leers out at her. *Chloe Cooper.*

Another shard of shattered memory cuts through her. Bubbles. Prosecco. Two glasses . . . *Gloria.* She's in Gloria's gallery. Where is

Gloria—what happened? Panic deepens into a raw primal terror. She pulls herself upright and this time manages to stand, bracing on the table, wobbling. Her gaze scans the room.

The place has been trashed. The prosecco flutes are broken. Glass shards shine among the blood on the floor. Stools lie on their sides. Blood streaks down the white door that leads into the gallery showroom. That's when Chloe sees her—Gloria. In a loose-limbed heap on the floor below the blood and handprints streaking down the door.

What happened, Chloe? Think! Remember! What did you do?

She was showing Gloria her art. Adam arrived. Threatening. She remembers feeling a surge of uncontrollable rage and terror. Tears slide down her face. She can't remember what happened next, what she did.

She stumbles over to Gloria and slides down to her knees. She moves Gloria's hair away from her face. Dead eyes stare at nothing. A sob racks through Chloe. She feels for a pulse. Gloria's neck is cold. Very cold. There is no life.

Chloe scrambles on all fours to Adam. She reaches for his shoulder and pulls him over. He slumps onto his back. She jumps as his eyes, glassy, stare at her. His jaw hangs open, slack. Gritting her teeth, she feels the surgeon's neck with her fingertips. No pulse. His body is cold.

Focus, Chloe. Think. You're in the gallery. With two dead lovers. Adulterers. You came here . . . for Jemma. To ask questions to help Jemma.

Another memory slinks into Chloe's consciousness. She hears Jemma's voice in a distant part of her mind.

There's an alley behind the gallery with loading bays. If you exit via the back of the building, turn left into the alley, and go to the end where it intersects with the street, I'll be waiting right there.

Chloe stumbles toward the door that leads into the rear vestibule area. Her coat is there. On a hook near the door. She takes it off the hook, sways, and steadies herself against the wall with her injured hand. With great effort she then maneuvers her arms into the sleeves of her coat. To keep from fainting, she slides her hand along the wall as she makes her way toward the back door.

The door is slightly ajar.

She slips out.

It's night outside. Very dark. A fine mist of rain kisses her face. The air is fresh, mercifully cool. Chloe stands for a moment, orienting herself, trying to breathe.

The alley is silent. Save for a raccoon near the opposite wall. It stops to study her. As the animal's eyes meet hers, Chloe feels as though she's slipped into a fantastical, dark netherworld. A Grimm's fairy tale where the protagonist ends up being devoured by a wolf. The raccoon turns and trundles silently into blackness.

. . . go to the end where it intersects with the street, I'll be waiting right there.

Using her phone as a flashlight, Chloe moves to the left and staggers to the end of the lane. Safety waits for her there.

But when Chloe reaches the bay in front of a brick wall, it's empty. Another faraway siren sounds in the city somewhere. A truck rumbles down the road nearby. She starts to shiver. Is her memory of Jemma picking her up even real? Did she really say she'd wait for Chloe here? Did she actually park and wait, and when Chloe didn't arrive, she went home?

Chloe peers at her phone. It's just after 2:00 a.m. She lurches toward the rear wall, leans her back against the wet bricks, and slides down to the cracked paving. She huddles there, shaking. The drizzle turns colder, more insistent. She's too terrified, too confused to call 911. She leans forward and peeks back down the alley—she can't even see the gallery exit from here. She thinks of the dead couple inside, lying in blood and broken glass, pools of blood. Chloe opens her phone again. The battery is almost dead.

She calls the only person she can think of.

It rings.

"Hello? Chloe?"

The sound of Stavros's kind voice—the memory of his warm, enveloping hug—sends a guttural sob up from her belly into her throat. Tears pool in her eyes.

"Chloe? Is that you? Is everything all right?"

"I—I need help. Stavros. Please help me. I—I need you to come get me."

AFTER THE MURDERS

Chloe hears tires crackling on the wet paving—a car approaching. She huddles tighter against the brick wall in the loading bay. The slight overhang on the roof high up is not protecting her from the misty sheets of rain, and her teeth chatter as she shivers uncontrollably from cold and shock. Monsters prowl along the shadowy periphery of her mind, darting in, reaching for her, grasping, almost becoming visible, and then they duck back into dark unconsciousness. She has a sense they're laughing at her from the shadows, that they are memories trying to surface but are too terrifying to be allowed fully in.

She hears the car turning slowly into the alley. It begins to creep closer. Rain glints in headlights. The car is a dark metallic green—Stavros's old Pontiac Sunfire from the nineties. She gets unsteadily to her feet as it comes to a stop.

He gets out immediately. "Chloe. Shit. What's going on—your face. Lip. Christ, you're bleeding. What in the hell happened?"

"I—I got hit. Stavros. Mugged."

"How—I mean, what are you even doing out this way?"

"Can you please drive me away?"

"Come, come get in." He takes her arm and helps her toward the passenger side. She winces in pain, but he's gentle. He opens the passenger door. "Can you manage? Can you get in? Where do you hurt? Oh man, look at your hand."

He quickly shuts the door behind her and climbs into the driver's side. It's warm inside. A cocoon. Smells like him. That woodsy and mint scent from those awful things he chews all the time. Weird-looking Stavros with his overly long, narrow face, lanky legs, big feet, bouncy gait never looked so welcome to Chloe.

He regards her with the engine and heater running. She shudders. "Can you drive? Go. Now. Please, Stavros?"

He shrugs out of his jacket, drapes it around her shoulders. His body warmth—still trapped in it—envelops her.

"You need to buckle up, Chlo."

But her hands are shaking too hard to get the metal end into the receptacle. He leans over and does it for her. He puts his car in gear. "We're going to the Lions Gate ER. It's just a few blocks away."

"No! No, please, just drive."

"Chloe, you're injured. That hand needs medical attention, and we need to call the cops to report the mugging."

"No. No." She reaches for the handle, opens the door.

"Christ, stop, Chloe. Just close the damn door."

She wavers.

"Close it, Chloe."

"I'm not going to the ER. No police."

Consternation creases his face. "Okay, okay. No ER. No cops. I—I'll drive a bit. You can warm up. We can talk, figure out what to do."

They start to drive. He navigates through the quieter side streets, and Chloe realizes he's heading north. Toward the bridge. He's taking her home.

"Not this way."

"I'm taking you back to your—"

She panics. "*Please*, Stavros, I beg you. Just drive away. Far away."

"Why?"

"I—I need to go away."

"Where to?"

"I don't know. Away from the city. I've got to get away. Far away . . ." Her words die on her lips as some snippet of memory hearkens back to her childhood. She's inside an old car. Her mother driving. Saying, *Got to get away, Zoe. Far away from this place. He'll try to come after us . . . he's coming after us.* Her mother is crying, shaking, as she fists the wheel of the old car that smells of cigarettes and stale beer.

The memory triggers something fundamental at Chloe's unconscious core. Flee. Run. Bad things after them. A man. Who has done terrible, heinous things. Palest ice-blue eyes. Black hair. Big man. Cunning man. Evil man.

Adam?

Stavros turns into a side street, drives around the block, then heads east, toward the other bridge that will feed them onto a highway and eventually lead them all the way out of the sprawling metropolis of the Lower Mainland and up into a twisting pass through the mountains. Instantly Chloe feels relief, and it eases her panic. She's also getting warmer. Suddenly she's sleepy—so incredibly, deeply bone tired. She begins to nod off, wrapped in the comfort and safety of Stavros's jacket. He's silent as he drives, and he keeps glancing at her. Worried. Horrified, perhaps. Maybe he's afraid she's done something terrible.

After they cross the Second Narrows and make it through the sprawl and are heading through a more rural area toward the small town of Hope, she dozes off. As she does, more memories awaken, rise, start knocking, trying to get in.

"Chloe," he says finally, rousing her. "What happened?"

"I was mugged," she says again.

"By who?"

"A man. He had a hoodie. Tall. He had . . . a knife. He took my wallet."

He throws her a glance. Streetlights and headlights from the odd passing car cast a sickly glow over his face. "Good thing you didn't have your phone in your purse."

He says it like he's unsure whether to believe her.

She realizes her wallet is zipped into the side compartment of her portfolio case that lies under the table at the gallery. The only reason she still has her phone on her is because she slid it into her pocket after texting Jemma. She wonders what happened to Jemma. Is she worried that her husband has not come home?

What about Gloria's little boy? Oliver. He has no mommy now.

God help you, Chloe, what in heaven's name did you do to them?

She clenches her teeth and balls her hands into fists, ignoring the screaming pain in the palm of her right hand. A defensive carapace hardens around her. Compartments go up inside her mind—separate rooms of mental concrete where she can park and lock away uncomfortable thoughts or things that might or might not be memories. It was these mental firewalls that started to crumble the night her mother died, and when she was trapped with Adam Spengler in the elevator, going down, down, down. Something about him, his eyes, pulled a trigger, and horrible memories started to leak out of the cracks between her brain compartments.

She opens her hand and glances at her cut palm. The wound looks black in the darkened interior of the Pontiac. "My phone was in my coat pocket," she says softly. "Mom always said I should keep my mobile on my person in case I was attacked, or needed to drop my purse and run or something."

Stavros casts another sharp glance her way.

"What were you doing in North Vancouver, in that alley?" he asks.

She closes her eyes, trying to replay it all. Jemma picking her up. In the white van. Dressed wrong. Walking into the beautiful gallery. Feeling as though her whole life was shifting. Then Adam . . . she inhales shakily as the memory dissolves into a billion little gray pixels.

"I was showing a gallery owner my art."

He looks askance at her. Like he can't believe someone would want to see her art.

"You did say I had talent, Stavros. Why should it appear so outlandish that someone might want to see more of my work?"

"Of course you're talented, Chlo. I was just—"

"Thinking it was out of my reach? A fantasy? A fabrication? Well, it wasn't. A woman who owns a gallery and is an art dealer came into the Beach House and asked me who the creator of the painting Bill hung in the entrance was. She also said it reminded her of a famous Edward Hopper work. So obviously my art does remind people of his pieces. And she gave me her card, and I called her. And I went in. And when I came out in the alley, I was attacked." She's silent awhile. "I think that's what happened," she says softly. "I—I don't really remember exactly."

"It's okay, Chloe. You must have taken a bad knock on the head. It could come back to you later, but this is why you should see a medical professional. What if you have a concussion? And you really should file a police report. If there's a mugger out there assaulting women, he could hurt someone else. You need to help stop that from happening."

She says nothing, just stares ahead into the few oncoming lights and darkness as the electric glow of the city fades behind them.

When she sees a road sign pointing the way to Hope, she stops clenching her teeth. Her muscles soften a tiny bit. She feels sleepy again.

After a long while of driving, Stavros says, "Did she like your work, then, this dealer?"

Chloe startles awake. Confusion, dissonance, swirls through her brain. She tries to bring reality back into focus. He waits.

"Yes." She offers nothing more.

A few moments later, Stavros says, "So, did she offer to hang some pieces in her gallery?"

Chloe's heart begins to race again. She strains to piece all the bits together: the nice feeling Gloria gave her, how much she loved Chloe's work, the welcome aura in the gorgeous gallery with all those fabulous pieces. She remembers Jemma's texts.

How are you doing? Everything okay?

NO RUSH! Just want to nip out for a coffee and was wondering
if I had time—if you are still going to be a while?

She was supposed to be digging up information, asking Gloria personal questions. That's why Jemma suggested she take Gloria her art.
Now that she's here, driving away in Stavros's car—Jemma's request feels
strange. Wrong. Sweat prickles across Chloe's lip.

"I think so," she says softly. "I think she really liked my work."

"You think? Or did she say?"

"She said—" An image slices across her mind—her canvases on the
floor, lying in blood and spilled prosecco and broken glass. Another
image rides on the back of the first—Gloria's body slumped at the base
of the door, blood streaking down from the handle. Chloe remembers
coming conscious, a bloody knife falling out of her hand.

"Stavros," she whispers as tears slide down her face and sting into
her cut lip. "I—I can't really remember at all what happened."

"Perhaps we should find an ER now, and talk to the police."

"I'd rather you stop the car and let me out."

He shoots her a fast glance, then looks at his dash. "I tell you what.
I need gas. There's a station in Hope up ahead. We'll pull in there."

"I'd rather we didn't stop."

"If we keep driving past Hope, there's no gas station again for miles.
I do have to fuel up. And we do, too—some snacks, something warm
to drink. You can stay in the car. You'll be safe."

She studies his odd profile. She believes him.

"Thank you, Stavros."

He inhales deeply. Clearly troubled, he flexes his hand on the wheel.
Gently he says, "Where is Brodie, Chloe?"

Panic pierces back into her heart. Her breathing becomes rapid.
"He—he's at home. He needs to go outside. He'll be—"

"It's okay. I'll call my uncle George on speakerphone and ask him to
go fetch Brodie. He knows Brodie, and how to look after him. Okay?"

"Okay. Thank you, Stavros. There are tins of dog food in the kitchen cupboard. George will need the code for the lockbox—there's a key inside that my mom's carers used."

"Right, what's the code?"

She can't recall. Her memory is completely funky. She's having trouble with the simplest of mental things.

He waits.

Slowly it comes to her—images of numbers swirling in her head, arranging and rearranging themselves. She recites the same code she called out to George when the ambulance came. Stavros phones George, who sounds worried because it's so very late. Stavros tells him everything is okay. He will call George again later and explain.

They enter a valley, and mist begins to sift over the highways, and the temperature drops. Their headlights illuminate a green sign with white letters that announces they are arriving into Hope.

She's not certain whether she's been here before. But she knows Hope is where they filmed *Rambo* many years ago. And he was a fugitive who went into the mountains, and it feels right. Mist thickens. When they see the bright neon sign of a gas station up ahead, nestled in the lee of a mountain, Stavros engages the indicator. It *tick tock tick tocks* in the quietness, and he turns off the highway.

AFTER THE MURDERS

September 30, 2019

Jemma is roused from the groggy depths of medicated sleep by her dogs' barking. Begrudgingly she surfaces to hear the *ding dong dinging* of the doorbell and her dogs barking more frantically. She blinks, momentarily confused. *What time, what day is it?* She takes a second to register the brightness outside the window, the blueness of a clear sky. Thanks to Adam they still have no blinds.

Adam?

She stretches her hand to his side of the bed. Empty. Her pulse kicks. She sits bolt upright. On his side the sheets are still smooth, the pillow unwrinkled. A flick of dread shoots through her belly.

He never did come home last night. She really is alone now.

The doorbell rings again and a loud knocking starts. Jemma swings her legs over the side of the bed and glances at the bedside clock. The red digital numbers reveal it's 10:28 a.m. Alarm flares through her. Her gaze shoots to the container of pills beside the clock.

How many sleeping pills did I take? Why am I so fuzzy and unable to move?

An image hits her—Chloe walking away from the white van with that cumbersome portfolio at her side, and disappearing into the gallery. Butterflies skitter through Jemma's stomach. She lurches up and lunges for the bedroom window that looks out over the laneway. In the street, parked across their driveway, is a familiar brown, unmarked sedan. She grabs her dressing gown off the chair and hurries barefoot into the passage as she pushes her arms into the silky sleeves. She quickly descends the stairs as she belts her robe. Boo and Sweetie are going berserk at the back door.

Jemma orders her dogs to go sit in their beds. They remain agitated but obey—thanks to months of private dog training. She smooths back her hair with her left hand as she opens the door with her right. Air, cool and fresh, drafts into her home.

Detective Maeve Havers stands there in a shapeless raincoat, a grim expression on her face.

"Detective Havers," Jemma says as nerves coil and boil through her. "Sorry, I—I was still asleep. What can I do for you?"

The detective's features remain inscrutable. Jemma leans forward and peers out the door in search of her partner. Axel Pederson is once more peeping into the garage windows, on the side where Adam parks his Tesla.

Detective Havers says, "Can we come in, please, Mrs. Spengler?"

"I've just woken up. I know it's late, but I had a headache and took medication, so—"

"We need to talk to you, Mrs. Spengler. I'm afraid we have some bad news."

"What news?"

"Please. Can we step inside?"

Jemma regards her as fear rises in her chest. She thinks of Adam's empty side of the bed. Of their plan. Her plan. Could something have gone wrong? "I—sure, come in." She steps back and holds out her hand. "Take a seat in the living room."

Pederson joins Havers, and together they head into her living room, wearing their heavy, wet shoes. Jemma follows and seats herself gingerly on the edge of a chair as the cops lower themselves to the sofa.

Carefully, hesitatingly, she asks, "Is this about Adam? He—he didn't come home last night."

"I'm afraid so, Mrs. Spengler. Your husband has been found deceased at an art gallery in North Vancouver."

A strange noise escapes her as her body reacts viscerally. Instantly her throat turns dry. "What . . . where? How?"

"The Bergson Gallery. There is evidence of a violent altercation. There will be a postmortem to determine cause of death, but it appears your husband was stabbed, Mrs. Spengler. Another person was also stabbed and died at the scene."

"W-who?"

"Identity has not been officially confirmed, but we believe the second victim is Gloria Bergson, the gallery owner."

Jemma feels lightheaded. She reaches for the arm of the sofa to steady herself. Her heart beats so fast she fears she'll pass out. "Are—are you sure? That it's Adam? I—he can't possibly be dead."

"A wallet with his credit cards and his hospital ID card with a photograph was found on the body. We will, however, need you to make a formal identification as well."

Jemma stares at their faces. They watch her intently in return. Her dogs creep over to her bare feet. She bends down and draws them both up onto her lap for comfort. Cuddling them close, she says, "I—I don't understand. What happened?"

Calmly, Detective Havers says, "An investigation into the fatal assaults is underway. There is a lot of evidence at the scene to work through, but we're not making any assumptions at this point."

"Do you know Gloria Bergson?" Detective Pederson asks.

Jemma reaches into her robe pocket for a tissue and blows her nose. "Adam was—I learned recently he's been having an affair with Gloria Bergson. They have a child." Jemma can't help the tears that suddenly slide down her cheeks at the bite of sharp, raw pain—the fact Gloria has a child and she does not and cannot ever make a baby again. That Oliver is Adam's, and not hers. That her husband is dead.

"Were you aware your husband went to the gallery yesterday?" Pederson asks.

272

She shakes her head and inhales deeply. "Adam told me yesterday our marriage was over. Our marriage of thirty-four years. Done, just like that. He said he was leaving me for Gloria and his son. That he no longer loved me. That our union had been loveless and empty for him for years. I—he left the house yesterday, and he said I should call a friend. He told me he'd come back later to collect some of his things. He—they have a house. Him, Gloria, and Oliver. In North Van. He bought it for her some time back. Magnolia Lane. I only recently learned about it."

"I'm so sorry, Mrs. Spengler," Havers says.

Pederson says, "I imagine learning of their affair made you very angry?"

Her gaze flares to his. "What?"

"Your husband leaving you for another woman—it must have enraged you."

Her jaw drops. She glares at him. "How *dare* you," she whispers. "What in the hell are you insinuating?"

Silence.

"How would *you* feel, Detective?" she asks. "Of course I was angry. As well as deeply, desperately, crushingly hurt and utterly broken. I tried to argue, to reason with him. I pleaded, got mad, yelled. All of it. But he walked out." She blows her nose again.

"What time was this?" Pederson asks.

"Around lunchtime yesterday. I didn't check the time exactly. I was a mess."

He makes a note in his little book. "And what did you do after he left?"

"I went for a long walk along the beach path with my dogs. Trying to clear my head enough to process it all. Then I came home, opened a bottle of wine. Then another. Drank far too much. Drunk cried, and then took sleeping pills."

"You didn't call anyone?"

273

"I—I wasn't even prepared to admit it to myself. I thought maybe he'd still come back to me by morning." She swipes away tears. "I felt humiliated. Discarded. Ashamed."

"And what time did you return from your walk?" Pederson asks.

"Are you seriously asking me this—like I could have—"

"Just procedure, Mrs. Spengler," Havers interjects smoothly, still without a hint of emotion—no tell, no clue, no giveaway as to what she's thinking. An old pro.

"It was about five, I think."

"Did you walk or drive to the beach?" Pederson asks.

"I drove."

"Where did you park?"

"At the Jerrin Beach lot."

"Pay parking?"

"Yes."

"So you have a receipt, with the time stamp?" Pederson asks, glancing up from his notes.

"I paid with the app."

"So you have the app history on your phone?"

She gets up, goes to her purse on the counter, and takes out her phone. She opens the app and shows Pederson. "I paid the rate for the full day. If you stay more than two hours, it starts to cost as much as the full day anyway."

He studies her phone screen, nods, and makes another note in his pad. Jemma returns to her chair.

"So you were home alone for the rest of the evening, and during the night?" Detective Havers asks.

She blows her nose again, nods.

"No one to vouch for—"

"No, no one," she snaps. "Unless someone saw me through these damn windows without blinds—" She stops suddenly and glances out the window toward the building across the alley. "You could go ask her. The neighborhood snoop. She watches us from up there on the third floor with binoculars. She's been stalking Adam, and he told me he noticed her following him on a few occasions. Go ask her."

Maeve Havers studies Jemma, then glances toward the window. "You mean Chloe Cooper?" she asks.

"So you do know her?" Jemma says.

Havers says, "Have you met Ms. Cooper?"

"I made the mistake of having her dog sit for me. I caught her on our doggy cams snooping around our house while I was away, fiddling in Adam's jacket pockets, putting things in them, opening our drawers, going through our things. She went through our laundry basket, even. And she took photos of all the rooms in our home, God knows why."

"What kinds of things did she put in your husband's pockets?" Pederson asks.

"Napkins from the restaurant where she works. With lipstick on them. And a note. I—I think somehow she knew Adam was having the affair with Gloria and wanted me to find out."

The cops exchange a quick glance. Jemma feels uneasy. She shifts in her chair and blows her nose again.

"Has this cam footage of Chloe Cooper snooping around inside your house been saved?" Havers asks.

"Yes. I can show you, or give you a copy."

Pederson asks, "Can you think of anyone who might want to harm your husband, Mrs. Spengler?"

"You can ask Chloe Cooper that, too. The freak."

"What do you mean?" Havers says.

"I don't think she was impressed that Adam was having an affair. When I met with her to discuss the dog sitting, she said she hated—detested—all cheats and liars and adulterers. At the time I was unsure what she was referring to."

Pederson says, "From outside your house it appears that your husband's Tesla is still parked inside the garage."

"He left in an Uber. He'd had something to drink with lunch, and I presume he was going out to drink more, with her. Or alone. I don't know."

"Can we take a look in the garage?" Pederson asks.

She gets up, goes to the door that leads into the garage, and opens it. "Be my guests."

Jemma folds her arms and stands in the doorway while the detectives walk around the Tesla. Anxiety whispers through her as she watches Havers cup her hand against the glass and peer into the back window.

"There are bags on the back seat," Havers says. "Mind if we take a look?"

Jemma shrugs, but her heart beats fast. "Go ahead."

Havers opens the car door. She calls Pederson over and shows him a large green gym bag with its zipper open.

Jemma hears Havers say quietly to her partner, "Wet suit. Booties. Hood. Gloves. Goggles. And these." She points to two Idaho license plates, plus the bunch of clearly marked keys to Narek's estate.

Havers glances at Jemma. "There's a bunch of keys with his belongings in the back. Do you know what they are for?"

She moistens her lips and says carefully, "Narek Tigran's estate on the North Shore, across the Burrard. He's an old friend of Adam's, and he asked Adam to keep an eye on his property while he's away on business."

AFTER THE MURDERS

Chloe stirs awake in the midst of a nightmare. For a few moments she hangs there—in that vague and syrupy state of altered perception between dead sleep and wakefulness. She hears it again—her mother's voice—coming from the depths of a place she can't identify.

Zoe, quick. He's coming. Get inside—in there. Safe cave.

But it's not a cave.

It's a closet with a prickly blanket inside. She remembers it now. Or does she? Is she still dreaming? She slips deeper into the dream again.

A closet with a folding door. The doors have louvered slats she can peer out of. Her mother pushes her inside, sits her down in the corner, puts small headphones on her head. Chloe feels the Walkman clutched in her hands. Her mother takes her finger and guides it to press PLAY. A lyrical, soothing voice comes through the headphones and fills her head. "Once upon a time, there was a selkie in a land where the grass was green as emeralds . . ." Her mother places the blanket over Chloe's head, and now she's truly in a cave. A prickly, hot one. Just her and the selkie story wrapped together. She can't see through the closet slats now, can't see what he's doing to her mother. She just lets her mind go to the land where the grass is green as emeralds and the ocean heaves with storm-gray waves crested with white foam, and the selkie leaves her skin on the rocks . . .

Chloe comes awake fully. She blinks. There is pain in her upper arm and her hand. She's in a room and it's dark. Suddenly it hits her— Stavros. The gallery. Bodies. Blood. She jerks upright in bed. Her heart races as her gaze shoots around the room. She's in a double bed. Beneath the window is a sofa piled with a rumpled blanket and pillows where Stavros slept. She recalls how they pulled into the motel parking lot after the gas station because Stavros said he was tired, and it wasn't safe to drive this way. He got them a room while she waited in the Pontiac. She made him promise not to give the motel person her name. He wanted to know why, but when she insisted, he agreed. Stavros is not in the room now. A thin slit of light shines between a gap in the blackout curtains. Chloe glances at the clock. Almost 10:30 a.m.

She pushes back the covers and realizes she's in a T-shirt with panties. How embarrassing. She can't let Stavros see her like this. She wraps the bedsheet around her waist and starts toward the bathroom. When she passes the counter on which the TV stands, she sees a note. Chloe picks it up.

Gone to find us some breakfast and decent coffee. Back soon.

Stavros.

She stumbles to the bathroom, shuts the door, and looks in the mirror. The yellow light above the mirror makes her look sallow and ghostly and awfully ugly with her fat, swollen mouth. She leans forward and presses a finger to the cut on her lower lip. It cracks open and starts to bleed again. She wads up toilet paper and presses it to her mouth to stop the blood.

Holding the wad on her mouth, Chloe sits on top of the toilet seat for a while, trying to sort out the disjointed shards of memories slashing through her head. Fear rises in her chest. She really can't remember what she did at the gallery.

She recalls only the bloody knife in her hand when she came round lying on the floor. And she remembers the hate and rage that overcame her when Adam walked into the gallery and surprised her.

Maybe if she takes a shower and cleans herself up, things will come back to her.

She turns on the shower, and while she waits for the water to get hot, she examines her cut hand. It's not too deep, but it's swelling and turning red around the edges. She's going to need some disinfectant. She looks into the mirror and angles her body slightly to examine her upper arm. There's a red mark. The skin around the mark is swollen, too. She presses it tentatively with her fingertips. It feels as though she was punched, but as she leans closer, she sees a pinprick of a mark. She frowns as another memory tries to get through, but can't.

Chloe climbs into the shower and allows the water to sluice over her head as hot as she can stand it. As the steam boils up around her, she sees Adam in her mind again. Entering the gallery. He comes at her with something in his hand as she tries to escape.

She goes dead still. *It was a syringe.*

A noise sounds on the other side of the bathroom door. Chloe quickly turns off the water and listens. She hears the sound of the television. Stavros is back. She pulls back the shower curtain, climbs onto the bath mat, and towels herself off carefully so as not to hurt her injured hand.

Chloe pulls her T-shirt and panties back on, wraps a towel around her waist, hesitates, then reaches for the door handle. Nervously she exits the bathroom. Stavros has drawn back the drapes to reveal a bright, clear day, and she sees his Pontiac parked outside their window in the motel parking lot. She smells coffee, and something sweet and buttery that makes her mouth water. Stavros has his back turned to her. The TV is on loud, and he hasn't heard her come out of the bathroom. The remote is in his hand. He's riveted to the screen as the words BREAKING NEWS run in a banner across the bottom. The footage shows a reporter in a mustard-colored coat. Behind the reporter yellow police tape flaps across a street that Chloe recognizes—it's where the gallery is. Fear closes a hand around her throat and squeezes.

The reporter says, "Police have still not released the identities of the two victims killed in what appears to be a violent and bloody assault at the well-known Bergson Gallery in North Vancouver. A source close to the investigation has confirmed it was Gloria Bergson's nanny who made the shocking discovery early this morning when she went to the gallery with Bergson's young son after his mother did not come home."

A noise escapes Chloe's throat. Stavros spins around in surprise. He stares at Chloe, his mouth open and his eyes wide with horror. She wills herself to speak, to utter something—anything—that will remove that fright and disgust from his face. His fear. Of *her*.

"What have you done, Chloe?" he whispers.

She steps toward him.

But he moves sharply backward, raising both hands in front of him, the remote in one, as though it's a weapon he might brandish to ward her off. His other hand goes for his cell in his pocket.

"Leave your phone, Stavros," she says.

But he slides it out of his pocket.

"Don't do it, Stavros—do not call anyone," Chloe says quietly as she reaches behind her, fingering the surface of a cabinet for something heavy. Just as she did in the gallery. Her fingers touch a stone ashtray. She hooks it with her middle finger and inches it closer, until she can curl her hand around it.

IT'S CRIMINAL: The Chloe Cooper Story

The screen shows George Vasilou in his barber's chair
with his hand clasped over the evil eye pendant at his
neck. His dark eyes are liquid. He stares at the painting on the opposite wall.

TRINITY OFF CAMERA: When did you first hear the news?

GEORGE: On the Monday morning after the murders. I saw on the
TV about the gallery killings. Two people dead. Still no names released.
Later that day reporters started talking about a third person who fled
the scene. By Monday evening the bodies were identified on the news as
being Gloria Bergson and Dr. Adam Spengler. And a massive hunt for
the third person was initiated. Police said on the news they wanted to
question a woman named Chloe Cooper in connection with the violent
homicides. They said anyone who came into contact with Chloe should
not approach her, but call the number on the bottom of the screen or
report to their nearest police station. That's when I knew.

TRINITY: Knew what?

GEORGE: My Stavros. He'd gotten involved in something terrible. He'd called me around three a.m. on that Monday morning. He was in a car with Chloe. They were driving somewhere—he didn't say where. He asked me to go get her dog, Brodie, and to look after it. He didn't say when they would be coming back.

George pauses. He releases his hold on the evil eye pendant and reaches for his coffee cup. His hand trembles ever so slightly. He takes a slow sip, clearly gathering himself.

GEORGE: I contacted the police immediately. I told them about Stavros's call. That night, Stavros did not report for his shift at the Beach House, and he was still not answering his phone. The next day I learned the news about the third person's DNA found at the scene. How it matched all those earlier terrible killings.

AFTER THE MURDERS

Jemma meets Detective Maeve Havers in the sterile corridor outside the morgue. The detectives offered to drive her to the facility, but she needed to be alone in her car with Boo and Sweetie in order to process and ready herself.

"This way," says Havers.

A set of doors slide open, and Jemma accompanies Havers into a room where a body lies covered by a white sheet. A morgue technician in scrubs and gloves stands beside the body. Blood drains from Jemma's head, instantly rendering her dizzy. She stumbles.

"You okay?" Havers asks.

She gathers herself and nods.

The tech lifts the top of the sheet and moves it carefully away from the head. Jemma presses her hand to her mouth and nods again as tears sear into her eyes. It should never have come to this. This is not how it was supposed to be. When she married Adam, she truly believed it would be her and him, happily ever after. She *needed* it to be that way. She *needed* to be the center of his world. Forever.

"It's him," she whispers shakily. "It's Adam. My husband."

This is your fucking fault, Adam. You did this. I loved you. We had a life together, and you threw that all away.

"Have you found her yet?" Jemma manages to ask.

"Who?" asks Havers.

She meets the detective's unreadable brown gaze. "The person who did this. The woman you've launched a province-wide hunt for. Our stalker from across the alley. Chloe Cooper."

"Not yet."

"Do—do you have any leads as to where she is?"

"We do." Havers pauses. "Are you able to come into the station, Mrs. Spengler? To answer some more questions?"

"About what?"

"Your husband. His affair with Gloria Bergson. Your respective relationships with Chloe Cooper. It will help us put a timeline on things, and also possibly throw some light on Ms. Cooper's movements leading up to the incident."

Anxiety rises in Jemma. Did anyone see her picking Chloe up in the van?

"Sure," she says quietly. "When?"

"Now would be good."

She hesitates, feeling a wave of anxiety, trepidation. But she decides it's best to get it over with. "Fine. I'll drive myself to the station. I have my dogs in the car, and I need to let them out first."

Jemma holds Boo's and Sweetie's leads as she stands on a tiny strip of lawn next to the hospital parking lot, waiting for her dogs to relieve themselves. She feels weak, edgy, as she mentally runs through possible questions the cops might ask her. She is rehearsing potential responses when she notices an older woman and Detective Havers coming out of the same doors she just exited herself.

The woman could be in her eighties, chic—silver hair—impeccably tailored jacket and matching linen pants. Havers walks at her side in her clumpy boots and misshapen coat. The women are talking closely. Havers places her hand on the older woman's arm. The woman takes a tissue from her purse and blows her nose. Curiosity rustles through Jemma.

Havers leaves, and the woman enters the parking lot and moves through the parked cars toward a white BMW. As she nears, the passenger side door of the BMW swings open. A small dark-haired woman gets out with a black-haired toddler. The child dashes toward the older woman, who crouches down to gather him into her arms.

Shock immobilizes Jemma.

The child's movements, shape, skin, and hair coloring, everything—it's Jackson. Alive again. A toddler again. The boy buries his face into the woman's neck, and emotion floods into Jemma's face. It dawns on her who the woman must be. Gloria Bergson's mother. She's Oliver's grandmother. And the small dark-haired woman must be Oliver's nanny, who found the bodies. The realization is a raw gut punch. Gloria's body is in the same morgue with Adam. Lying in death alongside her husband on a metal autopsy slab.

Unable to stop herself, Jemma tugs her dogs' leads and hurries toward the group, her attention riveted on the boy.

"I'm so sorry to intrude," she says as she reaches them. "I . . ." Her voice fades as the toddler looks up at her with big, innocent, pale-blue eyes. Her Jackson's eyes. She can't bear the pain in her heart. Every nanoparticle in her body—every memory of being his mother—screams, aches, to touch, to hold him, smell him, take him away for herself. Adam should have lived. Then they could have taken him, kept him. She could have made this little boy wholly hers. They could have started over. A family again.

She realizes both women are staring at her, expectant, waiting for her to finish what she started saying. And Jemma can't even recall what she was saying.

She clears her throat and swipes away tears she hadn't even realized were wetting her face. "I'm sorry. I saw you come out of there—" She gestures toward the building. "My name is Jemma, and my husband is in there. Adam. He—he was with her. Gloria. Are you her mother?"

The woman comes erect as surprise registers on her face. She regards Jemma intently with eyes red rimmed from crying. Finally she says, "I am. I'm Ruth Bergson."

"I—I'm sorry for your loss, Ruth," Jemma says. She clears emotion from her throat. "I only learned recently about Gloria in my husband's life." She glances down. "And Oliver."

"I don't know what to say. I'm sorry for your loss, too. Gloria was our only child."

"Did you meet my Adam? Did you know him?"

Ruth swallows, nods. "He visited our house on several occasions. We knew it was serious between him and Gloria, and we liked him. We also knew he was involved in a prior relationship he was in the process of ending, and it was just taking a bit of time."

Jemma reels as though physically struck. Her world crumbles further. "He—Oliver—looks so much like Adam and our late son. Jackson—his name was Jackson. He died just over two years ago. Around the time Oliver was born."

Ruth looks uncomfortable. She places her hand protectively on top of Oliver's head. Oliver continues to stare up at Jemma.

"Did—ah—did the police say anything to you about what they think happened?" Jemma asks. "Do they know who did this?"

"They're still searching for that woman, Chloe Cooper," Ruth says. "Her wallet with her ID was in the side pocket of a portfolio left at the scene, and her signed canvases were all over the floor. She was also caught on Gloria's CCTV camera entering the gallery just before it closed at six p.m. Apparently the woman is a stalker who expressed a hatred for Adam. The police told me she's unstable, with mental health issues and a tenuous relationship with reality." Tears fill the woman's eyes. She reaches into her purse for another tissue. The nanny takes Oliver's hand.

"Come, Olly, let's get in the car," the nanny says.

"Wait!" Jemma can't let Oliver go. She crouches down. Her gaze meets his, and she offers him the biggest smile she can muster. "You look so much like my boy when he was your age." She touches his chubby wrist, strokes his soft skin, but he yanks his arm away from her and shoots his gaze up to his grandma in alarm.

Pain stabs. Worse than a knife. Worse than death. Jemma says gently, "Would you like to say hello to my dogs, Oliver?"

He shakes his head and presses himself firmly against his nanny's legs, farther away from Jemma and her dogs.

"Come, Olly, let's get into the car," the nanny says. Oliver turns eagerly, and his nanny helps him up into the car seat and begins buckling him in.

Suddenly Jemma is hotly, fiercely glad Adam is dead, along with that adulterous whore.

"What will happen with Oliver now?" she asks Ruth.

I can take him. I will look after him. I can make him mine.

"He'll come live with us. He's familiar with our house. He loves his gramps, and he will have his nanny for some continuity and stability." Tears flood Ruth's eyes again. She blows her nose. "Poor boy. My heart—it will take a long while, but at least he's with family. And he won't want for anything." She hesitates. "There was something else the detective just mentioned—it seems Adam was worried, and the detective was asking why."

"What do you mean, *worried*?"

"He very recently transferred all of his financial assets to a new account and changed his will."

Surprise slams through Jemma. "I don't follow."

"Well, with Gloria gone, everything of his father's now goes to Oliver in trust until he's older. Including the Magnolia Lane house, the gallery that Adam was part owner of, and his Tesla—which he left instructions for an executor to sell. Even a new home he apparently owns in Crow's Point."

Jemma stares. Her brain spins. "How—how do you know this?"

"His lawyer from Ontario called us. Apparently Adam left the lawyer—who has limited power of attorney—instructions to initiate the asset transfers and to alter his will. The detective was asking me if I knew why he would do this. As though he knew he was in danger." She pauses. "Do you have any idea?"

Jemma shakes her head, unable to speak. Her brain races as she recalls how Adam bought the house in Crow's Point without her. He put it in his name. She hadn't even really thought about the implications at the time, hadn't got around to talking about who was on the title. She hasn't checked their joint bank accounts recently, either—she doesn't know what he might have moved out of them, or for how long he might have been moving funds. She also knows he had his own private accounts. She just assumed everything would come to her as his spouse.

Ruth Bergson says goodbye and takes her leave, and Jemma, stunned, watches her climb elegantly into her BMW with Oliver strapped in the back. Her gaze follows the car as it drives out of the parking lot.

Wind gusts and blows hair over her face as Jemma realizes that everything she has fought so desperately to preserve for herself is now gone: her youth, her marriage, her husband, her possessions, her children, life as she knew it. In front of her lie all her fears. Isolation. Loneliness. Age. She has been brought down by her own desperate actions to keep hold of it all, and instead she has lost it all. Every last thing.

IT'S CRIMINAL: The Chloe Cooper Story

The screen fades to Detective Maeve Havers in her chair.

MAEVE: The identifications of Gloria Bergson and Dr. Adam Spengler were confirmed by next of kin, and immediately the gallery slayings case became very high profile. Both the victims were well loved in their respective fields. And both sets of the victims' parents were wealthy and extremely well connected. Dr. Spengler's father was recently deceased, but before his death he was a respected and distinguished federal court judge. His mother—still alive at the time of her son's death—was a well-known and influential Ontario socialite and benefactor of numerous social causes. Bergson's parents—both alive at the time of her murder—were founders of the Bergson Corporation, which owns hundreds of local and international media outlets. Media coverage of the killings exploded worldwide.

The image of Detective Maeve Havers segues into a shot of spinning tabloid headlines.

LOVERS TRYST LEAVES BLOODY TRAIL. GALLERY KILLINGS EXPOSE AFFAIR. LOVE CHILD ORPHANED

AFTER BRUTAL SLAYINGS. BELOVED SURGEON KILLED
WITH LOVER IN ART GALLERY. MEDIA MOGUL'S
DAUGHTER MURDERED WITH JUDGE'S SON. VIOLENT
DEATH FOR FATED LOVERS. HUNT IS ON FOR THEIR
KILLER. DNA OF ARTIST WHO FLED THE SCENE BEING
ANALYZED.

*The images fade back to Detective Maeve
Havers.*

MAEVE: Intense pressure came from all quarters to solve the violent
homicides that occurred in the quiet neighborhood, and because of
the victims' high-profile connections, additional funding was made
instantly available to the investigative team. This enabled us to fast-track
forensic analysis by accessing a new private forensic lab partnership with
Lower Mainland law enforcement.

TRINITY: Two-tiered justice on full display?

MAEVE: Unfortunately that's how it works. Funding and staff resources
are always an issue when prioritizing cases and processing evidence. It's
why, for example, some cold cases will never be solved. Ordinarily,
obtaining DNA results from crime labs can take anywhere from several
weeks to months, but in reality, DNA processing—depending on com-
plexity and the tests required—can take a day or two.

TRINITY: So, in terms of evidence, you had the fingerprints on the
knife, which the pathologist determined was the murder weapon?

MAEVE: Yes. The wound shapes were consistent with the carving knife
found on the studio floor being the murder weapon.

TRINITY OFF CAMERA: You also had the bloody handprints and fingerprints on the walls. You had saliva DNA from the pieces of champagne flute glass. Plus, you had blood DNA from the third person. And you had the portfolio and signed paintings—this all pointed you to Chloe Cooper?

MAEVE: Correct. The first indication Cooper was at the scene was her wallet containing her ID found in a portfolio on the floor. And as you mentioned, her canvases were signed. I also immediately recognized the swimmer painting from her apartment. Additionally, Cooper was captured on the gallery's CCTV cam when she entered the premises carrying the portfolio. Blood swabs and saliva samples from the pieces of champagne flute—along with the hand and fingerprint latents—were all expedited at the private lab. We had the initial DNA results within the day.

TRINITY: What did the results immediately tell you about the third donor?

MAEVE: Nothing. At least not immediately. A DNA profile is only of use if you can match it against something. The profile was run through our National DNA Databank—or NDDB—which contains two indices: the Crime Scene Index—or CSI—and the Criminal Offenders Index—or COI. The CSI stores coded profiles taken from crime scene investigations, and the COI contains profiles lawfully taken from offenders who have already been charged and convicted of serious crimes. We got a shocker hit from the COI. A real doozy. It stunned us all, and it was somehow leaked to the press. It hit the media ball clean out of the park.

AFTER THE MURDERS

"I'm begging you, please don't call anyone, Stavros," Chloe says as she moves the stone ashtray behind her back.

Stavros swallows. His face is sheet white, and his eyes are huge, dark hollows. He clutches his phone in his hand, and his gaze flicks to the motel room door, as though he's calculating whether he can escape. The fact that he's frightened of her hurts.

"Chloe," he says very softly, "why don't you just talk to me? Tell me what happened at that gallery."

"Then you'll call the police."

He holds his phone out from his body and carefully, slowly, sets it atop the dresser next to the TV. He shows her his palms. "See? No phone. I won't call them. But you do need to tell me what's going on." He sits on the sofa, his gaze locked on hers. Stavros is not going to flee, or jump her and wrestle her to the ground and tie her up. He still on some level trusts her, so why can't she trust him?

Shame, humiliation, washes up through Chloe's chest.

Because you don't even know what you did, Chloe. You can't even trust yourself.

She moves the heavy ashtray back to the counter and releases her hold on it. Emotion fills her eyes. "I can't tell you, Stavros, because I don't know . . . I'm confused. There's this noise in my head, and I can't seem to think straight."

She needs something stiff to drink. Fast. It'll calm the crazy crinkling patterns of light and sounds in her brain. It'll ease her rapid breathing. She's going to have a panic attack. Like in the elevator when she was trapped with Adam Spengler.

"I don't *think* I'm a bad person, Stavros."

He regards her. Weighing her. Slowly, quietly, he says, "I think you're a kind person, Chloe. A person who has had a difficult life, and a rough struggle with a sick mother for a long, long time."

Tears release and slide down her face. Kindness hurts—really hurts in a terrible whole-body-aching kind of way.

Stavros leans forward on the sofa and clasps his hands together in a nonthreatening avuncular fashion. "But something happened in that gallery, Chlo. You told me you took your portfolio in for the owner to appraise, and next thing you recall is being outside in the dark alley around two a.m., with your hand and lip cut, bleeding, confused. And now the police want to talk to you urgently in connection with two brutal homicides, and I suspect that the longer you try to run away from the cops, the worse it will get for you. We need to go back."

She stares at him as her mother's voice rises in her head.

You see? You silly little imbecile. Did I not say you would rue the day you called the cops? If you had kept your stupid little mouth shut about the Jet Ski accident, none of this would have happened. Your call started all the dominoes tumbling, and look where you are now, little spy, little snoop. Did I not say the police would end up blaming you for everything? You, the stalker. The watcher. The weirdo with your binoculars in the window.

"I'm not ready to go back," she says flatly. "Don't force me, Stavros."

"Fine, fine. Okay. How about we talk it through, then? Maybe your memories will surface if I ask you questions. No need to answer them, but they can serve as prompts. How about that?"

Claustrophobia tightens her chest. The walls of the room close in. She glances at the door.

"Can we maybe do it outside? Go into that park next to the motel?"

His eyes flicker. She can see this idea makes him uneasy.

"I'm not going to run away, Stavros. Where would I run to? And I can't drive. And I need some vodka. I need it to help me relax, because otherwise I can't think or remember anything at all. We can drink vodka in the park. It will help me think."

Twenty-five minutes later Stavros has bought vodka—a big bottle—at the motel off-sales. They walked along a small and narrow trail and now sit in the forest atop a granite mound high above a river frothing with white water. Chloe sips from the plastic cup she brought from the motel room. Stavros cradles his drink in an ugly brown mug he got out of his car.

It's probably a dangerous place to drink vodka, thinks Chloe. One little slip and either one of them could topple off the rock and fall all the way down to drown in that ferocious little river. But she actually feels okay here to talk—on a precipice above water rushing free and away to the sea. She's already a bit warm and fuzzy, thanks to the first few burning gulps of her drink, and it strikes her suddenly that she really is like the girl she paints with her feet stuck inside rock, always searching for a way into the sea. Gloria's beautiful words surface in her mind.

There's also a word in German, Sehnsucht, *used to describe an indefinable and intense yearning for a person, or place, or an experience, or state that is unattainable or beyond one's current reach . . . This loneliness resides deep inside every one of us, whether a person is in a relationship, a marriage, or a group, or a city—it's a shadowy part of who we are as humans. That's what I see in your work.*

Her hands begin to tremble again, and she raises the cup to her lips and swallows deeply.

"I know you've had a really hard time with your mom, Chlo. All those months of caregiving on your own."

"I had the carers."

"Still, it was ultimately all on you. And then losing her." He sips from his mug. "I know it was also always just you and Raven for most of your life." His gaze meets hers, and she almost breaks the eye contact, but doesn't. He says, "I have a feeling you've had a difficult life—maybe even something really big and traumatic and horrible occurred in the past. And . . . maybe it's made you uneasy about the world around you."

She feels heat in her face and takes another gulp from her cup.

"And that's okay, you know? Emotional injuries can make people a bit knobbly in the places they try to heal."

"Knobbly?"

He gives a half smile. "You know, like a tree trunk that got damaged. It weeps sap, then it grows over the wound, and it's knobbly."

Chloe dares a smile. "You'd make an odd shrink, Stavros." She hesitates. "Has something happened in your past? Because you make it sound like you know about these things."

He's silent for a long time. All Chloe hears is the sound of rushing, chortling water, and the soft whisper of wind in the conifers around them.

"Stavros?"

"Yeah. I suppose."

She's curious now.

Ah, but curiosity killed the cat, Chloe. Look where curiosity has landed you now. You would not be here if you had controlled your curiosity about the new neighbors.

So she doesn't press him. But after a few moments he sucks in a deep breath and says, "I lost my mother in a car accident when I was eight. My father was driving, and he always blamed himself for her death. He started drinking. A lot. He sank deeper and deeper into himself." He glances at her cup, which is almost empty. "To escape, you know? From feelings he couldn't deal with." He sips his own drink, swallows, and falls silent again for a few moments. "I guess he basically neglected me. Stopped caring for me, taking me to school. Just sat there in his chair drunk all day. Neighbors called social services. They took me away. He died eight months later. Fell down some stairs to the basement and hit his head. He was impaired at the time."

"Oh, Stavros, I'm sorry."

He gives a shrug.

"What happened to you then?"

"My uncle George—my father's younger brother—flew out from the small town where he lived on the south side of Crete. My mother's family is also from there. He opened his barbershop on Main and took me in. He cared for me until I moved out and got my own place." He rubs the tuft of hair under his lip and offers her a sad, lopsided smile. "I was lucky. George is a very good man. And look at me—I turned out okay?"

Chloe regards him.

"Right?"

All of a sudden, all those weird things she doesn't like about Stavros sort of just *are* Stavros, and her heart does a funny little squeeze.

"Right?"

She clears her throat. "Well, I suppose so."

"That's not a helluva endorsement, Chlo."

Stavros makes a lot more sense to Chloe now. It stirs a feeling of kinship in her.

"And yours?" Stavros asks.

"My what?"

"Father—you never mention him."

"Well, you never mentioned yours, either."

"But now that I have, it's your turn."

"I don't know who he is."

He waits for her to say more. She finishes her drink and pours more from the bottle in the brown paper bag. She sips and watches a stag that has appeared on the far side of the river. It grazes in the grass along the bank, oblivious to them. Like something out of a folktale, she thinks.

"My mom told me she brought me from England when I was a toddler. I don't know any more than that. After we got here, we went to live on a farm. I was homeschooled my whole life. Well—sort of. I never did graduate. Not officially. I am an autodidact, though."

"What's that?"

"Self-educated person. I studied on my own. I do know a lot of things. Probably more than some people who finish high school."

"So where was the farm?"

"A ranching area inland, near Williams Lake. Quite isolated. Long, cold winters."

"Just you and your mom? Like, on someone else's farm?"

She nods. "Just us. We rented a little cabin from the rancher. We had a vegetable garden in the summer, and a root cellar. She worked as a receptionist for a municipality in the small town nearby. I made the big move to the city on my own, and got the apartment. She warned me not to go. She always said something horrible would find me, and that I wasn't equipped to live on my own. But I went." She swirls the clear liquid in her cup. "Then my mom got sick, and I couldn't not bring her to live with me, close to the cancer agency and the big-city hospital where she needed so much treatment." She sips, thinking. "Maybe I was even a bit relieved that she came, because it was scary in the city at first. And she brought Brodie, and he's good company."

"And what happened with the gallery?"

She tenses and quickly downs the rest of the vodka in her cup and hurriedly pours more. He watches and looks worried, but he doesn't try to stop her, and Chloe is very grateful to be able to get drunk in front of him and not have to hide somewhere alone where no one can see.

Slowly she tries to broach the incident. "I—I met Gloria Bergson at the bar when she came into the Beach House and asked about my painting. She invited me to come to her gallery with my portfolio." She glances at him. "And Jemma Spengler, the swimmer from across the alley, my new neighbor, encouraged me to do it. She drove me there . . ." Chloe falls silent. It all seems too complicated to explain. But she tries again, and proceeds to tell Stavros everything, right up to how she entered the gallery prepared to hate Gloria, and how nice Gloria actually turned out to be, and about how nervous-excited she was to think that her life at forty might be changing after all, and then Adam Spengler entered via the back door. And when she tried to leave, he blocked her exit and came at her with a syringe.

"I remember that part now. He had a syringe with a needle. He stuck it into my arm as I hit him with a tool from the framing table. It was self-defense—I was scared and wanted to get out. And—and that's when everything seems to go fuzzy."

"So you did assault him?"

"Only when he lunged at me with the syringe."

"Can you show me your arm?"

Chloe slips off her coat and pulls down the shoulder of her long-sleeved T-shirt. She shows Stavros the pinprick mark surrounded by swelling. He touches it gently with his fingertips, and tears gleam in his eyes.

"What's wrong?" she asks.

"I was worried that you were lying to me, but I think you might have been drugged, Chloe. And that's why things are fuzzy. Those people—the Spenglers—what Jemma asked you to do, sounds weird, suspicious. We need to go back to the city, Chlo. I think you did nothing wrong."

She inhales deeply and stares at the river and the stag on the bank. "Can we just stay until tomorrow?"

"I don't know, Chlo. It could get—"

"We have to, Stavros. I like it here. I *need* to stay one more day. You can't make me go."

IT'S CRIMINAL: The Chloe Cooper Story

The screen shows a large black headline across the top of a tabloid:

DNA FROM GALLERY MURDERS LINKED TO INFAMOUS SERIAL KILLER ROBERT AUTAIN

Two more headlines scream:

CROW'S POINT BARTENDER WHO FLED GALLERY BLOODBATH TIED TO SEX KILLER FROM QUEBEC KNOWN AS ABATTOIR AUTAIN

INCARCERATED KILLER LINKED TO HIGH-PROFILE GALLERY SLAYINGS

The image fades back to Detective Maeve Havers.

MAEVE: The link was familial. Robert Autain—dubbed Abattoir Autain by the media—a pig farmer from rural Quebec who abducted, sexually assaulted, and murdered eleven known victims over a period of thirteen years, is Chloe Cooper's father. He usually found his victims hitchhiking along a particular stretch of highway he routinely traveled to transport his livestock—pigs—to the abattoir, for slaughter. On his return trip he would pick up a woman—usually a young hitchhiker, sometimes a sex-trade worker. He'd drug her, put her in the livestock trailer, and drive her back to his remote farm. After several months of torture and abuse, he would kill his victim and either bury her body parts on his farm or feed the remains to his swine. One of the women Autain abducted outside a truck stop was Jennie Smith, a tourist from the UK. She was seventeen years old. He kept Jennie on his farm in a converted shipping container covered with dirt for six years. During that time she gave birth to a baby girl she named Zoe. When Zoe was almost five, Jennie managed to escape with her child.

The screen fades to show archival news photos of Robert Autain. A large man with a coarse but almost handsome face, thick, shiny black hair, and eyes such a pale blue they are eerie. Text below the images reads:

THE BLUE-EYED BUTCHER. ROBERT "ABATTOIR" AUTAIN.

TRINITY: What happened to Jennie Smith?

MAEVE: She fled barefoot with Zoe through frozen fields. She hid in a farm outbuilding with her toddler for almost a week. She was found by a neighboring farmer, who took her and her child to the hospital. Jennie would only testify against Autain after being promised some form of witness protection for herself and her child. There was a lot of pressure to put this guy away—authorities ended up agreeing. Her court testimony sealed his fate. She helped lock him up for life, and her assistance was critical in identifying the other eleven known victims he assaulted. She was even able to show authorities where some of their remains were buried. Jennie helped bring closure to the families of those missing women. And she said she did it for Zoe. She said she was able to dig deep enough and finally find the courage to escape and run from her captor because of her daughter. She wanted to save her, protect her, above all else.

TRINITY: Zoe is Chloe?

MAEVE: We know this now, yes. Her mother, Jennie, changed her name to Chloe and her own to Raven Cooper when she moved west after the trial. While authorities helped facilitate their move and name changes, Raven and Chloe never really got the psychological help they needed. Some part of Raven was always running and hiding from Robert Autain, even though he was incarcerated. In her mind he was almost superhuman. Which is one of the reasons she homeschooled Chloe. She imprinted her daughter with her own terror and fears of the world, and Chloe already had deep childhood trauma of her own—things she saw she was not able to remember, or did not have a narrative for, so she was never able to articulate her swirling anxieties about the world even to herself.

TRINITY: Generational trauma. Passed down. And as fate would have it, her trauma was triggered by her new neighbor Dr. Adam Spengler's superficial resemblance to this evil monster from her childhood—the sexual sadist and killer from whom she hid in the closet when he came to abuse her mother. A man she couldn't remember with her mind, but her body knew all too well.

Detective Maeve Havers nods.

MAEVE: She recalled how the man with those eyes made her feel. And she projected those feelings onto Adam Spengler.

TRINITY: What happened to Stavros Vasilou that day?

The screen fades to a photo of Stavros Vasilou with his uncle, taken before the Spenglers arrived in Crow's Point and crossed paths with Chloe Cooper.

AFTER THE MURDERS

October 1, 2019

It's almost 10:30 p.m. Chloe exits the motel bathroom in her T-shirt with her face washed and a towel around her waist, ready to make a beeline through the dimly lit room for bed. Once in bed, she will discard her towel. Stavros is on the sofa, and she's still loath to let him see her running about in her panties.

She and Stavros spent this first day of October nursing hangovers, and Stavros called into work to say he needed some mental health days off, but as the hours wear on, she can see he's growing increasingly tense and agitated about being with her. She suspects tomorrow morning, one way or another, Stavros will hit the road. She's unsure what to do about this.

As she scuttles through the room to the bed, Stavros stares at her.

"Don't watch me like that, Stavros. I do need some privacy," she says as she climbs under the covers.

He continues to stare. The TV is on but muted. It's showing a commercial for a medicine designed to combat psoriasis.

"What is it, Stavros? Why are you looking at me like that?" She pulls the covers up around her neck as she leans against the headboard in a sitting position.

"I think they found your father, Chloe."

"What?"

"It's all over the news. It—it's just breaking." He points at the flick-ering TV, which is now trying to flog home insurance. "Someone at the private lab doing forensic analysis of the gallery evidence has leaked the preliminary results from the blood DNA left by the person who fled the scene."

"I don't know what you're talking about, Stavros. What does this have to do with my father?"

"It's *your* DNA they were analyzing, Chloe. From blood *you* left at the scene—it has to be. They ran it through the National DNA Databank, and it's a familial match to a man currently serving a life prison sentence in Quebec." He pauses. "For eleven known murders."

Tension rises thick in the room. Her heart begins to gallop. "Who is this man?" she whispers.

He gets up, comes to sit on the side of the bed. Too close. She clutches her knees tightly to her chest, both terrified to hear the truth and desperately needing it.

He touches her knee.

"P-please don't touch me, Stavros."

He retracts his hand and rubs the hair tuft under his lip. "He abducted your mother when she was seventeen. He kept her prisoner on a pig farm for six years before she escaped with you."

Chloe stares at Stavros, uncomprehending. "My mother came from England when I was a toddler."

"Chloe," he says gently, "they're saying on TV that the woman who left blood DNA at the scene is the daughter of this man, and his name is Robert Autain. He abducted seventeen-year-old Jennie Smith, a British tourist, and she had his baby while in captivity. A baby girl. She escaped with her daughter when she was a toddler. Jennie Smith had named her daughter Zoe."

She feels all the blood drain out of her head. The room swirls as her mother's British-accented voice rises faintly from far away.

Run for your life and hide, Zoe!

Zoe, quick. He's coming. Get inside—in there. Safe cave.

She lurches out of bed and lunges for the television remote, not caring now if Stavros sees her old panties and chubby legs. She bumps up the sound. The commercial break is over, and the footage returns to the news. Slowly she sits on the edge of the sofa and watches a pretty reporter talking to the news anchor in a studio.

"This is truly astounding news," the anchor says.

"Shocking news indeed," admits the reporter. "An internal investigation has now been opened as to how the DNA link came to be leaked, but if this is true, the gallery murders have opened up an old media mystery about the whereabouts of serial killer Robert Autain's daughter, Zoe Smith, who vanished into a protection program with her mother, Jennie, after Jennie testified at Autain's trial. According to news reports from the time, Jennie Smith told reporters she found the courage to finally defy her captor and that she escaped because of her daughter. She became consumed with protecting her child from the killer. She wanted to find a way to give her a proper life, a safe one, with a future. If it were not for her child, Jennie said, she might never have been able to dig deep enough to find the will or strength, because Robert Autain dominated her both physically and psychologically. He controlled every aspect of her existence, from what she ate to when she could bathe, or see sunshine, or eat, or read, or go to the bathroom. She was terrified of disobeying him on any level."

Behind the newspeople in the studio is a huge photo of a man with shiny black hair and pale-blue eyes. Under him are the words:

Robert "Abattoir" Autain, convicted for abducting, sexually assaulting, and murdering at least eleven known victims over a period of thirteen years.

The image fades to show another: a grainy old newspaper photograph of a skeletally thin young woman with bare feet, a torn dress, and wild hair. Her arms and legs are scraped and bruised, and she clutches a child as EMTs wrap a blanket around both of them. The headline reads:

JENNIE SMITH FOUND ALIVE WITH AUTAIN'S CHILD

The subhead reads:

Assault victim held captive for six years flees pig farmer's prison with daughter born in captivity.

Chloe starts to shake. She looks at Stavros. She can't make words come.

"We need to go back, Chloe."

AFTER THE MURDERS

October 2, 2019

Chloe sits at a table in a GVPD interview room. Across from her are Detectives Maeve Havers and Axel Pederson. Seated beside her is Samantha Chang, a lawyer provided to her free of charge through the province's legal aid system. Chloe has voluntarily surrendered her phone to the police. They now have access to the detailed images she shot inside the Spenglers' home. Officers also took her clothes and shoes, and they've given her a sweatshirt and pants to wear. She's been fingerprinted, her photo has been taken, and her injuries have also been documented and photographed, including the cut on her hand and the needle mark on her arm. They took a blood sample, plus scrapings from beneath her nails. She feels numb and unsure whether she should have listened to Stavros about returning, but she was consumed with a need to know more about who her father might be. Either way, she's here, and it's too late to change anything now.

Havers told her that the interview will be recorded, and Chloe glances up at the CCTV cam in the corner of the room, near the ceiling. She wonders who all is watching her from somewhere else in the building. It feeds her anxiety, so she fiddles with her fingers under the table. Where is her mother's voice inside her head when Chloe most needs it? Her mother seems to have fallen silent. Perhaps because Chloe doesn't know who she is anymore—Raven Cooper or Jennie Smith. She tells herself it'll all be okay—Stavros will be outside, waiting for her. Brodie is safe with George. She's not wholly alone.

Havers turns a laptop screen to face Chloe and her lawyer, hits PLAY. "Is this you, Chloe?"

She watches the CCTV footage of herself nervously entering Bergson Gallery with her portfolio clutched at her side. She nods.

"Could you speak your answers out loud for the recording, please?" Havers says.

"Yes, that's me."

"The clip is time-stamped," says Havers. "You arrived at the premises at 6:02 p.m. Is that correct?"

"Yes." Her counsel has advised her to stick to simple yes-and-no answers, where possible.

"Shortly after you entered the Bergson Gallery, we see you here, going into the back room with Gloria Bergson," Havers says as she points to the footage. Pederson just watches Chloe's face. She figures he's looking for little tells and trying to judge if she's being truthful, or he's determining what might be stressful for her. And when he does detect a trigger, he will leap in and twist the interview knife. The bad cop–good cop routine. She's seen it on TV.

Chloe watches the image of herself entering the rear of the gallery with Gloria. She says nothing.

"Can you tell us what transpired from this point on?" Havers asks.

Chloe glances down at the table. There's a brown cup stain on the surface. She stares at the mark as she tells them that Gloria poured prosecco and appraised her work, and told her that her paintings had real merit. That Dr. Adam Spengler arrived via the back door, and that it sounded like he'd let himself in with a key.

"How did Gloria Bergson react when she saw Adam?"

Chloe glances up slowly. "She was surprised but also seemed excited to see Adam. She asked if he had good news. I thought maybe she was anticipating him to say he had finally ended it properly with Jemma."

"Why did you think this?" Havers asks.

Chloe glances at Samantha, who nods for her to continue. She clears her throat. "Because of what I overheard that night between Adam and Gloria outside the Spenglers' house. I told you about that already. She gave him an ultimatum. She said he had to finish with Jemma or he would never see her and his son again."

"What happened next in the gallery, Chloe?" Havers asks.

A noise starts to sound in Chloe's head. She fights to silence it. "Adam made me nervous, scared. And he was looking at me weirdly as he came closer. I perceived danger and tried to escape, but as I moved toward the rear door, he stepped in front of me and barred my way. I reached behind me for a tool to defend myself with. When he came at me with a syringe, I struck him on the side of the face." She pauses and reaches for the cup of water in front of her. She sips and sets it down carefully, because her hands are still shaking. "He got the needle into my arm before he went down. I tried to run, but I felt drunk, unable, and fell to the floor." She flicks a glance to her lawyer, who nods again for her to continue.

"When I was on the floor, I think I saw him get up and take a knife from the deep pocket on the side of his cargo pants. I can't remember anything after that. When I woke up, it was late, and they—Adam and Gloria—were both dead."

Havers says, "How did your prints get on the knife?"

Nerves bite. She glances at her lawyer again. Samantha Chang says softly, "Go ahead, Chloe."

"When I woke up, it was in my hand, and my palm had been cut. It was bleeding."

Havers regards her. A thickness fills the room. Chloe feels the walls closing in and the roof pressing down. Her blood pressure rises.

"How did you get that cut on your palm, Chloe?"

"I don't know."

"And your lip—how was that cut?"

Tears prick into her eyes. "I—I can't remember."

Detective Havers leans back in her chair. She taps the back of her pen on the table. "How did you get to the gallery, Chloe?"

She explains how Jemma picked her up. In a white van. And how she felt nervous about that. She explains why Jemma wanted Chloe to go to the gallery—to dig for dirt from Gloria. She tells them how she was invited to Jemma's house for wine, which was when they discussed the plan.

"She *invited* you?" Pederson asks.

"Yes. She phoned me and asked if I wanted to join her for wine and to talk about walking her dogs. Over wine she confided to me about her husband's affair."

Pederson crooks up a pale brow. "And why would she do this?"

Chloe's jaw tightens. "Are you asking me because you think it's impossible a woman like Jemma might want to befriend someone like me?"

"Just curious."

Her skin heats. She glowers at Pederson.

He's trying to rile you, Chloe. He's assessing your temper. Take it easy. Control yourself. Say nothing.

She doesn't respond, but her hands fist against her thighs under the table.

"So this was *after* you dog sat for her?" Havers asks. "After you snooped around their house, took photos of all the rooms, and put things in Adam's pockets."

Her skin goes hotter. Samantha shifts beside her—a silent warning.

"Yes," she says simply. Through her lawyer Chloe knows Jemma has given PetGuardian footage to the cops that shows her doing these things. Her lawyer said Jemma is accusing Chloe of having motive to kill Adam and Gloria. She has told the cops Chloe is mentally unstable and that she detests adulterers, had a particular hate-on for Adam, and has been watching and stalking them both. Her mother was right. It has come down to this—she's being blamed. It's so easy to blame an outsider, isn't it? Why would anyone believe *Crazy Chloe Cooper* over the wealthy Spenglers?

Pederson makes notes in his pad and says, "Why did you put things in Adam's pockets, Chloe?"

"I thought Jemma should know her husband was being unfaithful."

"So you didn't like Dr. Spengler?"

Samantha says quickly, "What does this have to do with the homicide investigation?"

"Goes to motive," Havers says.

"You hated him, didn't you, Chloe?" Pederson says, leaning forward. "Because you abhor cheats and liars. You hated them both, right? Gloria *and* Adam. The adulterers. You went to the gallery to help Jemma, and you wanted them both gone—dead—for Jemma's sake? Because you had an unusual fixation with her, didn't you?"

Chloe's breathing gets fast. Her skin goes hot. She shoots her gaze to her lawyer in desperation.

Samantha says, "Can we stick to facts? I know this is not a court of law, but Chloe's personal opinions about liars and cheats are hers to keep."

Havers purses her lips and says, "After you had wine with Jemma, what did you do next, Chloe?"

"I went home. Jemma phoned me later that night. She said she really needed me to make an appointment with Gloria for Sunday evening, to get dirt on Adam. I think it was dawning on Jemma that it was Adam who killed the swimmer because he assumed Marianne Wade was Jemma in her pink cap. Plus, he had those fake plates on his Tesla. You can see the Idaho plates in the photos on my phone that you took from me. I took a photo of the display hanging on his garage wall."

Havers and Pederson exchange a fast glance. Chloe senses the energy in the room shift. She feels scared. Her breathing is growing even shallower, and her skin is itching hot. She glances at the door, desperate to escape. She cannot abide being trapped in small spaces. She feels she's back inside a tiny closet with a hairy blanket over her head and not allowed to come out, and she hears pigs screaming and squealing and smells manure.

Havers says, "Let's go back to your claim that Jemma drove you to the gallery."

"She *did*. In a white van. She said her car was in the shop, and the van was a rental."

"Any distinguishing marks on the van?" Pederson asks. "Anything you recall that would help identify it?"

She shakes her head. "Only that it smelled new inside, freshly detailed. And there was a bag in the back with blue nitrile gloves sticking out."

Pederson scribbles another note in his pad.

"Jemma told me she'd wait for me at the end of the alley out back. But there was no one there when I got out."

"Presuming what you claim is true, Chloe," Havers says slowly, "you didn't feel any of Jemma's requests were strange?"

Tears pool in Chloe's eyes. "I—I did, I guess. A bit. But I wanted to help her. Very badly. I wanted to protect her from that man."

"You mean from her husband, Adam Spengler?" Havers confirms.

"Yes."

Havers consults her notes, turns a page, looks up. "And you say you called Stavros Vasilou from the alley?"

"Yes."

"Why did you and Stavros flee after he arrived to pick you up?"

Tears escape Chloe's control and run down her cheeks. "I—I don't know. I was scared. I couldn't remember anything—my head was fuzzy, like I was drunk. And I didn't know what I had done, because the knife was in my hand when I woke up, and I just had this terrible urge to flee. I—I heard my mother's voice from far away, from when I was little, just saying, *Run, Chloe. Run for your life. He's coming for us.*" Chloe pauses, swipes tears from her cheeks. "Except she called me Zoe."

AFTER THE MURDERS

Stavros was not waiting for Chloe outside. The detectives are interrogating him now, so Chloe finds a bench in a small corner of the park across from the police station, and she sits down to wait for him. Together they will go to pick Brodie up from George.

The autumn air has turned crisp, the sky is very blue, and a pale sun lies low in the sky, tingeing everything with an otherworldly gold. Chloe is overwhelmed, exhausted, and for a moment she watches an old woman in a brown coat, tossing crumbs to pigeons from a brown paper bag in her hand. The birds coo and peck calmly in green grass. Chloe closes her eyes, listening to them, just feeling the soft sun against her skin. A breeze stirs. She hears the dryness of turned leaves rustling in the trees, and she feels a cool touch, like a fingertip on her face.

She startles but doesn't open her eyes.

Mom?

There is no answer.

Wind stirs again. Fallen leaves clatter and skitter across the ground at Chloe's feet. She opens her eyes. The old woman in the coat is gone. In her place a fat brown squirrel is busy hulling something.

Chloe, what have you gotten yourself into?

Relief washes through Chloe at the sound of the familiar voice in her head. Her mother has not totally abandoned her. Not yet.

I know, Mom. That you were Jennie Smith. That I was Zoe. I see how I fit now. She pauses, unsure of how to proceed. She still hasn't even begun to properly process the startling and awful revelations about her father and mother.

I saw on the news what happened to you—how you were abducted by the Monster, and how he fathered me when you were so young. And in the car, on the drive back to the city with Stavros, I read everything I could about it all on my phone—archived news stories, the breaking ones now, and I saw what people on social media are saying about my DNA and the gallery homicides. In the old news stories they say you were so brave. You told reporters you did it for me, that when you became a mother—even though it was the Monster's baby, I was still yours, and my existence gave you a superhuman maternal courage to defy him, and to get away, even though he was so terrifying and controlling and sick and dangerous.

I also saw photos of him online.

She swallows, watching the squirrel, whose busy little hands seem to go still as it watches her in return.

He has different facial features from Adam Spengler, but the coloring is the same. The thick, shiny black hair. His stature. Those eyes. I remember those pale eyes. I think that's why, when I looked into Adam's eyes, I was hit by a sense of Evil with a capital E. It's starting to make sense now, Mom. Me. You. Why we functioned the way we did in the world.

Well, Chloe, you did say you wanted these things sorted out when you turned forty.

You sound different, Mom.

Like how?

You're not calling me stupid, or an imbecile with a thick skull. Do you know that by calling me those things, you made me afraid, unworthy—

I wanted to protect you from the world, Chloe. I was worried he'd find us.

But look what you made me, Mom.

You're alive and safe, aren't you? Chloe, the Monster broke me. He was a violent, murderous psychopath, and he crushed my body and my mind. I never did come right, but I tried. I did my best. For you. And sometimes best intentions—well, sometimes the best we have to give just doesn't work out. I always wanted you. I love you, my Chloe.

Chloe sits for a while, pondering this. And how she read in an old news story that Jennie Smith's parents thought their daughter was dead after she'd been missing so long. When she escaped and they discovered she survived, they wanted to bring her home to England, but only if she got rid of the heinous Monster's offspring first. They couldn't face the "bad seed" that was little Zoe. They wanted the child farmed out for adoption. When Jennie refused, they cut her out of their staunchly religious lives. And she had no more family. And she became Raven Cooper. And it was just them. Chloe Cooper and her mom. The two against the world.

"I know," she whispers softly, out loud. Leaves rustle around her feet and in the branches above her head. "I love you, too, Mom."

I still think you stuck your nose in where it doesn't belong, Chloe. Look what happened. Curiosity almost did kill the cat. You were dragged into the quagmire of a love triangle with a murderous couple.

Chloe sees a figure approaching from the police station across the street. Skinny. Long. Funny lopey walk with a bounce. Stavros. Her heart feels a spurt of familiarity, comfort.

Well, I do not rue the day that I called the cops, Mom. The detective is quite kind. She's just doing her job.

Stavros comes closer, moving across the lawn to her bench. The squirrel darts for a tree.

And you know, Mom, sometimes you do actually have to let certain people in and tell them your fears and hurts and hopes, or you will never have friends. I'm alone now. I need friends.

Be careful, Chloe. Cross the road to the other side if someone gives you a bad feeling, no matter how small. Listen to the little whispers. And make sure you look after Brodie nicely in his final days, Chloe.

Are you leaving, Mom?

Silence.

Mom? Are you there?

Silence.

A desperation, a panic, rises in Chloe.

Stavros reaches her. He gives her a lopsided smile. "You doing okay?"

She feels suddenly bereft. But she nods. He holds his hand out to her to help her up from the bench. She places her hand in his. His palm is a little rough, his fingers strong, wiry. She comes to her feet beside him.

"How did it go with you and the detectives?" she asks him.

"The interrogation?" He shrugs and pops a mint in his mouth. "How about we talk in the car on the way to fetch Brodie? Uncle George is making us all dinner."

"All of us?"

"Of course."

Emotion burns into Chloe's eyes at the fact she's included.

"I do feel rather hungry now," she says.

He puts his arm around her shoulder. They begin to walk back to where he parked his old Pontiac Sunfire. Gently he says, "And you, Chlo? How'd it go with your interrogation?"

She hears the caution in his voice, and his concern. He's worried about her.

She looks up into his kind eyes. "You know what, Stavros? I think it's all going to be okay. Actually, I'm pretty certain it will work out okay."

"Oh? What makes you say that?"

"My mother's voice inside my head has stopped telling me it won't."

He breaks his stride, stops, looks down at her. "What do you mean?"

"I don't know exactly. I just think maybe her job is finally done. She kept me safe. She got me here—to the truth in the end. We all have our issues, you know? She certainly had hers. But I believe she did her best. And now I know who I am."

He gives her an odd look, as though trying to figure her out.

"I do realize I have a lot ahead, Stavros. It will take time."

A slow smile crosses his face and moves that clump of hair under his lip. His dark eyes brighten. "You are a curious one, Chlo. Come, let us go and get little Brodie. He must be anxious to see you by now."

As they walk, the words Gloria mentioned float softly into Chloe's thoughts. *Saudade. Sehnsucht.* That universal sense of longing for something. And she realizes that in many ways the opposite to *longing* is *belonging.*

AFTER THE MURDERS

Jemma is in the GVPD interview room with Havers and Pederson for a second time. They have located Chloe and brought her in. This much was on the news. Jemma doesn't know what Chloe told them, but the detectives want to question her again, and this time she has come with Greg Ford, a top criminal defense lawyer. She's not taking chances.

As she sits at the table, she reminds herself of what she told Adam, that the burden of proof is entirely on the detectives. Even if they do believe she's committed some crime, if they can't find evidence to support it, they cannot charge her.

Havers says, "Chloe Cooper claims you drove her to the Bergson Gallery in a white van. You picked her up on Main Street, dropped her off near the gallery. And you said you'd wait for her in the rear alley."

"She's fabricating," Jemma says. "I already told you what I did that day."

Pederson says, "So you claim you did *not* drive her there?"

"Of course not. Why would I? What for? Where would I even get a white van from? She's lying—she's unhinged from reality."

Havers says, "Chloe claims you asked her to visit the gallery and get dirt on Gloria, your husband's mistress, because you wanted to know what you were up against."

"It's not true." They have no proof, she thinks—otherwise they'd be coming at her differently. *Relax. Stay calm. Take your time.*

Havers says, "We have records from Chloe Cooper's phone that show you called her twice on Friday. Once in the evening, to invite her over for wine—"

"I never invited her for wine."

"And once later that night urging Chloe to contact Gloria Bergson stat and arrange to meet with her specifically on Sunday at the close of her business day. And you said you would drive her there. Why did you ask her to meet with Gloria on Sunday?"

Jemma glances briefly at her counsel, inhales deeply, and says, "I phoned Chloe that first time to cancel our dog-walking arrangements after I realized she was the woman up in the window across the road who'd been watching us with binoculars. Adam also told me she was stalking him. I phoned her again later that night because I saw her once again, outside our fence, peeping into our house while she was walking that old dog. I told her during that second call that if I ever found her peeping or stalking us again, I would file for a restraining order." Jemma leans forward over the table. "Honestly, Detectives, your lines of questioning are offensive and hurtful. I have recently lost my husband in a most terrible fashion, and I'm struggling with grief. Plus, the media is hounding me. And that woman is fabricating things. She's a pathological liar, a snoop with an obsessive fixation on her neighbors, and she fled the scene of my husband's murder. She's dangerous, and now you know exactly what her bloodline is." Jemma hadn't seen *that* one coming.

"These things can be hereditary, you know? Just the generational trauma alone that must have come out of her childhood is enough to send anyone over the edge if triggered. An abused victim often becomes an abuser. A victim of violence learns to engage in violence. I even heard she kept the oxygen compressor in her apartment running long after her mother died. She made food daily for a dead mother who wasn't there."

"Where did you hear this?" asks Pederson.

Jemma holds his gaze. Her heart pounds, but she maintains her cool, collected exterior. "One of Raven Cooper's carers also works shifts as a maid for a woman who approached me in the supermarket. She recognized my photo from the news coverage, and she came up to me to offer her condolences. She told me what her maid told her. Chloe Cooper is not in touch with reality—I don't know how many times I need to say this."

Havers and Pederson regard her as silence settles over the room. Jemma tries not to fidget, or shift in her chair. Her lawyer makes notes.

Havers starts tapping the back of her pen on the table. Pederson leans forward and says, "When we asked whether you or your husband had access to marinas on the North Shore—"

"I honestly didn't think of Narek's place at the time."

Pederson says, "You knew your husband had a display of vehicle registration plates on the garage wall, yet when we asked what had been on that wall and he claimed there'd been nothing, you didn't contradict him."

Greg Ford clears his throat and says, "What does this have to do with the gallery homicides?"

"Goes to possible motive. If Jemma suspected her husband had tried to kill her with a Jet Ski, it could predispose her to murdering him," Havers says coolly.

"Christ. You're not serious?" She glances at her lawyer. "Do I honestly have to sit through this, Greg? It's clear what happened here—that crazy woman witnessed the Jet Ski accident and is now claiming it was Adam? Trying to kill me?"

Before Greg can respond, Havers says quickly, "We do have Adam's Idaho plates. And a photo from Chloe's phone of the license plate collection that was on your garage wall. We also have Adam's wet suit, gloves, booties, goggles. We have CCTV images of his Tesla with the Idaho plates crossing the bridge early in the morning before the Jet Ski hit-and-run, and returning after. Plus Chloe's testimony that she saw the Tesla with the Idaho plates returning to your Crow's Point garage. And one of the keys in the bunch found in Adam's Tesla opens the boathouse at Narek Tigran's estate."

Pederson slides a photo across the table toward Jemma. "And this blue-and-white Jet Ski was found inside Narek Tigran's boathouse. Damage on the hull is consistent with striking a swimmer, twice. Plus, the damaged hull contained microscopic pieces of a pink silicone bathing cap with trace amounts of DNA from deceased swimmer Marianne Wade."

Greg says, "Whatever criminal act Dr. Adam Spengler may have engaged in that day bears no relevance to my client's actions regarding the gallery homicides. Whereas Chloe Cooper is obsessed with my client, and if she believed Adam was the Jet Ski murderer as well as a lying adulterer, she'd have every reason to lose her cool with Adam when he arrived unannounced in the gallery. She also had reason to kill Gloria Bergson."

Pederson takes another photo from his file folder and slides it toward Jemma and her counsel.

"Do you recognize this van?"

She studies the photo of a white van, looks up. "No."

"This van was parked inside Narek Tigran's garage."

She shrugs.

"Did you ever drive this van?" Pederson asks.

Jemma glances at Greg. His eyes tell her that if the cops had evidence she did, they would say so.

"No. This is absolutely ridiculous." She turns again to her counsel. "I don't have to stand for this, do I, Greg?"

"Unless you are going to charge my client, Detectives," Greg says, "I think we're done here. Mrs. Spengler has been as helpful as she can under the tragic circumstances. We respectfully ask that you now allow her to grieve in peace."

Jemma pushes her chair back and rises. Her lawyer does the same. She walks out the door.

A free woman.

IT'S CRIMINAL: The Chloe Cooper Story

The screen shows Detective Maeve Havers now sitting opposite Trinity Scott.

MAEVE: Everything in our investigation pointed to Chloe Cooper having stabbed to death both Dr. Adam Spengler and his mistress, Gloria Bergson. She had opportunity. Motive. Means to do it. And we had the trace evidence to support it. Once we learned she was the daughter of Robert Autain, a man with a strong resemblance to Adam Spengler, there was additional reason to believe she was triggered by Dr. Spengler himself due to her childhood trauma and possible repressed memories of a violent Autain and her mother's response to Autain. According to trial transcripts, Jennie Smith told the court she would hide her toddler in the closet and force her to listen to an audio recording about a selkie with a blanket over her head while Autain raped her repeatedly.

TRINITY: And she lost her mother at the same time she encountered Adam Spengler. In the same hospital.

MAEVE: Which must have been additionally triggering. And she fled the homicide scene. So, yes, everything pointed to Chloe Cooper as being the killer. We had nothing to prove her claims about Jemma

Spengler were in fact true. Plus, Chloe was an unreliable witness at best. I saw with my own eyes that oxygen compressor feeding air into a cannula lying on an empty bed, and the bowl of congealing oatmeal on the bedside table.

TRINITY: What about Chloe's claim that Adam injected and drugged her?

MAEVE: There was physical evidence she'd been injected—pricked—with something sharp, likely a needle. Toxicology revealed nothing in her blood sample. Although something like ketamine—to which Dr. Spengler had access—has a short half-life. There wouldn't have been evidence in her system by the time we took biological samples.

TRINITY: Ketamine would explain her memory loss and confusion.

MAEVE: Yes, it would, and there were missing vials of Ketalar—or ketamine hydrochloride—unaccounted for at Dr. Spengler's place of work, but this still did not implicate Jemma Spengler in any way. The advice from prosecutors—Crown counsel—was that we had nothing to support charging Jemma Spengler, and certainly nothing that would secure us a criminal conviction in court. We did, however, have what we needed to charge Chloe Cooper for both the murders of Gloria Bergson and Dr. Spengler, and we certainly had a narrative to support it.

TRINITY: Yet you didn't charge her?

MAEVE: I'm retired now, but at the time of the gallery homicides, I'd already been a major crimes investigator for a long time. I'd come to rely on my gut, my instincts as a cop. Sometimes the little tells are not always apparent to the conscious mind, yet some part of your brain has perceived them, and they're whispering things to you. They add up.

TRINITY: So you believed Chloe?

MAEVE: More than I believed Jemma Spengler.

TRINITY: You think Jemma did it? You believe she killed her husband and his mistress and framed Chloe?

Detective Maeve Havers falls silent awhile. A slow, wry smile curves her lips.

MAEVE: As Jemma's friend—Sophia Mancini—told us, people don't just leave Jemma. Mancini's words to us were, She's all needy—she will fight to remain the center of attention, until a line is overstepped, and then she's just furious, filled with hate. If she can't have undying affection from her love interest, no one else can.

TRINITY: Sophia Mancini was referring to an old boyfriend of Jemma's who dumped her in favor of Sophia?

MAEVE: Yes. There were rumors about how he died, and investigators at the time did look into whether Jemma might have pushed him over the cliff into the quarry. However, there was no proof. There was talk about her father's death by fire in his trailer and the door being locked from the outside, but the coroner ultimately ruled it an accident. Then there were the rumors about the death of her own son—Jackson Spengler—but again, no proof, and no formal investigation was opened at the time, either. All we had back then was clear forensic proof that pointed to Dr. Adam Spengler being the Jet Ski killer.

TRINITY: Do you think it was possible that Jemma and Adam at first conspired to kill Gloria together, and frame Chloe, but after setting her husband up and getting him to the gallery, Jemma double-crossed and turned on him, eliminating him, too?

MAEVE: It was definitely one of our investigative angles at the time. But, again, nothing was found to support this theory.

Detective Maeve Havers pauses.

MAEVE: Like the mythological Furies. Like Agamemnon's wife, Clytemnestra, one should never underestimate a deceived wife's capacity for revenge. Clytemnestra welcomed her husband home from battle a hero; then that night, when he was in the bath, she stabbed him to death. Mythology and reality hand in hand, as old as time.

TRINITY: So Jemma walked free.

MAEVE: Free. Alone. And broke.

THE SWIMMER

Now

It's Jemma Spengler's sixty-sixth birthday, and she's alone in a small basement room in a lower-income area of the city. The ground-level windows are narrow and grimy, and the air is cold and dank. It's all Jemma can afford, since almost everything that was not specifically in her name went in trust to Oliver Bergson. Of course she challenged this, and sued, but she lost, and the legal fight served only to sink her deeper into financial despair.

The only reason Jemma can even cough up enough for this dump is because she was able to access a rent-subsidy program designed to assist low-income seniors. She has since been wait-listed for a government-funded assisted-living facility because she's having mobility issues now, after a fall last year. But it could be years before her name moves to the top of the housing list. Jemma no longer swims. Swimming in open water triggers panic attacks.

Jemma has chosen this day—this anniversary of her birth—to pluck up the courage to finally watch *IT'S CRIMINAL: The Chloe Cooper Story*, streaming on Netflix and receiving buzz around the globe. Trinity Scott and Gio Rossi did contact her at the outset to ask if she'd participate in their production. Naturally she refused. She knew she'd be portrayed as a villain. A pariah—the shunned, broke, and broken woman once poised to be a world-famous dancer and now rumored to have killed her husband and his mistress, and possibly even her child and an old boyfriend. There are even rumors about her having set her drunk father's bedding alight before locking him inside his trailer. She's fully aware that Detective Maeve Havers and the rest of the homicide team remain convinced she killed Adam and Gloria. They just couldn't prove it. So Jemma walked free.

But she's not free, is she?

She might as well be in a cell. Sometimes Jemma wishes she were. At least she'd have company in a prison. There would be programs she could access. She wouldn't fear where her next meal was coming from, as terrible as prison fare might be. Another deep-rooted part of Jemma's psyche feels things might even have turned out better if she *had* been charged, tried, convicted—if she'd been forced to atone by society's rules and been able to say, *Look, society, I am paying for what I did.* Perhaps karma might have been kinder to her then.

As she watches the show's introduction on the small television screen in her basement room, her mind slides back to September 29, 2019, and the hours before the murders—those fragile moments when she could have stopped, done something different, and changed it all.

It's Sunday afternoon, and twilight gathers while Adam walks up to Main Street to wait for an Uber to take him to a destination one block down from the gallery. Jemma, meanwhile, dresses in baggy old clothes that she'll dispose of later. She tightly braids her hair and pulls on a baseball cap.

"I'll be back soon," she tells Boo and Sweetie as she shrugs into a shapeless jacket. She picks up her bag of gear, which includes nitrile gloves and booties to cover her shoes. "When Mommy comes home, everything will be fixed. Perfect. Just us."

She exits her garage in her car and drives down to the beach parking lot. She pays for parking using the app. Jemma locks her car and pulls the bill of her cap down low over her brow. Darkness is beginning to gather when she finds Narek's van, which Adam parked under some trees. She crouches down, feels around inside the rear wheel hub. For a tense moment she can't find the fob. A group of people approach along the sidewalk. She quickly gets up and pretends she's crossing the road. When they round the corner, she hurries back to the van. Her heart races now. She drops to her haunches and feels under the hub again, moving her hand higher. Her fingers touch the cool surface of the fob. Relief surges through her.

Jemma climbs into the driver's seat and checks the time. She's beginning to run late. Chloe will be getting agitated. She navigates out of the tight parking space and drives up to Main Street. When she sees the bus shelter, she slows, and pulls into the bay. Chloe has already started to walk away with her cumbersome portfolio.

Quickly Jemma slides down the window and calls out to Chloe as she inches the van forward, keeping pace with the younger woman's stride.

Chloe peers inside, and looks uncertain. Jemma smiles broadly and tells her to place her portfolio case in the back.

Jemma drops Chloe a short way away from the gallery. It's Sunday. Quiet. Chloe grows nervous. She seems unsure why Jemma is not stopping closer to the gallery entrance.

"I don't want her to see me."

Once Chloe has entered the gallery, Jemma drives around to the alley. She parks at the far end, but on the opposite side from where she told Chloe she would wait. From here she can see the gallery exit at the rear of the building. Keeping an eye on it, she pulls the booties over her shoes, tucks her braid into her jacket, and pulls on the nitrile gloves. From her bag she takes a kitchen carving knife. She needs it to appear as though this was a sudden act of violence, and the weapon must look like one of opportunity—something Chloe might grab from Gloria's kitchenette drawer. Adam also has a carving knife on him, along with the ketamine syringe. But Adam doesn't know the full plan.

When Jemma sees her husband entering the gallery from the rear, she exits the van and moves rapidly toward the gallery door. It's dark now. Raining. There's no one about.

When she enters the studio at the back of the gallery, Jemma sees Chloe on the floor, still conscious, but unable to move. Adam freezes at the sight of Jemma. He's holding Gloria by the arm. They appear to be trying to escape together via the door into the showroom. Rage, disgust, hardens Jemma's resolve.

"I knew you were too weak, Adam. A lost cause."

She moves swiftly forward with the knife.

"Go, Gloria, run!" Adam screams as he tries to step in front of Jemma.

But Jemma sidesteps him and lunges toward Gloria, who reaches for the handle of the door to the front showroom. Gloria twists the handle and pulls, but the door is still locked.

"Jemma, no! Stop!" Adam screams. "You don't have to do this!"

As Gloria fights to unlock the door, Jemma sinks the blade of the carving knife into her back, deep, aiming for the liver. Gloria screams and goes rigid. Adam yells and barrels at Jemma. Panting, Jemma yanks the blade out and plunges it in again.

Adam freezes in his tracks as Gloria slides to the floor with a soft moan. Blood pools onto the floor around her. Jemma spins around to face Adam.

"Fucking loser," she growls at him. "I knew you couldn't follow a plan, Adam. I knew you wouldn't do it."

Adam raises both hands as he fixates on the blade she points at him. Fear, horror, widens his eyes. "Okay, okay, Jem. It's done now. You got what you wanted. Let's just get out of here. We stick to the rest of the plan. Chloe takes the blame. By the time she wakes, by the time the cops find her, the drugs will have cleared through her system."

Jemma's pulse races. She's panting hard. Her body is drenched in sweat. She nods and says breathlessly, "Fine. Go on then, go to the van. I'll sort Chloe."

As Adam turns, she lurches forward and plunges the knife into his back, then again. He slumps to the floor, tries to crawl away on his hands and knees, slipping in his own blood. Adam comes to a stop in the kitchenette area. He raises his hand up to her, as though to plead for help.

"Is that what Marianne Wade did, Adam? Is that how the swimmer lifted her hand, called for help, before you turned around and plowed over her again?"

"J-Jem, please—"

She sinks the knife into his neck. His eyes bulge. His hand goes to his neck as she pulls out the blade. Blood wells through his fingers and he slides to the floor.

Breathing hard, Jemma waits to ensure he's not going to move again, that he really is dead now. He remains still, and she's amazed at how easy it is, in the end, to take a life. How vindicated she feels in meting out deserved retribution. As she did for the boyfriend who abandoned her for Sophia. As she punished her father. She hurries over to Chloe, who has now passed out.

Carefully, Jemma slices the tip of the blade across Chloe's palm. She needs Chloe to leave blood at the scene. Then, with her gloved hands, she wraps Chloe's bleeding palm and fingers around the knife hilt, ensuring prints.

Jemma hurries to the exit. She tries to catch her breath before she peers out into the dark alley. Nothing moves. Rain falls softly and silently. She exits and hurries back to the van.

Jemma drives to the storage facility. Inside the storage locker she removes her shabby clothing and bags it, along with the nitrile gloves and booties, in the black garbage bag she brought with her. She knots the top of the bag closed and changes into fresh gear. She leaves the bagged crime scene clothing in the unit, but collects Adam's wet suit and the plates and places them in a large carry bag. She relocks the storage locker, then drives back to Narek's place.

Inside Narek's garage she wipes down the van seats and vacuums the van using the vacuum cleaner attached to the garage wall. Adam told her Narek's staff use this van, and that it's detailed after each use. Narek is anal that way. There is every chance this van will be used and cleaned out again before cops ever think to look here.

She hesitates, hooks the large carry bag over her shoulder, walks back up the driveway, then briskly strides several hundred meters along the Eagle Cove Road. Outside someone else's estate, she calls for an Uber.

Jemma asks the driver to take her to a restaurant on Main Street. She's dropped off there, pays the driver in cash, hooks her bag over her shoulder, and moves toward the restaurant entrance. But when the cab disappears around the corner, brake lights flaring briefly, she turns and hurries toward home.

She places Adam's wet suit into the back of his Tesla, along with his gloves, booties, goggles, and the Idaho plates, plus the bunch of keys to Narek's estate, including the one marked *Boathouse*. Jemma lets her dogs out, showers, then goes downstairs and opens a chilled bottle of her best white wine. She sits on the sofa—in soft candlelight—finishing the bottle as she mentally rehearses her story for the police and tries to calm herself.

When her wine is done, she leaves the bottle and her glass out on the kitchen counter, takes two sleeping pills, and lets the dogs out to pee again. As she stands at the open glass slider, waiting for Boo and Sweetie to do their business in the dark and drizzle, she glances up at the third-floor window across the alley. No woman looks out. Her apartment is in darkness. Empty. Boo and Sweetie skitter inside and shake raindrops from their coats. Jemma slides the door shut and locks it, wondering when the blinds will arrive. No matter. She plans to sell this place as soon as is reasonably acceptable. She must at least appear to "grieve" long enough. Jemma goes upstairs to bed, dogs in tow.

It had become clear to her that Adam was never going to break it off with Gloria—certainly not after trying to kill her. She'd never make

Adam wholly hers again. She once loved him so very deeply. She was committed to their marriage, their pact, their lifetime vow. In sickness and in health. But once he crossed the line—that point of no return— once he showed her the sheer depths of his deceit and betrayal, and once Jemma saw in her heart of hearts that she'd never make herself the center of his life again, she tipped from love to hate. Just like that. They are so close, aren't they? Those polar ends of passion for someone. And if she couldn't have him, no one would.

It was supposed to be a perfect murder.

Except it cost her everything.

THE GIRL BY THE SEA

Now

"I watched it," Chloe tells Trinity.

"All of it?" Trinity asks.

Chloe nods.

They sit at a table in a nice café, facing the sea. It's been six years since the Jerrin Bay hit-and-run and the horrendous gallery slayings. Sometimes it feels like yesterday. At other times—like now, sitting in a sunny window in a quiet café corner with a person like Trinity—those dark days feel an entire lifetime away, or as though they belong to someone else.

"What did you think?" Trinity asks, reaching for her mug of coffee and sipping, her gaze holding Chloe's.

Chloe studies Trinity's face and thinks again how nice she is. This is not her first meeting with the creator of *IT'S CRIMINAL*. She met with both Trinity and Gio back when the duo first started work on *The Chloe Cooper Story*, when they approached her to ask whether Chloe would be a part of the production.

Chloe said no. Trinity then asked if she'd be open to them buying the exclusive rights to her story, for both novelization and a television series. They made her an offer with a very large sum of money attached to it.

After discussing the offer with Stavros and George, on their advice, Chloe got agent representation. She ended up signing an impressive deal that hit headlines in the entertainment and publishing worlds.

"I think you and Gio did a good job, Trinity. But the actress who plays me in the fictionalized segment doesn't look like me. She's actually quite nice-looking—not unattractive."

Trinity smiles. "Sometimes we really can't see ourselves the way others might, can we, Chloe?"

It's at this point Chloe's mother inside her head would historically pipe up and caution her not to be seduced by the false words of strangers who flatter you because they want things. But her mother's voice really has gone quite silent since their last little chat and final goodbyes. No more inside English accent tries to govern and control Chloe's life. Chloe's therapist had all sorts of academic-sounding reasons why this might be the case. But Chloe just feels that her mother must surely know her job of keeping her child safe and finding her a home, a family, a place to belong, has been done.

"I also watched the whole season of *The Leena Rai Killing*," Chloe says. "I was particularly riveted by the episode where you learned that the man convicted for killing Leena was your father, Trinity. It was touching and rather well portrayed," she says. "It made me realize that doing *The Chloe Cooper Story* really was personal for you."

Trinity nods. "We share that, you and I. Criminal parents. Young Oliver Bergson does, too—his father murdered the swimmer."

"But you went to the prison to meet your father." Chloe pauses and twists her cup in its saucer. She meets Trinity's eyes. "Was it worth it?"

"Are you asking whether I think it's a good idea for you to go meet Robert Autain?"

She inhales. "Well, no—not really. I—I was just wondering if there is such a thing as proper closure, you know? If looking into someone's eyes helps you, or if it makes things worse."

"Everyone and every situation is different, Chloe. For me, I didn't make that choice. It sneaked up on me when the man convicted of killing Leena Rai wanted to be on my podcast. What I can say is that positive things did come out of my experience. I was able to open up, and I grew close to Gio through it all, and it's turned into a lifelong relationship with the best partner I could ever imagine. We wouldn't be where we are now, producing successful true-crime series, if not for that period in our lives. And it brought me here. To you. To you agreeing to give your side of the Chloe Cooper story."

"But I didn't *participate* in the show. I didn't appear on camera myself, or anything."

"You gave us your blessing. You spoke off camera. It made our show possible."

"I suppose my mother would be horrified and turn in her grave if I did try to meet Robert Autain. She fought her entire life to keep me away from that monster, and Evil with a capital *E*."

Trinity assesses Chloe in silence. Then carefully, quietly, she says, "If it's any help, Chloe, we did try to gain access to Robert Autain. He refused to see us or talk to us."

She bites her lip because, inexplicably, it's starting to wobble. "Did he—did he say anything else? Anything about me? Or my mom?"

Trinity hesitates. Then leans forward and takes Chloe's hands in hers across the table. "I'm only telling you this because I don't want you to get hurt by a dangerous, manipulative psychopath." She inhales. "He relayed a message to us that said he's *not interested in anything to do with that Jennie bitch or her offspring.*"

Chloe bites her lip harder. Blood thuds in her ears. She has to wait several minutes until she's ready to speak with an even tone. "Right, then. That's sorted. At least I know where I came from, and how I fit, and why I am like I am." She feels a catch of emotion in her throat. She waits for it to pass. "And I know my mother wanted me. She did everything she could to save me. And to keep me safe in the only way she knew how. My therapist really helped me understand how much I was wanted by her. And how difficult it must have been for my mom, all alone."

"She was a child herself, really," Trinity says, "who managed both to survive Abattoir Autain and escape him, and then faced him in court and put him away. If anyone failed, it was a system that couldn't support her better at the time."

Chloe nods. "She certainly was a brave woman, and I'm so glad I did everything I could to look after her into her end days. To be with her."

"So how are things with Stavros on Crete? When are you guys flying back?"

Chloe feels a warmth just thinking about her new home in Greece, and the great big eccentric extended Vasilou family she has found there. And how money from the *IT'S CRIMINAL* deal helped fund a little taverna by the sea—an azure-blue sea in which Chloe learned to swim, and where she now swims every morning at sunrise.

"Very good." She hesitates, because sharing intimate thoughts remains difficult. "Like you found Gio—I also found a friend. Like, a real one. I don't think I ever really had one before."

"You mean Stavros?"

She nods.

"When is the wedding?"

"You mean our big fat Greek event with all the straggles of relatives?"

Trinity laughs. "Yes, that."

"Next spring. Before the summer tourist season starts and our little taverna gets busy. You should come visit sometime. Stavros really is a most excellent cook. Since he was a child, he dreamed of a taverna on the Libyan Sea, on the south side of Crete, where generations of his family come from. I guess that's why he liked working at the Beach House. And we have two little dogs now. They will never quite fill the space in my heart that I hold for Brodie, but they are cute rescues."

"Not cavapoos?"

"Heavens no! Although one should never judge dogs by their owners, Trinity. Boo and Sweetie were really sweet."

They finish their coffees and pastries and are about to say their goodbyes when Chloe, a little embarrassed, says, "Oh, I have something for you."

She reaches under the table and brings out a small portfolio case. She holds it out for Trinity to take.

"What is it?"

"Open it."

She does. Inside is a painting of a girl leaving jagged rocks and stepping into an ocean that is not gray and dark, but aquamarine and indigo blue and filled with shimmering luminescence. And flowing into the ocean with the girl are streams of gold—veins of Jungian treasure, finally set free—and the gold pools on the surface of the water, mirroring the rising sun.

Trinity looks up, and her gaze meets Chloe's. Emotion gleams in her eyes.

"Thank you," she whispers. She gets up and hugs Chloe.

Chloe allows it. She's better with hugging now.

ABOUT THE AUTHOR

Loreth Anne White is the Amazon Charts, *Bild*, and *Washington Post* bestselling author of *The Unquiet Bones*, *The Maid's Diary*, *The Patient's Secret*, *Beneath Devil's Bridge*, *In the Deep*, *In the Dark*, *The Dark Bones*, and *A Dark Lure*. With more than three million books sold worldwide and translations in over twenty languages, she is an ITW Thriller Awards nominee, a three-time RITA finalist, an overall Daphne du Maurier Award winner, an Arthur Ellis Award finalist, and the winner of multiple other industry awards. A recovering journalist who has worked in South Africa and Canada, she now calls Canada home. She resides in the Pacific Northwest, dividing her time between Vancouver Island, a Coast Mountains ski resort, and a rustic lakeside cabin in the Cariboo. When she's not writing or dreaming up plots, you'll find her in the water or on the trails, where she tries—unsuccessfully—to avoid bears. For more information on her books, please visit her website at www.lorethannewhite.com.